W9-BYF-378

Desert Wives

Other books by the author

Desert Noir

Desert Wives

A Lena Jones Mystery

Betty Webb

Poisoned Pen Press

Poisoned Pen Press

Poisoned Pen Press
6962 E. First Ave. Ste. 103
Scottsdale, AZ 85251
www.poisonedpenpress.com
info@poisonedpenpress.com

Printed in the United States of America

For Max McQueen, who first told me about the blonds;
and for my cousin Virginia Lawler,
who kindly allowed the use of her name for a major character.

And, of course, for Paul.

Acknowledgments

The author is indebted to Kathleen Tracy's excellent *The Secret Story of Polygamy*, Sourcebooks, Inc., and Tapestry Against Polygamy (www.polygamy.org), an organization founded by a group of brave women who have escaped from the polygamist lifestyle.

Ever faithful with their helpful criticisms were the Sheridan Street Irregulars: Sharon Magee, Ed Dixon, Judy Starbuck, and Eileen Brady. Marge Purcell also provided invaluable advice.

Thanks also to the cover photograph's blushing brides: Amanda Kingsbury, Erinn Figg, Stephanie Jarnagan, and Theresa Curry; and their proud groom, Andrew Long. Their contributions (long photo shoots in Arizona's hot, dusty desert) went way beyond the call of duty.

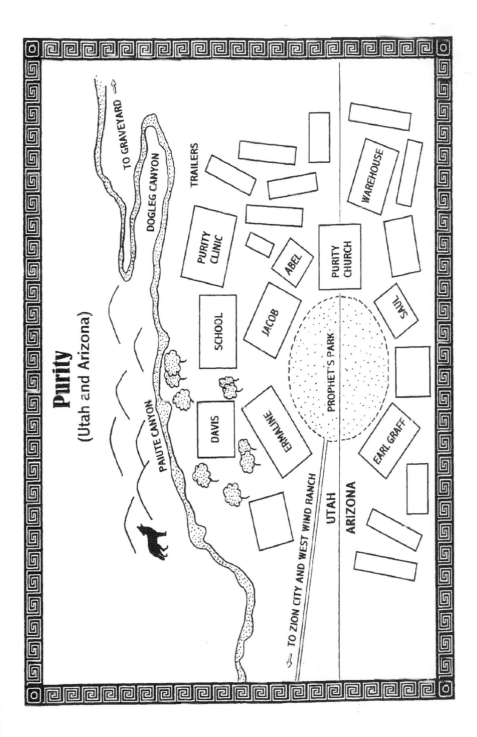

Purity
(Utah and Arizona)

Chapter 1

What do you call a dead, sixty-eight-year-old polygamist?

In the case of my thirteen-year-old client, you call him your fiancé.

"Oh, Lena! Prophet Solomon's been hurt!" Rebecca Corbett gasped as I pulled her away from his body. "Shouldn't we stop and help him?" She was such a nice girl.

But I'm not a nice girl. Few private detectives are. We see too much of the dark side of human nature, such as fathers who would trade their beautiful thirteen-year-old daughters in exchange for two not quite as beautiful sixteen-year-old girls. Kind of like baseball cards, I guess.

Besides, "nice" was a luxury I couldn't afford. The cool September night had clouded over and the full moon all too infrequently illuminated the inky sky. Impenetrable darkness carpeted the floor of Paiute Canyon, where loose shale, sliding gravel, and humped boulders conspired to break our legs at any moment. Yet Rebecca and I still had more than a mile to travel before we reached the piñon pine thicket where my partner waited.

We had no choice. The dirt road above, which paralleled the canyon for almost twenty miles, would soon swarm with the men from the polygamy compound at Purity, all eager to take back what they saw as their property: a breeding-age girl.

"Lena? Didn't you hear me?"

I shook my head. Maybe a nice person would have sat down with Prophet Solomon Royal and waited for help, but when I aimed my flashlight beam, the condition of his chest informed me that the old man was a lost cause. His stiff arms crooked upward, as if embracing the moon. The flashlight showed me something else: a double-barreled shotgun lying among rocks at least twenty feet away from the body.

This was murder.

"He's dead, Rebecca," I told her, not taking time to cushion my words. "Once we get on the Arizona side of the state line I'll call the Utah State Police so the coyotes won't..."

I stopped myself. Thirteen-year-old girls didn't need to hear what coyotes would do to a dead body. I had seen that once and it still gave me nightmares. I started again. "I'll call so Prophet Solomon won't have to lie here alone all night. But for now we've got to keep moving."

"Can't we at least say a prayer over him?"

"We don't have time." I gently pushed her ahead.

Twenty minutes ago, Rebecca had slipped out of bed to meet me in the canyon. She had sworn no one in the compound had seen her, but I was in no mood to take chances. If Prophet Solomon's henchmen caught up with us, they certainly wouldn't take the time to pray. They all claimed to be religious men, but what kind of religion forces polygamous "marriages" on girls still playing with Barbie dolls?

I heard the call of a nightbird, then the rustle of wings. Something shrieked in the darkness. The Arizona Strip, a one-hundred-mile stretch of badlands between Utah and Arizona, was no place to be caught out alone at night. I had already learned its dangers during the three days and nights I camped out in the canyon, waiting for a chance to signal Rebecca as she walked from her father's house to the compound's schoolhouse. One night a black and white king snake had slithered across my foot, but since it was nonpoisonous, its presence did not bother me. I had been less enchanted with the seven-inch-long centipede crawling up my leg.

"Hurry, Rebecca!" This time I did not bother to lower my voice.

Rebecca did her best, but in the darkness she ran straight into a straggly mesquite jutting out from the canyon wall. Bless her gallant heart, she didn't make a sound. As she disentangled her bleeding face and hands from its grasping limbs, she took a final backward glance toward the body.

"Oh, Prophet Solomon, I'm so sorry!"

"You've got nothing to be sorry about," I said, wiping her blood away with the hem of my T-shirt. "You didn't kill him, did you?" I tried to turn it into a joke but she didn't laugh.

Come to think of it, neither did I.

It took us almost an hour to make it to the stair-stepped boulder cascade leading out of the canyon and onto the desert floor, but we found Jimmy waiting exactly where he'd promised to be, where he'd waited for us every night since I had gone down in the canyon to rescue Rebecca. His Toyota truck was parked, lights off, in a piñon pine grove several yards back from the road. A cloud picked that moment to slip away from the moon and as we approached; its silvery glow highlighted the curved lines of the Pima tribal tattoos on his temple.

Rebecca pulled back in shock. "Who...?"

I patted her shoulder. "There's nothing to worry about, Rebecca. That's Jimmy Sisiwan, my partner at Desert Investigations. He's a detective, too."

Jimmy's smile transformed his fierce face into beaming beneficence. "We Pima Indians aren't into scalping, Rebecca. We're just peaceful farmers. Want some lima beans? Some squash? Or how about a nice barbequed rabbit?"

She didn't laugh, but at least she relaxed enough to crawl into the truck beside him. I followed and as I did, the wind picked up. Piñon needles scraped against the cab. In the distance, something muttered crossly. A mountain lion? Or a polygamist seeking blood atonement for his fallen prophet? Given a choice, I would take my chances with the mountain lion.

"There were complications," I told Jimmy, forcing my voice to remain steady. "A shooting. We'd better get the hell out of here and across the state line. Don't stop for anybody, you hear? *Anybody*. Especially not Rebecca's father."

Abel Corbett, damn his hide, had caused all this mess in the first place. Fourteen years ago, he and Rebecca's mother had run away from Purity, married, and moved to Arizona where they had led as normal a life as possible for people with their backgrounds. But the marriage eventually fell apart when Abel, who had kept in touch with his polygamist father and uncles, began to pine for multiple wives. After his father wrote that Prophet Solomon had promised him two sixteen-year-old girls if he returned to Purity with Rebecca, Abel promptly kidnapped his daughter and took her back to Utah with him.

Jimmy's hand froze on the way to the gearshift. "Did you say there's been a shooting?" He looked down at my hip where my own .38 was secured in its holster. During the past three days I had not fired it once.

"Prophet Solomon's dead," I told him. "And no, I had nothing to do with it. We discovered his body in Paiute Canyon while we were making our escape. Now let's get going, okay? I'll give you the details later."

Jimmy gave me another worried look but for once heeded my advice. He flicked on the headlights and threw the truck into gear. The tires spit a small avalanche of pine needles and rocks as we shuddered northwest, leaving the sheltering piñons far behind. Facing us now were empty miles of desert and scrub, where we'd be easily spotted by pursuers. I threw a glance over my shoulder and saw nothing but blackness, but that did not mean Prophet Solomon's body hadn't already been found. I wondered if the law hanged fiancé thieves in Utah. Or was that just horse thieves?

The Toyota took a nasty dive into a deep rut, almost bottoming out. Rebecca fell against me.

"Can't you be a little more careful?" I complained.

Jimmy's gaze didn't shift from the road. "Fast or careful, Lena. Take your pick."

I said nothing.

The Toyota dove downward again. Reflexively, I put my arm around Rebecca. She shook worse than the truck.

As the crow flies, less than two miles separated us from Arizona, but after leaving the compound which straddled the Utah/Arizona state line, the dirt road veered sharply northwest toward Zion City and didn't cross the two-lane blacktop heading south to Arizona for another twenty miles. But the terrain, gullied by sudden canyons and drop-offs, was so treacherous that even if we'd had a four-wheel vehicle we wouldn't risk leaving the road at night.

As we bumped along I tightened my arm around Rebecca's thin shoulders. "I've got a surprise for you, a really good surprise. Your mom's back on the Arizona side of the border, at the motel. She came with us because she didn't want to wait until we returned to Scottsdale to see you."

For the first time that night, Rebecca's face crumpled. "I want my Mommy!" she wailed.

When we finally pulled into the parking lot of the North Rim Motel, I saw a colony of bats diving for moths in the incandescent light. Rebecca didn't look at them once. She barely waited for the truck to stop before she climbed over me, pushed open the cab door, and ran across the parking lot into the arms of the wild-looking woman pacing back and forth in front of the open door to Room 122.

"Mommy!" Gasps. Sobs. Muffled love words.

Damp-eyed myself, I watched them for a moment, then whispered to Jimmy, "Let's give them a few minutes alone. They've got a lot of catching up to do."

So Jimmy made a big, slow deal of wrestling the truck into a parking space beside Esther's Geo, which was so coated with dust that its green paint barely peeked through. I frowned. The trip to the motel from Scottsdale, although long, had been by interstate, then blacktop; we'd never once left asphalt. Surely she hadn't disregarded my orders and driven out toward the compound.

But I kept my concern to myself. As Jimmy took his sweet time, I gave him more details on the night's adventures.

"Do you have any idea when it could have happened?" he asked, when I finished. "I mean, did you hear the shot?"

"I'm no coroner, but since he was in full rigor, I'd say he could have been dead anywhere from five to twelve hours. Maybe even more. And yes, I heard a shot. Dozens of shots. Hunters are always in that canyon, and I'm telling you, keeping away from them for three days wasn't easy."

"Is there any chance it could have been a hunting accident? Maybe he dropped his gun and it went off?"

I snorted. "He had no powder burns on his chest, and the shotgun was too far away from his body for it to have been merely dropped. No, someone grabbed it, shot him, then discarded it. It was murder, all right. We need to report the death, but let's get Rebecca and her mother further away from Utah first. We're still too close to Purity for comfort."

Jimmy said something under his breath in Pima but when he switched to English, he sounded all agreement. "You'd better use a pay phone on the way, then, because cell phones…"

"Can be traced," I finished for him. "Now let's get moving."

We bailed out of the Toyota and hurried over to the motel, where Rebecca still stood wrapped in her mother's arms. The sight brought a lump to my throat. This was how normal mothers were supposed to behave, not as my own mother had thirty-two years earlier when she'd shot me in the head and left me to die in a Phoenix street. I'd been four years old. I survived only because I had been found by an illegal

Mexican immigrant, who without concern for her own precarious position had carried me to a nearby hospital.

Swallowing hard, I forced away the memory of my mother's betrayal. I did not know where she was now and I did not care, or so I told myself. I had put my past behind me. After all, most of my foster homes hadn't been too bad.

When I thought I could trust my voice, I explained our latest problem to Esther. "Prophet Solomon is dead. We found his body in Paiute Canyon, and I might as well tell you straight out, that it looks like murder."

Her face paled but she said nothing, so I continued on. "It's only a couple of hours to sunrise, and pretty soon now someone's going to notice that Prophet Solomon and Rebecca are missing. When that happens, they'll form a search party and it's my guess they'll figure out the Rebecca part pretty quick. Then the shit will hit the fan."

Esther nodded, her strawberry blond hair slipping out of its barrette. It was easy to see from which parent Rebecca had inherited her beauty. Even with the stresses of the past few days, Esther's perfect face remained as flawless as a Botticelli angel's. Her pale blues eyes, though, looked guarded.

"You're saying Solomon was shot?"

I frowned. I had said nothing of the kind.

Rebecca tore herself away from her mother's arms and gave me a terrified look. "I already told Mother about the Prophet. About the hole we saw in his...in his..." She hiccupped, then attached herself to her mother again.

I directed my next words to Esther, careful not to say too much. "Yes, I'm sure you did. But this is no time to be worrying about assisting the police with their inquiries, at least not before we get back to Scottsdale and get your child custody mess cleared up. Then you can help the authorities all you want."

"I have no intention of helping the Utah authorities with anything," Esther said. "They never helped me or Rebecca when we needed them." She gestured into the room behind her, and I saw several suitcases sitting on the bed. "We're already packed."

"Then let's get moving."

Since we had paid a week's rent in advance for the room, we simply threw the luggage into our vehicles, and within seconds our two-car caravan peeled out of the parking lot. Fifty miles slid by before I directed Jimmy into a truck stop. As I ran up to the bank of pay phones to relay my information to the Utah State Police, I saw the taillights on Rebecca's Geo disappear over a ridge. I didn't blame her for not stopping. After six months' forced separation, Esther and her daughter had a lot of catching up to do.

What I didn't know was that they would soon be separated again.

This time, by jailhouse bars.

Chapter 2

A week after my return from Utah, my old boss walked through the door of Desert Investigations.

I blinked in surprise. Usually, when Captain Kryzinski, head of the Scottsdale Violent Crimes Unit, wanted to see me, he simply phoned and asked me to come down to Scottsdale Main, where his glass-walled office was only ten feet away from my old cubicle. Then I noticed two other men behind him, one of them wilted from the 115-degree heat. They were in their early thirties, both well over six feet, both blonds. Mr. Wilted's muscles bulged like a professional wrestler's, but Mr. Cool, the man who did not have a bead of sweat on him, looked more whippet-thin than buff. If I were a betting woman, I'd lay three-to-one odds that Mr. Cool could beat the crap out of anybody in the room.

Cops. But not from any Arizona law enforcement agency that I knew of. With their plain gray suits and Temple white shirts, they looked like Utah.

Jimmy turned away from his computer and stole a worried glance at me before wiping all expression from his face.

I forced a smile. "Why, Captain Kryzinski, you old hound. It's been a coon's age." Actually, it had been two days since we'd run into each other at an art opening just down the street. After we'd both worked together on a case involving the murder of an art dealer, Kryzinski had developed an interest in painting.

Today the usually affable Kryzinski wasn't smiling, a bad sign. He merely gestured toward Mr. Cool. "Lena, this is Sheriff Howard Benson from Zion City, Utah, and his deputy, Scott Yantis. They're here about a homicide with Arizona ties, and I want you to know that the Scottsdale P.D. is extending them every courtesy."

Of course. In Scottsdale, just about one in every four passers-by had Mormon relatives. Those who didn't knew enough not to offend those who did, because Mormons counted among the state's major power brokers and held controlling interest in several industries and banks.

I stood up and held out my hand. Deputy Yantis stepped forward and shook it in friendly enough fashion, but when I held it toward Sheriff Benson, he let my hand hang in the air until I finally lowered it.

Kryzinski gave him a dirty look but his voice remained neutral. "Sheriff Benson here says he wants to ask you and Jimmy some questions. How about we go into the conference room, Lena? We got lots to talk about."

I liked Kryzinski but I didn't feel like making nice, so I motioned to the hard wooden chairs scattered around the office. "Sit, stand, whatever."

Jimmy frowned. Like most Pima Indians, he was very polite. Left to his own devices, he would not only have ushered Sheriff Benson and his deputy into the conference room, but would also have offered them cold drinks of his own private stock of organic prickly pear cactus juice.

As Kyrzinski and Deputy Yantis sat down and started mopping the sweat off their faces with wrinkled handkerchiefs, I stole a glance through the window. They must have driven up together because I could only see Kryzinski's blue-and-white parked at the curb. The rest of Main Street's gallery row appeared deserted, a not unusual situation for early afternoon, when heatstroke could fell the unwary art lover within minutes. Most Scottsdale folk wouldn't troll the galleries until sunset. The tourists, well, for them Scottsdale employed a state-of-the-art Medi-Vac system. I figured that to brave this heat, the lawmen from Utah had to be in one all-fired rush.

When I returned my attention to the room, I saw that Benson remained standing. He towered over my desk in the old I'm-Bigger-Than-You-Are game that certain men seem to love so much.

"Ms. Jones, we have reason to believe you have some knowledge about the murder of Mr. Solomon Royal, of Purity, Utah."

But Benson wasn't the only person who liked to play games. Smiling, I put my jeans-clad legs up on my desk and leaned back, nice and slow and lazy. I folded my hands behind my head and smiled. "Solomon who?"

"Oh, I think you've heard of him, Ms. Jones. Solomon Royal, Prophet Royal, as he was known in the area. Before his death, Mr. Royal was the leader of a religious group just north of the Arizona border."

I was enjoying this. "Oh, *that* Solomon Royal. I think I remember reading something about him in the Scottsdale *Journal.* When you say he was the leader of a 'religious group,' don't you really mean those Mormon polygamists?"

Benson's face tightened, as I knew it would. Members in good standing of the Church of Latter Day Saints don't like it when someone describes modern-day polygamists as Mormons. I knew full well that the official church had renounced polygamy more than one hundred years earlier, but after the hand-shaking incident, I wanted to yank Benson's chain. I had never liked smug men, and with his prim, ferret face and ramrod back, Benson looked way too full of himself for me.

"Mormons? You know better than that, Ms. Jones!" Benson snapped. "Solomon Royal's group, the Church of the Prophet Fundamental, is not part of the Church of Latter Day Saints and never has been. The people at Purity belong to a heretic sect which has absolutely nothing to do with our modern church. By taking plural wives, they are breaking the law."

I wasn't impressed. "So why don't you arrest them? I mean, you *are* the sheriff."

Jimmy stared at me steadily from across the table, as if warning me to be careful. He had been adopted by a Mormon family and raised in Utah, and although he had returned to his Pima Indian relatives on the reservation that abutted Scottsdale, he still retained strong ties to his adoptive parents and the Mormon community.

Captain Kryzinski's voice intruded upon my game. "Lena, I told you I've guaranteed the Scottsdale P.D.'s cooperation."

"Good thing I'm not Scottsdale P.D. anymore, then, isn't it?"

After receiving a bullet in the hip from a drug dealer, I had left the force almost a year earlier. I was my own boss now at Desert Investigations and no longer had to take orders from anybody, especially not from some badly dressed man. But Kryzinski couldn't seem to get our changed relationship through his thick skull. He kept trying to order me around like he had done since I'd been a rookie. The fact that we frequently worked opposite ends of the same case did not help.

"C'mon, Lena." He wiggled around on the hard chair, his corpulent body stuffed into one of his many too-small Western suits. Today's howler was pale blue with chocolate piping on the lapels and pockets, the ensemble completed by a black bola tie and purple ostrich-hide cowboy boots. Kryzinski's clothes had caused mirth around the station house for years, giving rise to many hummed choruses of "Rhinestone Cowboy." Originally from Brooklyn, Kryzinski, like many other imports to Arizona, had taken to the Western lifestyle with a vengeance.

Jimmy took pity on him and fetched some bottles of prickly pear from the office refrigerator. Kryzinski and Yantis gulped them gratefully. I noticed that he did not offer any to Benson.

Oblivious to the slight, Benson leaned over my desk and continued his attempt at intimidation. "Mr. Royal was shot to death a week ago and we know there's an Arizona connection. A Scottsdale connection, to be exact. That's where you come in. Our sources tell us that an attractive blond woman with a scar above her right eyebrow was seen hiking in the area three days before he died. That certainly describes you, doesn't it? And we were also told that a woman who used to live in Mr. Royal's religious community hired you to pull her daughter out of there. Now, you can continue to play cute if you want, but in the meantime, somebody's getting away with murder."

Well, there's murder and there's murder.

"Tell me why I should care anything about one of those Purity men getting murdered," I said to Benson. "And while you're at it, answer my question. Why don't you and the rest of you Utah law enforcement types round up the whole bunch of them and throw their asses into prison where they belong? After all, as you so succinctly pointed out, polygamy is against both church law and state law. So what does that make you, Sheriff Benson? A double scofflaw for knowing about it and not doing anything?"

The healthy tan on Benson's face darkened in an angry flush. "It's not rape if there is consent."

I laughed. "Come on, Sheriff. In Arizona, when a sixty-eight-year old man has sex with a thirteen-year-old girl it's called statutory rape. We don't believe that children are mature enough to give informed consent."

The red intensified. "Polygamists don't marry girls under sixteen anymore. Not since the law was changed in 2001."

"That's just Utah Tourist Commission bullshit and you know it. They're still doing it."

A tic got busy at the edge of Benson's right eye but the rest of him didn't move. "That's another conversation for another time. We're trying to solve a murder here."

"I'd like to give the murderer a medal."

"Aren't you interested in justice, Ms. Jones?"

"I certainly am interested in justice, Sheriff. That's why I'm not crying any crocodile tears over baby-rapers."

Benson's right eye jerked so much it almost closed. "That's a pretty harsh term."

"Old men forcing themselves on little girls, then covering up their crimes by calling it marriage, is pretty harsh, if you ask me."

The tic eased off and the smug look returned. "What makes you so certain the marriage, was being forced? Or do you have some information we don't?"

Benson was no fool. In my anger, I had come close to admitting that I'd been the one who rescued Rebecca from Prophet Solomon Royal. Before I could make another mistake I went back on the offensive.

"Maybe I'd cooperate if you'd tell me, since you're so interested in justice, why these polygamy compounds are allowed to continue? Or is the rape of young girls just Utah's version of safe sex?"

Benson's face tightened. "Not that it's any of your business, but there have been prosecutions. Tom Green is doing time for child rape and a member of the Kingston clan is doing six years for incest."

"You know as well as I do that the only reason Green and Kingston were prosecuted at all was because they were high profile cases that made it to the national media just before the Salt Lake Olympics. Now the Olympics are over, and you've still got polygamists spread out all over the map."

I could swear I heard his teeth grinding before he took a deep breath and finally answered. "My job is to investigate the murder of Solomon Royal, Ms. Jones. Nothing more, nothing less. Now, if you have information about the night he died, you need to share it with us. Otherwise…"

"Otherwise what?"

Benson said nothing, just stared at me through icy eyes.

Captain Kryzinski, looking worried, broke into the silence. "Lena, please cooperate."

"Cooperate?" If I had been any more furious I would have imploded. I snuck a sideways glance at Jimmy, who along with the deputy had listened carefully to this exchange.

I uncrossed my hands from the back of my head and made a big show of looking at my watch. "Gentlemen, you arrived without an appointment, and while our little talk has been educational, I need to get back to work."

"Lena…" Kryzinski leaned forward in his chair, his round face sagging in disappointed folds.

Benson cut him off. "Ms. Jones is right, Captain. Our work here is done. We might as well return to the station and start the process."

Start the process? I didn't like the sound of that, but since I didn't want the Utah boys to know they worried me, I kept fussing with my watch.

Deputy Yantis threw a look of dread outside at the waves of heat rising from the pavement, but Kryzinski just sighed and struggled out of his chair. Benson strode to the door, giving me one more baleful look before he opened the door and let the asphalt-scented breeze in.

"We'll speak again, Ms. Jones."

"Only if you subpoena me, Sheriff."

He managed a smile. "Oh, don't worry, Ms. Jones. We folks up in Utah are pretty good with paperwork." Then he braced himself against the blast furnace that passes for September in Scottsdale and exited the office, his sweating deputy in tow.

I watched until Captain Kryzinski's blue-and-white disappeared down the street, then went back to my desk and called Esther Corbett. After filling her in on what had just happened, I told her that if she had any vacation time coming from her job behind the cosmetics counter at Neiman-Marcus, this might be the time to take it. With Rebecca.

And preferably in some country that did not have an extradition agreement with the United States.

For the rest of the morning Jimmy continued his personnel investigations at a nearby semiconductor plant, where someone had been walking off with shopping bags full of computer chips. I, having no computer skills at all, drove to South Phoenix in order to get the owner of a discarded tire dump in South Phoenix to admit that, yes, he knew burning tires leaked pollutants into the atmosphere, and yes, hiring his son, who had racked up two juvenile arson convictions by the age of sixteen, had been a lapse in judgment. The South Mountain Citizens for Clean Air had hired me, pro bono, of course, in hopes that I could do something about the continued fires, but so far, the dump's owner refused to admit that his son was the source of the problem.

I could almost hear the vinyl upholstery in my 1945 Jeep sizzle in the triple-digit heat as I cruised west on the 202, happy to put Esther Corbett's problems aside for awhile. The glass-fronted high rises of downtown Phoenix provided no shade worth speaking of; they only succeeded in blocking the view of the White Tank Mountains. Not that the White Tanks looked particularly scenic at this time of year. Like everything else in the Sonoran Desert, they'd been burned almost black by the unrelenting sun. Only hardy creosote bushes and saguaro cactus survived on their slopes.

I exited the freeway at Nineteenth Avenue and headed south into the Barrio, where a motley collection of mesquite trees and palms did what they could to relieve the desert's omnipresent browns and umbers. Unlike most Scottsdale residents, I maintained a fondness for the Barrio, and not only because the family which had once saved my life lived close by. The small adobe homes, some of them a century old, were a welcome respite from Scottsdale's pseudo-Mediterranean mansions, as were the Barrio's pink flamingos, the garden gnomes, and the occasional live chicken scratching for its buggy dinner.

Despite its charm, the Barrio could be a risky place for a leisurely drive. I kept a lead foot on the Jeep's accelerator as I drove past the graffiti-covered walls which proclaimed that the turf belonged to the Crips, the Bloods, and the West Side Chicanos. This hard-core gang territory seldom failed to lead off the ten o'clock news broadcasts.

Even more insidious, South Phoenix remained the site of too many commercial waste dumps and industrial parks. The people who lived there suffered from respiratory ailments rarely found in the rest of the valley.

South Mountain Tire Storage, with more than six hundred thousand tires destined for the state's recycling program, had long been one of the neighborhood's chief offenders. In the past couple of years, it had belched huge columns of smoke on an almost regular basis. The Environmental Protection Agency proclaimed itself not amused, but so far, the fines they levied against Dwayne Alder, the dump's owner, had not solved the problem.

As I drove into the storage yard, I could still smell burning rubber, even though the last fire had been put out three months earlier. The stench emanated from the three-story-high mound of tires known sarcastically by the locals as Black Mountain. The smelly heap did not appear all that stable, either, and looked as if it would topple over any minute. I was just thinking that I would make this visit as brief as possible when a nasty-looking Rottweiler the size of a Shetland pony trotted from behind a mound of bald Firestones to greet me with bared fangs.

"What a good dog," I said hopefully, remaining in my Jeep while awaiting rescue. "And what nice, sharp teeth you have."

Good Dog informed me in his rumbly voice that he hoped to use them on me, but his hopes were dashed when a middle-aged man sporting a belly the size and shape of a bowling ball exited the single-wide used as the dump's office. The man's face had been so burnt by the sun that it almost matched his red hair and scrawny beard.

"Ringo, sit!"

Ringo sat, although he did not look happy about it. I climbed out of the Jeep, giving him a wide berth. His eyes followed my every move.

The man studied my Jeep with the same amount of beady fascination as Ringo studied me. Not long ago, some of Jimmy's relatives had decorated the Jeep with a series of Pima story-telling designs, and now the entire history of the Pima Indians marched across its hood, doors, and rear. A set of steer horns mounted on the hood finished off the Jeep's fashion statement.

"I'm Lena Jones, the private detective," I said, when the man finally faced me again. "If you're Dwayne Alder, we've already talked on the phone."

His eyes gave me the usual lustful once-over, then stopped when they reached my face. I was used to it. I had been told that the one-inch-long scar from the bullet that had almost killed me was the only flaw in an otherwise perfect set of features. The scar could have been removed in one short visit to any plastic surgeon, but I'd chosen to keep it, hoping that someone might eventually recognize it and tell me my real name. You see, the name I use is not really mine. It had been given to me thirty years earlier by a particularly unimaginative social worker.

"Are you Mr. Alder?" I tried again.

"Yeah, yeah, that's me," he said, finally shifting his eyes away from my forehead. "Call me Dwayne. C'mon, let's get inside the office before we fry. Ringo, you stay."

Ringo whined, but sat obediently in the shade of the tires.

It was much cooler inside and the purple faux leather chairs surprisingly comfortable, but the reek of burnt rubber that blended with the smell of stale tobacco kept my breaths shallow.

"I'm here about your son," I said. "Your neighbors aren't too happy with him."

"I don't care about the neighbors. Miles is a good boy."

He shifted around on his chair as if fleas bit his butt, and plucked nervously at his scrawny red beard. "Sure, Miles got hisself into some trouble years back, but he was runnin' with a rough crowd then."

If I had a dollar for every time I heard the parent of some felonious teen blame it on his friends, I would be skiing in Switzerland right now, not melting in the Arizona heat.

"Two stints at Adobe Mountain Correctional Facility aren't exactly a little trouble, Mr. Alder. And as for that rough crowd you say corrupted your son, my sources maintain that Miles was the ringleader. Whatever mischief they perpetrated, he initiated. It's time to face facts and get that kid some help, because he's not going to recover from his attraction to fire without it. Now, I know the ATF hasn't been able to come up with enough evidence for an arrest, but don't you think you have a moral obligation to your community? Every time that dump goes up, hundreds of little babies suck in lungs full of toxic fumes."

Alder hitched his pants. "Yeah, that's too bad, but there ain't nothing I can do about it."

"Couldn't you get Miles another job? Some place where he wouldn't be exposed to, ah, flammables?"

More beard-plucking. "Like flipping burgers at Mac-Donald's or something? The kid's gotta learn how to run the business. My health ain't so good. Emphysema. I'm going to have to retire pretty quick now."

"You don't have any other children?"

"Two girls. Why?"

"How about training one of them to take over?"

Alder looked at me like I'd just grown two heads. "Let a girl run a tire dump?"

I tried not to sigh. "Better a girl than a firebug. Look, Mr. Alder, in a day and age where women fly the Space Shuttle, I think with the proper training one of your daughters might be able to run this place."

Yep, I'd grown two heads, all right. "I don't need you to be telling me how to raise my family, sister. Miles stays."

My sigh finally escaped. "So you refuse to do anything about your son?"

"I don't need to do nothing about that boy. He'd be fine if people would just stop leanin' on him. Now you go on back to them Citizens for Clean Air fools and tell them to mind their own business. Maybe they ought to be looking at their own kids, cause it sure ain't my Miles been settin' these fires. Now, it's been awful nice talking to a pretty lady but I got me a ton of work to do here."

Just then a young man entered the office, Ringo slobbering happily at his heels. Miles. I recognized him from the news reports, where, in typical firebug behavior, he always bellied up to the camera to hold forth about the fires. It was easy to see how he'd become the apple of his dad's eye. Where Alder looked and sounded like the product of a hard-scrabble upbringing, Miles, with his designer hair, broad shoulders, and even features, could have posed for a Ralph Lauren ad. But I thought his blue eyes were just a trifle too steady. Con man eyes.

Since reason hadn't worked with the father, I doubted its effectiveness with the son. I decided on a more direct approach. "Listen, you little shithead. The neighbors are tired of the fires. They want you to stop."

Miles smirked. "Why, ma'am, I honestly don't know what you're talking about."

"Yes, you do, and I'm telling you right now, if those fires don't stop, I'm going to be all over your butt like a bad pair of pants until your firebug ass gets locked up permanent. And, Miles? Now that you're eighteen, you're too old for

Juvie. The next time you go down it'll be to the State Correctional Facility in Florence where the big boys live. You'll be the sweetest piece of ass they've seen in a long time."

The blue eyes blinked rapidly, then shifted to his father.

"Pop?" Miles whined, now sounding decidedly non-Lauren-esque. "Are you going to let her talk to me this way?"

Dad rushed to his baby's rescue. "You got no call to talk to my boy like that! Get the hell out of here!"

I nodded, but directed a parting shot to Miles. "Remember what I said, little boy. One more fire and you'd better start stocking up on K-Y Jelly."

When I stood to leave, Ringo, who had been lying adoringly at his master's feet, stood too. He looked at my own butt, perhaps envisioning a rare rump roast for dinner. Miles' eyes flicked toward his dog.

"If that dog bites me I'll shoot it first and ask questions later." I punctuated my words by patting the carry-all that served as my purse. A *thunk* revealed my .38's presence. Like so many Arizonans, I was licensed to carry.

My threat worked.

"Ringo, sit," Papa Alder ordered.

I made it to the Jeep in one piece.

Back at the office, things had slowed down. Jimmy had spent the day running background checks for the semiconductor company, and he had narrowed the thief down to three suspects, all of whom had criminal records.

"I don't know why employers don't do this themselves," he said. "Just think of all the money they'd save."

"They don't do it because they're not as good as you are, Slick."

Jimmy snorted. "It's so easy a child..."

"...could do it," I finished for him. Yeah, sure, a child with an I.Q. of 156, who'd grown up playing with computers the way other children played with Matchbox cars.

He pushed away from his keyboard and faced me. I had noticed long before that his tribal tattoos tended to darken when he was worried, and they looked almost black now.

"Lena, those guys from Utah. I don't like that they traveled all the way down here."

I nodded. "I'm worried, too. I told Esther to take a trip somewhere, anywhere, but I'm betting she won't. She has this ridiculous belief in Truth, Justice, and the American Way."

"What's so ridiculous about that?"

I snorted. Recently, a Maricopa County judge had forcibly returned a fourteen-year-old AIDS patient from Arizona, where she lived with a beloved aunt, to Minnesota to live in an adult AIDS shelter. Why? Because her father, who stayed in a Minnesotan rehab center after his release from a stretch in prison for child neglect, wanted closer access to his daughter. Following a long tradition in the addled Arizona court system, the judge decided that parental rights superseded the rights of the child, regardless of how sleazy the parent. Truth? Justice? The American Way? Not for Arizona's children.

But I simply said to Jimmy, "If those Utah cops catch up with Esther, she'll be extradited to Utah before you can say Brigham Young."

Jimmy turned back to his computer without saying a word.

Two hours later, my prediction came true. As I was closing up the office, the phone rang. It was Esther Corbett, calling me from the Scottsdale City Jail, where she was being held pending extradition to Utah.

For the murder of Solomon Royal.

Chapter 3

Under the glare of the cell's harsh light, Esther Corbett looked ten years older. No trace of the glow that had been painted across her face when I had returned her daughter to her a week earlier remained. Unhealthy shadows crept into the hollows under her cheekbones and eyes.

"Lena, you have to do something," she rasped at me, her voice raw, probably from crying. "Rebecca's father is driving down from Utah to take her back to Purity." She clutched at my hand as if we were mountain climbers and her safety line had broken. I'd have bruises tomorrow.

"At least Rebecca's safe for now," I said, tapping my notebook, where I'd written down the address and phone number where the girl was now staying. "Your ex-husband doesn't have custody, so we've got some time to maneuver."

Esther had told me that when she had seen the police car pull up in front of her rented house, she'd sent Rebecca out the back door with her roommate. The roommate had taken the girl to a friend's house, but warned that the arrangement could only be temporary. Another place had to be found for Rebecca or she'd wind up with Child Protective Services.

Esther shook her head. "The legal system in Beehive County is a mess, Lena. Abel filed a motion there last week, and since I didn't respond to the summons the court served on me, the judge actually awarded him custody by default!"

I hid my alarm. The whole thing flew in the face of the Uniform Child Custody Agreement recognized by every state, but weirder things have happened. Rebecca was in trouble, all right.

"Lena, I don't have money for bail or to drag this extradition thing out like you told me to over the phone. They'll probably send me back to Utah right away where you know I'll never get a fair trial. The polygamists *own* the courts there. And Rebecca, now that Solomon's dead, she's already half-forgotten how bad it was at the compound. She keeps talking about how many friends she made in just the short time she was there. I'm afraid…"

She chewed her lip so hard that a bright spot of blood appeared. "Lena, I'm afraid they're going to get to her."

"Get to her? What do you mean?"

Esther's eyes, which despite her distress had been dry, now teared up. "The men in Purity, even the women, they have their ways. They talk to you, they tell you things, they confuse you. They did it to me when I was growing up. They convinced me that marrying the man they ordained was God's will and that if I resisted, I'd go to Hell. I saw grown women so afraid of that threat that they married men they couldn't stand. Oh, Lena! Rebecca's just a child!"

I remembered Rebecca's face when we discovered Prophet Solomon's body. The man who'd been about to rape her was dead, and yet she reacted with an odd mixture of grief and guilt. Had the brainwashing Esther described already taken hold?

It wouldn't help Esther to know that I shared her fears, so I kept my worries to myself. "Look, first thing we do, we'll hire a good attorney. You'll need one here in order to stop the extradition process."

Frustration crossed Esther's face. "I don't have any money left. I used everything I had for the custody case."

No surprise there. Esther's had been yet another pro bono case for Desert Investigations. In fact, I worked so many pro bonos that Jimmy was in danger of being our company's only moneymaker. Not that it mattered. Unlike most detective agencies, we had an angel. Desert Investigations existed due to the financial goodwill of Albert Grabel, the Scottsdale computer magnate whose innocent son I had managed to get out of prison while I'd still worked for the Scottsdale Police Department. When Grabel heard I'd opened my own agency, he promised to finance the cases of others I believed were unjustly accused.

Grabel's largess didn't necessarily extend to exorbitant attorney's fees, though. If we left Esther's extradition case to a public defender, she would be Utah-bound in a heartbeat. Fortunately, Grabel was not the only person in Scottsdale who owed me.

But first, I had to get my client to tell me the truth for a change. "Esther, what kind of case do the Utah authorities have against you?"

"Nothing but lies." She lowered her eyes and pretended to find something of interest on the cell floor.

I waved her own lie away. "When Rebecca and I got back to the motel, I noticed that your car was covered in dust. You drove out to the compound, didn't you?"

She shook her head, but kept her eyes lowered.

I grabbed her by the chin and forced her to look at me. "Esther, I'm on your side, remember? But I can't help you if you don't tell me everything. That includes your movements while Jimmy and I were waiting outside the compound."

Her eyes filled with tears again. "All right, all right. Yes. I drove out there."

"And?"

"And nothing." She jerked her chin away. "What did you expect me to do, Lena? You'd been gone for days and I was desperate to see my daughter!"

"When was this?"

She looked away. "The same day you brought her to the motel. Around dinner time."

I tried not to groan. "Tell me exactly what you did and what you saw."

She met my eyes again. Now I was going to get the truth. "I hid my car in a stand of creosote bushes about a mile away from the compound and hiked down into the canyon. I thought I might even run into you, but I guess you were over in the other direction."

I nodded. I'd camped far enough back into the twenty-mile-long canyon to make discovery difficult. But Esther had placed herself right at the murder scene. Could her situation have been any worse?

She must have seen the consternation on my face. "All I wanted was just a glimpse of Rebecca, Lena. You'd told me how dangerous it would be if I tried to grab her myself."

"You ran into Solomon, didn't you?"

The tears came back. "Yes," she whispered.

Only the pain in her eyes kept me from screaming at her in frustration. "Tell me what happened. Don't leave anything out."

"We…we argued."

"I'll bet you did. Give me the gory details."

Her voice trembled but she managed to maintain control. "He was out hunting with two other men, and when I saw him walking along like that, looking so self-satisfied and arrogant, knowing that he wanted my daughter, what he was going to do to her, I…I just lost it."

"How badly did you lose it?" I had visions of Esther wresting the shotgun away from old Solomon and giving him both barrels in the chest. It was probably what I'd do if Rebecca had been my daughter.

"I started screaming at him, calling him all sorts of names. I told him he'd marry Rebecca over my dead body. It became ugly enough that he told the other men to leave us alone. I think he was afraid of what I might say. About him. About Purity."

I thought about this for a minute. "And did they leave you two alone?"

She nodded. "They went further up the canyon, in the direction of Zion City. But not so far that I couldn't hear them stomping around in the brush."

I pulled my pen and notebook out of my carry-all. "Give me the men's names. They'll probably be called as witnesses, so we need to be prepared." I waited expectantly.

Nothing.

"Esther?"

Her lower lip quivered. "Earl Graff was one of them. We never got along."

I jotted the name down. "And the other man?"

"My father."

I sat up straight. "Your father? That's good, then. He won't want to testify against you."

She shook her head miserably. "Before my father left me with the prophet, he called me the Whore of Babylon."

Not so good. "Your father called you the Whore of Babylon and then he and that other guy, Earl Graff, left you and Solomon alone. What happened next?"

She didn't say anything for a second, then finally took a deep breath. "I called him a pedophile. He slapped me. I started crying and ran back to my car."

I frowned. "Do you think the other men heard him hit you?"

She shrugged. "What if they did? Women get slapped around all the time up there. It's how the men keep them in line."

I frowned. The story sounded reasonable, more or less. I would have liked to learn the real reason Solomon had sent the two men away, but the hard edge in Esther's voice told me the interview was over. Still, for all the holes in her story, I doubted if Esther had killed Solomon. If she had, Graff and her father would have heard the shotgun blast and nabbed her on the spot. Then they might have indulged themselves in a little Wild West justice. The kind with a rope.

I put my notebook away and prepared to make my exit. Forcing a smile, I patted her hand. "Don't worry. I'll make sure you have a damned good attorney before Abel gets down here. We'll have your ex-husband so tied up in red tape on this custody and extradition business that he'll look like Houdini."

Hope leapt into her eyes. "Do you really believe you can prevent Rebecca from being forced back to Utah?"

"I know I can."

I'm such a liar.

Jimmy had left for the semiconductor plant again when I arrived back at Desert Investigations, so I rushed straight to my desk and began making phone calls. I soon discovered that I'd forgotten that Scottsdale's rich and famous tended to flee our hideous heat every summer to hole up in cooler places, such as London or Copenhagen. But after an hour of punching in numbers, I finally hit pay dirt.

Serena Hyath-Allesandro, one of the Valley's richest women, remained in town. She had just been released from rehab with her doctor's warning not to dance the European tango with the fast crowd she usually danced with. Even though I had recently been involved in a murder case which devastated her family, Serena and I had nonetheless developed a wary friendship.

"Polygamy?" she breathed at me over the phone, her voice as thin as Arizona's ozone layer. "In this day and age? Surely you can't be serious."

I told her that I was very serious indeed, and brought her up to date on Esther's case. When I reached the part about Rebecca's possible return to Purity, I could almost hear her spine stiffen.

"Well, that's simply not to be allowed," she said, her voice firmer. "Tell you what. I'm on the board of My Sister's House, a shelter for victims of domestic abuse, and another board member, Ray Winfield, you know him, he's the attorney who got Craig Merryweather off when he was accused of murdering that topless dancer. Ray and I..." She let the sentence trail off, but I could have finished it for her. According to the society pages, Ray Winfield and Serena had become an item, and rumors floated around town that they would marry as soon as her divorce from her third Euro-trash husband came through. "I can promise you that Ray will be down at the jail in less than an hour."

When Serena Hyath-Allesandro said she would do something, it was as good as done, so I thanked her and hung up. For a moment I sat looking out the window, just thinking about families and the trouble they could get into.

"Lena? Lena?" Jimmy's voice snapped me out of my reverie. He'd returned while I'd been on the phone with Serena. "How's Esther?" The look on his face hinted at more than concern, and I realized that my soft-hearted partner had fallen for yet another client.

"Her ex-husband is coming down from Utah to take Rebecca back with him. The kid's with a friend of Esther's roommate right now, but it's just a matter of time before she's handed over to CPS or her father. I think Esther's more worried about that than the murder charge."

Jimmy's tribal tattoos darkened. He loathed the prospect of returning Esther to Purity as much as I did. No surprise there. Pimas respected women, and their culture vilified the seduction of young girls.

Then a small smile tugged at the edge of his mouth, and the tattoos lightened. "You know, Pima land is sovereign territory. We have our own police, our own court system."

I frowned. "Your point being?"

His smile broadened. "My point being that Utah couldn't pick up so much as a stray dog from Pima land, let alone a little girl spending some time with her Pima friends."

I got it. "Which Pima friends?"

"Oh, let's say for instance her dear friend Tiffany Sisiwan, who just happens to be my niece. Utah shows up at Tiffany's house, well, Tiffany's dad will get real irritated and show Utah the quickest way off the rez. Maybe even at gunpoint."

I smiled back at him. "Jimmy, you are the most under-handed noncriminal I know. I can't begin to tell you how much I admire you for it."

Thought being father to the deed, Jimmy immediately called his brother and explained the situation, while I called Esther's roommate and told her what we planned to do. Within minutes, Curtis Sisiwan and his wife were on their way to pick up Rebecca.

Rebecca's safety now guaranteed, Jimmy returned to his computer. Exhausted after flying in the face of so many child custody laws, I tried to relax by watching a herd of sunburned tourists exit a chartered bus and begin strolling along the neighboring art galleries on Main Street. It was something like watching the buffalo roam, except that tourists moved with less purpose. They drifted, sweating, into one gallery and out the other, emerging with bad paintings of Italian-looking "Indians" and plaster statues of howling coyotes.

I understood why Scottsdale was considered an Eden in the midst of winter, when as the rest of the country shivered in sub-zero temperatures, we barbequed by the pool. But in summer? Why on earth would someone from cool, shady Minnesota visit Arizona, where asphalt had been known to melt as early as May?

This conundrum cleared my mind wonderfully, and so I began to relax, my eyes following the tourists until they climbed back onto the bus.

Jimmy began straightening his desk. "I think I'll head over to Curtis's house. Anything you want me to tell Rebecca while I'm there?"

"Tell her not to worry, that her mother will be out of jail in no time."

It wasn't bad enough that I had lied to Esther. Now I was lying to her child.

After a little more fussing at his desk, Jimmy was out the door, into his souped-up Camaro, rumbling down Main Street toward the Salt River Pima-Maricopa Indian Reservation, where tribal law ruled and the rest of the world could go hang.

The afternoon shadows lengthened into darkness, and for a moment, I thought about changing into jogging gear and heading out to Papago Park. But since I had already worked out at the gym that morning honing my karate skills I gave it a pass. Besides, I still felt parched from my three days in Paiute Canyon, where I had learned to my surprise that Utah's daytime temperatures climbed almost as high as Scottsdale's.

Instead, I decided to call Dusty, my boyfriend, and invite him over for the evening. He worked forty miles north on a dude ranch at the backside of Carefree, but now that the Pima Freeway was finished, the drive took less than forty minutes, even with traffic. After a bumpy beginning to our relationship, much of it my fault, we'd recently grown closer.

I picked up the phone again and punched in the number.

"Happy Trails." The voice at the other end of the line belonged to Dusty's boss, Slim Papadopolus, the owner of the ranch.

"Hi, handsome. It's Lena."

"Ah, the most beautiful blond in the world." Before buying the dude ranch, Slim had been a jockey on the top racing circuits and his flattering ways had helped him become as popular with women as with the horses' owners. None of them seemed to mind that he stood no more than 5'3" in his built-up cowboy boots.

"What can I do for you, sweetheart? You want to come up here and ride tomorrow? You do, I'll get Lady saddled first thing in the morning. Unless you want to try that new Appaloosa we just got in. I figure you can handle him."

The prospect appealed, but I declined. "I'd love to, but I'm in the middle of a case and can't spare the time. I was just calling to see if Dusty was through for the day and wanted to be treated to a home-cooked meal."

Slim usually laughed when I said something like this, because my inability to cook was legendary. This time, though, he just said, "Dusty, he's, ah, he's not here."

That was odd. Dusty seldom went anywhere. Other than the times he took tourists out on a trail drive, his excursions to the nearby country-western bars or down to Scottsdale to see me tended to be the sum total of his worldly travels.

I wasn't Dusty's baby-sitter. He'd probably taken that old truck of his out for a tune-up. "When he gets back, tell him I called."

"Will do." Slim sounded relieved.

I hung up the phone and prepared for my nightly ordeal. Hating myself for my weakness, I reached down into my carry-all and took out my .38 revolver. I turned off the office lights, leaving only the neon sign outside to glimmer "Desert Investigations" to an empty street. Since it was not an Art Walk night, the one evening during the week when the art galleries stayed open until nine o'clock, all the businesses had already closed. I was alone.

But, hey, I'd been alone almost all of my life, so what was the big deal?

Plenty, a mean little voice inside me hissed. *Plenty.*

I locked the office and, revolver pointed before me, started up the narrow staircase at the side of the building to my apartment. Even though I had taken every security precaution possible, every time I entered my apartment all my childhood fears returned. Not too surprising since at the age of nine, I'd inadvertently locked myself in my own bedroom with my foster father, who then celebrated the occasion by raping me. The near-misses I'd endured during my last murder case hadn't helped my nerves, either.

The metal door with which I had replaced the wooden one looked solid enough to withstand an elephant stampede, but I examined the locks and the hinges carefully. As on other nights, my paranoia remained unfounded. I saw no gouges around the door's frame; the locks and hinges remained intact. Still, I pressed my ear against the door and listened. Silence.

Taking a deep breath, I unlocked the upper and lower deadbolts, shoved the door open with my foot, and entered the apartment gun-first, leaving the door ajar behind me in case I needed a fast exit.

As usual, I had left the lights on before coming downstairs to work that morning, but I still checked every corner for telltale shadows. My mainly beige living room, the only spot of color being the huge George Haozous painting, proved free of lurking assassins. So did the hall closet, kitchen and bath.

But the bedroom had always scared me the most, and as I approached it down the short hallway, my breath hitched as if I had run a four-minute mile. With a kick, I slammed the door back, hoping to injure anyone who might be lurking behind it. No one was. Then I walked over to the bed, jerked the spread away and knelt down, revolver thrust forward. All that greeted me there were a few harmless dust bunnies.

But now came the worst part: the long, dark closet. My foster father had hidden in a closet.

Gun still before me, I rolled back the sliding door and jumped away, ready to blast anything that moved.

Nothing did.

I sighed in relief, and after double-checking to make sure no one had crept into the apartment behind me, I returned to the front door and double-locked it.

Now I was safe, or at least as safe as my .38 and my fortress of an apartment could keep me. I wandered over to the stereo, inserted a John Lee Hooker CD, then went back to the kitchen. As John Lee sang about empty beds and lonely nights, I put my gun down within easy reach on the kitchen counter, took a Michelina's Lasagna with Marinara Sauce out of the freezer and nuked it. I ate my dinner standing up, my back to the sink all the while, keeping a steady eye on the front door.

A girl can never be too careful.

Later that night I lay awake until the wee hours, watching the light show on my ceiling made by the headlights of passing cars. I knew that as long as I could see them I was safe. But at some point I drifted away, lulled by the noise of tires on pavement and the sweet whisper of the air conditioner.

I awoke to find myself on a bus filled with singing people. A woman who looked like me held me in her lap, her fingers tightened into claws. Something cold pressed against my forehead.

"I'll kill her! I'll kill her!" the woman screamed, pressing the gun closer to my head. *"You just see, I'm going to kill her right now!"*

A sound of thunder, a gunshot. Pain.

Then I was thrown away into the night, only to awaken in my Scottsdale apartment.

I sat up and kicked the sweat-dampened sheets away.

"Damn you, Mother," I whispered.

Chapter 4

"We'll fight extradition as long as we can, but in the end, Ms. Corbett will have to return to Utah to face murder charges," Ray Winfield warned, as we spoke over the phone the next morning. "We can get a Utah attorney as an assist once she gets up there."

"How long can you stall for?" I noticed out of the corner of my eye that Jimmy paid close attention to my side of the conversation.

A pause. Then some throat-clearing. "A couple of weeks if we're lucky. You know, Ms. Jones, the Utah officials appear pretty confident about their case, which gives me some concern. Just how much do you know about Ms. Corbett's movements that night?"

Damned little, I realized. I thought back to that night at the motel and Esther's oddly prescient question, "Solomon was shot?" True, this was the twenty-first century and many unanticipated deaths arrived by gunshot, but still, there had been absolutely no surprise in Esther's eyes at the news of Prophet Solomon's death. Even Rebecca, in all her panic, noticed it. How could a woman so transparent ever hope to outwit the Utah court system?

"Ms. Jones? Ms. Jones?" The attorney's words startled me out of my reverie.

"Lena." I picked up a pencil and began drawing a hang-man's noose on a scratch pad.

"What's that?"

"Call me Lena, Ray. I'm not into formality."

"I asked how much you know about Ms. Corbett's movements that night. You're certain to be subpoenaed when this case goes to trial, and it's better to tell me now so there won't be any ugly surprises later."

I gave him my rehearsed answer. "As far as I'm concerned, there won't be any ugly surprises. Esther was waiting for us when we got back to the motel."

"This is just a supposition, but is there any way she could have been at Purity that night and made it back to the motel before you did?"

I didn't answer right away. Instead, I drew a man's head in the noose.

"Let me rephrase that, Ms. Jo…uh, Lena. How well do you know the area up there?"

"This is privileged information, right? Nothing I tell you can be used in court?"

"Right."

In order to forestall one of those ugly surprises he had cautioned against, I told him what I knew. "There are several paths leading out of Purity and into the desert, but there's really only one way to hook up with the road. To smuggle Rebecca out without anybody seeing us, I chose the path into Paiute Canyon. It's not only the shortest, but it provides the best cover, too. Juniper, mesquite, and brush all over the place. Hell, you could hide a giraffe in there. Anyway, we headed south down the canyon until it hooked northwest, and that's where we just about fell over the body."

He phrased his next question carefully. "When you all drove up there, Ms. Corbett took her own car, right?"

"A bright green Geo with Arizona plates." I began shading the male figure's head, trying hard for a resemblance to Prophet Solomon.

"Are there any other roads leading to the compound, especially any paved roads?" he asked.

"Naw. Just the dirt road." Satisfied with my drawing's resemblance to the prophet, I added a bullet hole between his eyes, then sketched in a shadow box frame.

"So if Ms. Corbett drove along that road she would pass you at some point, right?"

As much as I wanted to answer in the affirmative, I couldn't. "Not necessarily. You forget that all those nights Jimmy was waiting for me, he'd pulled the truck several yards off the side of the road and hid it in a stand of piñon pine. He told me he heard several cars and trucks going to and coming from Purity that night, but he was more concerned with staying hidden than he was with car-spotting. Technically speaking, if Esther left the motel just after Jimmy, she could have driven all the way to the compound without him seeing her, done the deed, and beat us back. The timing would be tight, but with a little luck she could have managed it."

"It was night. And way out in the badlands." Winfield's voice sounded distant, like he was deep in thought. "To avoid being seen, all she had to do was turn off her lights."

I wiggled the pencil between my fingers and explained. "Cars driving along dirt make a lot of noise, which is why Jimmy was able to hear all the traffic. But here's my thinking. If Esther had driven within a quarter mile of Purity that night and yet not gone in, someone would certainly have heard her and gone out to investigate. Also, where the dirt road ends at the blacktop? There's an all-night gas station/café combo sitting right there on the northwest side of the intersection. Lots of traffic and lots of nosey people. They probably pay pretty close attention to any strange car they see going out to the Purity compound, and a green Geo is a pretty strange vehicle for that area because almost everyone else drives pickups. If nobody's come forward yet to say they saw the Geo, we're probably all right."

When he spoke next, he still sounded worried. "We'll find out during the discovery process, won't we?"

"I guess." I thought we'd finished the conversation, but then Winfield dropped a bomb.

"Ah, Lena, I have some other news you need to know about. Abel Corbett, Rebecca's father, arrived in Scottsdale this morning, custody papers in hand from Utah Family Court."

The pencil in my hand broke in half.

"Mr. Corbett insists on taking his daughter back to Utah with him until this situation is cleared up," Winfield continued. "We have to comply."

"Does he have another dirty old man he wants to sell Rebecca to?"

"No crime has been committed yet. Rebecca has to be proven to be in danger before we can successfully challenge the Utah custody order now that her mother's in jail."

I tossed the pencil's remains into the wastebasket. "What does that mean? Do we have to wait until Rebecca's in some old fart's bed and *then* go to court? Where's the sense in that? You know as well as I do that the Utah court system won't remove a little girl from a polygamy compound. It's been tried before by worried relatives and they've failed every time. The court always rules that the parents, whatever freaks they may be, have custody over the child until she turns sixteen. And by then, it's too late."

"Lena, the law is the law, and as an officer of the court, I have to comply with it. In Utah, parents are God until proven unfit, and that's pretty tough to do unless they're serial killers."

"Well, I'm not an officer of the court, and as far as I'm concerned, you can put the law where the sun don't shine."

"Nice sentiment, coming from a former police officer."

I brought myself back under control. There was no point in alienating him. "Sorry about that, Ray. For now, just tell Abel Corbett that his daughter's in a safe place, a place arranged by her mother. And remind him that according to *Arizona* law, her mother is still the custodial parent, jailed or not. Those legal tricks he pulled in Utah are just so much bullshit."

"Child Protective Services might not see it that way."

My laugh was ugly. "Oh, yeah, Child Protective Services. Sometime when we have a couple of hours or, even better, a couple of days, remind me to tell you about my own experiences with CPS." The seedy foster homes I'd endured reared up in my memory. "I wouldn't turn a snake over to CPS."

"While I'm certain there have been abuses..."

"The answer is no, a flat-out no. Rebecca stays where she's put until her mother either changes her mind or gets out of jail. If you do your job properly, that'll be sooner rather than later."

Although unhappy, Winfield let it go. Uttering dire warnings about custodial interference and the Uniform Child Custody Agreement, he hung up.

I replaced the receiver and stared at my hand. It was shaking.

"I didn't like the sound of that conversation," Jimmy said from across the room. I'd forgotten he was there.

"Neither did I. What do you think the chances are that Utah has a witness who saw Esther near Purity? It's too bad one of us wasn't able to stay with her at the motel."

"Yeah, it is. But I couldn't be two places at once, could I?"

He'd had to wait for me near the compound every night, until I finally showed up with Rebecca. I'd thought I could trust Esther to do what she'd promised when I allowed her to tag along with us to Utah. Still, moping over my own culpability in Esther's current situation accomplished nothing. The woman stood accused of murder, a murder I was pretty certain she hadn't committed. If Esther had wanted to kill Solomon Royal, she'd have gone into the compound in daylight, gun blazing, shouting to God and all his angels that the Prophet was getting what was coming to him. There would have been none of this sneaking along dirt roads at night, leaving her beloved daughter to discover a very messy dead body.

Which reminded me. "Jimmy, have you seen Rebecca yet today?"

He smiled. "I stopped by on my way in. Curtis is teaching her 'The Corn Song.'"

I smiled back. Jimmy had taught me the old Pima harvest chant when we had first started working together. Those words from another time had never ceased to calm me. Maybe I needed that now: a good run, a few bars from "The Corn Song." Esther's and Rebecca's woes had knocked me off my usual schedule, and now my nerves were paying the price. My workouts at the gym made a pretty poor substitute. Besides, my sore hand complained that it didn't care much for karate.

I looked up at the clock and discovered to my surprise that it was still early afternoon.

Jimmy broke into my thoughts. "Lena, we've got to help Rebecca. That little girl…"

"I know, Jimmy. I know."

With a grunt, he turned back to his computer and tapped away on the keys, escaping into one of his cases. I tried the same, but it didn't work. All I could think about was Rebecca and what awaited her if she returned to Utah. With her mother in jail, getting her out of Purity again and keeping her out would be impossible. Because of religion.

Yet after my last case I could no longer call myself a blatant atheist. Too many odd things had happened as I lay near death on the desert, not all of them attributable to hallucinations.

I was still musing on the mysterious ways of God when the door opened and a tall, thin man in his mid-thirties entered. Hallelujah, another client. Then I noticed his faded, long-sleeved, high-necked shirt and his shiny-kneed slacks. Not a paying client.

"May I help you?" I asked.

The man ignored me and addressed himself to Jimmy. "I'm here about my daughter."

I stiffened. He'd spoken to Jimmy, a tip-off that he didn't take women seriously.

The look on Jimmy's face proved he knew who confronted us. I'd never seen him indulge in violence before, but I wondered if that was about to change.

"Better talk to her," Jimmy muttered, turning back to his keyboard. His hands shook.

Abel Corbett stood in the center of the office for a moment, obviously loathe to speak to a lowly woman. Then necessity conquered philosophy, and he looked down at me. *Really* down, as if at a bug.

"You must be Lena Jones." Nature, having one of her little jokes, gave him a girlishly high voice. It sort of tickled me.

"That's me, sure enough."

"Where's my daughter?" With his almost-white hair and light blue eyes, he bore a vague resemblance to Sheriff Benson, and I wondered briefly if the two were related. It wasn't impossible. The gene pool ran pretty small on the Arizona Strip.

"Danged if I know." I smiled.

For a moment he didn't know how to respond to my denial, then male supremacy reasserted itself. "Don't hand me that. I demand that you turn Rebecca over to me. Now."

"Why? So you can pimp her out to some other prophet?"

I thought he'd faint from shock. From the stories Esther had told me about Purity, women never challenged men. Then again, Abel must have become used to it once he moved away.

Maybe that was why he'd returned to the compound.

He sputtered for a few seconds, then leaned over my desk, not noticing Jimmy rise quietly from his chair and begin toward him. "Tell me where my daughter is or I'll..."

"Get your skinny white ass out of this office before I party on it." Jimmy stood right behind him.

Abel Corbett twirled around and for a moment, it looked like he was going to throw a punch. But after taking note of Jimmy's own height and considerably heavier bulk, he obviously thought better of it.

"The law's on my side," he squeaked, as he backed away from my partner.

I motioned toward the door. "Leave."

He looked at me, then at Jimmy. He left.

"Oh, Jimmy, what are we going to do?" My voice trembled, but I didn't care.

Jimmy thought a moment, then said, "I have this cousin, Donny, he's in one of the reservation gangs, the Rez Bloods. His posse could take care of Abel for us."

I didn't say anything. For a long while, neither did Jimmy. Then he sat back down and put his head in his hands. When he finally looked back up at me, he said, "Well, we've got to do something."

"Yeah."

He turned back to his computer and tapped fitfully at it. I tried to immerse myself in paperwork, but the names and numbers jumbled together until they looked like Cyrillic.

I studied them for probably another half hour, then gave up.

"Jimmy?"

He turned around so quickly I knew he'd had the same trouble concentrating. "What?"

"I have to go back to Utah. The only way to prove Esther didn't murder Solomon Royal is for me to find out who did it. That Benson clown certainly won't."

To my surprise, Jimmy nodded. "I'll go with you."

Shaking my head, I said, "We're in the middle of several investigations here, including that damned firebug and the microchip thefts. Someone has to handle them."

He nodded. "Then take Dusty. That place is too dangerous for a woman alone."

I rolled my eyes. "Oh, please, not you, too. Besides, I haven't been able to reach Dusty for days. That's why I'll need a special favor from you. You used to live in Utah and you still have contacts up there."

"Yeah, my parents, for instance." You don't often get a chance to hear a Pima turn sarcastic on you, but when they do, it can be cutting.

"Then help me find a place to stay near the compound, someplace even closer than the motel. But not Paiute Canyon. I have no way of knowing how much time it'll take me to figure out this mess, and I'll need access to a phone and other modern conveniences. Hell, if you can somehow get me into the compound, that would be ideal."

He scowled, another Pima rarity.

"Jimmy? If you won't help me, do it for Rebecca. And Esther."

He picked up the phone.

Chapter 5

Jimmy worked his magic again, and two days later I was on my way back to the Arizona Strip.

The drive up I-17 toward Flagstaff was pleasant, watching the low Sonoran Desert evolve slowly to high chaparral, then miles and miles of sweet-scented Ponderosa pine. But once I turned out of Flagstaff on Route 89 to circumvent the Grand Canyon, the terrain morphed back into high desert. By the time I'd looped around the canyon, took 89A over the mountains, then dropped back down to the Kaibab Indian Reservation, the scenery looked as bleak as the Sonoran on a very bad day.

Then the scenery flipped on me again when I cut north on 389 into Utah and headed up toward Zion National Park and West Wind Guest Ranch. As the Jeep bumped along the long dirt road leading to the ranch, I remembered what I'd read about the area.

Rivaling the nearby Grand Canyon in beauty, Zion National Park had originally been home to the Anasazi Indians. When the Anasazi disappeared, the Paiute moved in, and many remained. Anglo settlement began in the 1850s, when the Mormon pioneer Isaac Behunin saw the area and named it "Zion," which meant "beautiful resting place." Old Isaac hadn't been given to hyperbole, either.

Sheer cliffs towered more than three thousand feet above the forested plateau below, where the Virgin River wound its way through red and white sandstone. Lush Ponderosa pine, sycamore, piñon and cottonwood covered the valley, complemented by scarlet plumes of Indian paintbrush and blue columbine.

Although the tourists who flocked to Zion kept West Wind Ranch in business, Jimmy had told me that the ranch, owned by Leo and Virginia Lawler, acquaintances of his adoptive mother, also served as a safe house for polygamists' runaway wives. The women would arrive exhausted from their escape, rest up for a few days, then Virginia would drive them to Zion City, where groups such as Tapestry Against Polygamy helped ease them into mainstream society by finding them apartments and jobs.

After the road took a final dogleg around a massive column of red sandstone, West Wind Guest Ranch came into view. Built entirely of logs, the multi-building complex appeared to have been part of the canyon for more than a hundred years. Jimmy's mother had told me, though, that only the ranch house was an original structure, and even it had undergone extensive renovation. The outbuildings, all new, had been designed to look as old as the house. In the manner of all dude ranches, a few well-fed horses milled around a split-rail corral, their grumpy expressions hinting they didn't much like their prospective riders.

Tourists limped across the grounds, looking spiffy in their new, pressed jeans and expensive cowboy boots. Driving into the yard, I heard a smattering of German, some Japanese. Just like Scottsdale.

I eased the Jeep into the gravel parking lot, weaving through a plethora of BMWs, Mercedes and Lexuses. It takes real money to vacation rough.

A woman dressed in Levis and plaid Western shirt waited for me on the ranch house porch. About forty-five years old, she was a big-boned, comfortable brunette, but as I grew closer I saw that her green eyes belied her sturdy physique. They were shadowed with sorrow.

She glanced at the scar on my face, then said, "Howdy, Lena. I'm Virginia, and I don't let guests tote their own luggage." Before I could protest, she grabbed my suitcase, but when she reached for the carry-all which secreted my Arizona-only licensed .38, I stepped quickly out of her reach.

"Pleased to meet you," I said, smiling.

She grinned back, dimming the pain in her eyes. "An independent woman. Good. You're gonna need to be."

The ranch house's interior lived up to the exterior's rustic promise. The walls on either side of the ancient stone fireplace were tapestried with knotty pine and antlers. Bright Navajo rugs lay scattered across the oak plank floor, softening the distance between a series of low, leather couches. Overhead, black beams girded a whitewashed ceiling. The room was empty of tourists.

"A gaggle of guests are out trail riding with Leo," Virginia explained, leading me up the stairs and down a softly lit corridor. "They'll start drifting in soon with sore butts, whining for martinis."

She gestured toward the wet bar, her sour expression reminding me that Mormons were non-drinkers. But as many Mormon hoteliers had done during the Salt Lake Olympics, the Lawlers apparently indulged their gin-guzzling guests.

"You want something?" she asked. "Beer? Whiskey? Any other kinda strange brew?"

When I told her I didn't drink, I earned a smile of approval. I didn't tell her, though, that my teetotaling ways had nothing to do with religion or dietary philosophy. Not knowing what kind of genetic load I carried, I never drank anything stronger than Diet Coke. For all I knew, both my vanished parents had been druggies or alcoholics, and I didn't want to risk traveling the Addict Highway. I'd already lived through Hell and didn't feel the need for a return visit.

"I'm gonna put your stuff in Number Eight, but don't bother unpacking," she said, stopping before a door at the very end of the hall. "You might not stay all that long."

I frowned. Jimmy's mother had given me the impression I'd be operating out of West Wind for the next couple of weeks, using it as my home base while I interviewed anyone who would talk to me. Had something changed?

"Uh, Virginia, I'd planned..."

"Man proposes and God disposes," she said vaguely, putting my suitcase down and unlocking the door to Number Eight. When she pushed it open, the afternoon sun streamed in through the window, revealing a pine dresser, armoire, and a bed with a Navajo-print spread. The Bible and the Book of Mormon rested on the night stand next to the phone. Photographs of at least a dozen young women, all wearing old-fashioned clothing, adorned the walls.

"It's very nice," I said, studying the photographs.

She put my suitcase down on the bed, then answered my unspoken question. "Those are girls we helped after they ran off from Purity."

"How often has that happened?"

She gave the photographs a cursory look. "Not as often as we'd like. Problem is, Purity's a long way away from everything, even West Wind. A woman's got to walk, what, twenty-something miles down that old dirt road before she makes it to the highway. But some gals have done it. Nobody carrying babies ever has, though."

I looked at her, puzzled. "Why don't they just call you to pick them up? Surely even Purity has phones."

She sat down on the bed with a thump, making the springs squeak. "Sorry, but my feet are killing me. Tourists expect us all to wear these Western boots, but I never even rode a horse, so it's kinda silly. Phones. Yeah, Purity's got phones. And electricity, indoor plumbing, and satellite TV, too. But the men keep all that stuff locked up. Every now and then they'll let the women call family in other compounds, but they always listen in to make sure they're not up to funny business."

Funny business such as what? Talking to divorce attorneys? I felt my blood pressure spike, so I crossed the room and stared out the open window, breathing in the sharp tang of juniper. The call of a canyon wren fluted over a bilingual conversation below then died away as more voices emerged from the stable area. The trail riders had returned.

Over my shoulder, I asked, "If they're so cut off, how do the women find out about this place?"

"Fliers." A deep male voice.

I turned around to see a lanky man of about sixty standing in the doorway. With his straight black hair and weathered face he could almost have passed for a Native American, but his blue eyes revealed Anglo ancestry. The scent wafting off his faded jeans and brown, snap-front shirt was pure Eau de Horse.

He walked toward me, spurs jingling. "I'm Leo, Virginia's husband." He held out his hand.

His callused hand enclosed mine gently. "Fliers? How would women back in Purity get their hands on any fliers?"

He let my hand go and grinned, revealing teeth so white they almost looked false, a feature not uncommon among Mormons since they didn't indulge in such teeth-staining substances as coffee, tea or cigarettes. "I leave fliers all over the Zion City grocery stores and other shops. Down by the welfare office, too. The women pick them up when they're driven into town, but they have to grab them pretty fast before their husbands catch on."

I leaned against the window sill. "Considering how controlled the women are, why are they allowed to go to town in the first place? Surely not to shop. I thought the polygamists were self-sufficient."

Leo chuckled. "You weren't raised in the country, were you?"

"Mainly Phoenix and Scottsdale."

"Ah, a big city gal!" He flashed those white teeth at me again. "Well, Lena, not even self-sufficient country folk make their own flour, sugar, and baking soda. But the women have to go into town for more than groceries. Tell you what. You've had a long drive and maybe you'd like to freshen up some. Then why don't you come down to the office and we'll have a nice long talk about lots of things. Forewarned is fore-armed, right? Right now I have to go back downstairs and play bartender. I've got me some pretty sore Germans down there."

With a groan Virginia heaved herself off the bed, explain-ing that she also needed to get back to work. "Consuelo, that's our maid, she's feelin' sick, so I'm pretty much on my own. I need to finish up some cleaning and after that, I gotta help Leo with the bookkeeping. At least the cook's okay. Don't know what I'd do if Juan turned up sick. I'm not much of a cook, myself. Maybe I'd just draft a stable hand, though I bet the guests would get awful tired of franks and beans."

She started to leave, then turned around. "Remember, now, don't you unpack. Leo and I, we've got something in the works." Then she left.

Something in the works? Virginia's final words worried me. Both the Lawlers seemed nice enough, but their devotion to anti-polygamy activities could pose a problem. If they thought I was up here to become their foot soldier, I'd have to set them straight. I'd already noticed how emotional I became when thinking about Purity. Captain Kryzinski had once warned me that an emotional detective was a sloppy detective, so I needed to remain cool. After all, my purpose here was to find out who killed Prophet Solomon, not obsess about the fate of women I didn't even know.

To keep my mind off the women's troubles, I took my pistol out of the carry-all and checked the closet and the space under the bed. Then I relaxed with a leisurely shower. By the time I changed into fresh jeans and a T-shirt, I felt ready to get to work. Leaving my carry-all and gun in the room, I wandered downstairs in search of the office. A few tourists still lingered in the living room sipping drinks and singing little snatches of "Home, Home on the Range" in deeply accented English. A Frenchman, his dark eyes dancing, offered to share his Pernod but when I told him I had business in the office, wherever that was, he pointed helpfully down the hall.

"The office, it is just to the left of the dining room. And then, when you are finished in there, perhaps you would care to join me on that secluded little patio in the back? It is so very pleasant with the afternoon breeze, much more private than in here. My wife, she is hiking in the Zion Park, and will not be back until the evening."

The Frenchman was cute, but not that cute, so I headed down the hall.

I found the Lawlers seated at a no-frills steel desk, frowning at a computer. While the thing beeped and whirred at them and they muttered back, Leo motioned me to a chair. I looked around in amusement. With its modern office equipment, including a copier and a fax machine, and almost total lack of Western paraphernalia, the office could have belonged to an insurance company.

"I hate that uppity thing," Virginia growled over her husband's shoulder as he shut down the computer. "We just paid all the bills and now it's tellin' us we're broke!"

Leo managed a wry smile. "You being in business yourself, Lena, I'll bet you know all about that."

It would be cruel to tell the couple about Albert Grabel's largess, so I just smiled. "Self-employment can be tough, that's for sure. Now, what did you want to talk to me about? Do you have some information about the murder of Solomon Royal?" Hopefully, this pointed question would steer the Lawlers away from the recruitment speech I feared they'd rehearsed. I had no intention of driving to Zion City and handing out anti-polygamy leaflets.

"We've got some ideas about that, but first we want to give you some background on the way things are run at Purity," Leo said, as the couple moved from the desk to the frayed sofa across from me.

I suppressed a sigh of impatience and settled myself more comfortably into the chair.

"The legal situation is a little convoluted, but here's the short version," Leo continued. "The polygamists circumvent bigamy laws by divorcing one wife before they marry another. Of course, the relationship with all the other so-called ex-wives remains exactly the same. The guy sleeps with every one of them, but that's not all. Most of the husbands keep a record of each woman's menstrual cycle so that they can 'catch' her at her most fertile. Making babies is the name of the game, Lena."

I didn't get it. "You mean they're purposely impregnating all those women? But *why?*"

Leo gave me a wry smile. "Two reasons. One, the official reason, is religious. The polygamists believe that the more children a man has, the higher level of Heaven he'll be sent to when he dies and the more servants he'll have to wait on him."

He made a face, then continued. "But that's not the real reason, which is that the more babies the women pop out, the more money the compound gets. See, the women are divorced, and that makes them single mothers. In this state, single mothers collect hefty welfare. The more children, the more welfare they collect, so when you figure that there's about three or four hundred single women out there, each of them having an average of a baby a year..." He let his voice trail off.

I suddenly understood. "Holy shit! That's a lot of money!"

Leo's frown reminded me that I was in the presence of good Mormons.

"Excuse my French," I muttered. "But, Leo, that's got to be a small fortune!"

Virginia stared at her husband, and for a moment, I thought she might say something, but she didn't. For such a loquacious woman, she remained oddly silent.

Leo continued. "The women never see a penny of it, either. All the compound's welfare money, all the profits from their cattle, mining and gaming interests—yes, they own a couple of casinos—is funneled through the Purity Fellowship Foundation, supposedly a charitable trust. Even the homes at Purity, they're all owned by the Foundation. It's been estimated that the Foundation controls anywhere from $150 million to $300 million, but nobody knows for sure. Not that it makes any difference, because as the financial arm of a religious organization, it's tax-exempt."

My jaw dropped so low I was surprised it didn't fall off my face. Any decent detective knew that the two primary motives for murder were love and money. So my next question was a no-brainer. "Who manages the Foundation?"

"Prophet Solomon Royal used to manage everything, but the job's been passed to the new Prophet of Purity." Leo paused and looked at me in anticipation.

I dutifully asked the next no-brainer. "And the new prophet is…?"

"Davis Royal, Solomon's favorite son." Leo sat back against the sofa cushions with a satisfied smile, having made clear his own suspicions about the murderer's identity.

Virginia looked up from the floor, her face tense with irritation. "Money, money, money, all the time you talk about the money. What about those poor girls?"

I sympathized, but I saw Leo's point. Sons had killed their fathers for a lot less money than the Purity Fellowship Foundation controlled. It would be interesting to find out exactly how well Solomon and his son had gotten along, but in the end, I doubted it made any difference. One of my recent cases had shown me how little love mattered when big bucks entered the picture.

Virginia wouldn't drop it. "The girls, Leo. Tell her about the girls. She needs to know before Saul gets here."

"Saul?"

Leo smiled again. "Oh, just an old friend. He's joining us for dinner tonight, and he has a very interesting proposition for you. But Virginia's right, you do need to know more about the women."

I was becoming more and more uncomfortable with this. "Look, I'm just here to catch a murderer so I can get my client out of jail. I'm sorry life is so hard for those women, but I don't have time to get involved."

Leo grunted. "Trust me. You're going to need to know exactly how the women in Purity are treated and how they behave. But we'll hold off on that until Saul arrives. For now, there's something you might find more directly useful about the political situation."

I leaned forward and listened.

"We're beginning to suspect that the polygamists are in collusion with certain government officials."

I frowned. "Name names."

"For starters, Jepsom Smith, the governor himself, is descended from polygamists. He issued a press statement once to the effect that polygamy, because it's a religious belief, is protected under the First Amendment. Good thing nobody's sacrificing babies to the great god Baal, right? Given Smith's weird interpretation of the First Amendment, we'd sure have a lot of dead babies around Utah. But he's not the only nut. Some of our legislators are even trying to get the anti-polygamy laws repealed."

Utah sounded goofier than Arizona, with its flying saucer landing pads and New Age vortices. I told him so.

"You don't know the half of it," he said. "There are anywhere from thirty to fifty thousand people still practicing polygamy, mainly in Utah, but some in Arizona. Maybe even more. At least ten thousand of them live right here in Beehive County and we can't get anybody to do anything about it.

Now tell me, Lena, let's say you dismiss Jepson Smith's drivel about freedom of religion. Think you can come up with the real reason government officials are playing the hands-off game with the polygamists?"

I remembered Sheriff Benson's excuse. "Polygamy is considered a victimless crime, is that it?"

Leo laughed, but the sound wasn't pretty. He was a man with a mission, all right. "Oh, that's the official excuse, but remember the money, Lena, always remember the money. Those polygamy prophets are rich men and we suspect they've spread a few dollars around to avoid prosecution."

I frowned. "Do you have any proof?"

He shook her head. "Nope. Getting the proof is *your* job. You're the detective."

I threw up my hands. "Whoa! I'm not the U.S. Attorney General. What you're describing here could range anywhere from graft to organized crime."

Leo's face was grim. "Exactly."

Chapter 6

Virginia disappeared into the kitchen and directed the cook to serve us an early dinner on the back patio, that secluded little spot so dear to the randy Frenchman. In the distance, the red pillars of Zion National Park flamed with the late afternoon light. I heard the chi-ci-go-go of quail as they scurried through the underbrush, the cooing of doves from the nearby grove of sycamore. The chatter of tourists gathered around the big fireplace only now and then penetrated the pine-scented air.

"Boy, I sure don't get cornbread like this at home," said Saul Berkhauser, the Lawlers' dinner guest. A retired contractor, Saul appeared to be in his seventies and sported a weathered face so deeply lined it could have served as a plat map for the Grand Canyon. Yet his voice contained the energy of a much younger man.

"I've been living at Purity for eight years now, and believe me, that's eight years too long," he said, waving away an inquisitive fly. "Still, I'm staying until they run me off."

He shoveled another wedge of crumbly cornbread into his mouth with the fervor of a man who hadn't been cooked for in a long time. I was amused until I looked down at my plate and realized I had done exactly the same thing. The high desert did wonders for the appetite.

Although the sun was still a good two hours away from setting, the day had already begun to cool. Fortunately, the glowing outdoor fireplace on the patio kept us warm as Saul related the series of events that led to his involvement with the polygamists. He explained that the death of his wife several years earlier had left him feeling adrift. Seeking a cure for the empty place inside, he embarked upon a religious pilgrimage.

"I tried Buddhism, the New Age stuff, and once I even showed up at a Catholic mass," he said, waving his fork like a schoolroom pointer. "Nothing rang my chimes.

"Then one night I went down to the local senior center where Prophet Solomon was giving a talk. He started off by talking about the skyrocketing crime rates, the escalation of drugs, disintegrating families, and children who didn't honor their elders. Since my kids couldn't be bothered visiting me as much as I thought they should, he pushed all my buttons."

Saul crammed more cornbread into his mouth, then followed it with a huge bite of honey-baked ham. His eyes closed momentarily in pleasure. Before speaking again, he helped himself to another slab of ham and placed it carefully in the center of his plate, where he gazed at it lovingly.

"I didn't move to Purity to marry some little teenager, if that's what you're thinking," he finally continued. "I just wanted to find a community I could be a part of, and yes, maybe a willing woman who'd help me start a new family to replace the one I'd lost. No fool like an old fool, right?"

"And a common story," Leo agreed. "But you eventually redeemed yourself, didn't you?"

"How?" I asked.

Now it was Virginia's turn to speak. "Saul showed up here once in the middle of the night, bringing these two little scared things wrapped in blankets. Just kids! Maybe fourteen, fifteen at the most. They was about to be married to Solomon's brother, and they didn't want any part of it."

Saul nodded. "Yeah, that was a wild night. If those guys at the compound ever find out it was me that helped those girls get away, my ass'll be grass and they'll be the lawn-mower."

Which was why his continued residence at Purity didn't make any sense to me, and I told him so. "Why don't you leave?"

Saul remained silent for so long that I was relieved when the fly returned and he had to swat it away again. At least the irritation made him look less, well, foolish.

"Go on, tell her," Virginia urged. "She's a detective. I bet she's heard dumber stuff."

Saul sighed. "All right. Here it is. The reason that I don't leave Purity is because they've got my money."

I frowned. "What do you mean they've got your money?"

Saul sighed again. "Solomon told me that in order to become eligible to receive Purity's benefits, I'd have to turn over my assets to the Purity Fellowship Foundation. So when I moved to the compound, I sold my business, my house, I even cashed in my stocks, bonds, and IRAs. Then I signed over my Social Security checks."

I almost choked on my cornbread. "You mean you gave Prophet Solomon everything you owned?"

"Solomon let me keep enough to build a simple house, but the house itself and the land it stands on belong to the Foundation."

Seeing the expression on my face, he nodded. "Yeah, I know. Stupid, stupid, stupid. But that kind of setup isn't unusual on the Arizona Strip. For some folks, it's not that bad because the prophets take care of all the legal fees everybody's always racking up for one reason or another, and let me tell you, some of those legal bills can look like the national debt. So anyway, I rationalized my stupidity by telling myself that giving my money away was a fair enough price to get rid of my loneliness."

Loneliness. Now there was a buzz word for you.

Of all human emotions, loneliness ranked third only to hatred and love as the most powerful. The fear of loneliness kept battered women with abusive men, and cuckolded husbands with wives who didn't give a damn about them. For some of us, the prospect of loneliness was so terrifying that it kept us *alone*, which was not the same thing. It's my theory that you can only suffer the worst forms of loneliness if you've experienced its opposite—love. I hadn't.

Like many children raised in foster homes, I had always resisted forming attachments. Becoming attached to any foster family could bring a whole truckload of pain, because any day you could be wrenched away. Foster families, by their very nature, were temporary. Jobs changed, necessitating the family's move from the state, leaving their foster children—wards of the state of Arizona—to find new homes. In some cases, foster mothers developed breast cancer.

I wondered how Madeline was doing now. If the cancer that had separated us had recurred.

Loneliness? Oh, yeah. I understood Saul better than he realized. "I get the picture," I told him.

His craggy old face showed relief. "Once I finished building my house Solomon told me I'd have to wait for a while to get a wife. He said that I had not yet been 'tested in the Faith,' whatever that meant. The real reason, I soon found out, was that all the unmarried women in the compound had been promised to other men, mostly Solomon's relatives and cronies. Eventually, though, Solomon kept his word and gave me a wife."

Now his eyes looked as sad as Virginia's. "That didn't work out, either. Let's just say Ruby and I never hit it off."

At this point, a Hispanic man wearing an apron emerged from the ranch house, carrying an immense steaming cobbler. The smell wafting from the deep dish had me nearly swooning with delight.

Setting the cobbler down, the man said to Virginia, "This is the last of the peaches. Tomorrow we will start on the blackberries, and after that, the apples."

"Thanks, Juan," she said. "Hey, how's Consuelo doing? She any better?"

"Consuelo will be able to help you tomorrow, she thinks. She is very sorry she has caused so much trouble for you."

"Phooey. She didn't do any such thing. You just tell her to take care of herself. If she needs somethin', juice or tea, you let me know and I'll take it up to her."

Juan nodded. "I will do that. The guests in the other room are drinking now. Is that all right?"

Leo chuckled. "Just as long as they don't start rehashing World War II."

"Please?"

Virginia smiled. "Just one of Leo's jokes, Juan. Once you finish up in there, you go on upstairs and help Consuelo out. Take the evening off. I'll go make nice with the guests."

Juan's face broke into a big smile. "Thank you, Mrs. Lawler. I will do that."

He went back into the house, a happy man.

The conversation, minor as it had been, reminded me of something that had puzzled me earlier. Mormons liked large families, but nowhere throughout the ranch house had I seen any evidence of children or grandchildren. Could their absence have anything to do with the sadness in Virginia's eyes?

I eased into the question. "I have a friend, Slim Papadopolus, who runs a dude ranch back in Arizona. He tells me it's a lot of work."

"Sure is," Leo said. "Hiring ranch hands is easy, because young people always want to work with the horses, but when it comes to house help, it's another story. We were very lucky to find Juan and Consuelo. And before you ask, yes, they're legal. We have enough problems running this place without INS breathing down our necks."

Since an illegal alien had once saved my life, I didn't care if Juan and Consuelo were legal or not. I kept the conversation on track. "Slim has it a little easier than you guys. He has five children and they all help out."

An uncomfortable silence greeted this information, but I burrowed on. "Virginia, why don't any of your children help run the ranch?"

She didn't answer. Instead, she made a big show of fussing with the peach cobbler. Leo wouldn't look at me.

I felt a hand on my arm. Saul's. "Lena, Virginia's only child died some years ago."

"I'm so sorry. I didn't know."

Without asking, Virginia ladled a big scoop of peach cobbler into my dessert dish. When she finally spoke, her voice trembled. "I don't like to talk about it, okay?"

To ease us over the awkward moment, Saul left his own helping of cobbler cooling on his plate and resumed his story. "Anyway, Solomon had already taken my money and there wasn't really anything else I could do for him. He figured I was even too old to help the other men add extra bedrooms onto their houses every time they got a new wife. So eventually I figured out that the 'new family' Solomon promised me was never going to happen. That's when I started making a stink and the Purity Fellowship Foundation filed eviction proceedings with a Beehive County judge."

To hide my expression, I turned and looked through the lengthening shadows toward the corral, where a stable hand was dumping flakes of hay into the feed bins. The horses crowded around him, nipping at each other. Their squeals, mingled with the harsh tat-tat-tat of a woodpecker, drifted toward us on the freshening breeze.

When I was confident that my face would give nothing away, I looked back over at Saul, who'd just revealed an excellent motive of his own for killing Prophet Solomon. Something else bothered me, too. Saul had referred to the dead child as "Virginia's," not "the Lawlers'." Had the child not been Leo's?

Keeping my tone neutral, I said, "Maybe the Foundation will drop the eviction proceedings now that Solomon is dead."

"Naw. Davis Royal's hell-bent on throwing me out of the compound, too, especially since I've stopped turning over my Social Security check to those thieves."

Maybe he was telling the truth, maybe not. "If they do succeed in evicting you, is there a chance you'll be able to recoup any of your money?"

He snorted. "As Prophet Solomon once explained to me, that money was a gift to God, and God isn't into Indian giving."

I thought about what he'd told me. Saul Berkhauser would not be the first sheep to be fleeced by some flock's phony shepherd, or the last. Still, men had killed for weaker reasons.

Virginia rejoined the conversation, but with less joviality than she'd shown earlier in the day.

"Solomon ripped Saul off, just like one of them con men you see on TV," she said, her voice rising in anger. "But there's a bigger shame goin' on in Purity. You heard him tell how Solomon was out there giving talks at libraries? Guess where those guys been showin' up for the last couple of years. Homeless shelters! The welfare office! Even the court house! It ain't always too hard to convince some woman that if she moves to Purity her nutty ex-boyfriend won't find her and beat her up again. And it ain't hard to convince others they'll find true love at Purity, either. By the time they find out it's all a big lie, they've been cut off from everybody they know and they've got new babies they can't bear leavin' behind."

Leo put a restraining hand on her arm. "Hon, we can talk about this until Doomsday, but I doubt if it's going to make any difference to Lena. She's seems pretty focused on her own assignment, not donning a suit of armor to join our little crusade."

Aptly put. So aptly, in fact, that I found myself wondering how the rough-cut Virginia had wound up with the much smoother Leo. But when I studied her face more closely, I saw the remnants of considerable beauty. That explained everything. Educated men like Leo had married uneducated beauties before, and would again.

"I'm no Joan of Arc, that's for sure." I offered an apologetic smile.

Saul looked at me. "Don't say that yet." Then he transferred his glance to Virginia. "Seems like a good time to ask her, don't you think?"

Virginia nodded. "I'd say so."

Saul chuckled with the rusty sound of someone who hadn't laughed in a long time, then astounded me by leaving his chair and getting down on his knees. "Well, Miss Private Detective, seeing as how you look to be of child-bearing age, how'd you like to come and live with me in my little honeymoon cottage at Purity?"

I opened my mouth but no sound came out.

"Of course, we'll have to get married before we get there, otherwise our new Prophet Davis might want to snatch you up for himself. He likes tall, skinny blonds. In fact, all six of his wives are blonds! So how about it, Lena? If you're worried about Ruby, well, she won't mind me dragging home another wife. She was born in Purity and knows that sharing a husband is her God-ordained duty."

My voice faltered. "I don't think, I don't think…" I looked at Virginia for help, but she'd hidden her mouth behind her hands. Those sad eyes were laughing, though.

Leo rescued me. "Lena, posing as Saul's new wife is the perfect way to smuggle you into the compound. You can't find out who murdered Prophet Solomon if you don't talk to the people involved. And the only way to do that is to go to Purity."

Now that I'd recovered from my initial shock, I realized the plan made sense. Yes, Saul might have his own reason for wanting Solomon dead, but that didn't matter to me. Pretend-marrying him would certainly bring me up close and personal with all the other people who had motives, too. I did see one weakness in the plan, however.

"Let's say, just for argument's sake, that I do this. How would you explain me to the others? Would you tell them I was some sort of mail-order bride? Frankly, I can't imagine anyone with half a brain believing that."

Saul rose from his knees and returned to his chair. After taking a couple of more bites of peach cobbler, he told me he'd already figured that out.

He had been away from the compound for several days, supposedly on a trip to Salt Lake to visit one of his daughters, but in actuality, he'd been conferring with his attorney in Zion City. When he returned to Purity with a new wife, he would simply explain we'd been introduced by an acquaintance who ran a shelter for battered women, and that I'd leapt at the chance to have a permanent roof over my head while at the same time getting far, far away from the crack-head boyfriend who'd threatened to kill me.

"And I'll tell them that I took care of all the legal work through an attorney cousin of mine. I think they'll swallow it. After all, that's exactly the kind of stuff polygamists pull all the time."

Virginia's voice revealed her enthusiasm for the idea. "You'll need to act a little different, Lena. Kind of quiet. And obedient. Oh, absolutely more obedient!"

Quiet. Obedient. Two words seldom used to describe Lena Jones.

Noticing the doubtful expression on my face, she said, "Hey, it won't be that hard. Just pretend you've had a real bad life and it's left you all messed up."

Who had to pretend? I merely said, "I think I can manage that."

I mulled it over. Living in the compound would certainly be the best way to investigate Prophet Solomon's murder, but at considerable risk to myself. Although the Lawlers obviously trusted Saul, I knew nothing about him. Come to think of it, I didn't know anything about the Lawlers, either, just that Jimmy's mother liked them.

A little voice inside, a voice I'd heard a hundred times, warned, If you do this, you're *nuts*. The voice had never been wrong.

Then I remembered Esther's terrified face. Rebecca's. "I'll do it," I said.

When we finished eating, Virginia took me upstairs to loan me one of the dresses discarded a few months back by a runaway polygamist wife. I studied myself in the mirror, aghast at what I saw. The long-sleeved, high-necked, ankle-length calico made me look like a refugee from the *Little House on the Prairie* television series. And underneath all that clothing? More clothing. The wool Temple underwear favored by Mormons in the nineteenth century and poly-gamists in the twenty-first made me itch in crevices I hadn't even known were there.

Those ridiculous layers of clothing did have one benefit, though. Even the most careful observer wouldn't be able to spot the .38 holstered at my thigh.

Pulling my hair tightly behind my head, I bobby-pinned it into a sloppy bun, exposing my scar even more than usual. I looked like a half-skinned rabbit, but apparently the men of Purity had a thing for half-skinned rabbits.

I stepped back, studied myself again, and nodded in satisfaction.

After Virginia went downstairs to help with the clearing up, I picked up the phone, hoping Jimmy remained at the office. Luck, and his workaholism, were with me and he answered on the first ring. When I told him my plans, though, he made his displeasure plain.

"You've done some crazy things in your life, but this is probably the craziest," he said. "There's no way you'll be able to pass yourself off as some meek plural wife."

"But there's too much at stake for me *not* to try it."

After he finished lamenting my changed plans, I gave him a list of names I wanted run through the Lexis-Nexis Internet search. And if that didn't work, to hack into whatever he had to hack into. When it came to unearthing information, Jimmy wasn't always legal.

"Saul Berkhauser might be a perfectly nice man, but I want to make sure," I told him. "Same with Virginia and Leo. Yes, I know your mother likes them, but maybe they're just a little too good to be true. Virginia worries me a lot. She's down one minute, up the next. Maybe she's just bipolar or something, but I need to know what I'm dealing with. Saul mentioned she had a child who died, and the way he put it made it sound like the kid might not have been Leo's. So see how many times she's been married, okay? Maybe your mom knows her maiden name."

"Yeah, yeah." I heard the click of computer keys. He'd already begun searching the Internet. Then, "Lena?"

"What?"

"I'm begging you. Please don't do this."

"It's the only way to help Esther and Rebecca." I sounded braver than I felt.

He grunted. "Well, at least there's one polygamist you don't have to worry about up there. Captain Kryzinski brought Abel Corbett back in here this morning, demanding that we turn Rebecca over. That guy is really steamed at you."

"Which guy? Kryzinski or Abel?"

"Both, I guess." He sounded glum.

"I don't care how steamed they are just as long as Rebecca's safe. And she is safe, right?"

"Of course. And she's going to stay that way, too." He paused for a second, then added, "I went down to the jail this afternoon to see Esther. She's doing about as well as can be expected. I tried to cheer her up but I don't think it worked."

I thought for a moment. "How many trips to the jail does this make for you? Six? Seven?"

He mumbled something I didn't quite catch and my worries increased. Jimmy had a bad track record when it came to his love life. He always seemed to fall for felons. The very fact that he'd obviously taken a shine to Esther did not bode well for her innocence.

I opened my mouth to lecture him, then thought better of it. Telling someone whom they should or should not love was about as profitable as telling the sun not to rise.

"Watch yourself," I just said, and left it at that.

Mutual warning session duly accomplished, Jimmy filled me in on the day's events. There had been another fire at South Mountain Tire Storage.

"It was just a shed this time. The tires didn't go up, but I hear the folks from ATF are real antsy. They might be ready to make an arrest."

I wasn't hopeful. Even if the feds arrested Miles Alder, his dad would probably bond him out. In Arizona even people suspected of mass murder were set free to walk the streets if they had enough money.

"Stay on it," I said. "Firebugs always lose control at some point. Maybe we'll catch this one before anybody gets hurt."

I started to ask if Dusty had called the office, but changed my mind. I had more important things to do than worry about my own love life.

Chapter 7

"Remember, keep your eyes on the ground and never contradict a male," my new "husband" warned me as his '86 Chevy pickup trundled southeast along the private dirt road straddling the Utah/Arizona state line. The evening's lengthening shadows made the creosote bushes sprinkled along the flat desert floor appear twice their size, almost monstrous.

"I've been practicing," I said, breathing deeply, trying to quell my panic.

Since leaving West Wind Guest Ranch, we'd dropped enough in altitude to make all the difference between tree-bordered streams and an arid no-man's land. The terrain alone helped explain why so few women escaped from Purity. Nothing other than miles of sand, rock, and creosote bushes stretched to the south. True, the blazing reds and oranges of the Vermillion Cliffs rising steep-sided on the north furnished some visual drama, but otherwise, the landscape resembled the surface of the moon. And it functioned little more hospitably. The Arizona Strip was an alien landscape governed by men who recognized no laws but their own. The polygamists had chosen their paradise carefully. Because of the area's remote bleakness, tourists, whose curiosity might have proven problematic, never did more than pass quickly through.

Now I had willingly entered this desolation again, but this time "married" to a man I had just met. What if Saul's helpful demeanor had baser motives? After all, he'd told me the polygamists routinely used lies and manipulation to entice prospective brides. Had he followed suit with me? And would he, frustrated from years of an unhappy marriage, creep into my room tonight? I closed my eyes and counted backward from one hundred. It didn't help.

"Lena, can you cook?" Saul's voice halted the countdown somewhere around thirty.

I opened my eyes. "You must be kidding. My culinary skills run to ramen noodles and Michelina's TV dinners."

His expectant look faded.

We rounded the final turn in the road and Purity came into view. I'd seen the place before, of course, but I'd been too distracted by Rebecca's situation to pay much attention to the architecture. Now I noticed how dismal the place looked. With the exception of the sturdy brick church and one other brick building, Purity could have modeled the Before of a civic Before-and-After project.

Like most of the polygamy compounds on the Arizona Strip, half its buildings sat on the Utah side of the border, the other half in Arizona. This way, if the Utah authorities raided the compound, the polygamists would amble across the road to Arizona, only ten feet away. If Arizona raided, everyone would shuffle off to Utah. However, this simple but effective plan had never been tested due to both states' continued assertion that polygamy was a victimless crime.

The town's layout was simple, if drear. Two curved rows of houses, bisected by the dirt road, faced each other across the state line, with Prophet's Park, the bare circular area between, doubling as a children's playground and a graveyard for junked pickup trucks. Approximately thirty ramshackle houses the size of small hotels sat at odd angles on litter-strewn dirt lots, their roofs covered in an untidy mélange of tin and unmatched shingles. None were painted. Instead, tar paper siding fluttered in the evening breeze, making the shiny satellite dishes attached to each house look wildly out of place.

At the far end of the compound, just to the side of the square-steepled church, I counted four Quonset huts and a dozen battered trailers, probably used as overflow homes for Purity's extra wives. Behind these rusting hulks ran a series of chicken-wire paddocks containing chickens, pigs, goats, and a few cows.

The brick church, which normally would have provided some semblance of construction competence, hunkered under rickety-looking scaffolding and flapping canvas. It looked like some huge mythical beast about to pounce.

"The Church of the Prophet Fundamental," Saul said, pointing. "Someone got the bright idea of having a stained glass window made documenting Prophet Solomon's holy works, so they're spiffing up the joint first. Paint on the inside, sandblasting on the outside."

"Too bad they don't do the same for everything else around here," I observed. "But where do they hold Sunday services now?"

"Prophet's Park on nice days, the new prophet's house on bad days. In shifts, though. Davis's house is big, but not that big. Once family matters are settled, he'll probably move into his daddy's old house." Here he pointed to the only brick home in the compound, a structure so large I'd assumed it was an apartment building.

To the north of the compound lay gardens and orchards, offering the only swatches of green to relieve Purity's browns and blacks. Although almost dusk, a few granny-garbed women still toiled in the gardens gathering last-minute dinner vegetables.

Beyond the gardens, Paiute Canyon, my old hiding place, zigzagged along the base of the gaudy Vermillion Cliffs. I flinched as a shot rang from its depths, then reminded myself of the canyon's omnipresent hunters.

Ragged, unsupervised children ran everywhere. They climbed on the rusting cars, poked sticks through the fence at the chickens and goats, and skipped along the unpaved paths between the huge houses. Some scuffled in the dirt like wild things. One little boy of about four threw rocks at a skinny dog. No one came to its aid.

"Where are their mothers?" I asked Saul. "These kids look like they're on their own."

"If you had ten children do you think you'd be able to keep an eye on all of them?" He swerved to avoid a child's Big Wheel hunkered down in the middle of the road, its owner nowhere in sight.

"Probably not." Frankly I doubted I could mother even one child.

As we rolled by the gigantic but decrepit houses, we stirred up a dust cloud that made children scatter in all directions. Watching them, I was struck once more by their ragtag appearance.

"Saul, this place looks pretty slummy for a financial organization that's supposed to control millions of dollars. Are you sure that's not an urban myth?"

"It's no myth. I know at least twenty men here who work for some of the businesses managed by the Purity Fellowship Foundation. But you're right, very little money goes toward upkeep around here, other than for the church. At best, the Foundation dribbles out a few bucks here and there to add a room when some family starts outgrowing its house or trailers or whatever."

He waved toward a building on the Utah side of the compound which resembled a warehouse that had seen better days. "That house belongs to Jacob Waldman, Esther's father. He started building it fifty years ago. I think it had three, maybe four bedrooms then, one for each wife. They say it has twenty-two bedrooms now."

"For twenty-two wives?" I couldn't keep the shock out of my voice.

"Old Jacob's only got about ten wives at this point and considering the state of his health, isn't likely to get more. The rest of the rooms are dormitories for his kids. I think there's around seventy or eighty, I'm not sure, cause the older ones are all married off. That's kind of an average family size for most of the guys around here."

As I craned my neck to stare at the house where Esther grew up, something else began to bother me.

"Saul, the house doesn't have any windows! Almost *none* of these houses do."

Saul braked for a child chasing a ball. "Windows cost money. Prophet Solomon didn't believe in mortgages, except for the ones he held on other folks' property in Salt Lake, so everything built here is paid for in cash. The money gets deducted from each family's monthly allowance, which has always been doled out by Solomon. When folks are that strapped, windows are a luxury. Besides, most of the men work at their piddly little jobs all day, and at night, well, it's too dark to see anything anyway."

"Don't the women feel cooped up?" The thought of a windowless house horrified me. Since a murderer left me for dead in a car trunk, I suffered from bouts of claustrophobia.

Saul laughed at my question. "You think Purity's women have time to enjoy the view? According to 'The Gospel of Solomon,' and it's an actual book he printed himself a few years back, anything that gives pleasure is considered mere vanity. That includes looking out windows."

My feeling of horror intensified. "Saul, please tell me your house has windows. If I can't look outside…"

"Don't worry, before I handed over my money to Solomon, I made sure I kept enough for windows. I was a contractor, remember. None of this cheap-jack construction for me."

I relaxed as we drove up to a small wood-shingled house on the Arizona side of the compound which, unlike the other buildings, bore a semblance of style. Bright red flowers bloomed from window boxes painted the same blue as the trim on the large windows and front door. While not elegant, the little house and its tidy yard shamed its hulking neighbors.

As Saul helped me unload the garbage bags meant to pass for a desperate woman's luggage, I caught sight of a group of men leaning against a rusting Chevy Impala. The fading light didn't hide their frank stares.

"Show time," Saul grunted, then turned to face them. "You guys in the Circle of Elders wouldn't help me, so I went out and found me another wife in Salt Lake."

A portly red-headed man of about fifty, wearing a long-sleeved shirt, bib overalls and metal-rimmed glasses, approached, his face stern. He addressed Saul without greeting me.

"Brother Saul, you didn't get approval from the Circle to take another wife. Until you do, we can't sanctify the marriage." He narrowed his already too-small eyes at me, his expression a scarifying mixture of lust and loathing.

"Well, then, Brother Earl, you can sanctify my ass!" Saul snapped. "What's the matter with you people? Prophet Solomon said that no man can enter the Kingdom of Heaven unless he has more than one wife, so I'm merely following his instructions. You boys got a problem with that, you can take it up with me after I get my woman in the house."

My woman. Almost choking from outrage, I lowered my eyes modestly and stared at the ground. But not before I wondered if Brother Earl was the same Earl Graff who'd witnessed the argument between Esther and Prophet Solomon.

"Brother Saul, we'll deal with you at the next Circle of Elders meeting," Brother Earl said in a soft voice that almost, but not quite, masked his anger.

As Earl rejoined the others, Saul put his hand on my back and gave me a push that almost made me stumble. "Get yourself in the house, Sister Lena, and head straight for the kitchen. I'm hungry." His voice could have carried to the farthest building in the compound.

Although his performance was obviously for the polygamists' benefit, my gorge still rose and I almost slapped his hand away. But then I remembered Rebecca's terrified face, and hurried up the steps, garbage bag luggage in my hands and my new "husband" hot on my heels. Keeping my own voice low, I warned, "Do that to me again, Brother Saul, and you'll be whistling 'Dixie' out of a gap in your front teeth."

He snickered. "A Godly woman is an obedient woman, Sister Lena. She wouldn't dream of decking her jackass of a husband."

My dread increasing, I entered the house. Once inside, though, I was pleasantly surprised.

The house, as Saul had described earlier, had been furnished with bits and pieces left over from the big yard sale he'd held in Salt Lake before moving to the compound. Nothing matched, but the long, brown leather sofa coexisted comfortably with the green and blue armchairs. A multicolored rag rug lent an air of gaiety to the room that, in my present glum state, filled me with gratitude.

I walked around slowly, staring at the amateurish snapshots covering one of the pine-paneled walls. Children. Dozens of them. The girls wore Purity's nineteenth-century-style dresses; the boys, plain slacks and high-necked, long-sleeved shirts.

"Ruby's kids and grandkids," Saul explained. "Only a few still live here. The others married into other polygamy compounds, such as Colorado City and Hildale. Out here, one compound feeds the other."

Remembering the vast empty stretches we had traveled to get here, I asked, "Are those other compounds close by?"

"Hildale's the closest, and it's almost forty miles east, so she doesn't get to see her kids much. I think missing them is part of her problem. Hell, missing kids was sure part of my problem. If the stinkers had visited me more, I might not have wound up in this polygamist Sodom and Gomorrah in the first place."

The photographs on the opposite wall provided startling contrast to the bargain basement snapshots. Studio portraits of three attractive women with their spouses, surrounded by gaggles of kids, proclaimed that Saul spared no expense in documenting his family. A separate photograph portrayed a dignified man in a Naval uniform.

"The women are your daughters, right?"

"And the sailor's my son. Sarabeth's a nurse, Alexandra's an engineer, Toni teaches American Lit at BYU, and Gordon is chief petty officer on the *U.S.S. Enterprise*. Gordon's out in the Persian Gulf right now, but we still manage to keep in touch." He motioned to a small tape recorder that sat on a side table. "We make recordings and send them back and forth to each other. I never got the hang of email, but the tape recorder still beats letters. Uh, before you ask, my kids only have one spouse apiece, but I'm happy to report that between them, they've given me fifteen grandchildren and six great-grandchildren!" His elation vanished as quickly as it had arrived. "Sure wish they lived closer."

Besides the modern tape recorder, I noticed several other items that conflicted with Virginia's description of Purity's homes.

"Saul, you have a telephone, a big-screen TV, and a stereo! Right out here in the living room! I thought those accouterments of Satan were supposed to be locked away from us dumb, impressionable women."

He patted the TV, obviously his pride and joy. "Even in my beginning days out here, before it all went sour, I never paid much attention to that kind of stuff. I leave the telephone out so Ruby can call her family any time she wants, not that the girls are always allowed to talk to her." His voice lowered for a moment. "I'd be careful about using it, if I were you. The Circle of Elders knows too many details about my own phone conversations, and I don't think it's because Ruby's spreading the word. She likes to eavesdrop, but she's pretty loyal."

I lowered my voice to match his. "Are you warning me the telephone's tapped?"

"I wouldn't be surprised, and don't look so shocked. Do you really think the people around here care about legalities? So, ah, if you need to contact that partner of yours, you'd better ride into town with me when I go for supplies."

He began to speak normally. "Most of the men here tell their wives and kids that television is dangerous if not managed properly, but I don't mind if you and Ruby watch it every now and then. Just don't go tuning into Oprah or CNN and getting any dangerous ideas about a woman's proper place."

The thought of Oprah and CNN being dangerous not only took my mind off my anxiety, it made me smile. I bore little love for the boob tube, but knew the polygamists feared that too much exposure to what they termed the Outside would tarnish the blissful ignorance of their plural wives. Especially the younger ones. Speaking of plural wives…

I stopped smiling. "Where's Ruby? I'd like to meet her."

Saul and I had agreed earlier that Ruby should be kept in the dark about my true purpose in Purity, so meeting my 'sister wife,' as the polygamists' wives called each other, promised to be an interesting experience.

Just as Saul prepared to answer, I heard the squeak of a door down the hall, then soft footsteps advancing toward us.

"Sister Ruby? You come on out here, hon. I've got someone I want you to meet!"

I tensed, remembering that I was supposed to play the part of a fairly uneducated woman. I didn't see any problem with fooling the compound's men, but fooling a woman might prove more difficult. Even when a woman had little formal education, she could easily spot insincerity in another. I braced myself for a dangerous encounter, but when Ruby finally shuffled into view, pity washed away all my apprehension.

If a human being could truly be said to look like a whipped dog, Ruby did. Her coarsely featured face appeared oddly distorted, as if it had been taken apart and then put together again by inexpert hands. Her brown-and-gray hair was twisted into a tight bun as dull and lifeless as broom straw. We did have one thing in common though, our dresses. Both were long, poorly sewn, and unflattering.

She raised her eyes from a long perusal of my garbage bag luggage, and in a barely audible whisper said, "Brother Saul, it is good to have you home."

"Sister Ruby, I have wonderful news."

When Ruby looked at me, I thought I saw one brief flash of recognition when she saw the scar on my forehead. But she might merely have pegged me as another beaten spirit. "Yes, Brother Saul?"

"I've brought you a new sister wife to help around the house. Her name is Lena."

"Sister wife?" She lowered her eyes and studied the floorboards for a few seconds. Just when I thought she wasn't going to say anything else, she looked up. This time her eyes didn't focus on anyone or anything, just stared off into space. But her jaw clenched. "Yes, that is good news, Brother Saul."

I held out my hand but the scene with Sheriff Benson replayed itself. She wouldn't shake it. Feeling foolish, I dropped my hand to my side, wondering if there was a chapter on etiquette in Prophet Solomon's Gospel. If so, I needed to bone up. Maybe it said to kiss your new sister wife's cheek and shout, "Glory, Hallelujah!"

"It's nice meeting you, Sister Ruby," I mumbled, trying for timidity.

Somehow she managed to speak through that clenched jaw. "It's nice meeting you, Sister Lena." Then she turned around and stalked back down the hall. I heard the door squeak open, and a second later, a slam.

Baffled, I looked at Saul for explanation.

He smiled. "That didn't go half as bad as I thought it would!"

Had we been in the same room? "She's jealous, Saul."

"You're imagining things. 'Jealous sister wives will never see the jewel-bright halls of the Highest Heaven,' Solomon writes in the third chapter of the Gospels. Ruby was raised on it, and like all good polygamist women, she believes it."

Like I said, men are pretty easy to fool.

Formal introductions accomplished, he picked up my garbage bag luggage and led me down the hall to my room, next to Ruby's. After we shut the door behind us, I whispered, "You know, she's probably going to notice that you and I don't, well, that we don't..."

He whispered back. "In most polygamist families, the wife visits the man in his room, then after the guy has his fun the woman can return to her room. As long as you keep up some kind of pretense about visiting me every now and then, she'll never guess our guilty secret." Raising his voice, he added, "I'll leave you to put your things away, Sister Lena. When you're through, knock on Sister Ruby's door and ask her to show you where everything is in the kitchen. I'll want a nice big breakfast tomorrow."

I stared at him. "I told you I don't cook."

"If you can boil water, you're better than me. Or even Ruby." He winked, then left, closing the door gently behind him.

Bare as a monk's cell, the room held only one narrow bed and a small dresser, with a bright wedding ring quilt providing the only color. Created by Saul's dead wife? Or proof of Ruby's handiwork before she had disintegrated into the gray-on-gray creature she'd become?

Only with difficulty did I refrain from making a break for the front door. But remembering why I was here, I lifted my skirt, took out my .38, and began my usual reconnoiter.

"Rebecca, I hope some day you realize what I've gone through for you," I whispered, as I scanned the empty closet for a boogeyman. I didn't want her waking up in the middle of the night for the next fifty years, screaming from night-mares.

I had nightmares enough for the both of us.

Chapter 8

Someone banged on the door.

"Wife! Wife! Time to prepare breakfast!"

I lay there, trying to make sense of the words. *Wife? Time to prepare breakfast?* This was one crazy dream.

Then I remembered.

"Coming," I muttered, crawling out of bed and staggering to the door. I leaned into the frame and hissed, "I told you, Saul, I don't cook!"

"Better act like you're at least trying," he hissed back. "Ruby's already in the kitchen. You don't want to make her suspicious, do you?"

"All right, all right." I wrapped my housecoat around me, unlocked the door, and shouldered the grinning Saul aside as I darted past him into the bathroom. I showered in record time, then returned to my room, where I strapped on my gun and donned a granny dress made from a gray on gray print even drabber than the one I'd worn yesterday. Except for my face and hands, the dress covered me completely, with not so much as a pleat or ruffle to soften its severity. As I braided my hair into a tight plait which made the scar on my forehead stand out in bright relief, I stared at myself in the mirror: The well-dressed sister wife. I looked like puke.

"Sister Lena!" Saul's voice. From the kitchen. "The Lord is telling me that you are taking time for vanities."

Although I knew he said this for Ruby's benefit, it still ticked me off, a warning sign. The perfect sister wife displayed no impatience or temper. Her mind held no thoughts for anything other than the Lord, her husband and her children—in that order. She was a breeding machine, nothing more.

Gritting my teeth, I stuffed my feet into my Reeboks—for some reason not forbidden—and headed toward the kitchen.

Ruby waited by the stove, her dress and hairstyle mirroring my own. She did, however, look less pale today. Her cheeks were pink. "Sister Lena, how come breakfast wasn't ready a half-hour ago? The Lord hates sloth!"

Unless my radar had gone awry, Sister Ruby simmered in a jealous snit. I looked over at Saul to see if he'd noticed.

He sat at the head of the table with his back to her, oblivious. "Oh, Sister Ruby, our dear Sister Lena has lived on the Outside all her life, so she has much to learn." His voice carried enough conviction to scare me, but then he winked. "Now Sister Lena, I want three eggs sunny-side up, three strips of bacon, two slices of white, buttered toast, and a big glass of milk."

Cholesterol heaven. I doubted if a Godly wife corrected her husband even when it was for his own good, so I said nothing.

I did my best, but breakfast, after Saul led us in an obligatory prayer from Solomon's *Gospel*, proved disgusting. Cooking by myself with little assist from Ruby, I had somehow contrived to cook the egg yolks granite hard while keeping the whites runny. I burnt the bacon and cremated the toast. Even the milk seemed to curdle in my inexpert hands. Saul, obviously the possessor of a cast iron stomach, ate most of it, albeit with a pained expression. Ruby pushed the runny eggs around on her plate with all the enthusiasm of a full-bore anorexic, while I confined myself to a pear I'd found on the window sill.

"Fruit is good for you," I said. "It has a lot of fiber. Keeps you regular."

"Fiber?" Ruby knitted her brow as if the concept of a healthy gastrointestinal tract was altogether alien. "Our husband likes eggs and bacon. It's what he likes that counts around here, not what you think."

Meow. But I decided that the woman, who probably saw herself as shunted aside in her husband's affections, deserved sympathy, not sarcasm, so I didn't tell her that pleasing a husband by blocking his arteries was an odd way to show affection. Aloud I said, in a respectful tone, "Perhaps you can teach me how to cook, Sister Ruby. When I lived in the outside world I never cooked, other than to heat up TV dinners." No lie there.

She gave me a quick glance, then in a studied return to her former meekness, said softly, "Sorry, Sister Lena. The Lord told me my family duty is the laundry."

I blinked. "Huh? You mean *God* told you to do the laundry?"

Saul came to the rescue. "Before the Lord spoke to Prophet Solomon and gave Sister Ruby to me, she served as sister wife in a large family where each woman was given one specific duty. One wife cooked, one cleaned, one sewed, and Sister Ruby did the laundry."

A sly smile crept across Ruby's rough features. "Yes, Sister Lena, the Lord spoke unto my husband and told him that I was to wash clothes, and whenever necessary, help with the cleaning. But He didn't tell me to cook."

It irritated me so much I forgot myself. "Aw, c'mon, Ruby. The *Lord* didn't tell you to do the laundry. Your husband did!"

The sly look disappeared, replaced with one of genuine confusion. "Husbands speak for the Lord, so what difference is there?"

I felt a kick on my shin and looked over to see Saul's disapproving frown. My first morning in Purity and I'd almost blown it already.

Saul cleared his throat and addressed me in a stern voice more suited to a televangelist than a retired contractor. "Like any good sister wife, Ruby speaks the truth. The Lord quite rightly communicates with the husband, who then conveys the message downward to his wives. Why should this surprise you, Sister Lena? Prophet Solomon assured us no thing on Earth is too small for the Lord. He knows who's best suited at tilling the fields and who's best suited for the laundry. Because He can see into our hearts, the Lord never makes mistakes. Therefore, it's a terrible sin not to obey the Lord's message."

I glared. "You mean the Lord's message according to Prophet Solomon."

Saul glared back. "Damn straight I do."

I felt another kick.

Having duly chastised me, Saul turned to Ruby. "Ah, the Lord just reminded me that our Sister Lena is new to the ways of the Church of the Prophet Fundamental and that we shouldn't judge her too harshly for a while. He suggested that you and I, as Godly men and women, lead by example, so I'll rely upon you to help our new family member learn the ways of the godly. You got that?"

Ruby bowed her head, but not before I saw that jaw tighten again. "Of course, husband."

I managed a smile. "Thank you, Sister Ruby. Your instruction will be most appreciated." It says something about my commitment to Rebecca that I did not gag as the sycophantic drivel issued from my mouth.

Saul shoved his chair away from the table and stood up. "I've got a lot to do today, Sister Ruby, and I'll need Sister Lena's assistance. I received a phone call last night and was told that Prophet Davis has called a special community meeting up at his house. He wants everyone in Purity in attendance."

Ruby's mouth gaped. "You mean even *wives?* How will we all fit? His house is big, but…"

"He says he'll handle it like we've handled the Sunday services since they started working on the church. In shifts. We drew the first shift, along with the Circle of Elders, so I don't know whether to dance or cry." He turned to me, a dry smile on his face. "When he stepped into his father's shoes, Prophet Davis promised to bring reform to Purity, and I imagine that's what this meeting's all about. It'll be interesting, because from what I hear, the Circle of Elders plans to fight him every inch of the way. I hear he's curtailing their power, maybe even disbanding the whole group."

"I don't believe it!" Ruby burst out. "Reforms? God's word needs no reform!"

"Let's wait and see." Leaving Ruby fuming into the dish-water, Saul ushered me to into the living room. "It's just more bullshit," he said, as we sat down on the sofa. "These damned polygamy prophets are always having what they call 'revelations,' so who knows what crack-brained stuff we'll hear this time. The 'revelation' will probably turn out to be more about money than anything else. They like to talk God around here, but it's money and sex that really get their knickers in a twist."

He looked at his watch. "Tell you what. The meeting won't start until ten, so why don't you take a walk around the compound and familiarize yourself with things. But don't challenge anybody like you just did Ruby, okay?"

I bit my lip. "Yes, sir, Brother Saul."

He cackled, then slapped me on the rump. "Attagirl."

I left the house with a feeling of relief, swearing that when I got back, I'd have a little talk with hubby and remind him to keep his hands to himself. For now I relished the chance to explore the compound in broad daylight, something I hadn't been able to do during my days in the canyon.

There were fewer people abroad than I expected. Judging from the dearth of pickup trucks, some of the men had probably been working in the distant fields since sunup. Most of the children were in school. Just about the only sign of life I saw, other than the odd skinny dog or two, was a straggly line of people winding their way along the dirt pathway toward the kitchen gardens. Some carried baskets, some hoes. When I grew closer, I made out at least a dozen pregnant teenagers and a smattering of elderly men and women.

Suddenly the front door of one of the trailers located near the chicken runs slammed open. A man and four women, all dressed in Purity's turn-of-the-century garb, emerged to hurry after the gardeners. The man, heavy to the point of obesity, looked at least seventy. Three of the women with him were elderly, too. But the last woman!

Not yet forty, and although her waist had thickened, probably with repeated childbirth, she dazzled like a Nordic goddess. Platinum hair and sky-blue eyes intensified this Valkyrie image, while a rosebud mouth and small, straight nose lent softness to what might have otherwise been an almost masculine physicality. The old man's daughter?

As I watched, the man stopped, reached around her waist and drew her to him. While the other women pursed their lips with disapproval, he gave her a slobbering kiss she didn't return.

I shuddered in sympathy. In any other setting, Beauty would probably have been covered in diamonds instead of faded calico, but here in Purity she'd wound up in the rustiest trailer in the compound. Hers was hardly a love match, either. Judging from the way Beauty cringed away from Beast's kiss, she detested him. Not that Beast noticed—or cared. When he finally came up for air, I saw a look of utter self-satisfaction on his face.

The romantic interlude over (was Beast trying to make his other wives jealous?), the group resumed their hurried pace toward the garden. For a minute I thought about following them, then decided not to. The whole scene was too depressing.

Instead, I walked behind the group of trailers to the livestock pens, clucking at the chickens, mooing at the cows.

Still calling sweet nothings to the baffled livestock, I rounded the corner of a shed and saw a boy of about fourteen throwing flakes of hay into a goat pen.

"Shouldn't you be in school?" I asked, before I remembered that Saul had told me not to speak to anyone until I'd been spoken to, and definitely not to challenge any male, however young.

The boy jerked, dropping the hay outside the pen, which made the two goats inside bleat in irritation. Then he caught himself, scooped up the hay and threw it into the pen.

"Sister, you shouldn't sneak up on people like that." His voice began as a baritone but finished as a soprano.

I would have smiled, but the expression on his face was a study in despair. "Sorry about that. I'm Lena, Brother Saul's new wife."

His voice rocked and rolled for a moment, then settled down in the alto range. "I'm Brother Meade Royal. Pleased to meet you, Sister Lena. And not that it's any concern of yours, but I'm taking a little time off school this week." With his pale blond hair and vivid blue eyes, he was a younger version of the Valkyrie I'd seen being so unpleasantly mauled.

I pointed toward the rusty trailer. "You live there?"

He nodded. "Me and my mom, we just moved in. My father's…" A sniffle.

Boys his age never want you to see them cry, so I studied a ground squirrel scampering in a zigzag pattern across the ground.

After a few noisy gulps, Meade regained control. "My father died and Mother had to get married again. Brother Vern had a spare trailer so the Circle of Elders gave her to him."

Royal. "Was your father Prophet Solomon, by any chance?"

"Yeah. He was murdered. The police caught the woman who did it." He looked ready to howl with grief.

What a life. "I'm sorry, Brother Meade."

He thrust out his chin. "Why be sorry? Father Prophet attained the highest level of Heaven and we should be jubilant." However, reciting the party line didn't keep a tear from slipping down his cheek.

I wanted to hug the poor child, but since he was trying so desperately to act manful, I restrained myself. No wonder he wasn't in school. His mother probably thought goat-tending would be more therapeutic than algebra, a pretty good judgment call in my estimation.

His mother's hasty remarriage didn't seem like such a good judgment call, however. Saul said the Circle of Elders encouraged widows to remarry as soon as possible, but this was overdoing it. Solomon had been dead, what, a little over a week? For that matter, why did a woman as beautiful as Meade's mother plummet from being the wife of a wealthy prophet to the wife of a trailer dweller?

I had started to question him further when the crack of a rifle shot echoed across the compound and made me jump half out of my Reeboks.

Brother Meade walked over and patted my arm. "Don't be scared, Sister Lena. It's all right. That's just the men hunting down in the canyon. Fried rabbit's delicious. If you've never had any, you ought to try it."

I like a nice steak, but the thought of nibbling on some cute little bunny depressed me. "I think I'll give it a pass. Well, Brother Meade, it was nice meeting you. Maybe I'll see you later at the community meeting. I'll be at the first session, how about you?"

"Yeah, first session." I returned to my walk, leaving him with his goats. The warming day made me long for Paiute Canyon's deep shade. Purity's flat terrain, bordered by the glaring Vermillion Cliffs, served as little more than a heat sink for the sun's rays, and by the time I wandered back to the central dirt circle, sweat stained the underarms of my long-sleeved dress.

Apparently the day wasn't too hot for the few tow-headed toddlers who began filtering from their hotel-sized homes to play with the battered toys littering the grounds.

Threading my way through them, I noticed that the least rundown houses were situated on the Utah side of the border, the poorest houses in Arizona. Also in Utah stood the large schoolhouse and next to it, a two-story, warehouse-sized building whose wooden sign bragged "Purity Health Clinic." Fifty miles was too far to drive when a child needed immediate care, so this made sense. Still, what kind of medical care could the clinic really offer? I doubted the compound had its own doctor.

While I stared at the clinic, which was really no more elegant than the usual Purity Garbage Dump Modern, a man exited and walked briskly toward a gabled house that peeked through a stand of cottonwood and mesquite on the edge of the canyon. What I could see of the house looked almost elegant, but then so did the man. In his prime, the man stood well over six feet tall and had the broad shoulders of a movie idol. His pale blond hair, glossy as corn silk, revealed the same Nordic ancestors as the Valkyrie's, as did his eyes, which were the color of sky-reflecting fjords. His blue eyes perfectly matched his bright, high-neck shirt, making me suspect there might be a touch of vanity there. If so, he came by it honestly, because I'd never seen such a good-looking man, and I'd seen plenty in my time.

"That's Prophet Davis," a girl's voice said. "Handsome, isn't he?"

I turned to see a girl of around fifteen, her own considerable looks undiminished by her red-rimmed eyes and stained apron. Like other teenaged girls who'd drifted into Prophet's Park, she held a struggling toddler by the hand.

"He's a hunk!" I blurted, then slapped my hand over my mouth. Busted again.

The girl just smiled. "We're not supposed to notice a man's appearance. The body is just the physical casing for the soul. That's what the Gospel According to Solomon says, anyway. But the girls still stare." As she bent to pick up the toddler, a book fell out of her apron.

Since her arms were full of wriggling two-year-old, I reached down and retrieved it. A new paperback copy of E. L. Doctorow's *Ragtime*.

"You're studying this in school?" I asked, surprised. Wait a minute. She wasn't *in* school. Neither were any of the other teenagers in the park. Then I remembered Saul telling me the compound's girls weren't expected to attend school after the age of fourteen because they were needed as babysitters or wives. Sometimes they received their G.E.D., but usually not.

She grabbed the book and stuffed it back into her apron pocket. "Please don't tell anyone you saw this, okay? Brother Saul picks these up when he's in town, but we have to keep it a secret. Mom would have a fit if she knew I read such nasty books."

Nasty books? *Doctorow?* Well, of course. A community which didn't let its women and children watch television certainly wouldn't allow free access to literature. But I simply said, "Doctorow's not that all that racy."

Her eyes lit up. "You've actually read Doctorow?"

"Sure. We studied him in my American Lit class. My favorite was *The Book of Daniel,* but I liked *Ragtime,* too, even though the lack of dialogue just about drove me crazy. By the way, I'm Lena...uh, Sister Lena. And you are...?"

Her face, rapt while listening to my discussion of Doctorow, flushed. "Oh, gosh, I'm sorry. I'm Sister Cynthia. Brother Davis is my brother, my blood brother. Half-brother, anyway. We have the same father."

That explained her red eyes. "Then you're Prophet Solomon's daughter."

More gunfire, followed by a shout. Some poor bunny rabbit just bought the farm. But this time I was ready for the noise and hardly reacted.

"One of his daughters," Cynthia said. "I have forty-eight sisters and fifty-four brothers."

Somehow I kept my eyes from popping out of my head. The dead Prophet had been a randy old sod, but judging from the three offspring I'd seen, he'd either been a good-looking man himself or married the most beautiful women in the compound. Probably the latter, I decided. Like rock stars, prophets attracted the prettiest groupies.

"I'm very sorry about your father."

She nodded. "Thank you."

"I met your other brother a few minutes ago, and he's taking it pretty rough." Then I remembered her dozens of brothers. "I'm talking about Meade."

Her eyes looked away from mine, and she plucked at the plastic buttons on the bodice of her pale pink granny dress. "We have different mothers. Meade was close to Father Prophet, closer than I was, 'cause I'm just a girl."

Just a girl. Just a girl who had E. L. Doctorow smuggled into a polygamy compound. I wondered how many other bright young women were leading lives of quiet desperation. But there was nothing I could do about that now.

"Ah, I heard that your father was found in the canyon," I said. "Do you think it was a hunting accident?"

She murmured a few words to the toddler, then set him down. "They say it was murder, that a woman killed him, but I don't know. He liked to hunt for rabbits and stuff, so when he didn't come home for dinner, most of us thought that was what he was doing. But the men say he'd already started back home when that woman, when she…"

"When she killed him?" I finished for her. "But why…"

Before I could finish, a nearby child screamed and we both turned around. A little girl had tripped over an abandoned tire and lay struggling in the dirt. Cynthia ran forward and picked her up.

"Hush, sweetie," she murmured, as she tended to her scraped knee. "I'll kiss it and make it well."

The girl sobbed into Cynthia's apron for a few minutes, then finally ran off to rejoin her playmates, giving the tire she'd tripped over a wide berth.

"You'd think the men would haul this junk away," I said, gesturing to the tire, the junked cars, the other litter. "It's not safe."

"You'd think." For the first time her voice sounded bitter. "Last week one of the little boys slashed his leg on that old car over there." She pointed to a rusting sedan which looked ancient enough to have been driven by Henry Ford himself. "I carried him over to the clinic and it took fifteen stitches to close the wound."

"The clinic has a doctor?"

"No, but Sister Lovey and Sister Judith can both sew up cuts. They're teaching me, too. I'd really like to be a doctor, but only boys get to go to college, and they study law. You know, to help out with Purity's legal stuff. I wish…" Her voice trailed off.

I would have followed up, but my job here was to find out who killed Prophet Solomon, not investigate the level of Purity's medical care. Changing the subject, I said, "I've heard so many wonderful things about the prophet, so why would that woman want to kill such a great man?"

Her pretty face, which had momentarily lightened as she tended to the child, darkened again. "From what I heard, he wanted to marry Esther's daughter. Esther's the woman they think killed him. Anyway, she didn't want that. She'd moved to Phoenix and they say she grew away from the church."

I played dumb. "If Esther didn't live here, why was her daughter here?"

"Abel, Esther's husband, returned to the church. Leaving Purity, coming back, it's not that unusual for the young men. They have trouble finding wives, so they try other places. Father Prophet did the same thing when he was younger, but he came back, too. His parents called him the Prodigal Son, just like in the Bible."

I tried to hurry her along. "If Abel returned, why didn't his wife come back, too?"

"She divorced him. She'd been infected by the Outside. That made him pretty mad so he drove to Scottsdale, that's somewhere near Phoenix, and got his daughter."

"You mean he kidnapped her?"

She blinked at my question. "Oh, no! You can't kidnap your own child."

I could have disabused her of that idea, but decided instead to take the conversation as far as possible. Unlike most teenagers I'd known back in Scottsdale, she was amazingly pliable. A sign of innocence? Or had she been taught to respect her elders no matter what goofy things they said or did?

"You know, Cynthia, I think I remember reading something about this in the papers! That girl your father wanted to marry, wasn't she only thirteen?"

She looked at the Vermillion Cliffs, so red this morning they appeared to be on fire. "When a girl is old enough to have babies, she's supposed to get married. I'll have to get married soon, too. My mother's been nagging me about it for a long time now."

So no medical school. "How old are you?"

"I'll be sixteen in a couple of months. That's pretty late to get married around here."

"Sure seems young to me."

When she faced me, her face was as troubled as her voice. "Solomon's Gospel says women must be fruitful if they want to attain Highest Heaven." But she didn't sound convinced. Maybe she'd discovered other interpretations of life's purpose in all those nasty Doctorow novels.

"Sister Cynthia, don't you think…"

A woman screamed. Both Cynthia and I looked toward the mesquite grove where the sound seemed to have originated.

The woman screamed again. Then a man shouted, "It's Prophet Davis! He's been shot!"

After a quick glance toward the toddlers, who had already fled for the safety of closer girls, Cynthia, as pale as her apron, picked up her skirts and ran toward the canyon. I followed, soon passing her, even though my hip had stiffened through lack of exercise. When we reached the mesquite grove, we found a crowd gathered around an irate Prophet Davis, who, as it turned out, was fine. But his bright blue shirt hadn't been so lucky.

"This is inexcusable!" he snapped, fingering a bullet hole in his shirt sleeve. "I could have been killed! Who's responsible for this?"

No one came forward to admit culpability.

"Come on, out with it! Which one of you was stupid enough to shoot *up* from the canyon, rather than along it?"

The women stopped their twittering, the men their grumbling. Some, relieved that no blood had spilled, drifted away. I heard one hunter say to his companion, "Well, you gotta expect a bullet hole or two when you build your house so close to the brush. He's the stupid one, if you ask me."

One of the women, yet another pretty blond, pulled at him. "Let me get you inside, make sure you're okay."

He brushed her hand away, though not unkindly. "I'm fine, Sissy, but I'd better change my shirt. No point in showing up at the meeting looking like something left over from target practice."

Giving one last furious glance at the remaining crowd, he called out, "If I catch whoever did this, I'll make sure his gun privileges are revoked for a month!"

Cynthia shook her head. "He's fine, so let's get back to the park. I've already been away from those kids too long. Who knows what they've managed to do to themselves by now."

When we arrived back at Prophet's Park, the other teenagers, less curious about Prophet Davis's narrow escape, had taken up the slack. None of the children had sustained any more bumps or cuts.

"Seems to me you should be able to build your house anywhere you want without getting shot at," I said, as Cynthia picked up another toddler.

"You'd sure think so, but this has happened before," she answered, her face still pale.

"Are you talking about your father?"

She shook her head. "No, Brother Davis. Somebody just missed him the other day, too."

I stared at her. "You're kidding."

"I'm not kidding. You know what I think?" Her eyes looked scared, and she lowered her voice to a whisper. "I think somebody's trying to kill him."

When I returned to Saul's, I found him sitting in the green recliner, hunched turtle-like into his shirt, tape recorder in hand. Someone, guess who, banged pots and pans in the kitchen.

"Ruby want to know why you went out for a walk instead of making the beds," Saul said. He wouldn't meet my eyes.

"I'm supposed to make beds?"

"She wanted you to do the dishes, too. She even reminded me that one of the benefits of having sister wives was getting help with the housework."

I looked around. The house appeared perfectly clean to me, and I said so.

He flicked a quick, guilty look at me. "Beds aren't made, floors aren't swept, toilets aren't scrubbed…"

I held up my hand. "Somebody just tried to shoot Prophet Davis."

The tape recorder fell to the floor. *"Again?"*

I nodded. "Again. What the hell's going on around here? Why didn't you tell me somebody's trying to take out *all* the prophets?"

Saul leaned over and picked up the recorder. He turned it on for a second, testing it, and I heard someone talking about life onboard ship in the Persian Gulf. Satisfied, he turned it off.

"I never connected Solomon's death with what happened to Davis, but maybe you're right. Both men are, were, whatever, prophets of Purity. Hell and blazes."

"Please tell me someone's talked to the authorities about this?"

Saul gave a short, hard laugh. "You're kidding, right? Lena, if there hadn't been some poor woman handy to pin Prophet Solomon's death on, nobody would have cooperated with the authorities over that, either. They settle their own scores around here in their own way. They only drag in the cops if there's an Outsider around to take the blame."

Remembering that I was an Outsider made me so uncomfortable that I actually swept the floors to keep from thinking about it.

Chapter 9

By the time I'd hurried through the housework, Saul was ready for the community meeting. The prospect of watching Purity's leadership in action intrigued me, as did meeting the men who might have benefited from Prophet Solomon's death—or even from that of the new prophet.

I freshened up in the bathroom, making certain the top buttons on my long granny dress remained fastened. As I studied myself in the mirror, I noticed that the brisk housework had left my face flushed, making the scar on my forehead appear vivid. The only thing I needed to worry about was keeping my mouth shut.

I joined Saul by the front door, only to discover that Ruby had finally left the kitchen and disappeared into one of the rooms.

"Ruby! Time to leave!" Saul called as we waited.

Silence for a few moments. Then footsteps. Ruby appeared from the hallway. "I can't go," she announced, in a grim voice.

"What do you mean, you can't go? Prophet Davis wants as many people there as possible."

She threw an accusatory glance my way. "Sister Lena didn't sweep in the corners or vacuum the rug."

I protested. "The house is perfectly clean."

"No it's not."

"Yes, it…" A firm hand on my shoulder stopped me.

"Sister Lena, since she knows more about it, we'll have to defer to Sister Ruby in these matters. Perhaps when we come back, she can show you the proper way to clean."

Ruby shook her head. "It needs to be done now, not later."

What a tyrant. Even more irritating was the fact that Saul deferred to her. Did that happen in other polygamy households? I tried some fence-mending. "Sister Ruby, I really want to go to the community meeting so I can better understand the way of life here. I promise that when I get back I'll clean the way you want me to do."

"No. You do it now."

I finally understood. Ruby was First Wife, I was New Girl on the Block, and she was merely establishing the pecking order. If Saul let this behavior continue, though, it could damage my chances to find Prophet Solomon's killer. An article I'd once read had theorized that housework expanded to fill the time available, and unless I was mistaken, Ruby planned to try out that theory herself, only using me as the lab rat.

I had to nip her plans in the bud. Turning to Saul, I whined, "Oh, please, Brother Saul! I really do want to go to that meeting!"

"And you will." My obvious concern alerted him to the problem. "Tell you what, Sister Ruby. You finish the floors, and once you're done, fix lunch. We won't need anything fancy. Just put some meat on two slices of bread. With a little mayonnaise."

Ruby opened her mouth to protest then closed it again without saying a word, probably remembering that her husband spoke for the Lord, and if the Lord wanted mayonnaise, He'd get mayonnaise. After a second or two she tried again. "Can't she at least clean the toilets now?"

"The Lord wants *you* to scrub the toilets, Sister Ruby. He just revealed it to me." With that, he grabbed me by the arm and pulled me out the door, but not before I saw a glimmer of fury in Sister Ruby's eyes.

Saul headed toward the Utah side of the compound, towing me behind him. "That didn't go well," he said in a disgusted voice. "If you want to pull this off, you'll have to figure out a way to keep Ruby happy. Like the rest of the women around here, she may not have much formal schooling but she's a long way from dumb."

Knowing he was right, I nodded. For the first time it occurred to me that Purity's women lived an even more difficult life than I'd originally believed. Not only did they have to obey their husbands' every whim, but they had to guard against their sister wives, too.

Saul continued talking as we walked, trying to keep out of earshot of the other people scurrying across the compound. To the west, a long line of battered cars and pickup trucks streamed toward us on the dirt road.

"Rumor has it that our new prophet is going to initiate some pretty heavy changes in Purity," Saul said. "But I'll believe it when I see it. The Circle of Elders, which is made up of the most conservative of the conservative, will dig in its heels. Davis is going to have his hands full with them."

He gave me a brief rundown on the Circle of Elders and their relationship to Purity's prophets. Originally, the compound's government had functioned similarly to England's political structure, with the reigning prophet fulfilling the role of prime minister and the Circle of Elders behaving as Parliament. During the last few years of Prophet Solomon's reign, however, the Circle's role had waned.

"The Circle still arranges all the marriages and decides whose home gets fixed up or added to, but the prophet now negotiates all of the Purity Fellowship Foundation's business contracts. I'm not sure the Circle even knows how much money is coming in."

"Nice for the prophet," I said.

He winked. "Wait'll you see Davis's house. It's the second nicest house in the compound."

Davis Royal's house, surrounded by the grove of cotton-wood and mesquite that had kept me from seeing it earlier, was almost a city block long and appeared to be built out of the same red rock as the Vermillion Cliffs. Its green steel, copper-trimmed roof should have presented a gaudy contrast, but it didn't. Neither did the green shutters that framed the house's dozens of windows. A long veranda, furnished with expensive-looking patio furniture, ran the entire width of the house, playing host to the dozens of people gathered on it. Prophet Davis's humble abode looked like one of the more upscale Scottsdale resorts.

The new prophet's cars matched his house, too. In the circular gravel driveway sat a gleaming silver Mercedes ML55, a Cadillac Escalade, and three Chrysler Town and Country vans, the better to haul his brood, I reckoned.

"It sure doesn't look like Prophet Davis has taken a vow of poverty." Since we were approaching a large group of men also headed for the house, I kept my voice low.

"That'll be the day," Saul replied. "In Purity, the prophets have always lived well and nobody thinks a thing of it, not even when the rest of the folks walk around in rags and drive rust heaps. Now hush up before you start calling attention to yourself."

Following Saul's instructions, I kept my eyes on the ground, but every now and then I chanced a swift look up at the people around us. Most of the women, even girls who couldn't have been older than thirteen, were pregnant. Their bellies hiked up the front hems of their long granny dresses, exposing painfully swollen ankles. Some appeared ready to squat down in the dirt to give birth on the spot.

The men were all clad in an assortment of bib overalls, Levis, and long-sleeved woolen shirts buttoned up to their Adam's apples. Underneath, I knew, they wore their Temple undergarments. Given that the temperatures during the daytime topped the nineties, they had to be miserable—not that I cared how miserable any of them felt.

"Lena!" Saul's sharp command pulled me out of my thoughts. Then he lowered his voice. "Whatever you're thinking, stop it right now. You look like you're ready to pull a gun on someone!"

"Sorry," I whispered. "It's just that..."

He whispered back. "I know. It's exactly what I felt once I figured out what was really going on here under all this sanctimonious bullshit. But remember what I said. You have to act like a meek sister wife while you're here, not some pissed-off avenging angel."

The thought of me being anyone's avenging angel made me smile, and he smiled back. "That's more like it. A meek little sister wife is a happy little sister wife."

Still smiling, I whispered, "Thee can shove it up thine ass, Brother Saul."

He laughed, making several of the men waiting on Prophet Davis Royal's porch look at us curiously. A large group of women, probably their wives, stood in a huddle behind them. I couldn't help but notice the poor condition of the women's teeth. No dentists in Purity?

"We hear you have a new wife, Brother Saul," called one of the men, a thin-faced, pimpled blond scarcely out of his teens. Like the others, he was modestly clad and his ill-fitting clothes did little to disguise his too-short legs and concave chest. His large head and stunted limbs hinted at dwarfism.

"Yes, Brother Noah," Saul responded. "The Lord worked one of His miracles in my heart and swore He'd reward me for my righteousness with many children." Saul turned to me with a leer of such cartoonish intensity I had to lower my head again to hide my smile.

"Brother Noah is our departed Prophet Solomon's grandson, Sister Lena," Saul explained to me. "Treat him with the deference he deserves."

"Of course, husband," I murmured, allowing myself another quick peek at Brother Noah, only to find to my horror that Saul's leer had been matched by Noah's. The younger man's leer was the real deal, though, and as his watery eyes raked my body, he stopped just short of outright drooling. Apparently a man's lust wasn't considered a sin in Purity.

Noah finally turned away and began chatting with one of the other men. Saul took the opportunity to whisper into my ear, "Don't ever get caught alone with Noah. He once shot Solomon's dog just because it barked at him. The fact that it was his granddaddy's favorite dog didn't bother him one bit. "

I made a mental note to find out where Noah had been the night of Prophet Solomon's murder. Maybe Solomon had given his trigger-happy grandson a talking to and the ugly little hothead had killed him on the spot.

Saul shared a few words with an elderly man who bore an uncanny resemblance to a department store Santa Claus. His round, cherry-red nose peeked out from between snowy brows, and a lush white beard framed a cherry, sunburnt face. Santa's eyes, though, appeared vacant.

"Brother Jacob, I hope you're feeling better?" Saul asked politely.

"The Lord judges us from Highest Heaven and sends down blessings as well as vengeance," the old man responded, his voice holding no inflection. "We shrivel under His mighty gaze."

The other men fell into an uncomfortable silence, but Saul nodded in perfect seriousness, as if such Biblical pronouncements were the normal response to enquiries about health. "Yes, Brother Jacob, the Lord is a mighty Judge."

To me, Saul whispered, "Brother Jacob Waldman hasn't felt too good lately."

Jacob Waldman. Esther's father, the other witness to the argument between Esther and Prophet Solomon. I studied the old man's face more closely, trying to remember where I had seen that ain't-nobody-home look before. Then it came back to me. I'd once investigated a Scottsdale nursing home which had shown an unusually high death rate among its patients. The home specialized in the care of Alzheimer's disease.

A large man thrust himself in front of Jacob. I recognized Earl Graff.

"Brother Saul, I told you the Circle of Elders hasn't yet voted to sanctify the marriage to your new woman," he said, his face shaking in outrage. "Don't you think you should hold off bringing her into Prophet Davis's house until then? To bring an unhallowed woman into a prophet's house is a defilement."

The other men looked at each other, cleared their throats, and more or less tried to pretend they hadn't heard the insult, but Saul refused to be intimidated. "Since when would following the Lord's wishes be a defilement? It seems to me, Brother Earl, that you're attempting to place the Circle's desires above the Lord's."

Earl's face turned as red as his hair. "You're not a member of the Circle and you have no right to…"

Just then the door opened, and Purity's new prophet stepped out on the porch. "My, my, brothers," he boomed, his voice resonant as a televangelist's. "If I didn't know better, I'd think that I heard voices raised in anger. And right outside a prophet's front door, no less!"

Although I'd seen him earlier, I couldn't help but stare at him. On Prophet Davis, even the orange, high-necked shirt he'd changed into looked terrific.

"And who do we have here?" Prophet Hunk said to me, his amazing eyes crinkling with humor. He'd obviously recovered from his earlier near escape.

I lowered my head again and stared fiercely at the porch's redwood floorboards.

"Prophet Davis, this is my new wife, Sister Lena." A note of anxiety crept into Saul's voice. Davis certainly had an interesting effect on people, both female *and* male.

Davis's large, warm hand, free of calluses, engulfed my own. "Welcome, Sister Lena. The Church of the Prophet Fundamental is brightened by your glowing presence."

So help me I almost tittered. But I contained myself and looked modestly up at him. "Thank you, Prophet Davis. I seek only to serve the Lord and my husband."

Another large hand clasped mine as the Prophet delivered a caress thinly disguised as a handshake.

"Prophet Davis, their marriage has not yet been sanctified!" Earl said. "We in the Circle of Elders have grave doubts about its validity. No one knows this woman! Not who she is or where she came from!"

Davis tilted his head to the side and smiled down at me. His own showbiz teeth would have done a Scottsdale orthodontist proud. "I was taking care of some business in Salt Lake when you arrived, Sister Lena, or I would have been present to welcome you to Purity and help sort though this confusion with the Circle of Elders. Perhaps now that I am back…?"

He trailed off and looked questioningly at Saul. I couldn't help but notice, however, that Davis still held my hand. Not that I minded.

Saul noticed, too, and the anxiety in his voice increased. "Prophet Davis, I'd be happy to discuss the worthiness of my new wife with you. You just say where and when."

Davis caressed my hand once more, then gently dropped it. His voice, as smooth as his touch, purred. "I don't think you need to worry, Brother Saul. Your wife is charming."

With that, Prophet Davis went into the house and like good little Christian soldiers, we all trooped into the living room after him, the rest of the women following three paces behind. Muted children's voices could be heard somewhere toward the back of the house, but none, not even their toys, were evident in the startling sight that lay before me.

Davis Royal's huge, three-story living room looked like something out of the pages of *Architectural Digest*. A solid glass wall, which I hadn't been able to see from the road, offered a stunning view of the Vermillion Cliffs, and the cliff's colors had obviously inspired the room's decoration. Groupings of oxblood leather sofas and chairs hunkered on jewel-colored Persian carpets, which in turn topped what seemed to be acres of expensive oak flooring. Tropical fans dangled from the lofty, wood-beamed ceiling and stirred the ferns and palms placed around the room. I'd known billionaires with shabbier houses.

Virginia and Leo had been right. Regardless of the poverty most of Purity's inhabitants appeared to live in, the prophets themselves had access to plenty of money. Why did the Circle of Elders allow such disparity in lifestyle to continue? Religious intimidation—or something else?

But not everything in the room was elegant, such as the rows of folding chairs which faced the lectern at the end of the room. While people jockeyed for positions near the front, Saul and I found seats at the back, the better to watch the others while being less noticeable ourselves.

As I settled into my chair, Saul leaned over and whispered, "I think Davis is looking for a new wife, at least that's the buzz. Once the family situation over at Solomon's gets cleared up, he'll probably move over there. The house isn't as pretty, but it's a lot bigger."

Davis wove between the chairs, greeting each man personally, slapping him on the back, sharing brief comments. He didn't ignore the women, either. Each woman, even the oldest, homeliest, and most pregnant received that seductive two-handed greeting he'd given me. What a politician!

Saul nudged me. "Lena, didn't you hear me?"

"Sorry. What were you saying?" I watched Prophet Davis bend over a plain, dark-haired girl who looked much too young to be pregnant. When he patted her on her monstrous belly she looked up at him with adoration.

"I'm trying to tell you about Solomon's widows." Saul kept his voice low as the seats around us began to fill.

"Wait a minute. That girl Davis is talking to, she looks too young to be pregnant. What is she, all of fourteen?"

"That's Rosalinda and she looks younger than she is. She's sixteen. You've already had the non-pleasure of meeting her husband, Earl Graff. But please quit ogling our handsome prophet and listen to me. All of Solomon's widows are here, and I want you to pay real close attention to them. People say they weren't all that crazy about Solomon while he was alive, but they look plenty miserable now." He waved toward a group of silent women ranging from young teens to elderly grandmothers, sitting together in the middle rows. Like the women I'd seen earlier on the portch, their teeth were marred by untreated cavities and cheap bridgework.

"What do you mean?" I stopped watching Davis's meet-and-greet routine. Earl Graff's head suddenly turned toward us and I realized I'd spoken too loudly. I lowered my voice again. "Why are Solomon's widows so unhappy?" Toothaches?

"Because the Circle of Elders plans to divvy them and their kids up between other men," he whispered. "Martha Royal, his first wife, was the first to get a new husband, and from the way that's turned out, it's made the others plenty nervous. Vern Leonard, that's Martha's proud groom, is nobody's idea of a hottie."

I struggled to keep my voice down. "You mean the Circle of Elders is just *giving* the widows away like hand-me-down clothing?"

"It's usually about favors, not money. The Circle was probably in debt to Vern for something. Or maybe one of the Circle was pissed at Martha and figured this was a great way to get even."

"That's slavery!" My outrage made it difficult to keep my voice down.

Saul put his finger to his lips. "Careful."

I bit my lip, and to get my mind off the terrified widows, scanned the crowd. Approximately one hundred and fifty people had now filed into the room and taken their seats, and as I studied them, I noticed something odd. Almost all were blonds. In fact, so many blue-eyed blonds populated the room that it could have passed for an Aryan Brotherhood meeting. Then I remembered something I'd learned at ASU while studying the history of the Southwest. After the Mormons started their missionary work in other countries, they made many converts in Scandinavia. Many of those converts moved to Salt Lake city, which at this point was probably the blondest city in the U.S. In Purity, that tendency to blondness had magnified. No wonder Prophet Davis had looked upon me with such approval. Except for my green eyes, I fit right in.

While studying this profusion of blonds, I noticed Martha Royal sitting next to her new husband, his hand resting on her knee. If she leaned any farther away from him she'd topple off her chair.

Most of the other women in the room looked little happier than Martha but few displayed her utter disgust. Seeing this many women together, though, did make me finally put my finger on something that had nudged at me since I'd arrived in the compound. The women's granny dresses were sewn with various levels of competence. Some hems dangled and some showed the tracks of let-out seams. While clean, the fabrics were worn thin, with their former patterns faded into ghosts with repeated washings. Compared to these women, I was a virtual fashion statement.

"You'd think they'd at least dress up for the meeting," I commented.

Saul took a quick look around. "They *are* dressed up. Remember, most of these women are on welfare."

I bit my lip again to keep from saying more. One group of women, though, looked far from destitute. They stood in a little circle, chatting happily while waiting for the meeting to start. Their granny dresses glowed with bright colors and new fabric. While many of the other women were pale to the point of anemia, these women's faces radiated good health, and their teeth were as perfect as Davis'. As a group, they were the prettiest blonds in the room.

Saul saw me watching them. "Those are Prophet Davis's wives. Not bad, huh? He does have an eye for the ladies."

Ah, the old rock star perk. I recognized one woman from earlier in the day. About twenty, she was a younger, even more beautiful version of Martha Royal. Martha's daughter, perhaps? She wore a bright blue-and-yellow calico that set off her pale hair and azure eyes.

Saul saw me watching her. "That's Sissy Royal, Davis's sixth wife. He married her just after she turned sixteen, but she hasn't given him any babies yet."

I remembered that the more children a woman bore, the higher her family status appeared to be. Sissy, while beautiful, wore the strained expression of a woman who knows she's not measuring up.

"How many children does Davis have?"

Saul shrugged. "Around thirty, I think. Maybe more. Each of his other wives pops a baby out a year, and one of them even has two sets of twins. But I've got to say this for ol' Davis, his wives look a lot happier than the rest of the women around here. Even Ruby wanted a couple of her daughters to marry him, course that was mainly so they wouldn't have to marry guys living in some of the other compounds."

"What happened?"

He shook his head. "They weren't pretty enough for him. They got shipped off to some old guy in Sunset, about sixty miles away, and Ruby's hated Davis ever since." He jerked his head toward the lectern, where Prophet Davis, having finished the task of greeting everyone, rapped a small gavel on the lectern.

"Friends, before we begin today's meeting, let us pray," he said, sounding more like a televangelist than ever.

It was all I could do not to groan but I stood obediently with the rest of the group. The prayer was long, calling for God's help bringing strength and endurance to the men, obedience and humility to the women. I'd heard it all before, which was why I'd shied away from church all my life, but toward the end, Prophet Davis interjected some intriguing new material.

"As it says in Prophet Solomon's Gospel, 'For behold I reveal unto you a new covenant and unless ye adhere to this covenant, ye will never see Highest Heaven,'" Davis's voice rang out. "Our forefather Abraham received numerous concubines and they bore him many children, and therefore Abraham was seated by the Lord on the highest throne of Highest Heaven. Oh, children of Purity, that is our sacred commandment, to follow in Abraham's footsteps."

As everyone said "Amen," and sat down, I added a silent "Bullshit."

The self-serving prayer out of the way, Davis got down to business.

"First, I want to issue one more call for the man who shot at me this morning to admit his mistake. I am ready to confer forgiveness upon the sinner."

In the long pause that followed, I could hear people breathing. The silence must have continued for at least five minutes, but no one ever confessed.

"All right then," Davis said. "Here's what I'm going to do about it. The guns have all been returned to the armory, correct?" He looked over at the Circle of Elders, where each of those worthies nodded in unison.

"Brothers, bring your keys to me."

"What? What do you mean?" Earl Graff said. "The Circle of Elders has cared for the guns for a hundred years!"

"Not anymore." Davis's voice was grim. "Bring those keys here now, Brother Graff. From now on, when anyone wants to go hunting, he'll have to come to me and I will personally take him over to the armory and hand him a rifle. I don't like being shot at twice in one week."

Earl sputtered, as did the other members of the Circle, but in the end, they handed the keys over to Davis.

"The armory? Where's the armory?" I whispered to Saul.

"It's on the second floor of the clinic, where the Circle of Elders holds its monthly meeting. Like everything else around here, the guns are communally owned, but it sure looks like Davis is going to make it a lot less communal."

Davis spoke again, his voice carrying beautifully, even in this large room. "As you all know, brothers and sisters, things have been pretty tense around Zion City since Prophet Solomon's murder. The anti-polygamy media is trying to stir up a witch hunt again, and they're making our friends in government nervous. When you take those runs into town to sign those welfare and SSI forms, keep your wives and children as much out of sight as possible."

Noah Heaton, the dwarfish dog-shooter I'd met before the meeting, stood up. "Who cares what the Outside thinks? I'm more interested in what's going on right here in Purity. Maybe if things were a little fairer around here we wouldn't have so many problems. I mean, why should some men have ten wives while some of us still have none?"

Davis gave him a smile tainted with a trace of condescension. "Your point is well taken, Brother Noah, but this isn't really the time for such a discussion."

Noah refused to drop his complaint. "I want a wife! But the Circle of Elders refuses to give me one!"

Some of the women in the room giggled, but they fell silent when their husbands glowered at them.

Davis sounded pained. "You were offered one of Prophet Solomon's widows. It isn't the Circle's fault you refused her."

"But she, she..." His mongrel-thin face contorted in frustration. "She's too old to have any more children, so what good is she?"

Angry mutterings greeted this statement and one of the men near Noah shoved him back into his seat. Perhaps the men shared Noah's opinions about women's worth, but they still didn't like hearing them stated in such a bald fashion.

Davis's smile grew broader as he turned away from Noah and spoke to the rest of the group. "Actually, Brother Noah's comments give me an opportunity to bring up something else that's worried me.

"As we've seen with the firearms problem, the Circle of Elders has become slack," he said. "Like it or not, we live in the twentieth century, and by continuing to sanction marriages with girls as young as thirteen, these godly but sometimes improvident men have exposed us to even more media attention. Why, just look at the mess my father visited upon us! Brothers and sisters, you all know that in 2001 the Utah state legislature raised the marriageable age to sixteen. I'm informing you that from now on, Purity will operate within those parameters, too. Regardless of what the Circle of Elders had done in the past, I will no longer sanction any marriage when the young lady involved is a day under sixteen."

A chorus of male groans rose in the room. Davis had dealt a blow at the very heart of polygamy: child marriage.

He wasn't finished. "There's another problem we need to discuss. Of late, the Circle of Elders has also shown more interest than appropriate in the workings of the Purity Fellowship Foundation. This must stop. Just because you have a new prophet doesn't mean you have a weak prophet. I will continue the same strong financial leadership shown by my father, and I won't brook any interference from the Circle. Furthermore, if they continue to meddle in Purity's financial affairs, I'll disband the Circle completely."

The previous groans gave rise to angry bellows from the Circle of Elders, making me wonder which bothered them most—lessened sexual access to children, or to money. In the midst of their outcries, a shaft of sunlight burst into the room, lending a glow to Davis's pale blond hair. He reminded me of the Pre-Raphaelite paintings I'd seen of medieval knights starting off on a holy quest. Maybe he even saw himself that way.

Now he stepped back from the lectern and opened his arms, as if embracing the group. "I've noted your concern over these proposed changes and I sympathize. But brothers and sisters, look at yourselves! Are you happy your wives dress in rags? Are you happy with their rotting teeth? Are you content to raise your children in slums?"

The Circle of Elders stopped howling and watched carefully as Davis's voice grew even louder. "Folks, of course you're not happy with this state of affairs! Therefore, I'm going to rewrite the Circle's charter, and beginning next month, in my new capacity as CEO of the Purity Fellowship Foundation, I'll allow each family to keep a portion of their income. You men won't have to sign over your entire paychecks to the Foundation, just a percentage. That'll also be true for our senior members' Social Security checks and our sisters' welfare and SSI checks. Brothers, buy your wives some new clothes and take them to the dentist. Sisters, buy your children new toys!"

The room erupted into cheers, but the Circle of Elders remained ominously silent.

I hid my smile. Purity's new prophet wasn't just handsome, he was smart. In one fell swoop, Davis had reaffirmed his financial control over Purity, and at the same time, earned the approval of the vast majority of its residents. By doing so openly, he'd effectively forestalled any chance the Circle of Elders might have to retain their power. If the Elders were foolish enough to try, they'd have a riot on their hands.

When the noise died down, Davis stepped back to the lectern.

"Now let's revisit Brother Noah's concerns." He turned his blinding good looks on the young man. "Brother Noah, now that you understand you will be able to keep a portion of each wife's income, do you think you might reconsider the Circle of Elders' offer and open your heart to some lonely widows?"

Noah struggled to his feet. With his short, severely bowed legs, it gained him little height. "It all depends on what kind of a cut I'll get. If my cut's big enough, then the more the merrier."

More grumbling from the assemblage as Noah sat back down. Even setting aside the dog-shooting incident, it was easy to see why he wasn't popular. I felt sorry for the widows who wound up with him.

Davis appeared to disapprove of the young man's obvious greed, too, and a frown replaced his smile. "Stay after the meeting tonight and we'll discuss it."

Earl Graff jumped up, light glinting off his American Gothic spectacles. The sudden movement tore a side seam on his shirt, and he looked more like an overstuffed sausage than ever.

"Wait a minute!" he shouted. "You can't just start overhauling everything to suit yourself! The Circle of Elders will have something to say about that."

Davis pasted his smile back on. "We'll talk in a couple of weeks, at the next regularly scheduled Circle meeting."

Graff refused to be put off. "All these problems you're talking about, the media and everything, they'll all go away once they get that…that…*woman* back up here in jail where she belongs." The way he said "woman" made the word sound like an expletive.

Davis didn't address himself to Earl's overt misogyny. "I don't think we can relax until she's been tried and found guilty. In fact, the trial might be the worst part of all this. Her lawyer will have to come up with some kind of a defense, Brother Earl, which means there'll no doubt be some finger-pointing this way. Like I said earlier, everyone needs to be on their toes. Remember, my father was preparing to marry her thirteen-year-old daughter, and that might not play well in the media no matter what our friends do to hush it up."

With that, he looked in my direction. "You newcomers, I advise you to be especially careful. Keep modesty in your words and deeds at all times."

Modesty in my words and deeds. Too bad my partner Jimmy wasn't here. He'd fall out of his chair laughing.

But Saul and I dutifully nodded as Davis went on to recap what everyone already knew: that Esther was awaiting extradition to Utah; that her trial for murder would follow shortly; that her conviction was pretty much a done deal.

"There are two witnesses who saw her arguing with Prophet Solomon the evening he was killed," Davis continued. "And we all know that when she still lived here, there were times that she…"

A familiar voice interrupted him. I looked over and saw that old Jacob Waldman had risen to his feet, his eyes glinting with a mean, hard light. "The Lord will judge me harshly because I have raised up the Whore of Babylon."

Davis looked startled, then quickly recovered. "Now, now, Brother Jacob. We know you did your best to raise Sister Esther in the ways of the Lord, but sometimes, no matter how hard we try, our children disappoint us. Remember that she left the compound and lived Outside for many years. We shouldn't be surprised that she succumbed to Satan's wiles."

"She ate from the tree of Satan," Jacob Waldman agreed. "Perhaps with blood atonement…?"

Davis's eyes widened, and around the room, a dozen throats cleared at once. "Brother Jacob, there will be no more talk of blood atonement in Purity," he said firmly. "That manner of thinking belongs to the past."

"But God demands blood atonement for sins like hers! He's demanded blood atonement before, and on each occasion, we've complied."

Davis slammed the gavel against the lectern hard enough to make some nearby ferns wobble. "I said there will be no more talk of blood atonement, Brother Jacob! *Do you understand?*"

I was vaguely familiar with the old Mormon philosophy of blood atonement, which meant that a sin against God could only be erased by the shedding of the sinner's blood. Unless I had totally misinterpreted Brother Jacob's words, this philosophy, supposedly discarded when the official LDS church relinquished polygamy, was still being practiced in Purity. If so, whom had they killed? And why?

As I stared at the old man, his hard eyes began to lose their focus again. "God says…God says…"

With that, an elderly woman sitting nearby took him by the hand and, with the help of two burly men, hustled him away.

The room heaved a collective sigh of relief, not the least of which came from Davis Royal.

"We must pray for Brother Jacob." Davis's voice sounded shaky. Then, recovering, he said, "Now let's get this meeting back on track. Does anyone else have information that they might share about our recent tragedy? Anything we can tell the police in order to expedite the investigation and trial?"

So that we can get the cops and the media off our backs as quickly as possible, went the unspoken message.

"As much as it pains me to say this about a woman, Esther did always have a temper," Martha Royal offered, her Valkyrie face serene in its condemnation. "She was never a Godly child. Why, once I even saw her strike one of her brothers."

Davis lifted his eyebrows, aghast, no doubt, at such an unwomanly act. "When was this, Sister Martha?"

"Some years ago. Esther was around ten, I believe."

Earl Graff called out, "She showed her true colors even as a child!"

Oh, give me a break. What little girl hasn't hauled off and socked somebody at some point in her life? Maybe her brother had pulled her pigtails.

After Martha's damning accusation, one by one the other members of the compound offered to testify about Esther's evil ways at her trial. By the time everyone had spoken, Rebecca's mother had been accused of breaking each of the Ten Commandments, bedding Satan himself, drinking babies' blood during Black Masses, and funding abortion clinics. If Esther ever came up for trial, her goose was well and truly cooked. Abel Corbett would regain custody of his daughter and whisk Rebecca back to the compound in a heartbeat.

As I anguished over Rebecca's possible fate, I heard a groan, then a scraping back of chairs several rows in front of me. The groan was followed by a small shriek.

"Oh, Jesus!" A girl's voice.

I stood so that I could see over the heads in front of me. The cries had come from Rosalinda, Earl Graff's very pregnant young wife.

Graff stayed with the other men in the corner, but Davis stepped away from the lectern and hurried to her. Bending over, he said, "Sister Rosalinda? Is it your time? Do you need to go to the clinic?"

She clutched at his arm. "Yes! Yes! Please! Take me to the clinic!"

Davis snapped his fingers and several women rushed to Rosalinda's side. Between them, they were able to get the girl to her feet and out the door.

Earl Graff never moved.

Chapter 10

Shortly thereafter, the meeting broke up and the group dispersed, the women to their homes and the men back to whatever jobs called them. As Saul and I stood on Davis's huge front porch briefly enjoying the fresh air, I looked toward the clinic and saw several women hovering outside. A scream drifted through the open door.

"They're not taking that girl to Zion City Hospital?" I asked.

He grunted. "Old Solomon didn't think much of modern medicine, that's why he built the clinic. That girl will deliver her baby right here with the midwives."

I frowned. Although I was familiar with Arizona's midwife training program, I knew nothing about Utah's. Rosalinda seemed much too young to have her first baby away from a modern hospital with all the emergency equipment it could provide, not to mention some industrial strength painkillers.

Another scream rent the air. "Saul, what if there are complications?"

"Yeah, what if?"

When we stepped off the porch, I noticed Meade Royal in the yard, chatting with a girl about his age. A white-blond, like so many others in Purity, she nevertheless stood out because of the sublimity of her features. If she ever ran away from the compound, she could run straight to Hollywood, where casting directors would greet her beauty with open arms.

Meade smiled at me, his morning depression vanished. Ah, the resiliency of youth. "Sister Lena, this is Cora, my sister. My real sister, I mean. Not that the rest of you aren't, uh…" He trailed off, his face red.

I laughed. "I know exactly what you mean, Brother Meade. Hello, Sister Cora. It's nice to meet you."

She said nothing and her eyes appeared oddly blank.

Meade gave her arm a gentle squeeze. "Sister Cora, say, 'It's nice to meet you, too, Sister Lena.'"

The girl did as she was told, then turned to him and asked slowly, "Did…did I s-say it right?"

He beamed at her. "You sure did!"

I wasn't quite as buoyed by Cora's performance. Her lack of affect made me wonder if she might be mildly retarded.

Saul spoke up, interrupting my thoughts. "I don't know about you, Sister Lena, but I'm starved. How about we hurry back to the house and get something to eat?"

Now that he mentioned it, I was surprised to discover hunger nibbling at my belly, too. I waved goodbye to Meade and his sister, and followed Saul back to the house, careful to stay three paces behind.

Ruby waited for us on the porch. Ignoring my presence, she spoke directly to Saul. "I'm happy you have returned, Brother Saul. Lunch is on the table." But she looked more irritated than happy, which make me realize she didn't like to cook any more than I did.

Well, I couldn't fault her there. "That's very kind of you, Sister Ruby."

She dismissed my compliment and turned a smile upon Saul, making me look down to hide my own grin. If nothing else, my presence in the compound had apparently made Ruby come alive. Nothing like a good case of jealousy to make a woman feel like a woman again.

Lunch sat on the table, all right, but if it was possible to screw up chicken sandwiches, Ruby had discovered how. Rubbery pieces of chicken, skin and fat still attached, lurked between slices of stale, mayonnaise-drenched white bread. Like any true passive-aggressive, Ruby had found an innocent-looking way to punish us for making her "cook."

As before, Saul didn't appear to understand what was really going on. I watched with disbelief as he picked up a particularly nasty-looking specimen and gnawed at it. The pained look on his face told me all I needed to know.

I refused to eat the mess. "Um, I really appreciate this, Ruby, but I think I'll just have a salad. After that big breakfast we had this morning, I'm not all that hungry."

I scurried to the refrigerator and found a yellowing head of iceberg lettuce and, hiding behind a soured container of milk, a generic bottle of Russian dressing. Yum, yum. Nasty as it was, the goop I organized looked tastier than Ruby's sandwiches. Still, visions of savory Ramen noodles danced in my head. "You know, Brother Saul, I think a little grocery shopping might be in order," I said, finally putting down my fork.

"Might not be a bad idea. Tell you what, I've got a two o'clock appointment with my attorney in Zion City anyway, so why don't you just drive in with me?"

The idea of leaving the compound, even for a few hours, was appealing, but the thought of Esther sitting in her jail cell awaiting extradition weighed against it.

"I'll make up a shopping list." I began writing. RAMEN CHINESE NOODLES, MICHELINA'S TV DINNERS, BLUE BUNNY BUTTER PECAN ICE CREAM...

A few minutes later, Saul's truck bumped down the dirt road, leaving me alone with a woman who hated my guts.

"It's so good to have you in the family, Sister Lena," Ruby murmured, handing me a broom. "The housework has been such a burden."

While I glumly swept the kitchen twice in the same day, I wondered how often scenes such as these repeated themselves whenever a polygamist husband dragged home a new wife. A powerless woman was an angry woman, and an angry woman always found a way to exact her revenge.

Ruby wasn't through giving me a hard time. "Sister Lena, I am a light sleeper, and I noticed that you didn't visit our husband last night. Chastity after marriage is not God's will for a woman."

And here I thought I'd been so clever. I gripped the broom and tried to think of a suitable lie. It didn't take my devious brain long to find one. With all the old Biblical rules and regulations running amok in Purity, surely intercourse during menstruation was verboten as hell.

"It's the curse, Ruby. My time of month. But I am certainly eager to take up my wifely duties as soon as I can. Uh, speaking of chastity after marriage, though, our husband told me that you two aren't exactly burning up the sheets, either."

I thought her eyes would pop from shock.

"I have a, a *medical* condition," she stammered. "And anyway, unlike you I am past childbearing age. We in Purity never copulate for mere enjoyment."

Oh, sure. That's why thirteen-year-old girls were so popular with sixty-year-old men!

The subject needed changing, and fast. "Um, just how well did you know poor Prophet Solomon?" I asked, enveloping Ruby in a cloud of dust as I swept fiercely toward her. Two could play that old passive-aggressive game.

She coughed, stepping out of my path. "I knew him as well as anyone, I guess. The prophet was a great man."

"That's what Saul told me."

Ruby gave me an strange look. "Really? I thought our husband hated the prophet. You know, don't you, that Prophet Solomon was the one who originally demanded that Saul leave the compound, not the Circle of Elders."

I nodded, and to keep her talking, swept a little less briskly. "I'm sure you know that you can admire someone while still disagreeing with them."

The concept of loyal opposition appeared to be new to Ruby, for her lumpy little face assumed a look of horror. "That's impossible. To disagree with Solomon was to disagree with God. That's not admiration, it's blasphemy! I warned our husband about that many, many times, but you know how men are. They don't listen to women."

When the woman was right, she was right. In the listening department, men weren't much different on the Outside.

I don't know why I asked the next question, but I did. "By the way, did Saul by any chance have words with the prophet the day he died?"

She looked out the kitchen window, which she had closed against the dust that covered everything in the compound. The Vermillion Cliffs loomed in the distance and she made a big show of looking at them. "No."

"How about you? Surely you didn't agree with everything Prophet Solomon ever said."

The cliffs lost their interest and Ruby returned her gaze to me. When she spoke, her words were frosty. "As I told you, Sister Lena, Prophet Solomon spoke for God."

And to disagree with the prophet was to disagree with God. I didn't want to let her off the hook so easily. "Ruby, if Saul is evicted from Purity, what'll you do? Will you leave with us or stay here? You know the Circle of Elders will give this house away to someone else. Then what would happen to you?"

Perhaps Ruby believed that with Solomon dead, Saul would stay in Purity. I knew better. He'd already told me the old prophet's death had made no difference to the Circle of Elders, that Davis himself wanted to get his hands on the house, if not to live in, to use as a bargaining chip to accrue more wives.

Ruby didn't answer my question right away. When she finally did, her voice sounded faint. "Women are never abandoned in Purity. I will always have a home here. Just maybe not in the same house."

"But Ruby, think about what's happening now! If Saul loses his court case and insists that you and I leave with him, don't we have to do what our husband commands? What with husbands speaking for God, and all that shi…uh, stuff."

The confusion on her face was almost comical. "But God… But husbands…" Her voice trailed off.

A new thought popped into my mind and flew out of my mouth before I could do anything about it. "Sister Ruby, what happened to your first husband?"

"Gaynell? He died. It was a long time ago."

"How did he die?"

She looked down at the floor, and I couldn't read her face any more. "He just died."

"What did the doctor say?"

"Doctor?" She looked at me with unease. "Prophet Solomon said the Lord is the only doctor we need. When Gaynell got sick, we took him over to the clinic, where the Circle of Elders prayed for him." She paused for a few seconds, then added, "In the end, the Lord lifted my husband up to Heaven."

No doctor. While I wasn't surprised that old Solomon and the Circle of Elders believed a women's ailments could be dealt with by prayer, it hadn't occurred to me they felt the same way about men's ailments. At least they were consistent. Then I had another thought. Had an autopsy been performed, a procedure mandated by the state of Utah in the event of sudden death? Before I could figure out how to ask this indelicate question, Ruby scuttled out of the kitchen. Then I heard the door to her room squeak shut.

Call me suspicious, but I wondered which of Purity's men had inherited Gaynell's house. And how Ruby had felt about it.

I leaned against the broom and looked out the window at the landscape that had so fascinated my sister wife. Red cliffs, blue sky, your typical Utah postcard. But the very intensity of the colors now seemed almost artificial, like a Disney cartoon. And wasn't that a fitting description of the compound and everyone in it? When you didn't look too closely, life appeared picture perfect here: happy, God-fearing families revolving around a stern-but-fair patriarch. God's in His heaven, all's right with the world. But a closer examination of the pretty picture revealed institutionalized child molestation, property seizures, and unexplained deaths. The Disney cartoon was really a Tim Burton grotesquerie.

I shook the image out of my head and swept some more, but my heart wasn't in it. Housework and I had never been close friends, which is why back in Scottsdale I'd memorized the phone number of Merry Maids. No doubt Prophet Solomon wouldn't approve of my sloth, but the prophet wasn't around anymore, was he? Then I thought of his replacement, Davis Royal. Big hands, broad shoulders, bottomless blue eyes a woman could drown in.

Damn that dirty-minded Ruby for bringing up sex. For a while I thought of Dusty. Had he returned to the ranch yet? I remembered our nights together, the way his hands slid along...

The temperature in the kitchen rose considerably, so I opened the back door to let in a breeze, which worked all too well. The pile of red dust my broom had swept lifted off the floor and dispersed itself once again around the room. In disgust I threw down the broom. Thirty minutes of housework was enough for any woman, and I needed some real exercise. Back in Scottsdale I ran almost every day, but since arriving in Utah I'd been a sloth, and I could feel my muscles atrophying. I called to Ruby that I'd be back shortly, and without waiting for her answer, hurried out the door.

As I crossed the dirt circle of Prophet's Park into Utah, I noted that the compound seemed almost deserted again. Then I heard children's voices coming from the school. One of the most decrepit buildings in the settlement, the school looked like it had been patched together with throwaway lumber. The three-story structure didn't sit quite square on its cracked foundation, but unlike most of the buildings in Purity, the school at least had windows—such as they were.

Sheets of clear plastic substituted for glass, and all the windows were open to the heat of the day. I glanced up at the roof and saw a profusion of missing shingles but no air conditioner. Did they close the school when the temperature rose above one hundred? If so, they'd probably close it within minutes. Or maybe the kids would just swelter.

Maybe things would improve at the school when Prophet Davis initiated his reforms. A bitter chuckle at my own foolish hopes slipped out of my mouth before I could stop it. I began to hurry past the building, but as I slipped by one of the open windows, I heard something that stopped me in my tracks.

"The Great Mother is the mother most beloved by our Great Father," piped a child's innocent voice. "Because of the Great Mother's earthly sacrifice for her community, He allows her to ascend to the highest level of Heaven."

I raised my eyebrows. Religious instruction in a public school? Then I remembered. For the past few years, the polygamists had operated their own school system.

My urge to flee squelched, I stood on tiptoe and peeked in the window. The children, an almost equal mixture of girls and boys, appeared to be seven or eight years old. The teacher, an elderly woman with Coke-bottle bifocals, wore the compound's *de rigueur* faded ankle-length dress. It looked a hundred years old, but then again, so did she.

"How does the Great Mother earn her title, Sylvia?" the teacher asked.

"By giving birth to as many souls as possible," little Sylvia answered. With her blond hair, big blue eyes, and almost albino-pale skin, she could have been the clone of at least ninety percent of her schoolmates.

The teacher's smile took in the entire room. "Excellent, Sylvia. I am certain all you little girls will grow up to become Great Mother, assuring your places in Highest Heaven. Remember the law of God: no children, no Heaven. And you boys, you must do your part to enable these little ladies to enter Highest Heaven, because without your seed, Satan will find them and carry them away to the Underworld, where they'll burn forever in the Eternal Fire with all the other sinful, childless women."

Seed? Eternal Fire? Sinful, childless women? Holy literal shit!

"Boys, will you do your part?" the teacher asked again.

The boys responded enthusiastically. They yelled "Yes, ma'am!" and stomped their feet. Suddenly, the schoolroom full of innocents sounded like a troop ship nearing some sleazy third-world port. My stomach lurched. Those children were too young to truly understand what they were being taught but they weren't too young to be brainwashed.

My original idea had been to jog along the dirt road that led north through the fields, but after what I'd just heard I wanted cover. So I left the road and headed into the canyon as fast as I could, and didn't relax until its high walls rose above me, effectively shutting Purity out.

The rough path Rebecca and I had taken during our escape lay to the southeast, paralleling the dirt road to Zion City. When the compound had originally built the road, they had merely dumped the debris of rocks, boulders and dirt down into the canyon. The litter there made running difficult, but the northern branch of the canyon remained relatively smooth. As I walked along, the terrain flattened enough so that I could hitch up my long skirts and break into a slow jog.

The canyon was a separate eco-system from the compound's arid expanse, and was vivid with red Indian paintbrush and yellow daisies. Set beside the sage green of the shrubs and backed by the soft red of sandstone walls, the blooms provided vibrant contrast to the pastel palette around them. I heard the musical trickle of water, the tiny click-click-click of lush buffalo grasses waving in the breeze. Almost paradise. But, reminding me that the law of nature was kill or be killed, a red-tailed hawk rode the thermal overhead, searching for prey.

The tension fell away from me as I jogged past clumps of prickly pear cactus and gold-flecked creosote. Lizards scurried out of my way, prairie dogs popped back into their holes, and here and there, jackrabbits fled from me as if they feared *Fricassé de Lapin* topped my evening menu. I knew coyotes lived nearby, but since they were nocturnal, they were probably bedded down in one of the many caverns pock-marked into the canyon's walls.

Thanks to Davis's appropriation of the compound's rifles, I didn't have to worry about dodging bullets, and I had the canyon to myself.

I jogged for an hour, marveling at the length of the canyon. The Arizona Strip was laced with these long canyons, some leading south all the way to the Grand Canyon. Fortunately, they were broader and safer than the slot canyons found in the eastern part of the state, those steep, sheer-walled canyons which became death traps after a thunderstorm. I was in no danger now. It hadn't rained for days and the walls of Paiute Canyon sloped gently. Well-worn paths led up its sides and onto the desert floor above.

Finally winded, I slowed to a walk and turned around, lowering my skirts as I did so. Even the spectacular beauty of the canyon hadn't chased away the memory of the grotesque lesson I'd heard in the classroom. Part of me wanted to go back and slap the teacher upside the head, while the other part counseled restraint. Restraint won. Even if Miss Teacher didn't brainwash her charges, the job would still be accomplished by their fathers and mothers.

Mothers.

I touched the scar on my forehead, remembering the woman who looked like me, the woman who shot me at point blank range and left me for dead. Oh, yes, I knew that mothers could damage their children, too, not just fathers and prophets and teachers in crack-brained cults. In my career as a police officer, I had seen grisly injuries inflicted upon children by their mothers.

One day, when I had harped too loud and long about my own mother's sins, Jimmy had shut me up with an article he found in *National Geographic*. It described various tribes in Egypt, Kenya and Somalia, where mothers, in order to earn higher dowries for their little girls, cut off their daughters' sexual organs. These "operations," carried out by amateurs with no medical training using rusty tin can lids as knives, were not circumcisions. No, the article described the complete removal of all reachable sexual organs, clitoris *and* labia, performed without anesthesia. Many of the little girls bled to death during the procedures, but apparently their mothers believed death was a risk well worth taking. After all, a "cut wife" brought a higher dowry—even when the cut wife was numb from the waist down.

So in a way it was almost unjust for me to confine my rage to the males of Purity. Yes, the men held all the cards, all the power, but they could not maintain their illegal lifestyle without the women's collusion. So in the end, what kind of monsters wouldn't protect their own daughters? I touched the scar on my forehead again. Sometimes monsters were called mothers.

The singing of a cactus wren freed me from my dark visions. I could do little to help all of Purity's children, but at least I could save Rebecca.

Good investigators know that the solution to the crime of murder is to be found in studying the victim, so it was imperative that I begin interviewing Solomon's widows and children, not to mention his friends and business associates. Unfortunately, secrecy reigned in Utah's polygamy communities. There was a good chance, too, that many of my suspects might be moving soon. As I had learned in the community meeting at Prophet Davis's house, Solomon's wives and children would soon be parceled out to new homes, perhaps even to other compounds far from Purity. Somehow I would have to find a chance to talk to them before they dispersed.

A sharp movement caught my eye and I looked up again to see the red-tailed hawk plummeting toward the ground, its wings folded close to its body. As it dove into the canyon, I lost sight of it for a second, but then I heard a shriek, followed by sounds of a struggle behind a creosote bush. The hawk rose again, a bleeding prairie dog struggling in its claws.

My own quest felt as hopeless as the prairie dog's struggles. Given the difficulty of my task, there was a good chance that I might fail for the first time since opening Desert Investigations. But then I remembered Esther, the good mother, sitting in her cell while her daughter was in danger of being returned to the compound. Prophet Solomon might be dead, but I had no doubt that Abel Corbett, in exchange for some favor or other, would eventually hand her over to another old man. No matter how bleak my chances looked here, I couldn't give up. I had to save Rebecca, and if possible, do something to help the other little girls in the compound.

I was so deep in thought that I almost walked into Meade Royal.

"Sister Lena?"

My shriek sounded like the prairie dog's as I jumped back from the concerned-looking teenage boy in front of me.

"Sister Lena, are you all right?" In close up, Meade Royal's blue eyes were even more startling, the resemblance to his beautiful mother more stunning. He had a small rifle nestled in his arms, but since I'd heard no shots, I guessed he had just begun his hunt. Good. I'd already seen enough blood for one day.

I checked my dress quickly to make certain my skirts were all the way down and my buttons buttoned. Meade may have been little more than a child, but as I had seen, they started early here.

"Just daydreaming, Brother Meade. By the way, I thought Prophet Davis locked up all the guns."

He tried to form a look of disapproval on his angelic face, but it didn't work. Try as he might, he still looked like a Renaissance angel, albeit a disapproving one.

"I told him I wanted to hunt some rabbits so he let me have this. Regardless of what the other people think, my brother's a reasonable man. But what are *you* doing in the canyon? Have you no duties at home?"

The real Lena Jones would have smarted off to him, metaphorically spanking his uppity butt, but I reminded myself that the real Lena Jones was on hiatus. I forced a subservient smile.

"I finished the cleaning and cooking," I lied. "But the dust...I needed some fresh air. I, uh, suffer from asthma."

The disapproval vanished from his sweet face, and the concern returned. "I'll tell the Circle of Elders to pray for you. But the canyon's a dangerous place for a woman to be alone in, and I don't want you walking around down here by yourself. Come, let me take you home."

Before I could protest, he shifted his rifle onto his left arm, hooked my arm with his other, and began marching me back to the compound. Bemused, I allowed myself to be led. After all, this presented another interview opportunity. "Meade, why should it be dangerous now? Isn't your father's killer in custody?"

He gripped my arm even tighter. "You're not safe. There are, ah, other people about."

I raised my eyebrows. Did he mean whoever was gunning for Davis? "Oh?"

I was wrong.

"Indians," he said.

Purity's casual racism had been apparent from the beginning. Many of the Arizona Strip's polygamy compounds received an surge in population when the official Mormon Church changed its policy to admit African-American males to the priesthood, and Purity had been no exception. I wondered how Meade would feel if he knew that my partner and closest friend in the world was a full-blooded Pima Indian.

"What Indians?" I asked.

"Paiute. They're not friendly."

I tried not to laugh. Most Native Americans were friendly enough once you took the trouble to know them, but they were very protective of children. I doubted they bore any more love for the polygamists than the polygamists did them.

I gave Meade a grateful smile. "Thank you for the warning. I feel so safe with you! Perhaps you could tell me exactly where they live so I'll be extra careful not to go near them?"

He eased the pressure on my arm and slowed his step. "If you take the road northeast past the graveyard, and follow it for another four miles, you'll eventually see their village. They're in the canyon a lot."

"Hiking?"

He looked baffled. "Hiking? No, they hunt, just like I was doing when I ran into you. Other times they come down here to practice those pagan rituals of theirs. They went to court once to get the canyon taken away from us, saying that it was part of their holy ground, or some such nonsense."

I forwent the comment that Indians' holy ground always seemed nonsensical to certain Anglos. The proximity of the Paiute village to the compound sounded promising. Maybe one of them had seen something. For now, I pretended to be guided by a boy so innocent of the world that he didn't realize how many Indians wore Nikes, carried cell phones, and went to Christian churches on Sundays.

"Thank you for warning me about their pagan ways, Brother Meade. I certainly wouldn't want to fall into the hands of the ungodly."

As we walked back to the compound, I peppered him with questions, and for a while he even answered them. Yes, his sister Cynthia was unhappy, but conforming to God's wishes brought the only true happiness, not chasing after individual dreams. No, he wasn't aware of any major falling out between Prophet Davis and the Circle of Elders. At least not until this morning's announcement.

"Prophet Davis is a godly man," he assured me.

Then I remembered that Meade and Davis shared the same father. I asked him about that.

"Oh, yes," he said. "I'm the youngest son and he's the eldest, but we had different mothers."

"Was Prophet Davis's mother at the meeting?"

"Sister Lucy died many years ago. I never knew her."

"Did she get sick? Or was it an accident of some sort?"

"From what I hear, she died a few days after he was born, so our sister mothers raised him."

"Sister mothers?"

"Father prophet's other wives."

That was one good point about polygamy, at least. Their children seldom wound up in foster homes; they were just sent on down the line to new mothers. But I wanted more details about what medical care, if any, Sister Lucy had received. As we climbed the path out of the canyon and started through the mesquite grove that led past Davis's house, I asked a question I already knew the answer to. "Did she go to the hospital?"

"Of course not," Meade answered. "The Circle of Elders prayed over her, but God called her home…"

"To the Highest Heaven," I finished for him.

He shook his head. "Oh, no, not to the Highest. Davis was only her first child so she didn't have time to bear more children. Only Great Mothers achieve Highest Heaven."

Which the old crone in the classroom had made so clear. Before I could censor my words, I blurted, "That doesn't sound right, Meade. It's not fair that the poor woman didn't get her proper heavenly reward just because she died before she could throw a whole litter."

Meade gasped. "That's a wicked thing to say, Sister Lena! A good woman is an obedient woman. She doesn't question God's ways."

And a good woman should be slightly south of smart, I wanted to respond, but by then, I'd gained control over my mouth.

As we crossed Prophet's Park, a woman emerged from the clinic. In another environment, I'd have put her at thirty, but I'd learned the constant pregnancies the women endured made them appear older than they were. The woman's dishwater-blond hair, pulled tightly into a bun, did little to flatter her blunt features, but her rounded belly was proof that her husband, at least, found her desirable. As she hurried away from the clinic, I noticed something else. One of her legs was noticeably shorter than the other, making her gait resemble a series of ungainly hops.

My own hip, the one that had taken a drug-dealer's bullet and ended my police career a year before, twinged in sympathy.

When the woman neared us I saw tears. Concerned, I started toward her but found myself yanked back by Meade.

"Leave her alone," he said.

"But she…"

"That's just Sister Hanna, Brother Noah's sister. She's always crying."

"Why?"

He shrugged. "Who knows? Somebody told me she's had a lot of sadness in her life, but I don't know anything about it. People don't talk much about her."

I wondered if it had anything to do with her limp. An accident of some sort which had gone untreated? I tried once more to go to her, but Meade, proving surprisingly strong, pulled me along with him toward Saul's house as if I were little more than a recalcitrant puppy on a leash.

"But I want to help her," I complained.

"Sister Hanna's problems are none of your business!" he yelled at me. When this outburst attracted the disapproval of a knot of men standing on a nearby porch, he lowered his voice. "A curious mind is the Devil's mind, Sister Lena."

With that, he half-shoved me up the steps where Saul, just back from his grocery run in Zion City, had come out to watch our progress across the dirt circle.

"Your wife is sadly in need of instruction," Meade said, as he handed me over.

"I've noticed that," Saul said, hooking his arm around mine, much as Meade had done. "Come inside, wife. It's time for you to prepare supper."

Relieved to escape from Meade's clutches, I did as I was told. Soon a nuked bowl of Ramen noodles sat before each of us. After we'd slurped the noodles down I handed around some bananas and apples for dessert.

"This is it?" Ruby asked. Her face couldn't have been more aghast if Brigham Young himself had crawled out of his tomb and pinched her scrawny ass.

"Healthier than those chicken-fat sandwiches you made for us earlier," I shot back, my reserve of meekness depleted.

She flushed, whether in rage or embarrassment, I couldn't tell. Shifting in her chair, she turned to Saul and whined, "Husband, my dear sister wife must learn to cook or we will all starve." As if she did not have her own shortcomings in that department.

To my horror, Saul nodded. "I've been worried about that very thing, Sister Ruby, and I believe I've found a solution."

Not liking the direction in which we were headed, I said, "Hey, wait a minute..."

Saul raised his hand. "Silence, woman!"

It's a good thing no flies inhabited the room because one of them would have flown into my open mouth. While I gaped at him, Saul shoved his chair back and stood.

"Ruby, you see to the dishes, such as they are, and Sister Lena, you follow me."

That'll be a clean day on a pig's behind, I wanted to snap, but didn't. Leaving Ruby behind to her smirks, I followed him out onto the porch. Once we were out of earshot of curious ears, I let fly.

"Listen here, *husband.* Speak to me like that again and I'll shove a firecracker up your ass and light it with a blowtorch."

He winced, then gestured to the porch swing, which swayed slightly to a breeze drifting down from the canyon. "Have a seat, Miss Big Mouth, and let me tell you the arrangements I've made."

"I don't care what arrangements you've made," I huffed. Settling myself next to him on the porch swing, I added, "I didn't come to Purity to learn to how to cook."

His face assumed that smug look I'd seen on so many men in the compound, and it unsettled me even more. But with his next words my apprehension disappeared.

"You came here hoping to get Esther out of jail, and to do that, you'll have to do more than spend your time annoying Ruby and Meade. You need to talk to people."

His criticism stung because it was so on target. "That's what I've been trying to do, but it's harder than I thought it would be. These people are pretty tight-lipped, even with each other." In my ignorance, I had believed I could overcome the polygamists' reticence, and given enough time I might still be able to get some to open up. But that was the problem. I didn't have enough time. In a few days, Esther would be extradited to Utah.

Saul leaned toward me, a grin on his face. "So now, little Miss Sass, are you ready to hear what I've fixed up for you?"

"Lay it on me, brother." My voice sounded glum.

When he told me, I startled one elderly gentleman crossing Prophet's Park by jumping up and crowing in delight.

Chapter 11

Saul had arranged for me to be apprenticed to Sister Erma-line, one of Solomon Royal's widows, and reputedly the best cook in Purity.

"There's still a pile of women and something like fifty or sixty kids in that house, so if you pay attention, I'm sure you'll hear something that can help Esther."

I nodded and leaned back into the swing, my spirits rising for the first time since I'd arrived in Purity.

Saul's mouth assumed the grump position but his eyes smiled. "Play dumb. Watch your mouth."

I smiled back. "Me?"

"Yeah, you. They expect you there an hour before each meal."

"How'd you manage that? I thought everyone hated you around here."

"Correction, Lena. Solomon hated me and the Circle of Elders still hates me because I stopped turning over my Social Security checks to the Purity Fellowship Foundation. But a lot of the women here think I'm just fine. In fact, just before you got back, a couple of Solomon's widows came over, hinting that they wouldn't mind marrying me. So what do you think of that, Miss Priss?"

I grinned, not faulting their taste. Despite his age, Saul was a fine-looking man and a kind one besides. The women could do worse, such as with that pimply-faced Noah Heaton. I wondered if the widows Prophet Davis planned to give Noah were the same ones who had expressed an interest in Saul. Shivering, I looked up at the sun for warmth, but a dark bank of clouds had blown down from the north. After the midday heat, the freshening wind felt almost too cool for comfort. A hawk soared overhead, something struggling in its claws. The same hawk I'd seen during my morning run? Or a different hawk, different victim?

I tried to joke my sudden apprehension away. "Saul, Saul. Hugh Hefner has nothing on you."

He blushed and cleared his throat, started to say something, then stopped. At first I thought his discomfort came from my crack about his popularity among the compound's women. When he eventually spoke, though, he proved me wrong. "That, ah, brings me to the second thing I need to talk to you about. Ruby has been pretty nosey about your, um, monthlies."

"Monthlies?"

"You know. Your curse."

"Oh, you mean my menstrual cycle. What about it?"

His blush deepened. "She says, ah, that she hasn't found any indication that you are, ah…"

"Tell her I use tampons. And that I flush them."

He shook his head. "She knows better than that. She says you're just using your, um, period as an excuse to avoid sex with me. And that if you keep doing that, she's going to tell Prophet Davis and the Circle of Elders and they'll refuse to sanctify our marriage. Then you'll be out. Or maybe pawned off on some other man."

I groaned. "Damn, Saul. The woman's a jealous bitch."

Saul's glare reminded me that Ruby was still his wife. "Maybe she is a bitch, maybe she isn't. If you'd gone through what she's gone through…Ah, forget that. It's beside the point. But we're going to have to put on some kind of act if this thing is going to work. Tonight you come along to my

room. Here's how we'll handle it. Before I moved down here
from Salt Lake I saw this cute movie with Meg Ryan and
Billy Crystal. They were in some restaurant and she, um…"

"She faked an orgasm. Right there among the Caesar
salads."

He grinned. "That's the movie, all right. I hope you can
make it sound as authentic as Meg did."

I grinned back. "Oh, don't worry, husband. I'll make you
sound like the stud of the year. Which reminds me. Ruby's
your wife, your real wife, so what's the problem between
you two? If she's so interested in me carrying out my wifely
duties, why isn't she doing anything about hers? I didn't hear
her trooping down the hall to your room last night."

Saul looked up at the glowering sky, perhaps searching
for the hawk that had caught my eye earlier. It had vanished,
and only scuttling clouds filled the gray vacuum which
remained. When he found nothing there, he lowered his
eyes to the compound, where several men had gathered in
the dirt circle and stood chatting by a rusting Mercury. Every
now and then a sentence, carried by the wind, reached me.
They were talking about butchering goats.

"Hey, husband. I asked you a question."

Saul continued to pretend fascination with the bib-over-
alled men. "Question? Oh. Yeah, you did, but the problem
between Ruby and me doesn't concern you."

"In a murder investigation, you never know what's going to
turn out to be important. So tell me. What's up with Ruby?"

Saul finally stopped staring at the men and after heaving
a big sigh, told me everything I wanted to know. As with
most troubled relationships, his and Ruby's problems had
begun long before they even met. Ruby's dead husband had
been forty years older than she when he "married" her at the
age of thirteen. He had been brutal, too, turning her wedding
night into little more than rape. The next morning she'd
gone for comfort to her sister wives but found none. Instead,
they told her it was a woman's lot in life to submit to her

husband's demands, that a woman's hard life was God's curse for the sins of Eve. Impregnation was a duty, not a pleasure.

I watched several little girls playing hopscotch near the junked cars in Prophet's Park, their long dresses billowing in the wind. Was it my imagination or were some of the oldest girls trying to keep out of the men's line of sight? Maybe their own mothers had told them stories about God's curse.

"Ruby told me that she eventually figured out that her husband didn't like skinny women, so she learned not to eat," Saul continued. "She ate so little that she used to have fainting fits. He finally lost interest in her, but not before he'd soured her on sex forever."

Poor Ruby. No wonder she was a grump. I shivered again, but this time it had nothing to do with the lowering temperature.

"If Ruby's husband was so bad, and apparently the other wives thought he was, too, why didn't anyone do anything about him? These are supposed to be God-fearing people. Surely not even polygamists condone sadism."

Saul looked at me as if I'd lost my mind. "You're right. They're not all sadists, not by a long shot. Some of the guys around here are fairly good to their families. But you're forgetting that little human mind game called denial. People don't see what they don't want to see. But even if they did, there's no battered women's shelters in Purity."

"Battering? Is that common here, too?" I remembered Sister Hanna, the crying woman I'd seen limping from the Purity Clinic. Had she been beaten?

"Battering's as common as dirt in Prophet's Park," Saul answered. "It's how a lot of these guys keep their families in line."

"Then why don't the women leave?"

"C'mon, Lena, think about it. The women who've been raised here, they believe it's like this on the Outside, too, only worse. Remember, they don't watch TV, listen to the radio, or read magazines, so all they know about marriage is what they see right here."

His voice rose, and the men by the Mercury turned toward us. I recognized Earl Graff. Putting my hand on Saul's knee, I said quietly, "Husband, we have an audience."

When Saul spoke again, he'd lowered his voice but not lost his edge. "You have the same mind-set as most Outsiders. You think these women can just pick up and leave, but how can they do that? Most of them never learned to drive, and even if they did know how, their husbands hold the car keys. They have a bunch of kids, so what are they going to do? Carry a dozen kids twenty miles down that damned road to get help they don't even know exists? If they did manage to do that, where would they get the money for a divorce? None of these women has a dime.

"But let's say some benefactor gives them enough money for a divorce. It's happened. Groups like Tapestry Against Polygamy are always trying to help, but they're like David up against Goliath. Not only does the Purity Fellowship Foundation have a big bankroll, but it has a slew of attorneys in Zion City and Salt Lake on retainer. Some of those attorneys grew up in polygamy compounds. Hell, Purity's put six boys through law school. You think the women can compete with that? Oh, word gets around. The women are always hearing how the court took some jobless, homeless runaway's children away from her and sent them back to the compounds and their 'gainfully employed' fathers. So you tell me, Lena, what woman is going to allow herself to be separated from her children?"

I wanted to scream at him, *My own mother!*

But I didn't. I remembered Esther and her fight for her child. I forced my voice not to catch on my own memories. "You're right. Most women would die before they'd allow themselves to be separated from their children."

He nodded. "Until the authorities get off their butts and do something about these guys, the women's situation is hopeless."

I finally understood why some of Purity's women accepted polygamy even when they hated it. For a woman who still had some kind of normal feelings, *anything* was preferable to losing her children.

But in his summing up of the situation, Saul had neglected something.

"It's not hopeless," I said. "You've already helped two girls escape."

He looked glum. "Two unmarried girls with nothing to lose, not battered women with kids they couldn't bear to leave behind."

Depressed, I watched the men by the Mercury watch us. While I knew they couldn't hear us, their presence reminded me to always be on guard. And never more so than when I started my cooking lessons with Prophet Solomon's widow.

"What time am I expected over at Sister Ermaline's?" I asked Saul, deciding that it was time to change the subject before we both began to cry in frustration.

He looked relieved. "Five in the morning. Now let's get back into the house and pretend to be a happy married couple. And Lena? Try to look romantic."

Romantic. That was a good one. But then I envisioned Dusty's muscular arms wrapped around me, his thighs enveloping mine. Dusty might have been a couple hundred miles away but his memory was right here in my head. Oh, yes, I could manage to look romantic.

To Ruby's astonishment, I was holding Saul's hand when we entered the house.

We didn't have sex, of course, although to judge from all the moaning and groaning and spring-squeaking that night, we sounded like the floor show at an orgy. I could sense Ruby's ear pressed against the bedroom door as I jumped up and down on the bed, screaming, "Deeper, deeper, deeper!" while Saul sat in the corner chair trying not to laugh. After I had finally reached my Meg Ryan-inspired orgasm, he raised his voice for Ruby's benefit. "Told you I was hot, didn't I, wife?"

I raised my voice, too. "Husband, you are *such* a stud!"

A few seconds later, we heard Ruby's door close.

Saul used an old pile of blankets to make himself a nest on the floor, leaving the bed to me. Once I heard his snores, I allowed myself to fall asleep.

But the night brought dreams. Of my mother.

We rode in the big white bus and people were singing. My golden-haired mother, the woman who looked like me, raised her gun. She pointed it right at me.

"I'll kill her," she said. *"I'll kill her."*

"Mommy, no!"

A loud noise. Searing pain in my head, then in my stomach. Another scream. Then I began to die.

A sense of falling.

Then nothing.

"Jesus, Lena, you sound like Ruby used to. What the hell were you dreaming?" Saul stood over me, a concerned look on his face. It was still dark.

"Just the usual, no big deal," I said, glancing at the clock. Four-thirty a.m. Time to rise and shine.

"But Lena…" He didn't want to let it go.

"See you after the cooking lesson." With that, I slipped my housecoat over my pajamas and ran to the bathroom, where I showered away my memories.

Minutes later, I crossed the dark compound to Prophet Solomon's house. As I glanced over at the clinic, I wondered if Rosalinda had delivered her baby yet.

It wasn't quite five, but lights already blazed from Prophet Solomon's immense brick home, which looked only slightly smaller than the church. I'd been told not to bother knocking, to just walk in, and as I entered the Persian-carpeted living room, I saw and heard gangs of sleepy children in various stages of getting dressed.

The room, although obviously expensively furnished, was an environmentalist's nightmare. An entire cattle herd had probably sacrificed its life for the many leather sofas, chairs and leather-topped tables I saw scattered around. The wood paneling alone could have taken out half the Sequoia National Forest. Photographs of children covered every available wall and table. I would have counted them to see how many the old prophet actually had sired, but I didn't have the time. Maybe I'd try when I had a year or two to spare.

I did have time, though, to count the crosses hanging on the walls. Ten. And each one of them bigger and gaudier than the last. A painting of the prophet, looking meaner than he'd looked as he lay dead in the canyon, hung above the big rock fireplace next to an embroidered sampler which read, "I, the Lord thy God am a jealous God and I will allow no other gods before me." Remembering that Prophet Solomon frequently confused himself with the Deity, it creeped me out.

The din in the room was awful as the older children helped the younger ones dress. Even though most of the clothes being brandished appeared mismatched, I noticed that Solomon's children wore better clothes than the other children in the compound. I wondered how long that would last. Until the Circle of Elders parceled them out to new "fathers"?

As I settled into an overstuffed leather chair to watch the show, a pregnant woman wearing a purple-flowered granny dress and a clashing yellow apron that made her look like a giant Easter egg emerged from the kitchen. She held out another apron to me. "I'm Sister Jean, and you must be Sister Lena. Better get moving before Ermaline sees you sitting around."

Stung, I heaved myself out of the chair, slipped the apron over my head, and trudged toward the kitchen, all the while thinking that if I had been back in Arizona, I would still be sleeping. But considering my dreams, maybe making biscuits was preferable.

When I entered the kitchen, which was almost as large as the living room, the amount of activity so early in the morning amazed me. With its spotless ceramic tile floor and commercial-sized refrigerators, ranges and ovens, the kitchen looked like something you would see in a top Scottsdale restaurant, but the women preparing breakfast hardly looked like sous chefs. Most of Solomon's widows were blonds, which didn't surprise me, and they ranged in age from pubescent girls to grandmothers. Except for the very youngest and oldest, all were pregnant.

They worked in concert, their movements as synchronized as those of a ballet troupe. A platinum blond removed items from the pantry, a honey blond carried dishes from another cupboard into the dining room, and yet another blond hovered by the sink, snatching at the dirty pots being passed to her.

A severe gray-haired woman stationed at a tub-sized mixing bowl barked orders. "Get moving! You're like molasses today!"

None talked back. As they worked, I noticed that the women's long dresses were in much better condition than those I'd seen at the community meeting, and their snowy aprons were ruffled and beribboned. At least Prophet Solomon dressed his wives well, even though their dental care had been neglected. Every now and then one of them would sniffle in an emotion I first believed was grief, but on closer inspection saw to be fear.

The elderly woman at the mixing bowl looked up at me. "I'm Sister Ermaline, Prophet Solomon's first wife. Get over here and watch what I'm doing."

I took note of the swiftness with which she'd established her superior position in the family's pecking order. Although Saul had told me that Ermaline was in her mid-sixties, a life of hard work made her appear even older. She might once have been attractive but now her plump cheeks sagged into dewlaps and her pale eyes squinted through a pair of unadorned wire rim glasses.

When I didn't move quickly enough to suit her, she barked at me again. "Don't stand there gawking, Sister Lena. I expect you to work."

Reluctantly, I moved forward.

At one end of the long work table, Cynthia, the girl I'd met the day before, patiently instructed dull-eyed Cora how to roll out the biscuit dough. The task appeared to be more than Cora could manage, because she kept dropping the rolling pin, eliciting more fierce noises from Ermaline.

"Stop dropping things, you clumsy girl!"

Ermaline's barks made Cora even more clumsy and she dropped the rolling pin again. When Cynthia bent over to pick it up for her, a book fell out of her apron. She tried to grab it, but Ermaline beat her to it.

"What's this? *Gray's Anatomy?*" She flipped through it quickly, her dough-sticky hands soiling the pages. "Pictures of naked people! Just what you think you're doin', girl, reading this trash?"

"It's just a text book, Mother," Cynthia said, reaching for the book. "I told you I was interested in medicine."

"It's no text book your father ever approved! Your husband, if any man is foolish enough to ever want you, will teach you all you need to know about bodies. I'm throwin' it out."

"*No*, Mother!"

Ermaline slapped Cynthia's outstretched hand. "Don't you talk back to me."

Cynthia didn't make a sound but Cora began to wail. "Cindy hit! Cindy hit!"

This made Ermaline so angry she drew back her hand again, but before I could rush to the child's rescue, Jean stepped in front of her. Taking the book out of the surprised older woman's hand, she said, "Let me throw this thing in the dump where it belongs, Sister Ermaline. The longer it stays in here, the more minds it'll corrupt." She turned to Cynthia. "Apologize to your mother for reading this stuff."

For a moment I thought Cynthia would refuse, then she darted a quick look at Jean said quietly, "I apologize, Mother." She kept her eyes averted from Ermaline, however.

Jean then nudged Cora. "It's your turn. Apologize to Sister Ermaline for dropping the rolling pin."

"I s-sorry, Mother." Cora's voice held no more inflection than it had the day before.

"No, Cora," Jean said. It's 'I'm sorry, Mother Ermaline.' "

With Jean's coaching, Cora eventually delivered her line correctly. My heart went out to her. The poor little thing was so beautiful. And so damaged.

Ermaline growled, "What good are apologies when the rolling pin has to be washed again? And what good are apologies when a daughter reads trash instead of doin' a woman's rightful work? Sister Jean, on your way to the dump, why don't you get Cora out of the kitchen before she sets somethin' on fire and kills us all?"

"Certainly, Sister Ermaline." Jean whisked Cora away before she could enrage the older woman again.

I hoped Ermaline couldn't hear me grinding my teeth as I attempted to get my mind off the ugly scene by working out the compound's convoluted family system. The fact that Cynthia had called Ermaline simply "Mother" without the attached honorific "Sister" told me that the elder woman was her biological mother, but I could see no resemblance between the two. Their extreme difference in age probably accounted for that. Some quick math revealed that Ermaline had probably given birth to Cynthia at midlife. Maybe that was why she was so cranky.

To my discomfort, Ermaline turned her attention to me again. I stepped back. If she raised her hand against me...

But she didn't. "Well, Miss. I see Brother Saul picked himself a pretty lily of the field, all right, but you're one lily who's gonna learn how to toil and spin."

A half hour later, with scant help from me, the first breakfast serving made it to the table. Or rather tables. Since the house had been built to house up to twenty wives and more than a hundred children, it boasted several living areas, dining rooms and kitchens. Sister Ermaline managed the largest kitchen because, as she explained to me, not only was she Prophet Solomon's first wife, but she had also produced the largest number of children.

"Fifteen children!" she'd told me proudly, while lifting golden brown biscuits out of the oven. "All perfect, all thrivin'."

And all terrified of her, I thought, but at least they ate well. I snatched at one of her biscuits as she slid them off the pan and onto a banquet-size serving dish for the next go-around. The biscuit weighed no more than a snowflake, and it dissolved in my mouth like one, too. Ermaline could instruct me all she wanted, but I doubted that I could ever learn to make a biscuit like that. Good cooking was an art form, and I had no talent.

As the wives cooked, they ate. They had a bite of egg here, a sausage patty there, and helped themselves to biscuit after biscuit as they emerged from the oven.

"Feedin' all these kids don't leave time for much else," Sister Ermaline said, pointing out the obvious, as she whipped up another batch of biscuits. "But idle hands are the Devil's work, and ever since Satan tempted Eve in the Garden of Eden, idle women been sinnin'."

"That's what they say," said Jean, back from her sojourn at the trash heap. Somewhere in her thirties, with her pale red hair and Irish green eyes, she would have been easily the best-looking woman in the room except for the thin lines of discontent around her full-lipped mouth. Perhaps her swollen belly explained that.

Not that her advanced pregnancy cut her any slack with Ermaline. If anything, the elder woman tended to speak even more harshly to her than she did to anyone else in the kitchen, except for her own daughter. Some old quarrel perhaps?

Trying to stay out of everyone's way, I kept folding pea-sized pieces of shortening into the biscuit dough like Ermaline had showed me. Within a few minutes my right hand began to cramp and I looked at it sorrowfully. First I'd banged it up in karate practice, and now this. Hopefully, the tendons would adapt.

Ermaline's harsh voice interrupted my thoughts. "We'll soon knock the idleness out of her, won't we, Sister Jean?"

I hoped she spoke metaphorically, but I wasn't sure.

Sister Jean's face revealed nothing. "Oh, I'm sure you will."

Had Ermaline also knocked the idleness out of Jean? The older woman could quote Scripture all she wanted, but I recognized a tyrant when I saw one. And I was pretty sure I knew the reason for Ermaline's harshness. Maybe a woman's jealousy was considered Original Sin on the compound, but human nature was human nature, especially in Purity, where the more attention from her "husband" a woman received, the more likely she was to become pregnant. The more children a woman had, the bigger her household would be and the more power she would wield in the family. Sister Ermaline might have walked ten paces behind her husband, but among the household's women, she was top dog.

Until she stopped having children and they continued.

I wasn't here to make enemies, so I gulped down the last of Sister Ermaline's biscuit and gave her my brightest smile. "I know my past is cloudy, but I'm trying to be a good woman. Perhaps I can learn from your example, Sister Ermaline."

Mollified, she smiled for the first time. "See that you do. The Lord loves an obedient woman."

Oh, Saul, I'm going to kill you for this. Hoping to turn the conversation to less biblical matters, I asked Jean, "How many children do you have, Je...I mean, Sister Jean?"

"Three. This'll be my fourth."

Four children to Sister Ermaline's fifteen. That put her *way* down in the polygamy pecking order. Why so few children? Had Jean fallen out of favor with Solomon for some reason?

As more biscuits emerged from the oven, I helped Cynthia, who had returned to the kitchen, take them to the tables. Cora, she told me, was no longer allowed to carry food because of her habit of dropping things. Instead, the little girl now made sure the salt and pepper containers were filled.

"You should have been here the day she dropped the green bean casserole," Cynthia said, apparently recovered from the loss of her anatomy book. "Beans everywhere, even on the ceiling. Cora's a sweetie, but she has her limits."

With surprise, I saw Meade standing at the head of one of the tables, but when I said good morning to him, he hardly noticed. He was too busy holding a salt shaker steady so Cora could fill it. No matter where he positioned the shaker, the salt went elsewhere. To give the little tyrant his due, his voice expressed nothing but patience.

When Cora finally managed to fill the shaker, he made a fist and gave the table three sharp raps. The chatter in the room ceased.

"Brothers and sisters, it's time for prayer."

The mystery of his presence in his old home was solved. As a male, albeit an unmarried one, he was qualified to lead the family in prayer. Women weren't. Since the gigantic family ate in shifts, did he also pray in shifts?

I bowed my head and ran through the alphabet several times before the long-winded Meade finally quit. But I'll say this for him: he did manage to mention food a couple of times in between the Heavenly reminders of male superiority and female subservience. When we'd all muttered "Amen," I walked with Cynthia back to the kitchen.

"Does he do that every morning?" I asked her.

"Every morning, lunch and dinner. Brother Meade is very devout. That's why the Circle of Elders wanted to name him prophet, not Davis."

I stopped in my tracks. "You're kidding, right? A fourteen-year-old boy?"

She shrugged, stopping with me. "We believe a prophet is born, not made. After my father's funeral, the Circle of Elders met all night and by morning, Brother Earl said he'd had a Revelation that the new prophet of Purity should be Brother Meade, but by then it was too late. The night before, Brother Davis had his own Revelation, and the other men in the compound, the ones that don't like the Circle of Elders much, let him assume the title of prophet. Things were pretty ugly around here for a couple of days, but then they settled down. They always do."

I'll bet. A good old-fashioned power struggle, with everyone involved claiming to act for God. I wondered if the potshots taken at Prophet Davis from the canyon were signs that Earl Graff had organized a counter-revolution. Not that I cared what those fools did to each other. Cynthia's information did create a new suspect in the murder of Solomon Royal.

"How did Brother Meade feel about getting edged out for the job of prophet?" Kids had killed before, for stranger reasons.

Cynthia laughed. "The idea of being named prophet scared him to death, but he didn't want anyone to know that, especially not Brother Earl. After Brother Davis was anointed prophet, though, Meade looked like a thousand pounds had just slid off his back." She fell silent for a second. "Just between you and me, I think Brother Earl wanted to be prophet himself, but knew he wasn't popular enough."

Like his half-sister, Meade was no dummy. He'd probably guessed that Earl would use him as a figurehead only, and didn't want any part of it. Uneasy lies the head that wears the crown.

An hour later the last of the children had eaten and it was time for me to return home. "It's seven o'clock," I announced, slipping off the apron Jean had loaned me. "My husband must be starving."

"Oh, and how is Brother Saul?" Sister Jean asked, straightening her own apron. "You two getting along okay?"

"Sure, other than his complaints about my cooking."

She shoved a tinfoil-wrapped plate into my hands. "Here are some sausage, eggs and biscuits to take to Brother Saul, but by the end of the week you should be able to put together a decent breakfast for him."

I doubted that.

Keeping a humble expression on my face, I hurried the plate back to Saul's house so he could eat Ermaline's biscuits while they were still warm.

Ruby snatched the plate from me as soon as I entered the house. "It's about time," she snapped. Her eyes were red from lack of sleep, reminding me of my noisy performance the previous night. "It's a disgrace to make your husband wait so long for his breakfast."

Amused, I trailed after her. As I entered the kitchen, which now seemed tiny compared to Ermaline's, I saw Saul, freshly shaved, sitting at the table wolfing down a big bowl of Cheerios. An apple core and banana skin lay beside the bowl. I allowed myself a moment of housewifely pride. Maybe I couldn't cook, but I could sure write a mean shopping list.

"I actually helped make a couple of those biscuits," I said, as Ruby set the plate in front of him.

"The flat ones, probably," she grumped.

"Ladies, ladies, don't fight," Saul said, shoving aside his Cheerios and popping a butter-drenched biscuit into his mouth. "Sister Lena, this flat little biscuit tastes like heaven on earth. I can't wait to see what pleasures your lunch lesson will bring us."

Ruby said nothing, but I noticed that she ate as many biscuits as Saul.

After breakfast was over, Saul and I left an infuriated Ruby to the washing up and strolled onto the porch and out of earshot.

"Do you think it's going to work?" he said, as we sat down together in the porch swing.

"Learning how to cook or finding out more about Prophet Solomon's death?"

"Lena."

I grimaced. "Sorry. The stress of slaving over a hot stove must be getting to me. But in answer to your question, it's too early to tell." I gave him a brief rundown of the morning's activities, going into detail about the book incident. "By the way, I didn't know you were Purity's official book-smuggler."

"Oh, that. I've been doing it for years," he said. "Once Cynthia gets through reading them, she gives them back to me and I take them to the Salvation Army in Zion City so nobody'll spot things like *War and Peace* lying around on the dump. That Cynthia, she's a real bright girl and I'd like to see her make something of herself. She was talking about being a doctor there for a while, and I think she could manage it, too."

"She won't if Ermaline has anything to do with it."

He made a face. "Ermaline's got an attitude, but she makes a fine biscuit." He smacked his lips at the memory.

"Jean seems to look out for Cynthia."

"Poor Jean. She's never been happy up at that house. I think she used to be sweet on Davis Royal but then she had to marry his daddy."

"Had to?" I raised my eyebrows.

He chuckled. "Get your mind out of the gutter, girl. Jean didn't get pregnant out of wedlock or anything like that. That sort of thing doesn't happen much in Purity because the girls are usually married off as soon as they start their monthlies. No, what I meant was that some kind of deal went down having to do with a tractor her father wanted but didn't have the money to buy. But he got the tractor anyway and right after it was delivered, Solomon got Jean."

"That's terrible!"

"It was a nice tractor."

I gave him a look.

"The point is, Jean never could stand Solomon, so I don't think she was all that broken up over his death."

"Interesting."

"Don't go getting ideas about Jean. She's not the violent type."

"Lizzie Borden's neighbors used to say that about her, too."

"Lena."

"Sorry again." I sat there in silence for a few minutes, listening to the compound's children as they played on their way to school. They sounded like children anywhere.

"At least the kids seem happy," I finally said.

"Sure. Purity is great for kids, one big summer camp with hundreds of playmates to choose from. And don't forget, most of them have more or less intact families, weird as those families are. But when the kids grow up, things change."

I watched a little blond girl about ten years old cross the dirt circle from the Utah side to the Arizona side, her long, patched dress no match for her budding beauty. I understood what he was saying. "And when the little girls grow up, those changes can get tough."

"Yeah, somebody always needs a new tractor."

At eleven I headed to Ermaline's, first crossing over to the Utah side and the clinic. I'd planned to ask one of the midwives how Rosalinda was doing, but the groans I heard as I opened the door told me all I needed to know. I hurried to Ermaline's house.

Within no time I found myself grating heads of cabbage the size and density of bowling balls, all grown in the compound's massive kitchen garden, while Ermaline hovered over me, criticizing my every move. I worked until my hands cramped as I turned the stuff into coleslaw to be served with the luncheon menu's main dish: Sloppy Joe sandwiches. As Ermaline told me exactly how much vinegar, pepper, and mayo to add to the slaw's unholy mess, I edged toward my questioning.

"My heart was broken when I heard about Prophet Solomon's death," I lied. "I heard him speak at a library in Salt Lake City and he really turned my life around. It made me determined to come here, and so when I met Brother Saul, it was as if God himself had led me here."

The harsh expression on Sister Ermaline's face didn't lighten. "Our Great Father is living in the highest level of Heaven, waiting for all of us there. As first wife, I'll sit at his right hand, too."

Personally, I doubted that the dirty old man's waiting room was as comfortable as she believed, but I kept my cynicism to myself. Pulling a long face, I said, "Still, Sister Ermaline, it must be a great sorrow having someone you love so much taken away from you before his time."

"Don't be silly. In Purity we accept the blows life deals us. Add more vinegar to that. I don't hold with sweet slaw."

Our activities were interrupted once by a visit from Sister Hanna, who limped into the kitchen, eyes downcast, her pregnant belly looking almost painful.

"Sister Ermaline, I run out of flour."

"Poor plannin'!" Ermaline snapped, but directed Jean to fetch some from the pantry. "You need to start making lists and keeping them updated. God hates a woman who don't tend to business."

"I know, Sister Ermaline," Hanna said, almost cowering. "I'm trying. I just can't seem to..."

"Try harder!"

With a gentle smile, Jean handed Hanna a bag of flour. Before I'd come to Purity, I would have thought it was enough to feed an army; now I knew it wouldn't last beyond one meal.

"Thank you, Sister Jean," Hanna said, then limped out the door.

Ermaline stared after her, contempt in her eyes. And, strangely, fear.

Why?

As the morning wore on, I decided that Ermaline's entire interest in life began and ended with the kitchen. Unless she was a greater actress than I believed, she didn't appear to miss her husband. All she cared about was her coleslaw.

It intrigued me enough to try something. "Sister Ermaline," I began, "my sister died last year and even though I was a thousand miles away from her, I swear I knew the exact moment of her death. I was mopping the floor and suddenly I knew she was gone, just as surely as if I had been at her bedside. You'd been married to the Prophet for almost forty years and must have been close, so did you have a moment like that? A moment when you knew the Lord had taken him?"

Ermaline's busy hands stilled, and for a second I thought I saw a glimmer of sadness in her eyes. "I never noticed a thing. Not even the next morning. The prophet wasn't at the table, but I thought maybe he was still with one of my sister wives. Then after breakfast, when some of us was still in the kitchen cannin' raspberry preserves, Brother Earl came in and he said…he said…"

Was that a tear on her cheek? Or perspiration?

"But the afternoon before, Sister Ermaline, when it must have happened? Maybe one of the other wives felt something?"

She sniffed and her hands busied themselves again. "Sister Jean was in here awhile, but then she ran off to do something else. Sister Martha, she was here, too, but she didn't say anything about omens. Wait. I remember now. Martha wasn't feeling good, she had one of them migraines of hers. Somebody made her a potato poultice and she went off to her room to lie down."

Martha Royal, Meade's mother, now married to the old goat in that tin trailer. I'd wondered why the Circle of Elders had been so quick to find her another husband, and obviously such an unsuitable one. Now I wondered even more.

So Jean had been out of the kitchen on an errand, Martha had been lying down in a dark room, and Ermaline had remained alone in the kitchen. The section of the canyon where Rebecca and I had stumbled across Prophet Solomon's body was close enough to the compound that given enough time, a determined woman could have run down there, grabbed his shotgun and blasted both barrels at him, then get back to the kitchen before her absence was noticed.

As far as I was concerned, Ermaline was mean enough to kill anyone, but even mean people needed motives. No problem there. Ermaline had been effectively discarded in favor of younger wives, and although the wives of Purity professed to suffer no jealousy, I thought they all protested too much. But had Ermaline been alone long enough to actually do the deed?

"Sister Ermaline, it seems like you had a terrible amount of work to do all by yourself that day. Didn't anyone else come in to help you?"

When she shook her head, the bright kitchen light glinted on her granny glasses, shielding her eyes from me. The air in the kitchen was close and still. I wished someone would open a window.

"Me need help?" she finally said. "I don't need help. I never did."

"How'd it go, wife?" Saul asked me as I bustled into the kitchen, where he sat drinking a glass of orange juice. Ruby was nowhere to be seen, but that didn't mean she wasn't lurking about somewhere. After all, this was a woman who'd listened at Saul's bedroom door to check on the action.

"Fine." I put the plate Sister Jean had given me down in front of him. "Coleslaw. Sloppy Joes."

A big grin spread across his face. "And did my beloved wife cook all this for me?"

"You don't cook coleslaw," I answered primly. "You mix it. And yes, I mixed it with my own two hands. The Sloppy Joes come to you courtesy of Sister Jean. They're her specialty."

"Ah, Sister Jean." He smiled. As he ate with every indication of pleasure, for which I felt inordinately proud, he leaned toward me and asked in a low voice, "Find out anything interesting?"

"Only that Jean, Martha, and Ermaline all had the opportunity to kill the prophet."

He looked appalled. "Come on, now."

I leaned close enough to him to smell Sloppy Joes on his breath. "Prophet Solomon was shot, remember, and most women can use a shotgun if they have to. By the way, how much do you know about Ermaline? Was her marriage to Solomon happy? Or at least as happy as it could be, considering the situation here."

He chewed quietly for a while, thinking. Then, "Well, I've heard stories but you've got to understand that they're just stories. I don't know how accurate they are."

"Let me worry about that."

He sighed and put his fork down. "Ermaline might be crabby, but she's a good woman underneath."

Why was it that whenever someone started telling you what a good person someone was "underneath" you prepared to hear something nasty about them?

"Ermaline started having trouble with Martha a few years back over some little something, and Solomon took Martha's side. They say that Solomon stopped sleeping with Ermaline then and she took it pretty hard. I guess she wanted another baby, but at her age, that was pretty much impossible. Have you noticed that the women here compete over how many kids they have?"

I nodded. "It's kind of hard to miss."

"Anyway, people say Ermaline never used to be such a good cook, that she started studying all those cookbooks and stuff just to please Solomon, sort of like she was trying to lure him back to her bed with tuna noodle casseroles."

"You don't know what caused the original trouble between Ermaline and Martha?" I, for one, would hate to be on the wrong side of either Ermaline *or* the Valkyrie, who wouldn't have looked out of place strapped into armor and brandishing a sword.

Saul shook his head. "Maybe they had a falling out over a recipe or something, but so what? Prophet Solomon got murdered, not Martha or Ermaline."

And the beautiful Martha was handed over to a particularly unattractive man. Orchestrated by Sister Ermaline? Perhaps I needed to reassess my belief that women had no power in Purity.

Chapter 12

By the end of the week, thanks to Sister Ermaline's instruction, my biscuits weren't quite as lopsided and I'd even begun to master the basics of tuna noodle casseroles. I'd heard some gritty gossip, too, although I wasn't certain it would lead to Solomon's murderer.

Jean, for instance, described in grisly detail Rosalinda's bloody delivery of a healthy son, conveyed via a friend who worked at the clinic.

"You'd think Brother Earl would have a nice word for her after all that but all he did was count the baby's fingers and toes," Jean said. "The next day, while she was still lying there at the clinic, he told her she had five weeks to recover and then she'd have to resume her wifely duties."

I didn't have to feign my shock. "That's pretty creepy."

"He's a creepy guy," Jean said, her green eyes dark with concern. Like most of Solomon's widows, she obsessed over who her next husband would be, and both Earl Graff and Noah Heaton topped her list of dreads.

As she spoke, she stood by the stove, flipping sausage patties while Cynthia—who had been transfixed by Jean's detailed description of the birth process—transferred the cooked patties to a huge platter. Sister Ermaline was elsewhere in the house, probably torturing kittens.

"If I wind up with Brother Earl, I don't know what I'll do," Jean said.

"You don't really think the Circle of Elders will give you to him, do you?" I asked.

Jean smoothed away a stray wisp of her glorious red hair. Today she was dressed in a bright green dress almost the same color as her eyes. "Sister Ermaline has been talking to them, giving suggestions about who should go where. My name came up in connection with his."

Shades of Martha Royal. "I know it's none of my business, but why doesn't Ermaline like you?"

One of the other women vented a short, bitter laugh. "Sister Ermaline doesn't like anybody!"

Jean threw her a glance. "Especially not me. When I married the prophet, I was young and stupid, and I bragged about how many times he asked me to visit his bed. He even wanted me after I became pregnant."

"Lucky you," the other wife muttered sarcastically.

Another thing I'd learned in the week since I'd arrived at the compound was that sex after pregnancy wasn't considered necessary, although it was not unknown. The men kept charts of their wives' menstrual cycles and concentrated their sexual activities around fertile times. Once the wives became pregnant, the men usually moved on to the next unpregnant female. Ideally, by the time the last woman in the household had been fertilized, the first woman would have delivered her baby and be ready for action again. But it didn't always work that way.

I looked around to make sure Ermaline was still out of the room. "Why, Sister Ermaline was jealous!"

This time, all the women in the kitchen laughed.

Then Cynthia spoke up. I'd noticed earlier that her face seemed paler than usual, but at the time I didn't give it much importance—something I regretted later. "Father Prophet was still having sex with Mother when Sister Jean married him, but soon after that, he stopped asking Mother to visit."

Because reproduction was women's major function at Purity, I'd become used to their matter-of-fact discussions of sexual behavior. Still, I was shocked at this bald piece of information coming from the man's own daughter. "Your father stopped sleeping with your mother?"

Cynthia nodded. "She was unlikely to have any more babies, so what would be the point?"

Love, I wanted to say, but didn't. I had already learned that love had very little to do with sex in Purity. The women were brood mares, nothing more. And once a brood mare outlived her usefulness…

At least the men didn't take their aging wives to the slaughterhouse.

Later that day Saul told me he had another appointment with his attorney in Zion City, and asked if I needed to ride along. I jumped at the chance to return to West Wind Ranch to make some phone calls. I hadn't talked to Jimmy in over a week, and I was eager to find out what he'd learned about the list of names I'd given him.

When we arrived at West Wind, the ranch was full up with Swedish tourists, but as Virginia chatted with a man who looked like a professional skier, she motioned me to the office. First I phoned the ranch where Dusty worked, but after much hemming and hawing, Slim Papadopolous told me Dusty had phoned from Las Vegas and asked for another week off.

"He's not alone, is he?" I asked Slim, already knowing the answer.

"I'm sorry, Lena."

Well, this wouldn't be the first time Dusty had disappointed me. Not that either of us had taken any vows of faithfulness or anything old-fashioned like that, but a girl can still hope, can't she?

I forced a laugh. "It's no big deal, Slim. Dusty and I have an understanding not to have an understanding."

"If you say so."

"I do say so."

I replaced the receiver as gently as possible, surprised at the steadiness of my hand. But my old cop attitude stood me in good stead. When you weren't certain you'd return from your shift alive, a flamed-out relationship was no big deal. That was the theory, anyway. Besides, I didn't really love Dusty. Never had, never would. Repeating that like a mantra, I called Desert Investigations.

Jimmy's first words shocked me. "Lena, I want you out of Purity right now." The fiber optic line allowed me to hear the quaver in his voice.

"I can't leave until I've found Prophet Solomon's killer, Jimmy. Tell me what you found out."

As he related the result of his Internet searches, his anxiety to pull me out of the compound began to make sense.

"Some of those guys are convicted felons, Lena. They moved away from Purity when they hit eighteen and tried to make it elsewhere, but most never fit in. I uncovered several child molestation and lewd acts with minors convictions on a number of them, but right now I'm a little more concerned with one guy who might turn into a physical threat to you personally."

"Who?"

"Earl Graff, one of the witnesses against Rebecca. He left Purity and came down to Phoenix when he was twenty and wound up doing one to five in Perryville Prison for almost killing his first wife when she tried to leave him. When the next wife dumped him, too, he repeated his pattern and went to visit the Perryville boys again. That's when he saw the light and went back to Purity, where the women have to put up with that kind of stuff. He's dangerous, Lena. Really dangerous."

I waved it away. Graff's violent past didn't surprise me in the least. "What else do you have?"

"Oh, I'm just getting started. Have you run into some guy named Noah Heaton yet? His name came up in connection with Graff a couple of times, so I checked him out, too."

"I've met him. I can't say that he impressed me much."

"Prepare to be impressed. Up until five years ago, the compound's kids used to be bussed to the public schools in Zion City, which is why I was able to get the info on him that I did. It turns out that Heaton had a bad reputation in school. A very bad reputation."

"So did I, Jimmy. My teachers didn't know what to do with me. They called me uncontrollable and tried to get several of my foster parents to give me Ritalin."

"You've told me. But were you ever caught in the science lab dismembering frogs? *Before* they were dead?"

I winced. "Jesus, nothing like that." As a child, the only creature I'd ever hurt was myself.

He continued. "Heaton came to the attention of school officials several times, actually. He was always getting into fights and for a while wasn't allowed to even sit on the same side of the room with the girls. He was eventually expelled when the class's pet hamster turned up dismembered and one of its feet was discovered in his desk. After that, Heaton's mother had to homeschool him because no other school up there would take him on. About a year later, the compound withdrew all its kids from the public school system—afraid they'd get tainted by modern ideas, I guess—and Noah never came to the attention of the authorities again. I doubt if his animal-torturing career ended there."

I digested this. "How did you find out? Noah was a minor then, and even if he was in public school, his records should have been sealed."

"Not if your mother knows someone who knows someone who knows someone who taught at the school."

I found the information about Noah Heaton more dis-
turbing than that about Earl Graff's imprisonment for
battering. Graff was a thug, to be sure, but he was an obvious
thug. But Noah? Even given the dog-shooting incident I'd
been told about, I had considered him more whiney than
vicious. More fool me. Anyone in law enforcement knew
that serial killers began their careers by torturing animals,
eventually moving to human prey unless they received
intensive psychiatric treatment. Somehow I doubted that
the good people of Purity had driven Noah into Zion City
on a regular basis to have his head shrunk by an expert.
These people were more interested in hiding problems than
they were fixing them.

Struck by the futility of the situation, all I could say was,
"What a mess."

"You're telling me. But there's more, much more. Prophet
Solomon, for instance, certainly wasn't without his sins. He's
not on record for dismembering hamsters or beating women,
but he was one of those convicted child molesters I was telling you about. Back in the late Fifties, after he'd left the
compound for a while, he did two years in Idaho for inde-
cent acts with a minor. Even worse, I checked it out and
apparently the case was pled down from statutory rape. He
was twenty-five, the little girl was eight."

I felt a sharp pain in my palm. When I looked down, I
saw that I'd clenched my fist so hard the nails had dug into
it. Four crescent-shaped cuts sprouted tiny drops of blood.

"He also has a fraud conviction to his credit."

"A fraud conviction?" Not in the same league as child
rape, but still...

"Yeah, seems that after he got out of prison he took off
for Oregon, where he defrauded a group of Portland businessmen out of something close to six million dollars in a
fictitious land development deal. He served four years in a
federal country club, paid some of the money back, then
vanished for awhile. Next time we hear from him he's back

in Purity as God's very own prophet. Oh, and by that time, he'd already accrued five wives of record, one at a time, all legal."

"You think any of the people in Purity know about his adventures outside the compound?"

"Hard to tell, and even harder to tell if they'd mind if they did. They don't play by the same rules the rest of us do."

A thought struck me. "Did you get the names of the businessmen he defrauded? He only paid back some of the money, right?"

"Yes on both counts." He reeled off several names and I wrote them down. Warming to his theme, he continued, "Royal's victims recovered about two million and change, but the other four mill never turned up. It's my guess some of that money wound up in offshore accounts."

Who had the money now? Davis Royal? Or somebody else? "A lot of people would kill their grandmothers for four million dollars," I mused.

"Grandmothers? Try their mothers. And pet dog."

"Jimmy, you're starting to sound as cynical as me," I laughed.

"Maybe that's because I'm beginning to realize the number of crimes hidden in Purity. I hate to say it, even our client's own family may have blood on its hands. Jacob Waldman, Esther's father? My sources tell me it's rumored that one of his daughters went missing after she refused to marry his buddy Solomon."

I didn't like the sound of that. "What do you mean, went missing?"

"Exactly what I said. One day Jacob had a teenage daughter, the next day he didn't. No one knows what happened to her."

"Maybe she just ran off."

"Doubtful. She'd just turned thirteen."

I remembered Waldman's venomous display at the community meeting and his insistence on blood atonement. There was no telling how much of his raving was due to the dementia of Alzheimer's and how much to fact, but I made a mental note to watch the old man more carefully.

"Another thing, Lena."

"Yes?"

"That guy you're staying with, Saul Berkhauser? Well, about twenty years ago his business partner Micah Browning was found murdered up in Salt Lake. The case was never solved, but there were some pretty nasty things being said there for a while about Mr. Berkhauser."

I groaned. "Why didn't your mother know about all this?"

"I thought of that, too, so I called and asked her. Apparently, when it all went down, she was over in Bangkok with Dad trying to facilitate some adoptions. She said to tell you she's sorry she let you down, and that she feels awful for putting you into this kind of position."

I waved the problem away, then remembered he couldn't see me over the phone. "Tell her I'm a big girl and can take care of myself. But you said there were rumors about Saul. What kind of rumors?"

"Saul's wife Karen was fooling around with Micah Browning. I ran a search on her and found out that just before the guy turned up dead, she moved in with him and took out an order of protection against Saul."

It was hard to square the man who smuggled good books to knowledge-desperate girls with a man whose behavior merited an order of protection. "Are you sure?"

"I'm sure. The copy of the complaint I was able to get my hands on states that Saul threatened to kill both her and Browning. When Browning was murdered, shot in the head, by the way, Saul became the number one suspect for a while. The case was eventually dropped for lack of evidence, and Saul's wife went back to him."

"If Saul's wife went back to him it probably means she didn't seriously think he murdered Browning. Maybe she decided she was just overreacting."

"That, coming from you? Come on, Lena. You of all people should know that women can be battered half to death and still go back to their abusers. Have you forgotten the Clarice Kobe case already? But whatever was going on in Karen Berkhauser's mind, whatever she suspected, it became irrelevant pretty soon. She was dead within the year."

My stomach started doing the herkey-jerkey. "What did she die from?"

"Death certificate says heart attack. At home. Saul was the only one there when it happened."

People die from heart attacks all the time, nothing suspicious in that. What made me uncomfortable, though, was that many different modes of death—not all of them natural—could mimic a heart attack. Poisoning, for instance. Smothering.

"Was there an autopsy?"

"I didn't find any record of one. But listen, that's not all I've found, Lena. Virginia Lawler? Not that I think you're in any danger from her, but it seems that she once had a fourteen-year-old daughter who married a guy in the compound. Guess who?"

I felt overwhelmed by the onslaught of bad news. "You're going to tell me Virginia's daughter married Prophet Solomon, aren't you?"

"Right on, Sister Lena."

I remembered the dinner conversation at West Wind Ranch, when Saul had mentioned that the Lawlers had a "dead child." At the time, I'd thought he meant a *little* child, not a marriage-age woman. Although come to think of it, those words were frequently synonymous in Purity.

"What happened?"

"Her name was Alice and she died ten years ago. Her death certificate says she died due to a ruptured ectopic pregnancy."

Ectopic pregnancy, when the egg became fertilized while still in the Fallopian tube. The only way to save a woman who'd developed such a condition was immediate surgery, but as I'd seen, Prophet Solomon didn't believe in doctors.

"Lena, that's not all I have to tell you about Virginia."

"It can't get any worse."

"Wanna bet? When Solomon Royal married Alice, he was already married to Virginia! Solomon was Virginia's second husband, Lena. Her first husband, Alice's father, died in an accident."

If the situation hadn't been so sick, it would have been funny. Not only had Virginia been Solomon's wife, she'd been his mother-in-law at the same time! What was that old country song, "I'm My Own Grandpa?" No wonder Virginia didn't like discussing her dead child.

"Oh, crap, Jimmy."

He began listing the Purity men with child molest convictions in other states, and I recognized several names from the community meeting. None surprised me. Raise a boy believing a thirteen-year-old girl is a viable sexual partner and what could anybody expect? With such child molestation supposedly sanctioned by God, over the years Purity had become a virtual sanctuary for child molesters. No wonder the men turned over all their money to the prophet without a whimper. It was *protection* money.

"Any more?" I asked, after I'd taken down the final name.

"One piece of good news. You asked me to hunt around and see if any of my folks down here on the Pima Reservation knows any Paiutes up there. My great-uncle Arnold used to be good buddies with a guy named Tony Lomahguahu. He's one of the old-timers but he's still got all his marbles. Anyway, we called the rez and Mr. Lomahguahu is willing to meet you around nine o'clock tomorrow at the Purity Cemetery. You know where that is?"

"Yeah, it's not too far from where I used to camp while waiting to grab Rebecca."

"Mr. Lomahguahu seemed real interested when we told him about you. He's no fan of the Purity crowd."

"Tell him I'll be there. Now, anything more?"

"Murder, fraud, animal dismemberment, child molest. Nah, that's all."

Sufficient unto the day is the evil thereof, or some such damned thing. That's what my Baptist foster parents used to tell me, anyway. We chatted some more, then just before I hung up, I asked about Miles Alder and learned that yet another fire had broken out at the tire storage facility.

"This may be the beginning of the end of Miles' arson career, though," Jimmy said. "They caught him at the scene with second degree burns on his hands, reeking of gasoline. The police booked him into the Madison Street Jail."

I smiled for the first time that day. "Being kept out of temptation's way may save his life. It was just a matter of time before the kid went up in flames himself."

"Then I'm sorry to tell you his dad bonded him out."

When would parents learn? I hung up the phone, feeling sick for more reasons than one.

"Bad news?" I hadn't heard Virginia come back into the office, and now she stood over me, a concerned look on her face. How long had she been standing there?

I made sure she'd closed the office door behind her. "Virginia, why didn't you tell me that your daughter was one of Prophet Solomon's wives? And that you were, too? Considering everything, I find that an interesting omission."

She paled, and sat down heavily on the sofa. I didn't join her. Given what I now knew, I wanted as much distance between us as possible.

"I'm dying to hear your side of the story," I said, my voice sounding dangerous even to me.

She sighed. Or was it a sob? "I was *raised* in Purity!"

"That's your excuse for sending an innocent fourteen-year-old into the bed of a convicted child molester?" My hands shook so badly I dropped the pencil I'd been clutching.

Her lower lip quivered. "You don't know what it's like, livin' the way I did, being raised up like that. Your life's been too different from mine."

Right, just one party after another. "Then why don't you explain it all to me." I wanted to rip her eyeballs out and shoot pool with them.

She winced, as if she could read my mind. "Life at Purity was normal life to me, so I didn't think nothing about what was going on. Dale married me when I was thirteen and I had Alice the followin' year. I thought it was what God wanted me to do."

"When did Solomon enter the picture?"

"When a tractor rolled over on Dale and killed him. I was fifteen by then and Alice wasn't quite one year old. The Circle of Elders gave me to Solomon because Dale owed him some money and I turned out to be part of the repayment package. I didn't know about his problem with kids, I swear! When Alice turned thirteen and he told me he wanted to make us an even closer family, it just didn't sound all that strange to me. Not then, anyway."

She paused a moment, then added, "Lena, when everybody's told you all your life what's right and what's wrong, you never learn how to figure it out for yourself."

The office door opened and Leo came in, carrying a stack of papers. He took one look at our faces, and said, "Who died?"

Virginia gave him a despairing look. "Lena found out about Alice."

Leo threw the papers down on the desk and joined his wife on the sofa, putting his arm around her. "So what? You were a different person then." To me, he said, "You know what the Paiute say: walk a few miles in somebody's moccasins before you judge them."

I snorted. "You don't have to be a bull to know bullshit when it stinks."

He gave me a hard look. "When I met Virginia she'd been living in that hell hole all her life, hadn't read much other than her schoolbooks and that lunatic Solomon's ravings. She hardly knew up from down. But since then she's done what she could to make up for her mistakes. You wouldn't even be here if it weren't for Virginia."

Urged by her husband, Virginia told me the rest of the short, ugly story.

After three months of marriage, Alice became pregnant. Two months later she was dead. Half-crazed from grief, Virginia left Solomon's house one night and began walking up the dirt road. The next day, dehydrated and filthy, she reached the gas station at the highway junction, where Leo had just finished filling up his truck. He knew by her clothes where she had come from, so he drove her into Zion City and left her at the battered women's shelter run by a local church.

"She was so sad, so pathetic, I couldn't get her out of my mind," he said. "When I ran into her again a year later, it was like meeting a different person."

As soon as I trusted my voice, I said, "Virginia, you had one hell of a motive for killing Solomon Royal."

She looked me straight in the eye. "I never killed that man."

That's what all murderers say, isn't it?

I tried to act normal on the ride back to Purity but from the looks Saul threw in my direction, I knew I'd failed.

"You're awful quiet," he said, after we'd covered more than ten miles in silence. "Your partner tell you anything interesting?"

"Not much."

"C'mon, Lena. You haven't been yourself since we left Virginia's. I've heard more conversation from rocks."

While we barreled along the highway the arid landscape slid by with all the charm of the surface of the moon. I wondered how I'd ever found it beautiful. This was truly a no-man's land, filled with nothing but dried brush, sand, and rocks. Here and there, the desperate green of a prickly pear cactus added some color to the vegetation, but other than that, everything was beige, beige, and more beige. If the sky hadn't been blue and the nearby cliffs a fiery scarlet, I could have believed the hand of God had reached down and sucked all the color out of the land in Divine retribution. I was just thinking that my Baptist foster parents might have been right when they told me God punished the world for its sins when Saul pulled the truck over to the shoulder and stopped.

"What's wrong?"

I searched for a usable lie, but for once, came up empty-handed.

Saul settled back in the seat. "You found out about Micah and Karen, didn't you? And you've already tried and convicted me. Funny. I expected better from you."

I could probably have bluffed my way out of it, but what would be the point? If we were going to have a physical confrontation over this, I'd rather have it near the highway. Saul was no spring chicken and I figured I could handle him unless he was armed, and I'd never seen him carry a gun.

"My partner ran an Internet search on everyone in the compound and, yes, your name came up."

He didn't say anything for a few seconds, then burst out, "Goddamn computers are going to be the death of us all!"

A Dodge van passed us, going in the opposite direction. Just the knowledge that we were still on a public highway comforted me. That and my .38 strapped to my thigh under my dress. "Saul, is that all you have to say?" I figured it would take no more than two seconds to lift up my skirt, unsnap my holster, and pull my gun. Yeah, I could handle him.

After taking a few deep breaths, he said in a tight voice, "I didn't kill Micah, Lena. The Salt Lake police believe an old business associate of his killed him in retribution for a deal gone bad."

I took a few deep breaths of my own. "Then why didn't they arrest him?"

"Because he was killed in a head-on collision on I-80 before they could."

"How convenient."

The smile he attempted didn't quite come off. "I can't help that, Lena. And as for my wife, we'd been having some trouble, I'll not deny that. Yeah, she had an affair with Micah, but I didn't hold it against her. She'd finally become tired of my own running around and decided to show me how it felt. She was never in love with him."

"She *left* you."

His knuckles grew white as he clutched the steering wheel. Another van passed, a Japanese mini of some sort, followed closely by two pickups, both American-made. "Remember, she came back."

"Only after Micah died."

"She'd have come back anyway."

"So you say."

"Right. So I say."

Only fools and self-servers pretended to know the probable actions of dead people, and Saul was no fool. "Did Karen show any previous symptoms before the heart attack that killed her?"

Saul shook his head. "She'd never been sick a day in her life."

That gave me a brief moment of hope. If Saul had killed his wife, wouldn't he try to convince me that she'd been ailing for some time? Then again, maybe not. Maybe he believed it was more important right now to impress me with his "honesty."

He tried again. "Lena, if I was a killer, do you think I'd be stupid enough you bring you to Purity and actually let you live at my house? Wouldn't I try to stay as far away from the police as possible?"

Staying far away from the police was exactly what Saul had done for years. He'd left Salt Lake and moved to Purity, where the populace had lived outside the law for more than one hundred years. He might have stayed there, too, except for the land grab Solomon Royal and the Circle of Elders made on his house. Maybe he thought my investigation could somehow prevent that, so was willing to take the chance.

Which raised another point. "Tell me something, Saul. Would the women's situation in Purity bother you half as much if the Circle of Elders wasn't trying to get your house?"

He didn't answer right away, but when he did, it wasn't convincing. "The one thing has nothing to do with the other. But the real question, Lena, is—do you still trust me enough to go back to Purity with me, or do you want me to turn around and drive you to Virginia's? Your wish is my command. It's all up to you."

I didn't have to think about it. Another thing Jimmy told me before we hung up was that Esther's legal maneuvering had finally failed, and she was due to be extradited at the end of the week. Now that I'd seen firsthand how bad things really were for women in Purity, I couldn't take the chance that Rebecca would be brought back to the Arizona Strip, where her father would probably try to find her another husband.

"Take me to Purity," I said.

He pulled the truck onto the road. Neither of us said another word, just brooded on our respective paranoia until Purity raised its tar-papered head on the horizon. As we drove into the yard, the amount of activity in Prophet's Park amazed us. What seemed like almost the entire roster of Purity's male population was busily piling into cars and pickup trucks.

Saul stuck his head out the window. "What's going on?" he called to Earl Graff, whose swine-like face looked even redder than usual.

"It's Cynthia Royal! She ran away. Hellfire awaits her if she don't come back." The anger in his voice gave a clear indication of the hellfire he'd personally visit upon her if he found her.

Alarmed, I tried to calm him. "Brother Earl, the girl is little more than a child, and her father recently died. She's probably off crying somewhere."

Graff's mean little eyes narrowed and he let fly a most unreligious epithet. "Oh, yeah? Well, the little bitch was supposed to marry me two hours ago, and I notice that she wasn't crying too hard to run!"

Chapter 13

Where was Davis?

Purity's new prophet had promised that he'd allow no girl under sixteen to be married, especially not by force. Could it be he didn't know what was going on?

Or was he lying dead in Paiute Canyon?

"Drive to Davis's house!" I yelled at Saul. "If he's alive, he'll put a stop to this!"

"*If* he's alive?" Saul gave me a startled look, but he took a hard left and wheeled through the mesquite grove as fast as he could without clipping a few trees. As soon as he'd reached Davis's driveway, I saw that his Mercedes was gone.

I jumped out of the truck anyway, hiked my skirts, and ran up the stairs. Apparently hearing the commotion, Sissy met me at the door.

"Where's Davis? Cynthia ran off, and the Circle of Elders is after her! Earl Graff says she's supposed to marry him!"

Sissy blanched. "Oh, no! Not Brother Earl!" She shook her head. "Brother Davis left for Salt Lake City last night. He needed to do some banking."

I left her standing on the porch and ran back to Saul.

"Davis isn't going to help us, so we'll have to find her ourselves before Earl does."

For hours Saul and I drove around the perimeter of Purity in ever-widening circles, bumping dangerously over the desert itself. A couple of times we almost gullied out, but were able to rock the truck back and forth until we freed it. We searched the terrain for the slightest movement, but saw nothing other than a couple of antelope. It worried me. Although the high desert surrounding Purity was not as harsh as the desert surrounding Phoenix, it was harsh enough. A young girl could still easily die out here.

I trembled, remembering my own near death on the desert. Was anyone praying for Cynthia? Or just seeking to capture her?

We searched for hours but never found Cynthia. I comforted myself with the hope that perhaps she'd run to the Paiute and sought refuge with them. Or maybe, like so many other runaways before her, she'd headed toward West Wind Ranch. We drove halfway back to the ranch, scanning the sides of the blacktop for her, but we saw nothing to make us believe she'd passed that way. Eventually we realized she couldn't possibly have made it to the blacktop already, so we turned around and headed back toward Purity again.

"I should have realized something was wrong when I was at Ermaline's house this morning," I mourned. "But she didn't tell me!"

"Why should she?" Saul asked. "Remember, she thinks you're just another sister wife. But she should have had enough sense to come to me. Surely she knew I'd help her."

"We were gone all day," I said. "She didn't have *anybody* to turn to!"

Now that I'd had time to think, I could guess what happened. With Davis away, the Circle of Elders voted to hurry the marriage, figuring he wouldn't bother to annul it once the dirty deed had been accomplished. Whatever their reasoning, it was time to contact the authorities. But when I asked Saul to pull into a gas station so I could call them, he balked.

"I'm not sure you should drag the authorities into this," he said. "It might be best to…"

"To what? Just let her die in the desert?"

He shook his head, but stopped at the station anyway and gave me change for the phone. "Go ahead, then. But things might not work out the way you think they will."

Saul proved to be right. The minute I told the sheriff's dispatcher Cynthia was only fifteen and that I wasn't her mother, he lost interest. "She's a minor. If her parents are concerned about her, they'll file a report themselves."

"Her father's dead, and her mother, well...She, uh, she's out looking for her," I lied. "I imagine she was so worried that she didn't stop to call you."

The dispatcher remained unimpressed. When I kept insisting that Cynthia was only fifteen and could be in danger, he told me to have Ermaline call Dispatch when she returned. Then he hung up.

Fuming, I went back to the truck.

"Told you," Saul said.

Cynthia still hadn't been found when, several hours later, I walked to Ermaline's to help with dinner. The girl's absence was a good sign, I hoped. Maybe she'd already found help and was on her way to a new life. But just in case, I decided to skip my breakfast-fixing activities the next morning so I could look for her again.

In the kitchen, I was surprised to see Ermaline working away as usual. The other wives, especially Jean, looked much more upset than she did.

"Runaway girls are the men's problem," Ermaline said, kneading bread for what appeared to be a baker's dozen loaves. "As will be her punishment when they find her."

Looking up from the mess I'd made in the bowl by slopping lumpy mashed potatoes over the edge and onto the table, I asked, "Punishment?"

"Of course they're gonna punish her. But whatever pain steers a sinful woman away from Satan's gate is merciful in the end." Ermaline's voice was calm, her face severe. "The stupid girl's risked hellfire by not marryin' her God-chosen husband."

Appalled, I spoke before I thought. "God didn't choose Earl Graff for her, the Circle of Elders did!"

"Same thing."

I wiped my hands on my apron. "But Sister Ermaline, surely there are other prospective, ah, husbands who might be more to Cynthia's liking. And that Brother Earl, well excuse me, but he comes across to me as just plain mean!"

Ermaline's hands, as big-boned as a man's, I now noticed, kept kneading the dough until I thought it would scream for mercy. "Marriage is a covenant, Sister Lena, and covenants don't have nothing to do with liking or not liking. The only thing important for a woman is bringing more souls into the world, and she can't do that without getting married, can she?"

I opened my mouth to protest again, but noticed Jean's warning expression. "I guess I never thought of it that way."

Ermaline finally gave the bread dough a break and rested her hands on the work table. "Sister Lena, you're new around here but that don't excuse your ignorance of God's laws. You worry too much about feelings, but feelings are for the weak, not the Godly."

A harsh philosophy not worth arguing about, so I said nothing more, just busied myself with the mashed potatoes. The tension in the kitchen made it a more unpleasant place to work than usual. The day's heat, added to the full-bore ovens, had everyone sweating and snapping at each other like caged rats. No one dared to snap at Ermaline, though.

Sister Ermaline's casual attitude toward her daughter's welfare troubled me, but I wanted to give her the benefit of the doubt. Just to be sure, I decided to find out what she'd done, if anything, to see that her hellfire-bent daughter at least remained safe.

"Sister Ermaline, did you call the sheriff's office about Cynthia? It's pretty hot out there today and maybe she didn't take enough water."

Here Ermaline surprised me. "Of course I didn't, but when the men couldn't find her right away, Brother Earl came back and called the sheriff himself. There are patrol cars out looking for her right now."

I frowned. The deputy had pretty much told me that since I wasn't Cynthia's mother, I had no right to file a missing person's report. What made Earl Graff so special?

After that, we lapsed into silence, working quickly, if not cheerfully. Just when I thought I couldn't take the tension any longer, the household's older boys, led by Meade Royal, returned from the fields where they'd been working, and we carried the dinner to the table. After Meade led them all in prayer, I noticed with pride that no one refused my mashed potatoes.

When I finally left Ermaline's kitchen, loaded down with Salisbury steaks for Saul, I couldn't help but think that something obvious had slid under my radar while I worried about Cynthia. But what?

As I crossed the yard to Saul's house, I saw the men's pickup trucks were still gone, which meant they were still out looking for her.

Go, girl! Whatever you do, don't let them catch you.

Back at Saul's house, Ruby wolfed down her meal but refused to be drawn into a discussion about Cynthia. Saul said little, too, and I decided that his earlier anger at my suspicions of him had returned. When he finished dinner, he pushed himself away from the table, went into the living room and began recording another letter to his son. After finishing the dishes, Ruby stalked down the hallway and locked herself in her room, leaving me to listen to Saul tell his son about his current real estate problems. I felt totally alone, and for the first time that I could remember, didn't like it.

Then it struck me. I'd only been here a week, and yet I— a woman who'd always valued her privacy—now felt uneasy with solitude. How much more extreme would that unease be if I'd lived all my life in a house populated by at least fifty people? Did the simple fear of being alone factor into the women's odd acceptance of their fate?

Leaving Saul to his tape recorder, I stepped out onto the porch and collapsed into the swing. The sun set in its usual glory, tinting the Vermillion Cliffs with great splashes of red, orange and violet. But as pretty as it all looked, the compound remained eerily quiet. The men were still gone, and for once, few children played in Prophet's Park. Even the doors and windows to the homes were closed, as if by battening down the hatches, the occupants could keep Cynthia's rebellion from touching them. Not for the first time I suspected that the people of Purity were so locked into denial that they would probably never break free. It was as if they'd adopted the philosophy of "See no evil, hear no evil, speak no evil." Just the right environment for evil to flourish.

Just then I heard a rumbling from down the road, then saw a flash of headlights as the first truck topped the ridge. The men were back. Across the compound, a door slammed and Ermaline came out on the porch, followed by several other sister wives. Like me, they stood watching in silence.

I hoped Cynthia remained free and had made it to safety. In fact, I hoped so hard I didn't realize I was holding my breath until the pickups finally pulled into the yard and one of the men called out to Ermaline, "We couldn't find her!"

Then I finally exhaled. *Thank God,* I whispered to the Being I still wasn't sure I believed in. *Thank God.*

My joy didn't last long.

Early the next morning, as Saul and I started out to the truck to continue our own search for the runaway, we saw a sheriff's cruiser pull up in front of Ermaline's house. To my disbelief, a uniformed officer hauled a struggling Cynthia from the back seat and handed her over to her mother. As soon as Ermaline clasped her daughter's arm with one of those big hands, the girl stopped struggling and stood there, head drooping in defeat.

But that wasn't the only thing that shocked me.

The officer who'd brought Cynthia back was Howard Benson, the very man who had come into Desert Investigations and accused my client of murder.

Although I desperately wanted to go to Cynthia's aid, I couldn't let him see me, so I waited inside Saul's house until he'd driven out of the compound. In the meantime, I fumed. What the hell did Benson think he was doing, bringing the girl back to face a forced marriage? He was a sheriff, for God's sake, sworn to uphold the law, and the last time I checked, polygamy was illegal as hell. Since he'd brought Cynthia back, it could only mean he supported the polygamists. If so, I could never turn to him for help.

After Benson's car vanished down the dusty road, I ran across the yard to Ermaline's house.

Most of the household's children were already dressed, but strangely quiet, as if they knew something was wrong but weren't sure exactly what. Ignoring their baffled looks, I hurried past them into the kitchen, where the first load of biscuits was being taken out of the oven. No Ermaline, no Cynthia. The other women looked more scared than usual.

Sister Jean looked up from the sausage patties she was making. "You're late." No welcoming smile today.

"I overslept."

She raised a greasy hand and motioned to the other end of the long preparation table. "Ermaline's already measured out the ingredients. All you need to do is add them together, then cut the shortening into the mix."

I started work immediately, thrusting my hands into the huge bowl. But I was determined to find out what was going on. "On my way over here I saw Cynthia being brought back. Is she all right?"

"I think so," Jean answered, her voice so devoid of inflection that I couldn't tell if she was upset or relieved. "Don't concern yourself with her, Sister Lena. Just do your own job."

"But I was wondering..."

Jean glared at me. "Sister Lena, could you please shut up and work?" I noticed for the first time that her eyes were almost as red as her hair. She'd been crying.

"Yeah, yeah." No point in upsetting her further. I'd talk to Cynthia later. Jean was not only upset, but unless I was mistaken, she was terrified.

I'd just started patting the dough balls onto the cooking sheet when I heard the front door open and Earl Graff call out, "Sister Ermaline! We've come for Cynthia!"

We? I didn't like the sound of that so I wiped my floury hands on my apron and hurried into the living room, to see Graff standing there with a grim-faced posse of the compound's men. Then, to my disbelief, I saw Ermaline emerge from one of the bedrooms, dragging along an obviously terrified Cynthia.

"Mother, please, no!" the girl cried. "No!" She squirmed and struggled, but Ermaline remained implacable.

"Quiet, you wicked girl!" Ermaline hissed. "You gotta do the right thing or you'll burn in Hell forever!"

"Mother, no!"

I couldn't stand it any longer. I stepped in front of Ermaline. "You can't hand her over to these men!"

Sister Ermaline's big hand swatted me away as if I were no more than a fly trying to land on one of her precious biscuits. "Mind your own business, Sister Lena. Cynthia's sinned and she's gotta be punished. It's God's law."

I refused to let it go. "Sinned? Was she with someone else? Still, that's no reason to..."

Earl Graff slapped me. Slapped me so hard that little pinpoints of light danced around my head, like in the comic books. I staggered for a second, trying to keep my balance, and then, without even thinking about it, I spun around and smashed the karate-hardened edge of my hand against Graff's nose. A ragged blossom of blood and snot spewed forth as Brother Earl squealed, then hit the floor.

The other men stared in shock, and I heard running feet as the women emerged from the kitchen to find out what was going on.

"He hit me first," I pointed out, but it did little to erase everyone's stunned expressions, especially the men's. They looked like they'd just seen a rabbit transmogrify into a wolf.

"Sister Lena!" Ermaline was the first person to find her voice. "Go home to your husband right now! We'll take care of Brother Earl *and* Cynthia ourselves. You're no longer welcome in this house."

As I started for the door, the men and women huddled around the moaning Earl. All except for Ermaline, who studied me with narrowed eyes.

"Just who *are* you?"

I left the house without answering.

Chapter 14

"So you smacked the sonofabitch?" Saul asked, as he applied an ice pack to my face.

His expression made me suspect that given the right circumstances, he just might be capable of murder. I looked around and didn't see Ruby, but that was no guarantee she wasn't listening somewhere, so I kept my voice low.

"I did it without even thinking. I'm not used to being hit." At least not since I'd graduated from Arizona's foster care system, I could have added. But there was no point in burdening Saul with horror stories of my past.

"That eye's going to turn black," he said.

It wouldn't be my first black eye, so that didn't bother me. What did bother me was knowing Ermaline would turn her daughter over to the man who'd hit me—and he was probably a lot angrier at Cynthia than he even was at me. She had not only rejected him, but done it in such a public way that the entire compound and the authorities knew. How would he make her pay for such humiliation?

"As soon as I fix you up, I'm going to go over to Ermaline's and finish what you started," Saul muttered. "Damn creep's not going to go beating on *my* wife."

"I'm not your wife. And I took care of the problem, at least the immediate problem. If you pop Earl one, the rest of them will probably drop-kick both our butts out of here tomorrow even without a court order. So please calm down. Cynthia's the one who needs help, not me. Somehow we've got to stop that marriage."

He dabbed at my eye again, shaking his head. "How do you propose we do that, Miss Tough Nuts? You now see that our local sheriff won't do anything about it. Hell, Howard Benson's own family tree is filled with polygamists, so he's not going to get all hot and bothered over this deal. All he saw today was a runaway minor who needed to be returned to her parents."

"But Saul, she doesn't want to marry Earl Graff! It would be nothing more than rape."

"I know, I know. But there really isn't anything we can do about it now, is there? Not without blowing your cover even further than it's already blown. I'd grab the girl myself and drive her off to Zion City in my pickup if I thought I could get through the compound with her, but haven't you noticed how carefully they watch me every time I leave? For months now they've been afraid I'll do something like that, so they do everything but frisk me."

I tried again. "It's not a real marriage. The man already has a pile of wives."

He eased up with the ice pack for a moment and stared me straight in the eyes. "As far as these people are concerned, including Sheriff Benson, it *is* a real marriage."

My heart ached in admission that Saul was right. No wonder the law never prosecuted the polygamists. Too many of the law officers in Utah sympathized with them and looked the other way while they did their thing. With no cooperation from the law *or* her mother, Cynthia was doomed.

"Saul, there's something else I don't understand. Why did the Circle of Elders give Cynthia to Earl Graff? She's the daughter of the last prophet, and if I've been able to figure out the pecking order here, she should have been destined for a better marriage. Besides, Prophet Davis said that he wasn't going to allow them to force girls into marriage anymore."

His laugh was ironic. "Looks like a coup d'etat might be shaping up, doesn't it? Davis might be popular with the ladies, but you've seen what the Circle of Elders thinks about him. If you want the truth, I think they did it just to spite him. Cynthia is just the opening shot in a full scale war."

That sounded probable to me, too. I decided to think about that later. For now, I closed my eyes and let him continue attending to me.

I had almost fallen asleep under his tender ministrations when I heard him say, "Think you can remember how to make those biscuits?"

I opened my eyes with a start. "What?"

"I'm starved, Lena. And those biscuits you've been bringing home are all gone."

I stared at him in disbelief. "My face looks like hamburger, an innocent girl is being forced to marry a creep, and you're thinking of your *stomach?*"

"Lena, let me tell you something. I was in Korea, at Inchion Reservoir. We were surrounded by thousands of Red Chinese and weren't sure if we'd live to see morning, but we still ate our rations."

He had a point. Going hungry wasn't going to help Cynthia, so I reluctantly got up and went into the kitchen.

My biscuits turned out to be the size and density of hockey pucks. Saul and Ruby ate them, but with pained expressions. I contented myself with some Ramen and thought about Cynthia. There had to be a way to get her out of the compound and away from Earl Graff. I felt certain that if I worked on the problem long enough, I'd find a solution, but for now, my duty to my own client came first.

I'd been in the compound more than a week, yet I was no closer to finding Prophet Solomon's murderer than the day I arrived. Yes, Virginia had warned me that Purity's inhabitants were secretive, but she'd neglected to mention the almost harem-type seclusion the polygamists' women lived in, as well as their almost total separation from the men except for fertilization time. While I knew I needed to talk to the men, I didn't see how I'd manage, given my violent behavior at Ermaline's. They'd be even more on their guard. But perhaps not all was lost. Tomorrow I'd talk to Tony Lomahguahu and he might be able to give me more information.

After we'd finished the biscuits, Ruby spoke for the first time. "You need to get the Circle of Elders to pray over your eye, Sister Lena." She didn't ask how I'd received my shiner. She'd probably been cavesdropping.

The thought of Earl Graff and his henchmen in the Circle praying for my healing struck me as hilarious, but I refrained from laughing out loud. "I don't think so, Sister Ruby."

"God is the most wondrous healer."

I grunted. "God, maybe, but not the guys around here. And if I remember correctly, didn't your first husband die after being prayed over?"

Her indrawn breath told me that in my irritation, I had once again gone too far. Forcing myself to sound contrite, I said, "I'm sorry, Sister Ruby. Please remember that I am unused to the ways of faith."

Too late. Without another word, Ruby shoved her chair back from the table and left the kitchen.

"Nice going, Lena," Saul said. "Keep that up and pretty soon no one in Purity will talk to you."

I was washing the dishes when I heard the front door open and the sounds of men, all talking at once, enter the house.

"Sister Lena, you'd better get out here," Saul called.

I dried my hands and walked into the living room. Waiting for me were Davis Royal, looking more blond-on-blond gorgeous than ever, and ugly old Earl Graff. Saul had his fists balled as if ready to take a swing at Earl, but Davis had positioned himself between the two. Smart man. Sister Ruby, who'd emerged from her room, completed the party. She stood watching from the corner, her face blank.

"I try to get away to do some work on behalf of the compound, and things fall apart," Royal said, sounding aggrieved. "Sister Lena, Brother Earl has leveled a serious charge against you."

"Bitch hit me," Graff growled, his jowls trembling with rage. Was it my wishful thinking or had his nose already swelled to twice its size?

I took a step toward him, and he shrank back, a protective hand covering his nose. "Only because you hit me first, Brother Earl."

Was it my imagination, or did I see a twitch at the corner of Royal's gorgeous mouth? "Brother Earl, you didn't say anything about that. Is it true? Did you hit Sister Lena?"

Saul gestured toward me. I noticed that his fists were still clenched. "Look at her eye, Brother Davis. She sure didn't do that to herself."

Royal approached me. I'm a tall woman, but he had to stoop while he examined the area around my eye. His handsome face was so close to mine that I could smell mint on his breath. My knees began to buckle. But he gave my cheek a final soft caress and stepped back before I could make a complete fool of myself.

"Brother Graff, I haven't heard your answer."

Graff shuffled his feet for a few seconds, then finally muttered, "The woman needed correcting."

"So you hit her."

"Like I said…" Graff sounded like a weasel with laryngitis.

"I heard what you said the first time, Brother Graff. You don't need to repeat it." Royal's voice was still mild, but his blue eyes had grown cold.

I tried to explain myself. "Brother Davis, Sheriff Benson brought Sister Cynthia back, but she said she didn't want to marry Brother Earl, then Brother Earl threatened to punish her, so I said…"

Royal raised his hand to silence me. To my surprise, I shut up.

He turned to Graff. "It doesn't matter how great you felt the provocation was, Brother Earl, I will not have violence in Purity. I will not have violence of *any* kind, especially not against women."

Graff's jowls trembled as he nodded his head.

Royal wasn't through. "Yes, I know that under my father's leadership, it was sometimes thought necessary to correct our beloved sisters when they stepped out of line, but this is a new day, and there is new revelation. If you have trouble with any of Purity's women, and you do not feel you can handle that trouble without violence, you are to come to me. You will not strike *any* of them, not even your wives. *Do you understand me, Brother Earl?*"

Graff went white at the change in Royal's voice, and his own was barely audible when he replied, "Yes, I understand."

"One more thing, Brother Earl. Sister Cynthia is not yet sixteen. Do you remember what I said about marrying an underage girl?"

Graff's face looked like that of a child who had just lost his bag of candy to a tougher, bigger kid. "She'll be sixteen in a couple of weeks. What's the big deal?"

"The *law* is the big deal, Brother Earl. The *law.*" Then he turned to me. "Sister Lena, you say Sister Cynthia does not want to marry Brother Earl?"

Both Saul and I spoke at the same time. "That's why she ran off."

I added, "She's terrified of him! And with good reason!"

Royal shook his head. "I don't like this at all. Let's say Sister Cynthia truly was of marriageable age. Granted, a young woman seldom knows her own mind, but when she shows outright *fear* of her intended husband, well, the situation obviously needs to be examined closely."

Did I hear right? Was Davis Royal actually going to help Cynthia? My hopes lifted, so I decided to crawl further out on my limb. "Brother Davis, I must tell you that Cynthia's mother seems in favor of the marriage."

He shrugged. "What Sister Ermaline wants is of no consequence to me. She has her own sins to atone for."

What sins? I wanted to ask. But I didn't dare.

Deep in thought, Royal stood in the middle of the room, his muscular arms crossed over his broad chest. He looked like something you'd expect to see on the Acropolis. Just before I started to drool, he unfolded his arms and motioned to Earl Graff.

"Come back to my house with me, Brother Earl. We have much to discuss." Then he turned, nodded politely toward Saul and me, and ushered Graff out the door.

Silence gripped the room for a moment, then Saul said, "Lena, don't ever get yourself in a situation where you're alone with Earl Graff."

I nodded, having seen the look Graff gave me as he left. "Do you think Royal might stop the marriage?"

"Maybe. He seemed concerned about the situation." Then he looked over at Ruby, who still sat quietly in the corner. "Sister Ruby, Sister Lena has had a very bad day, and I think it might be nice if you made dinner tonight for a change."

"But I'm supposed to do the laundry! And maybe in an emergency, some housework," Ruby squeaked. "It's not my job to cook!"

Saul scowled. "It is today. We'll eat at five. The instructions are on the side of the Ramen packages."

Face livid, Ruby rushed out of the living room and down the hall, stomping every inch of the way. She slammed her bedroom door so hard the photograph of Saul's naval officer son fell off the wall.

Rehanging the portrait, Saul said, "We need to talk, Sister Lena. Follow me to the bedroom."

Like a dutiful sister wife, Ruby had made his bed. She'd even smoothed out my own night dress and draped it across the bedspread. I was touched by this evidence of thoughtfulness until I realized she probably hoped I'd get pregnant as quickly as possible, and thus be easier to control.

Saul perched on the bed, leaving the rocking chair to me.

"Are we going to have another hot night, Brother Saul?" I quipped.

He frowned. "If you don't start watching your mouth, we might not have any nights left in Purity at all. Look, Lena, most of the men around here hate me, and now they're beginning to hate you, too, yet you haven't even come close to finding out who killed Prophet Solomon, have you?"

"No, but…"

He interrupted me. "I wasn't going to tell you this because I didn't want to worry you, but you'd better start seeing some action on this case, because both of us may be gone soon. Remember why I drove into town yesterday, before all the offal hit the fan?"

I thought for a minute. "To see your attorney?"

He nodded. "Well, he told me I'll almost certainly lose my case, and even tried to get me to settle out of court."

My heart sank. "What kind of settlement?"

"The compound's attorneys have offered me ten thousand dollars to drop the case now and just walk away from the house."

I couldn't believe it. "But this house has to be worth ten times that!"

"Sure is, but the alternative is not only to lose everything, but to have to pay court costs, too. Apparently the agreement I signed with Solomon to hand over all my money in exchange for the 'protection and friendship of Purity' is legally binding." His voice was steady, but his knuckles, as he knotted his hands into fists again, were white.

"It can't be!"

He gave a hollow laugh. "That house where you're learning how to cook? Well, I didn't know this before, but my attorney says it used to belong to someone else before Solomon took it over and did all those add-ons. The folks that owned it originally, they had a falling out with the Purity Fellowship Foundation over the Social Security check issue, just like I did. They went to court, and they lost everything.

They lost the house, their cows, their farm equipment, everything. They even wound up having to leave a bunch of older daughters and grandkids behind when they moved. They're not even allowed to visit them now."

Saul didn't have any children to leave behind, but losing the house you'd built with your own loving hands had to be tough. Still, he'd walked into the deal with his eyes wide open, the rules laid out before him in black and white on the contract every new member of the compound was ordered to sign.

And he'd signed it.

I sighed. "Maybe you should take the offer and salvage what you can. If you do, how long will you have before you have to be out of the compound?"

"Thirty days."

Probably enough time for me to do what I needed to do, but my heart ached for Saul. Even if he was a murderer.

"What will you do about Ruby?" I asked.

"That's up to her," he said morosely.

Ruby served boiled chicken sandwiches again for dinner, and I didn't even attempt to eat them. Instead, I nuked myself some Ramen noodles, and when Saul requested it, nuked some for him, too. Ruby's sandwiches sat congealing on the platter.

After Ruby and I squabbled over who'd do the dishes and I lost, I finished them as quickly as I could. Then I left the house and walked around the compound in the fading light, admiring the flame-colored cliffs, enjoying the cool breeze wafting from Paiute Canyon. Cactus wrens called softly to one another, and in the distance, a coyote howled at the thin rising moon.

The evening radiated peace. Men leaned against the rusting hulks in Prophet's Park, talking softly to one another about the burdens of the day, while on the porches, their white-aproned wives stripped freshly picked green beans and tossed them into large kettles. I knew that in the poorest households, the beans would be boiled for hours with fatback and eaten as a main dish, the sparse meal rounded out by buttered slices of cornbread.

In this dim light I couldn't see the poor quality of the buildings, the drawn faces of the women, the pregnant bellies of girls who should be worrying about nothing more momentous than the latest boy band.

And I heard the voices of the children, hundreds of them, laughing, singing. I was struck by how happy they all sounded. They were untouched by school shootings, random crime, or live broadcasts of terrorists acts. Their families, however peculiar, remained intact, and they had all the playmates they could wish for—most of them well-behaved. While their haphazard education and lack of knowledge of the way the world worked would handicap them on the Outside, they functioned well here. Each child knew exactly what kind of life lay in store for him or her. There was comfort in that, I supposed, but was it enough to offset the abuses I'd seen?

A ball rolled toward my feet and I stooped down to pick it up.

"Is this yours?" I asked a little red-headed girl I'd seen at one of the dining room tables in Ermaline's house. She liked grape jam with her biscuits, no butter.

The girl nodded, but made no move to take the ball from my outstretched hand. The children she'd been playing with suddenly formed themselves into a defensive circle.

I decided that since the mountain obviously wouldn't come to Mohammad, Mohammad would have to go to the mountain. But when I approached the little girl, she stepped away, face apprehensive.

"Don't you want it?"

She shook her head fiercely. Then she moved backward and hid herself inside her circle of friends, leaving me alone with the ball.

Lena Jones, the Untouchable.

Chapter 15

After making breakfast for Saul and Ruby the next morning (instant oatmeal and raisins, I'd given up on biscuits), I hiked down into the canyon, not stopping until I'd climbed out of the dogleg at the eastern end and onto the desert floor beyond. Soon the Purity graveyard came into view, at first appearing as haphazard rows of upright sticks bleached white by the sun. Only when you walked closer did the sticks arrange themselves into the form of crude crosses.

Tony Lomahguahu hadn't arrived yet, so I lowered my skirts, settled myself down on a rock, and enjoyed the scenery.

Above, fat white cumulus clouds wallowed across the clear, hard sky. To the north, the Vermillion Cliffs loomed so close I could almost touch them, their scarlet walls plunging at a ninety-degree angle to the desert floor below. But there the beauty ended. On the flatland, a hundred miles of dirt, scrub and cactus stretched to the east, west and south, marooning Purity on a hostile beachhead. If the compound's fathers had searched for a hundred years, they couldn't have found a more isolated place.

"Miss Jones?"

He had approached from the opposite direction so quietly I hadn't heard him.

I stood and faced Tony Lomahguahu. He had probably been tall once, but age had bowed his back and the lined skin on his mahogany-colored face resembled a dry lake bed. His brown eyes remained alert. Like everyone I'd met in the past few days, he wore a plaid shirt and denims, but unlike the plain folks at Purity, he had spiffed up his outfit with a bola tie and several turquoise rings. He could have been anywhere from seventy to ninety, but he still cared about how he looked. I liked that in a man.

"Yes, Mr. Lomahguahu. I'm Lena Jones." I didn't extend my hand. I knew little about Paiutes, but most Indians I'd met didn't touch strangers.

He nodded, and said in a softly accented voice, "Hope I can help you, Miss Jones, but I don't know much about these folks. They don't make friends with anybody who isn't as white as they are."

I gave him a wry grin. "Yes, I've noticed. And they're pretty white, aren't they? But anything you could tell me would help. My client..."

He raised a gnarled hand to stop me. "Jimmy told me about the little girl you're trying to help, and he gave me this message. He said to tell you there's trouble. Somehow that girl's father found out where she was staying." His face darkened. Apparently he didn't think much of Abel Corbett.

"That man, he told Child Protective Services the girl had been kidnapped by Indians. The family's looking at jail time if they don't turn her over to him."

I was aghast. "He can't take her from Indian land!"

"White people have taken things from Indians before, Miss Jones."

He was right, of course. Abel Corbett's house at Purity sat on the Utah side of the state line, but if necessary for his legal standing with CPS, Abel could easily move across the road to the Arizona side of the border. All the trouble Jimmy and I had gone to had only gained her an extra week of safety. Maybe that week would be enough.

"Did Jimmy's relatives tell CPS what Corbett wants to do with Rebecca? Give her to some old man as a plural wife?"

"CPS said they'd investigate, but they've got a case backlog and it'll take awhile. They said to just be patient."

I wanted to scream in frustration. By the time CPS got around to doing anything, Rebecca would be back in Purity, possibly married. I suspected that CPS's handy "case backlog" excuse was the same old see-no-evil routine that kept American polygamy thriving despite its illegality.

Once again I felt like I had so many times as a child. So many forces arrayed themselves against me that I'd be a fool not to just give up. With surrender would come peace. After all, it was hope that kept you awake at night, hope that kept your hands trembling in the daylight. Hope that if you struggled hard enough, things would somehow, in some way get better. Peace came only to those people who had learned the bitterest lesson of life: acceptance.

"Never accept evil!"

With a shock, I recognized my mother's voice, long lost to memory. Bewildered, I looked around to see, of course, no one other than Lomahguahu and miles of cactus. My mind had merely been playing tricks on me again. Still, it seemed strange to think that the monster who'd almost killed me had said something so moral. Then again, maybe she'd been reading a super heroes comic book aloud.

I pulled myself back to the present to see Tony Lomahguahu watching me.

I flushed. "I thought...I thought I heard a voice."

He studied me carefully. "These voices, they can tell us important things."

"Not this voice, Mr. Lomahguahu." Too well I remembered the gun my mother had aimed at me, the sound of the gunshot, the terrible pain. No, my mother had nothing to tell me that I ever wanted to hear, vagrant memory be damned.

He shifted his eyes to the graveyard. "I hear voices, too. Young voices that cry out when the wind blows strong."

"Young voices? What do you mean, Mr. Lomahguahu?"

He didn't answer, just motioned for me to follow and set off across the hardscrabble ground toward a row of particularly shabby crosses, most of them smaller than the others.

"This is where the voices come from," Lomahguahu said. "They tell their stories to anyone who will listen."

"But I..." I was going to tell him that I didn't talk to ghosts, but then I remembered the time not so long ago when a murderer had abandoned me in the desert to die. For three days I had talked to all sorts of ghosts, the Hohokam, a coyote, even the ghost of a red-headed man who might have been my father. Hallucinations, of course. Nothing else.

"Speak to the dead and they will answer," Lomahguahu said. He motioned toward one of the small crosses.

I knelt down. The inscription, which appeared to have been carved by a pen knife, then stained with ink, was still read-able.

Annabella Royal, Nov. 12, 1991-Nov. 30, 1991, beloved daughter of Solomon and Martha. Next to it were three more small crosses carved by the same hand: Carolina Augusta Royal, Oct. 20, 1992-Oct. 25, 1992, beloved daughter of Solomon and Martha. Stephen Raymond Royal, beloved son of Solomon and Martha, August 31, 1993-August 31, 1993. Elias John Royal, Nov. 15, 1994-Nov. 15, 1994.

I counted the months between births. Martha had hardly time to recover from each one before she'd become pregnant again. So much for the theory that lactation protected women from pregnancy. The graves of the first two babies showed they had died after only a few days of life, but the last two had died the day they'd been born. Remembering Martha's robust appearance, her Valkyrie-like beauty, I was once again reminded that appearances could be deceiving. Not that her obvious health difficulties had made any difference to Solomon. Apparently, he'd just kept shoving those little buns in her overworked oven, leaving it to her to pop them out on schedule.

"The children's voices cry on the wind," Lomahguahu said. "Can you not hear them?"

I shook my head. "I don't hear a thing. But, *damn*, Mr. Lomahguahu, did you read those birth dates?"

He shrugged, his face betraying none of the outrage I knew mine did. "All the men of Purity believe that the more children they have, the better life they'll have in Highest Heaven. I imagine they think their wives' unhappiness is a fair trade for such riches."

A fair trade. I turned away from the tiny graves and faced him. "Are you serious?"

"That's the way they see it." He shrugged again, as if he had long ago stopped trying to understand the ways of his neighbors. Then he said something I didn't understand. At the time.

"The children will speak when you are ready to listen."

We stayed at the graveyard for several more minutes as I strolled among the handmade crosses. While I was no expert on the benefits of neonatal care, it was obvious that the women and children of Purity would have benefited from some. Too bad Solomon eschewed the advances of modern medicine and relied upon prayer to treat his flock. Maybe Davis would change all that.

Solomon himself lay buried on the cemetery's highest point, his professionally carved granite slab protected by a low, wrought iron fence.

Prophet Solomon Royal, God's Own Prophet to the Community of Purity. Lifted up into the Highest Heaven.

Highest Heaven, my ass. If an afterlife truly existed, the manipulative old goat was probably warming his toes in the deepest regions of Hell.

Saul sat waiting on the front porch when I got back, a grim expression on his face.

"Lena, I just received a visit from the Circle of Elders. They nullified our marriage an hour ago. They're saying that if you want to stay here, you have to find another husband. You've got twenty-four hours to do it in, because they can't allow two unmarried people to live together. That would be a sin."

I was so appalled that I forgot to hike up my long skirts as I mounted the porch steps, and caught my heel in the hem. If Saul hadn't reached out and grabbed me, I would have fallen on my face. As it was, he had to help me to the porch swing, where I sat in silence for a few moments, composing myself.

"Can they do that?" I finally managed. "Nullify a legally performed marriage?"

He nodded. "As far as the rules of Purity go, damn right they can. Remember, the Circle doesn't respect anyone's laws but their own, so unless Davis says otherwise, they can do anything they want. Don't get your hopes up there, either. I've seen Davis looking at you, and something tells me he wouldn't mind your being available, you understand me? Besides, I think he's biding his time until the next Circle meeting, where I hear he's really going to kick some ass. Cynthia's situation, well, that was an exception, partially because he doesn't much care for Earl Graff. Earl and Davis are cousins, you know. Had a bad falling out just after Solomon was killed, mainly over the more liberal direction Davis wanted to take the compound in."

"Cousins? Davis and Earl? The hunk and the pig?"

"Their mothers were sisters. Just about everyone around here is related in some way or another, you know that. Earl looks like his mother, except she was a lot prettier than him. Royal looks like his father."

I held my head in my hands. "Cousins. Oh, Jesus. It just keeps getting weirder and weirder." I sat in the swing for a while, letting the breeze whispering down the Vermillion Cliffs cool my hot face. When I felt collected enough, I turned toward him and asked the question I should have asked immediately.

"So tell me, my dear ex-husband, why did the Council of Elders take it upon themselves to nullify our marriage?"

He blushed, and after a few stammering false starts, said, "Um, Ruby, um, you remember that she does the laundry?"

I raised my eyebrows. "And?"

"Well, she, um, Ruby noticed, she noticed…"

He looked so miserable I decided to give him a break and finished for him. "She deducted, my dear Watson, that we weren't having sex because there were no semen stains on the sheets."

He smiled weakly. "She wasn't going to say anything, but Brother Earl cornered her when she was visiting one of her cousins at his house…"

"At his house?"

"Yeah, Earl's married to Pearl, her cousin. Anyway, Earl started cross-examining her about you and me, and he scared her so bad she broke down and told him. So Earl told the rest of the guys in the Circle."

Poor Ruby. Although we'd never hit it off, I sympathized with her dilemma. She didn't want to tattle on her husband, but at the same time, Earl could have scared Dracula. I sighed. "So I've got a big twenty-four hours to find a new husband or get the hell out of Dodge."

"Better start hustling, honey."

I stared off at the Vermillion Cliffs. Saul joined me and we both sat there miserably for a while. Then he eventually said, "I'm sorry it didn't work out, Lena. I really did try to help."

I reached over and took his callused hand. It felt cold. "I know you did. It's all been my fault, really. I just couldn't keep my mouth shut."

He squeezed my hand. "Or your fist out of another man's face."

"It was the edge of my hand, not my fist. But yeah, you're right. Maybe if I hadn't smashed Earl Graff's nose this wouldn't have happened."

We fell silent again, and after a while, saw several women carrying babies climb into a van that pulled into Prophet's Park. Among them I recognized Rosalinda, Earl's wife, and a couple of Prophet Solomon's widows. All had given birth since I'd arrived in the compound.

"You don't mean to tell me Earl's making Rosalinda go shopping already, do you? The poor girl just had her baby only a few days ago!"

Saul grunted. "That trip's about more important things than groceries, Lena. Brother Vernon's taking the new mothers to sign up for welfare."

"You're kidding."

"I'm not kidding. According to the law, they're unmarried, remember? That makes them eligible for Aid to Dependent Children, or whatever it's called these days. A couple of the older women there, they gave birth to Downs Syndrome babies, and their husbands are all excited. Downs kids bring more money, because not only does the mom get the ADC, she gets extra benefits because of their medical problems. Now that Davis is going to let these folks keep more of their welfare checks, a Downs baby is great news for the dads."

I felt revolted at this crass commercialization of tragedy, and told him so.

"That's the way it is here, Lena. You know Hanna, the gal with the bad limp? She's one of the Arizona contingent. She had her baby this morning while you were gone, and if it lives, she'll go to the county seat in Plattville next week to apply for her benefits. Her baby will get extra money, too."

I frowned. "What do you mean, if the baby lives?"

"None of her others did. She's had about six of them, I think, and all died right after birth. I hear this one's got some real serious problems, too. The Circle of Elders was over there at the clinic all morning praying over it."

I didn't even bother asking why Hanna and the baby hadn't been taken to the hospital. After more than a week in Purity, I knew why. Would proper medical care help the poor thing?

The van drove off but we continued sitting there until I heard a rumbling noise. I looked up at the sky and saw that masses of dirty-looking clouds had gathered. But they didn't appear dark enough yet for thunder.

"Saul, was that your stomach?"

He grinned. "Nobody nukes Ramen like you do, wife."

After we'd eaten, Ruby asked me to help with the dishes. I almost refused, but then I saw the expression on her face.

"I'm so sorry, Sister Lena," she finally said, as I dried the three forks and glasses she'd taken so long to wash. "I didn't mean to tell, really I didn't, but Brother Earl is pretty persuasive." Her eyes lowered to her wrist, bare now since she'd rolled back her sleeve to wash the dishes. I saw a man-sized bruise.

I clenched my fist. "It's all right, Ruby. I know what you're up against."

"No, you don't." She said little more.

The next morning I rose to a new resolve. After dressing hurriedly and pouring cereal for three, I headed out the door toward Davis Royal's house.

A bewildered Sissy Royal, overcome by my insistence, led me to his office. As soon as she shut the door behind us, I asked him the question.

"Brother Davis, will you marry me?"

Chapter 16

"Why Sister Lena, I didn't know you cared," Davis said, a bemused smile on his handsome face. "May I ask what brought about this sudden declaration of love?"

I sat down on the big leather sofa. "It's not really a declaration of love. It's just that…"

My voice trailed off. Davis wasn't stupid. To make him believe my wild tale, it needed to smack of reality, and the only way to do that was to tell as much truth as possible. But how much? I obviously couldn't tell him everything, that during the long, fearful night I'd come to the realization that to save Rebecca, I'd screw the devil himself. Not that Prophet Davis was the devil. Far from it. From what I had observed, he was the only polygamist who had shown a shred of compassion toward women. He certainly didn't have any thirteen-year-old "wives," and to his credit, had ordered the practice halted.

Start with the truth, then. I took a big breath. "Brother Davis, I'm a desperate woman." No lie there.

He lifted one blond eyebrow. Damn, the devil was good-looking. "Desperate? How so?"

I filled him in on the Circle of Elder's decision not to sanctify the marriage between Saul and myself, and then I added my own spin, mentally apologizing to Saul as I did so.

"Saul, well, he's an older man, and, well…"

Davis nodded. "I understand. It's a more common problem than women realize. But when it happens, the poor things believe it's all their fault."

Had the man been reading *Cosmopolitan?* Or did he speak from experience? My surprise must have shown on my face.

"Sister Lena, several women have discussed their marital relationships with me. You may not know this, but when I assumed the role of prophet, I married two widows, women who had been the wives of elderly men. They had both endured situations such as yours."

His smile was gentle, his blue eyes calming. Encouraged, I plunged ahead. "Then you understand it's so very, very wrong for the Circle to punish me." I threw out my hands, trying to look pathetic. "Brother Davis, I want to be obedient to the rule of Purity, but I'll admit that unlike the women who were raised here, I've been out in the world and sometimes those rules are hard for me. I've done wicked, sinful things, and I really messed up my life." Mimicking shame, I ducked my head.

When I peeped up again, the expression on Davis's Greek-god face told me I'd made an impact, so I continued my tale of woe. "If I have to leave Purity, God knows what's going to happen to me! I want to stay, I really do! I want to lead a good life, a Godly life. But I know that the only way I can stay here is to be married. You only have, what, six wives? I'd be a good wife to you."

A faint smile played about his well-sculpted lips. It was no trouble imagining them pressed to mine. But only if that's what it took to save Rebecca, of course.

"Sister Lena, I hear you're not a very good cook."

"No, Brother Davis, I'm not. But I can do other things." I allowed a sultry note to enter my voice and leaned forward, making my breasts strain against the cheap fabric of my dress.

Davis wasn't blind. A fine sheen of perspiration appeared on his brow. He crossed his legs and cleared his throat. "Other things?"

My performance would have done a hooker proud. "Believe me, Brother Davis, if you take me for your wife, you won't be disappointed. And if you want me to learn how to cook, I'll learn how to cook. I almost know how to make biscuits."

He threw back his glorious head and laughed. "That's not what I hear!"

I laughed back.

He wiped his brow and shifted in his seat. As if seeking to remind himself that my body wasn't perfect, his eyes flickered to the scar on my face. "Women can do other jobs around here, Sister Lena. You went to college, didn't you?"

I blinked in surprise. Was it that obvious? Yes, I had graduated with honors from Arizona State University, but there was no way I'd admit to that, so I hurriedly disavowed my alma mater.

"Well, I took some courses at a community college. History, mainly, and English. Some economics. I wasn't the world's greatest student, though." Actually, my grade point average had been 3.8, not bad for a kid who'd lived like a gypsy in more than a dozen foster homes.

"You could teach at the school."

"Without a degree?"

He leaned toward me, his knees touching mine. "Sister Lena, none of our teachers have even graduated from high school, and it's been a growing source of concern to me. Knowing that one day I'd assume his own role as prophet, my dear father sent me to Utah State University to study economics, but the experience transformed me in ways he didn't foresee. I came back a changed man. Now I'm convinced that so many of Purity's problems are traceable to lack of education. Yes, I know my father believed God would teach us everything we needed to know. But I think God needs a helping hand every now and then, don't you? After all, that's why God gave us brains—to use.

"Now here you are, an obviously educated woman, a woman seeking a higher calling in life, a woman so desperate to learn God's teachings that she is willing to marry a man she hardly knows, a man she does not love."

He leaned even closer to me and as he took my hand, I caught a heady combination of soap and sweat emanating from his pores. "Don't look so surprised, Sister Lena. I know you're not in love with me, but that is perfectly acceptable. After all, few marriages around at Purity begin with love, especially on the woman's side."

His hand closed tightly around mine. "Oh, yes, I am well aware it's panic and nothing else which brought you to me with your generous offer, but that doesn't mean I don't take your offer seriously. There's good sense in your desires, both the good sense of a woman's natural need for a man, and the good sense of a woman who with all her problems still desires to serve God. Admirable, truly admirable."

While one hand continued to clasp mine, the other slid slowly up my arm and caressed my shoulder in a soft, circular motion. When he drew me toward him, my body leaned forward to meet his. God help me, at that particular moment, I wasn't acting.

His lips, just before they closed on mine, whispered, "Sister Lena, eagles mate with eagles, not with mice."

Only half-acting, I reached toward him.

"Brother Davis! Brother Davis!" Sissy's insistent voice and loud bangs on the office door made us both jump.

Davis drew back but didn't let go of my hand. "I am counseling Sister Lena, wife," he called. "Please do not disturb me."

"But Brother Davis, the Circle of Elders is here," she called. "They need to see you right away! Something about Brother Saul and Sister Lena!"

Davis rose, pulling me up with him. "I can imagine what they want to tell me, can't you, Sister Lena?"

I pressed against him, inhaling his scent. It had been a long time since I'd been with a man.

"Yes, Brother Davis," I whispered. "I can."

When Davis announced our engagement, the Circle didn't like it, but most of them knew better than to argue with the compound's new prophet.

Earl Graff scowled, and I noted happily that his eyes were blacker than mine. And was it my imagination, or did he sport scratches on his face, too? I didn't remember putting them there. Maybe my nails needed trimming.

"You can't be serious, Brother Davis!" Graff protested, ignoring the warning whispers of the other men. "The woman is...she's..."

"Watch what you say about my intended wife," Davis warned. "She is dear to me and therefore must be dear to you. Do I need to remind you that you brought your problems with her upon yourself? Brother Graff, Purity's women are to be cherished, not struck."

"But..."

"Brother Graff, have you returned Sister Cynthia to her mother?"

"No, I..."

"Then do so immediately."

"But the Circle of Elders performed the marriage ceremony last night! *Sister Cynthia is now my wife!*"

Davis dropped his arm from around my waist and took a step toward Earl. He towered over the piggy man by at least eight inches, and it was gratifying to see the little thug shrink back. Not gratifying enough, however, to keep the image of the terrified Cynthia out of my mind. What had that monster done to her?

Davis grabbed Graff by the throat. "Then you disobeyed the direct order I gave you. Why did you do that?"

Earl gagged and choked until Davis loosened his grip slightly. "I…I convened the Circle of Elders, and we decided that since Prophet Solomon promised her to me, I might as well go ahead and marry her."

Davis's eyes narrowed. "That prophet is dead. I, as the new prophet, hereby annul your marriage and demand that you release that girl to her mother. To make certain you follow my orders this time, I'm returning to your house with you, and I'll escort Cynthia back to her mother's myself. Woe be to you, Brother Earl, if Sister Cynthia has one mark upon her person."

"But she…I had to…She…"

Without another word, Davis released his hand from around Earl's throat and grabbed his collar. Half shoving, half pulling, he hustled the cowering man out the door and toward his house. We all ran after them, across the dirt circle to the Arizona side, and up the stairs of the tar-papered hovel Earl called home. The front door, barely attached to its hinges, flew open with one shove of Davis's huge hand.

"Sister Cynthia!" Davis bellowed, as unkempt children scattered everywhere. Three very pregnant women stared at us, wiping their hands on their aprons. "Sister Cynthia. It's Davis Royal! I'm here to take you home!"

One of Earl's wives said nervously, "Our new sister wife isn't feeling well this morning, Brother Davis."

Another wife, a tall, sharp-featured woman who'd hung back in the doorway of the kitchen, threw a look of utter hatred toward Earl. "She had a bad night," she said. When Earl turned his eyes toward her, she pretended great interest in the worn linoleum, but her expression didn't change.

"Sister Pearl, you fetch Sister Cynthia," Davis commanded. "Now."

"Certainly, Brother Davis. But I might need a helping hand." Her eyes flicked toward me. "Perhaps Sister Lena…?"

I took my cue, noticing with interest that the woman knew my name. "Certainly I'll help, Sister Pearl. Where is she?"

"Follow me."

She led me down an unpainted, dark hall lit only by a single bare bulb dangling from a cord, and finally stopped before a cheap pine door.

"Don't be surprised at anything you see," she said, her voice flat. "Our husband isn't the gentlest of men."

When Pearl opened the door to the bedroom, I saw that what I had done to Earl Graff had been revisited a hundred fold upon Cynthia. The girl's beautiful face had been battered almost beyond recognition. Both eyes were swollen shut. Teeth marks covered her cheeks and neck.

"Brother Earl likes to bite," Pearl said, matter-of-factly. "You probably don't want to see what's beneath the covers."

I felt sick.

Pearl studied the wrecked room, the broken lamp, a shattered mirror, and a million feathers from shredded pillows. "Looks like she put up a fight, never a good idea with Earl. Those of us who've been around here awhile know it's better to just let him do what he wants and get it over with as fast as possible."

Maybe so, but I couldn't help but hope that Cynthia had taken a piece out of Brother Earl where it really counted.

I walked over to the bed and leaned over the girl. "Cynthia, it's Lena. Brother Davis just annulled your marriage to Earl. I'm here to take you home."

Cynthia forced her swollen eyes open, and I could still see burst capillaries in both of them. The whites had turned to blood. But her voice sounded strong. "I'm not sure I can walk."

"We'll help you, dear," Sister Pearl said, slipping an arm under her.

As Sister Pearl raised the girl up, the covers fell away. We both gasped. Bite marks sprinkled Cynthia's breasts and abdomen. Fist-sized bruises covered her entire body in huge, dirty polka-dots.

"My dress," Cynthia whispered. "Please."

Pearl reached for the torn garment at the foot of the bed, but I stopped her.

"No! I want them to see her. I want them to see what they've allowed to happen to women in Purity!" Turning back to Cynthia I asked, "Do you have the courage?"

Her poor, battered face contorted. "Let them see me? But I'm so ashamed."

"The shame is his, not yours. Let them see. *Let everyone see.*"

Pearl put her hand on my shoulder. "Sister Lena, are you sure about this? After what the poor child has been through it seems cruel."

"Cruel? Let me tell you what's cruel, Sister Pearl. Covering up situations like this, *that's* what's cruel! I'm so sick and tired of everyone pretending they're living in Paradise. There's plenty of snakes in this so-called Garden of Eden and I want them rooted out. I want…"

I forced myself back under control. What I wanted was the entire compound wiped off the face of the earth, the women and children sent to shelters and the men to prison— but not before I'd found Prophet Solomon's killer and removed Rebecca from harm's way.

I swallowed my rage as best I could. "Sister Pearl, I've talked to Brother Davis about the problems some of the women are having here, and he agrees with me that something needs to be done. If he sees how bad things really are, I'm sure he'll take steps. But…" I turned back to Cynthia. "But he has to *see* first! He has to see what happened to you. And the other men on the Council, they have to see, too."

Cynthia groaned. "No man has ever seen my body, I mean, until Brother Earl…"

Then Sister Pearl surprised me. "God created your body, dear, and God does not create anything of which we need to be ashamed."

Cynthia lay quietly for a moment, then took a deep breath and nodded her head. "You're right, Sister Pearl. If you think it'll do any good, I'll do it. My body's no different than any of the other bodies I've been studying in my anatomy books. Those men out there are all married, aren't they? They've seen it all before?"

"Yeah, they have." I would have hugged her for her courage, but I was too afraid I'd hurt her.

Sister Pearl wasn't quite so delicate. She leaned over the girl and said, "Put your arms around me, Sister Cynthia, and I'll help you up."

I rushed forward to help, and between the two of us, we managed to get the girl to her feet and wrap her in a flimsy robe we found in the closet.

"I'm going to close my eyes, though," Cynthia whispered, as we helped her walk to the door. "I don't want to see them...I don't want to see them see me."

Pearl gave her the hug I'd feared to. "You're very brave, dear. Don't worry. Sister Lena and I will make sure that you'll be okay."

Pearl threw me a pleading look and I nodded. Yes, I'd make sure Cynthia would be okay, even if it meant escorting her out of the compound with a gun. But hopefully, it wouldn't come to that. Royal was the wild card in the equation.

We shuffled Cynthia down the hall and into the living room, where the men waited with their backs to us as they spoke in low tones to Earl Graff.

I broke up their little party. "Do you see?" I shouted to them, opening Cynthia's robe so that her bitten, bruised body was visible. "Do you see what that bastard did to her?"

When they turned, their faces paled.

"My God. My God." Davis breathed. "I never thought..."

The other men gaped as if they'd never seen a battered girl before, although if I were a betting woman, I'd have bet they had: their own child-brides.

"Brother Earl?" one of them gasped, looking toward the little man. "Why did you do that to her?"

"She fell down!"

Before I could call him a liar myself, Davis moved swiftly across the room and punched Graff in his nose, felling him. But where I had smacked Graff just the once, Royal hauled him up by the shirt front and punched him again. And again. He kept punching him until the other members of the Circle of Elders pulled him off the bleeding, moaning man.

"Brother Davis, don't kill him!" one of them begged. "We can't have the sheriff called out again, it looks bad! Let the Circle take care of this problem."

I wanted to stay and find out what "take care of" meant, but Pearl whispered in my ear, "We've done what we needed to do. Now let's get the poor child cleaned up and dressed." To Cynthia, she said, "You've been a good, brave girl, dear. I'm proud of you."

Undone by Pearl's gentle voice, Cynthia finally allowed herself to cry.

Back at the house, Saul listened to the story in horror.

"I always suspected Brother Earl was rough on his wives, but damn, Lena! That's disgusting!"

"You'll notice that nobody said anything about taking Graff's other wives away from him," I pointed out. "Not even Davis."

"Lena, something has to be done about this!" Saul paced back and forth in the living room, his arms swinging in a jerky manner like a marionette's. "It can't be allowed to continue!"

I shook my head wearily. "It'll continue as long as the law allows it, you know that. As for me, Saul, I have a job to do and that job isn't to lead a revolution in Purity. It's to find Solomon's killer and get Rebecca's mother out of jail. Afterward, well, it may sound cold, but I've got a detective agency to run."

He stopped pacing and spun back around toward me. "So what about this marriage deal you've got going with Davis Royal? You really going to do it?"

I grimaced. "Who knows? I'll do whatever's necessary to help Rebecca. Anyway, my intended fiancé says I can stay here until he divorces Sissy, since my virtue's so obviously safe with you. Then the Circle of Elders will perform the marriage ceremony. Davis says that by this time next week, we'll be man and wife. Make that man and wives."

It didn't bother me that Royal would divorce Sissy, because the divorce meant nothing. The Purity system was about concubinage, not marriage. She'd still belong to him.

Saul interrupted my thoughts. "So you've got a week now to figure out who killed Prophet Solomon. That's not much."

"It's a week longer than I had this morning."

He dropped to the sofa beside me and gave me a bleak grin. "Sure wish you'd come up with a better reason to explain our lack of sex. You just put a major crimp in my social life."

I smiled back. "I don't think the story of your so-called impotence will leave Purity with you. Which reminds me. I've been so worried about my own situation that I've neglected yours. How's the lawsuit going?"

"The hearing is tomorrow, Lena, and my attorney says there's not much hope. There's a good chance I'll need to pack up and leave Purity by the time you get married, if that's what you're really going to do."

Now my glum face matched his. "Aren't we the happy couple?"

Jimmy had done his part by giving me the backgrounds of the Purity men, including Solomon himself, and now it was up to me to put it all together. Who had most benefited from the Prophet's death?

The answer wasn't long in coming.

Davis Royal. The new prophet of Purity.

Chapter 17

Since Prophet Solomon's death, Davis Royal had assumed total command of the compound's vast financial resources. And while Davis might be not quite as rapacious in his attitude toward the compound's young women, it was obvious he enjoyed the standard perks that came with leadership.

Who better to wear the mantle of murderer?

I tried to convince myself that I didn't care if Davis turned out to be the murderer, but I'm not sure I succeeded. Sure, he was as seductive as the Devil himself, but at the end of the day, what true value lay in good looks and a gentle touch?

Then again…

"Sister Lena, aren't you going to make lunch?" Ruby's voice interrupted my thoughts. She stood in the doorway to the kitchen, her long, faded dress almost trailing the floor. I recognized it as the same dress she'd worn yesterday. But now I also understood why. Many of the women in the compound had learned to make themselves look as undesirable as possible.

"Sister Lena?" Ruby tapped her toe impatiently.

But I had some serious thinking to do and couldn't be bothered with all that cooking nonsense. A good, long walk might help me collect my thoughts.

"You'll have to make lunch yourself, Sister Ruby," I said. "I told our husband that I'd run a little errand for him."

Saul looked up from the recorder, where he was taping another letter to his sailor son. "Yes. Yes, you did, Sister Lena."

Ruby's face tightened, but she headed for the kitchen as I headed for the door.

In mere minutes I had reached the silence of the canyon. I kept walking until I came to the small grove where Rebecca and I had found Solomon's body. Hoping that the site of the murder would give me more insight, I perched on a rock and stared at the small depression that remained in the sand. Solomon had been shot at close range, probably by someone he trusted.

Perhaps that was the key: trust. Solomon would have trusted his son Davis. Then again, with the naïveté of the truly self-centered, the old man probably trusted just about everyone at the compound: his wives, his other children, even the Circle of Elders. In fact, just about the only person Solomon deemed untrustworthy had been Saul, the compound's rebel. Try as I would, I couldn't imagine Saul finding Solomon in the canyon, asking to borrow his shotgun for a moment, then turning around and firing both barrels.

I could discount the compound's children, of course, but that still left me with dozens of men and their various and sundry wives. If I couldn't pin the murder on Davis, Esther and Rebecca would be in a world of hurt. I could theorize about Davis's guilt all I wanted, but theories didn't count in court. Only proof did. Not that any accusation I might make would even get to a jury in the state of Utah, where Prophet Solomon's body had been found. I'd already seen firsthand Sheriff Benson's collusion with the Circle of Elders. The sheriff would cut off his own right arm before he'd drag the polygamists into court just on the word of some out-of-state detective.

No, I couldn't go to Benson with a bag full of theories. I'd need to present irrefutable proof that Davis killed his father. But how?

As the breeze freshened, blowing down from the north with warnings of cool autumn winds to follow, I thought I heard voices. I held my breath and listened carefully, blocking out the sounds of the cactus wrens and hawks. Two men. As the voices came closer and I began to make them out, I could tell that one of the men was old, the other young. Unless I was mistaken, the older man was Jacob Waldman, Rebecca's grandfather. The younger one was Meade Royal. Hunting for rabbits again?

While I doubted that I had anything to fear from those two, Jacob being too far gone in dementia, and Meade being too young to entertain the requisite motives, my days on the compound had made me distrust most males. I looked around for a hiding place and soon found a shallow indentation in the canyon wall, half-hidden by a creosote bush and blooming snakeweed. Trying to keep my feet from kicking up any loose rocks, I hustled over there and squeezed myself into the shallow cave.

Just in time.

Jacob Waldman and Meade Royal rounded the bend in the canyon, deep in conversation. Meade carried a small rifle, and had two dead rabbits slung over his shoulder.

"Uncle Jacob, you must not blame yourself for anything that has happened. Some of these events must be left to God and his justice." Meade sounded wise for his years, even though during each sentence, his voice wobbled from tenor to baritone and back again.

"It is a father's duty to make his daughter obey!" the old man argued. "If I'd tried harder, I could have stopped Esther and Abel from leaving the compound. Then Rebecca would have been born here, under my protection, and none of this would have happened!"

Interesting. Old Brother Jacob was apparently having one of his more lucid moments, but time had taught me not to read too much into one sentence. As the two passed me and rounded another bend in the canyon, their voices began to fade. If I wanted to hear the rest of their conversation, I'd have to follow. I snatched up some of the yellow snakeweed blooms at my feet, hoping they would provide me with a good excuse for being in the canyon if the two became aware of my presence. As I hurried after them, trying to keep from dislodging any rocks, their conversation continued to intrigue.

"God is punishing me because I loved her so," Jacob said, his voice catching.

"Fathers are supposed to love their daughters," Meade's voice soothed. "There's no sin in that."

Suddenly Jacob's voice changed in timbre, assuming the eerie conviction of an Old Testament prophet. "There is if the daughter is Satan's whore!"

He was losing it again, but that didn't mean I wouldn't hear anything illuminating. Just the contrary. Under certain circumstances, even the ravings of madmen could be helpful.

More soothing sounds from Meade, tinged with an edge of fear, and I realized for the first time that the boy was afraid of his uncle.

"Uncle Jacob, God will punish Sister Esther for leaving us. You don't have to…"

"You are wrong, boy!" Jacob roared. "It is a father's duty to punish a wicked daughter, just as it is to punish a wicked son. The Old Testament in its wisdom talks about stoning disobedient children to death. God demands blood atonement! Only blood atonement can wash away the stains of evil! Without it we would *all* wind up in Hell, not just the sinner!"

"Please, Uncle Jacob…"

Now Meade sounded downright terrified and his voice broke on every other word. I patted my thigh to make certain my .38 hadn't dislodged as I scrambled through the canyon. Still there. Relieved, I continued to eavesdrop on Jacob's ravings.

"I meted out blood atonement to the other one and it freed her soul, so why was I so lax with Esther? Why did I allow her rebellion to continue?"

The other one?

"Sin is a virus which infects us all!" Jacob's rachety old voice rose to a screech, and I wondered if they could hear him all the way back at the compound. "The prophet himself, our own holy prophet! He was blinded by her beauty, blinded by her sin!"

Wait a minute. Who was he talking about now? Esther? Rebecca? Or someone else?

As quickly as Jacob's voice had risen, it lowered. Soon I had to strain to hear him.

"That's when our prophet gave in to sin himself, you know, and joined the ranks of Satan. If he hadn't sinned, he would have lived forever!"

"Uncle Jacob…" Meade's voice rose into falsetto. "You can't…"

"But unlike the prophet, I was wise to Satan's lures. I took the vengeance of God into my hands and washed her sins away in her own blood. The blood, the very color of the blood…"

"Uncle Jacob, please don't let anybody hear you talk like that! It, it could be taken all wrong!"

I killed her, I washed her sins away in her own blood. Had Jacob actually killed someone, and if so, who? Or was the murder merely a figment of his increasing dementia?

"Why, Meade! What are we doing here in the canyon?" Jacob's voice again, but this time calm. In the bizarre pattern of Alzheimer's, the old man's dementia had cleared, returning to a moment of lucidity. How long that would last was anybody's guess.

I heard Meade sigh. "We went to visit the graveyard, Uncle Jacob. And then we came up here and hunted for a while. See? I shot two rabbits? But after awhile you, uh, began feeling sick. We're on our way back home now."

Murmurs I couldn't quite catch. Then, "You're a good boy, Meade."

"Thank you, Uncle Jacob." Never had I heard such despair in a boy's voice.

The rest of the walk down the canyon proved uneventful. Jacob's Alzheimer's allowed him a time of respite, and his conversation with Meade appeared more or less normal—for a polygamy compound, anyway: who was marrying whom, the health problems of Sister Hanna's new baby, lamentations over a parasite that was attacking the stored grain.

There seemed to be little I could learn from them now, so I dropped back to make certain they'd arrive at the compound before me. A hollow rumble made me look up. Thunder. While I'd been in the canyon, fat black clouds had rumbled down from the north, bringing the promise of rain. With rain, I realized, came the flash floods that turned so many of the Arizona Strip's canyons into death traps.

Hurry, hurry, hurry, I mentally goaded Jacob and Meade, But they, too, had heard the thunder. Their footsteps quickened, then began to fade as they drew farther away from me. I gave them a few minutes, time enough to get back to the compound, then hurried my own pace, emerging from the canyon just as the first drops of rain began to fall.

I allowed myself a little jog trot as I hurried toward Saul's house. After the heat of the past few days, the rain felt cold and it reminded me that autumn, and then winter, weren't that far away. Winter would be a different season up here in the high desert than back in Scottsdale. A sudden wave of homesickness swept over me.

A battered Ford pickup truck I hadn't seen before drove into the compound just as I reached Saul's porch. I watched it pull in front of Jacob Waldman's house.

A young man and a girl emerged, but because of the increasing ferocity of the rain, it took me a minute to recognize the girl.

Rebecca.

Chapter 18

I ducked my head and ran into the house before Rebecca could recognize me and give me away. Fortunately, Ruby was nowhere to be seen, and Saul, after looking up briefly from the tape recorder, returned to it.

Confident that the shadows on the porch would make peering into the window difficult, I pulled back the window sheers and looked out. It was Rebecca, all right, and the man with her was Abel Corbett himself. She didn't appear frightened, either. When I'd first seen her alight from the truck, I'd taken it for granted that her father had kidnapped her once again, but as I watched her more closely, I began to doubt that scenario. Rebecca looked much too relaxed.

Happy to be with her father? Happy to be back on the compound with her friends? I couldn't help but notice the joy of the compound's children as they braved the increasingly heavy downpour and swarmed around their playmate as Rebecca and Abel hurried toward Jacob Waldman's house. Whatever the answer, I had to contact her somehow before she gave my presence in the compound away. If she hadn't already done so.

I turned from the window and cleared my throat. "Husband, could I have a word with you?"

He looked up. "Can't I just listen to this?"

"I need to talk to you about something, um, private."

Grumbling, he started down the hall to the bedroom. I followed, eager to avoid Ruby. The second Saul closed the bedroom door behind us, I told him what he needed to do.

"So you want me to go see Rebecca and warn her not to let the cat out of the bag? Considering the fact that I'm about as popular in this compound as you are, how do you figure I'm going to do that? Just walk over to Brother Jacob's and tell him I need to be alone with his granddaughter for a few minutes? Fat chance, Lena."

He was right. If Jacob Waldman had his wits about him today, he probably wouldn't even open the door to Saul, let alone allow a meeting with Rebecca. This meant I'd have to find a way to catch Rebecca alone myself, and as soon as possible.

For once, the Fates were on my side. An hour later the rain stopped. Children drifted slowly out of doors again and headed with Rebecca toward the playground. After making sure that no adults lurked about to hear any surprised exclamation she might utter, I left the house, forcing myself to look as if I were merely taking another of my canyon strolls. I ambled several yards behind the children until they reached a large open space between the houses, then quickened my pace until I caught up with Rebecca.

"Rebecca, please don't react or say anything," I said quietly, coming alongside her. "I don't want anyone to realize we know each other."

For a moment, I thought I'd blown it, because Rebecca stopped dead in her tracks, her face lit with joy. But then my words sank in and she smiled at her friends and started walking toward the playground again. Intent upon their own fun, they hadn't noticed the exchange.

"I'm going to continue on to the mesquite grove at the edge of the canyon. Play with your friends for a while, then come find me."

Her lips hardly moved as she whispered, "Don't go in the canyon, though, okay? It floods pretty bad when it rains."

Her concern renewed my confidence in her. "Don't worry. I know all about it."

About twenty minutes later, Rebecca joined me under a dripping mesquite, her face flushed and happy. She gave me a big hug. "Oh, Lena! It's so great to see you again! I missed you!"

"I've missed you too, but I can't say I'm happy to see you here. Don't you realize the dangerous position you've put me in? Your mother in?"

Her smile faded. "Yes, I know the position I've put my mother *and* Jimmy's cousins in. That's why I'm here. I heard the CPS people talking to them, saying they had to give me up. But Lena, they refused to! They said CPS could haul them all off to jail before they gave me back to my dad."

"Rebecca, CPS couldn't..."

She didn't let me finish. "My mom's already in jail and I didn't want the same thing to happen to them. Or you, either. I can't keep letting people get in trouble over me."

I shook my head. "The last thing your mother wants is for you to move back to Purity."

"But that's the whole point, don't you see? Everyone believes my mother killed Prophet Solomon to keep me out of Purity, but I figured that if I made everyone think I'm not afraid of this place at all, they'd realize Mom had no reason to kill him."

I digested this. "You really think that'll fly in court?"

She nodded. "It was the least I could do for her. So I called Dad at his hotel and told him to meet me at the old Circle K on the reservation, then I snuck away."

"Oh, Rebecca. Weren't you worried your dad might try to marry you off again?"

Rebecca assumed that look of teenage intellectual superiority that maddens parents as well as private investigators. "You just don't understand, Lena. All I had to do was talk to Dad and let him know my feelings. I didn't have time to do that before, you know. I thought the marriage stuff was all a joke, some silly thing these old people just talked about but didn't really do. By the time I realized Dad really did plan to make me marry that old man, you showed up. Anyway, I made Dad promise he'd drop the marriage routine."

I groaned inwardly at the folly of youth. What point would there be in telling her I didn't share her trust in Abel Corbett's ability to listen to reason? Any man so morally corrupted that he'd trade his thirteen-year-old daughter to an elderly man for a couple of sixteen-year-olds had moved far beyond wisdom *or* trust. So I said nothing. But I couldn't stop thinking of those two young girls Abel Corbett had been promised in exchange for Rebecca. Solomon might be dead, but the girls were still alive and available for trade. Abel wanted them. How far would he go to get them?

Then again, Purity had a new prophet. Davis had clamped down on forced marriages to little girls. Maybe...

I pushed that hope aside. "Listen to me, Rebecca. I know you think you're doing the right thing for your mother and Jimmy's cousins, and maybe it'll even work out the way you want it to, but you need to be very, very careful."

"Believe me, I'll stay away from the Circle of Elders. I don't want them to get any weird ideas. And I'll make sure nobody figures out we know each other."

She still didn't get it. "Rebecca, it's dangerous here! Somebody on this compound murdered Prophet Solomon. If your mother didn't do it, then who did?"

A little of that naive confidence faded from her face. "I guess...I guess...A passing tramp, maybe?"

Good lord, what had she been reading? Old Nancy Drew mysteries? I tried to keep my voice steady but I wanted to grab her by the shoulders and shake her. "There are no 'passing tramps' out here, Rebecca. We're miles from civilization."

"Maybe the whole thing was one of those hunting accidents."

I hated to say what I was about to say, but it was necessary. Teenagers, untried by life's tragedies, overestimated their powers of deduction, so I pointed out the obvious. "It would be pretty hard to have a hunting accident where Prophet Solomon was standing. He was in a clear spot, not surrounded by brush. And remember, Rebecca, he was shot by his own gun. What kind of hunting accident could that be?"

She bit her lip. "He dropped his gun, maybe, and it went off?"

"And maybe space aliens will beam Purity up to Alpha Centauri during Prayer Time tonight, but I don't think so." I reached out my hand and stroked her hair. "I don't want you to be frightened, but I want you to be careful. Don't take any walks alone, promise?"

"I promise."

I didn't believe her for a minute.

The next morning I woke up depressed, but I couldn't remember my dreams, which I counted as a blessing. I could say this for a bad childhood; it certainly put the sorrows of the present into perspective.

After grabbing a quick breakfast of Special K, I wandered over to Davis Royal's house. The front door was open and I almost entered, but I heard several male voices, so I paused on the porch to listen.

"Our lost bird has flown home!" Jacob Waldman said.

"I'm very happy for you, Brother Jacob," Davis said. "It is always..."

"Yes, Purity is Rebecca's true home." Abel Corbett's voice, sounding determined. "But I'm here, Brother Davis, to work out the arrangements that fell through when my daughter ran off."

"What arrangements?" Davis sounded cool.

"You know what arrangements. In return for offering Rebecca's hand in marriage, I was to receive two of Earl Graff's daughters. Just because Prophet Solomon died before the marriage actually took place isn't my fault. I've brought

Rebecca back and she's still available, so the Circle of Elders should fulfill their contract by giving me my two brides."

It was all I could do to keep from entering the house and slapping him, but I managed to stay put.

Davis snorted. "Brother Abel, you've been gone for a while so you don't know about some of the changes I've initiated. We are not going to have any more forced marriages, especially not of children."

Abel's voice became stiff. "My mother was only twelve when she married."

"An earlier time. I think the counter-offer the Circle made you is eminently fair, and I advise you to act upon it."

What counter-offer? I strained to listen.

"I'm a young man in my prime, Brother Davis, and I don't see why I should accept a couple of hand-me-downs."

"Hand-me-downs?" There was no disguising the anger in Davis's voice. "I don't think I care to hear two perfectly respectable women described in that manner. You were raised in Purity, and you know that we take care of our widows by finding them new husbands. Frankly, I see absolutely nothing wrong with your marrying Sister Jean and Sister Ermaline. Granted, Sister Ermaline is no longer of child-bearing age, but Sister Jean is still in her prime. Now that my father is dead, they're both destitute and need a husband's protection."

Abel's voice trembled with rage. "All those years I lived with Rebecca's mother I remained monogamous, so now I have to make up for lost time. I need younger wives or I won't be able to get enough children. I don't want to be stuck in Mid-Heaven, little more than a servant to the rest of you!"

Shades of Noah Heaton.

Davis didn't budge. "My mind's made up, Brother Abel. Before I consider your request for a younger woman, you must marry the two women I've chosen. Prove your worthiness for younger brides by having children with Sister Jean, and then we'll revisit this conversation. Now, good day to you!"

Jacob Waldman's voice again. "You see, Abel? That's what you get for defying God's Law! Instead of being fruitful and multiplying the earth, you gave yourself over to the selfishness of monogamy. Now you're reaping the harsh justice you deserve."

Selfishness of monogamy? What a topsy-turvy world these men lived in. If it weren't so tragic for the young girls involved, it would be funny. I had learned one new thing from the conversation, though. Rebecca's father sounded more afraid of eternal life in servitude than he was driven by lust.

The scraping of chairs signaled the meeting had ended. Not wanting to get caught eavesdropping, I tiptoed off the porch and away from the building. Since I was already near Ermaline's house, I decided to stop in and see how Cynthia was doing. I knocked, but the din of so many toddlers drowned me out, so I let myself in and wove my way through the herd. Some of the children were new to me, but like the rest, they sported various shades of blond hair, from towhead to cotton-white. Three of the palest had pink eyes. Albinos.

As I watched them, a honey-blond girl of around eight pushed a tiny chair into the path of an albino child, a cherubic looking kindergarten-age girl. Before I could call out a warning, the cherub ran full-tilt right into it and set up an ear-shattering wail.

I hurried over and picked her up. "There, there. It's just a bump."

Her pink eyes stared straight ahead, unfocused. I realized she was blind.

"Leave that child alone! She should be getting ready for school." I turned to see Ermaline standing in the doorway, hands on her hips. Flour dusted the front of her calico apron.

"She ran into a chair. I don't think she saw it."

Ermaline pursed her lips into a thin, hard line. "Of course she didn't. She can't see anything. Which one of the children moved the chair?"

When I didn't answer, Ermaline tightened her lips even further. She made no move to comfort the crying girl. "The children have been instructed to be very careful where they put things. Someone hasn't followed orders."

The honey-blond miscreant threw a desperate look at me.

I smiled at her and held the crying toddler closer. "I didn't see who it was, Sister Ermaline. It could have been anyone. So much is going on."

Another woman rushed into the room, apparently alerted by the child's squalls. Her hair was as white as the little girl's, her eyes as pink. But the woman could see.

"Give Judy to me," she said, stretching her arms out.

After giving her a quick kiss on the forehead, I handed the crying girl to her mother, who promptly left the room, the darker-haired child trailing at her heels.

All through this exchange, Ermaline frowned at me. She knew I lied, but could do nothing about it.

I continued to smile. "I just dropped by to see how Sister Cynthia is doing," I said, attempting to keep my voice non-judgmental. Apparently I failed, because Ermaline's scowl deepened.

"Cynthia's fine," she snapped.

"I'd still like to see her." Smile, smile.

Children flowed around our little Mexican standoff, laughing, whooping, singing snatches of songs, until Ermaline finally unbent.

"All right."

She led me down the hall, never once apologizing for the role she'd played in her daughter's rape. Like any good polygamist wife, she probably didn't think apology was necessary.

Ermaline opened the door to a dormitory-type room holding four sets of bunk beds. Bright posters drawn by children hung upon the walls, along with the *de rigueur* crosses and embroidered religious samplers. A gaily patterned quilt covered Cynthia, who appeared to be sleeping in one of the lower bunks. The bites and bruises on her face appeared even more vivid than the day before.

I whispered to Ermaline. "I'll just sit by her bed for a while."

Ermaline closed the door, the frown never leaving her face.

"She's gone," I said in a normal voice.

Cynthia's eyes opened. "Thank goodness. I'm so tired of hearing her beg for forgiveness."

I raised my eyebrows. "Your mother did that?"

Cynthia nodded, then winced as if even that slight motion had hurt her. "She swears she didn't know Brother Earl was that bad. And she gave me this." She pulled a couple of books out from under the covers. I crooked my head to read the title of the first one: *Boot Camp for Your Brain: A No-Nonsense Guide to the SAT.*

"As soon as I get well, she's promised to send me to live with my Aunt Bess in Salt Lake. Bess left Purity before I was born, but she's been back to visit, and every time she comes, she's tried to talk Mother into letting me stay with her so I can attend the University of Utah." She paused, then added, "So now it's finally going to happen—once I pass the entrance exam! Maybe someday I'll even make it into med school. I've already just about memorized this." She held up the second book: *Gray's Anatomy.*

"I thought Sister Jean took it to the dump!"

Cynthia grinned. "It's about the hundredth book she promised Mother she'd trash. But she always sneaked them back to me."

A happy ending for Cynthia, then.

We sat and chatted for a while until I finally got around to asking her about the blind child.

Her face became guarded. "That's Sister Sharon's child. She was born blind."

"How about the others? While I waiting out there, I counted several children with albinism. Are they getting the proper care?"

She looked down at *Gray's Anatomy* and caressed its cover. "I don't know."

I understood. Ermaline had promised Cynthia she could move to Salt Lake as long as she didn't discuss Purity with Outsiders. Maybe Cynthia would be more forthcoming later, maybe not. My betting was not. Most of the women and girls who escaped the polygamy communes didn't want to risk being cut off from their extended families, especially their mothers. Regardless of how badly Ermaline had treated Cynthia, a strong bond remained.

But I doubted that Cynthia felt as protective about the man who'd raped her.

"Okay. I can understand your not wanting to talk about the children, so I won't push that."

Her face relaxed.

"I'm curious about one thing, though, Cynthia. I've been racking my brains to figure out why in the world the Circle of Elders forced your mother to give you to a monster like Earl Graff, knowing all the while that his own wives were terrified of him. After all, you're Prophet Solomon's daughter, and that should have counted for something."

Cynthia looked up from her beloved anatomy book. "I was setting the table one evening and Earl was in the living room with Father Prophet, and, well, I heard an odd conversation. I couldn't make any sense of it, but at the end, Father Prophet told Brother Earl that if he kept quiet, he could have me." She stopped.

"And?"

She shook her head. "It made me so upset I ran into my room and cried. I didn't like Brother Earl, not even then. But I can tell you what he told me during our, uh, wedding night."

It was pretty much what I'd expected. Earl, after he'd finished raping Cynthia for the first time, completed the humiliation by crowing about his great coup over her father. During one of Earl's trips to Zion City, he'd run across a business associate of Solomon's. The man inquired about a particular business deal, one Earl had no knowledge of. Suspicious, he checked around and discovered that Solomon had set up a series of private accounts at various banks, and had been skimming money off Purity's operating accounts for years. Enraged, Earl confronted Solomon and demanded Cynthia and Saul's house in payment for his silence.

"My father sold me to Brother Earl, plain and simple," she finished, her voice sorrowful.

Usually, it's the blackmail victim who kills his blackmailer, not the other way around. But sometimes…

Brother Earl remained a viable suspect.

I struck Ermaline off the list, though. Before I'd begun to understand the compound's power structure, I'd believed she might have killed Solomon out of jealousy when she discovered he planned another marriage. I knew better now. With the prophet dead, Ermaline had lost everything. Sure, the men of Purity held all the power cards, but each polygamist household adhered to a strict pecking order. The first wife ruled the roost, with newly acquired wives falling into the power structure in marriage order behind her. As long as Solomon was alive, Ermaline, the first wife, maintained the highest status. She would not willingly give up that honor, because with it came great power among the wives themselves. Powerless people take their perks wherever they can find them.

As I sat there musing about the vagaries of fate, Cynthia's eyes closed and I realized how much my visit tired her. I told her I'd drop by later, then kissed her cheek and tiptoed out.

In the hall, I ran into Jean. After saying a few hard words about Brother Earl Graff, she invited me into the kitchen for a glass of orange juice and a chat.

"You're from the Outside, Sister Lena," she said, as I settled myself at the table and she poured me a glass of what appeared to be fresh-squeezed juice. "Is it really as wicked as they say? I can't remember much about it from my days there in public school, before the Circle of Elders voted to pull us all out."

I took a sip of my juice. Unsweetened. "Sure. Some parts of it are as almost as wicked as Purity."

She looked at me for a moment, her face blank. Then she began to laugh. "You are definitely a refreshing change. Sometimes it's a bit hard to believe that you thought marrying Brother Saul was a good idea. It seems to me that you're much too independent to need marriage."

Uh oh. Jean was sharp. Those few years in public school, perhaps? Or had she been reading Cynthia's books? I trotted out my lies again. "Well, I got myself into trouble, did some dumb things. Quite a lot of dumb things, actually."

She gave me a mischievous grin. "Dumb things with men, right?"

"Oh, yeah. Very dumb things."

Her grin faded. "Well, at least you were free to make your own mistakes. That's more than I can say for myself. Ever since I was a little girl, every move I made was dictated by others. I was told what to wear, what to say, how to pray, who to marry. If it'd been up to me, I would never have married Solomon. Never."

"But at least you got some wonderful children out of it, didn't you?"

She brightened again. "Oh, yes. I'd introduce you to them but they just left for school—or that hive of ignorance they call school around here. There's Kevin and Kyle, who are eight and nine, and Jennifer, seven. Jennifer's the bright one. She told me last week that she wants to be an attorney when she grows up."

I said nothing to that, and Jean noticed my silence.

"While I was still in Zion City Public School, we held Career Day, and a woman lawyer from Salt Lake drove down to speak. Her life sounded fascinating, but not long after that, the Circle of Elders built Purity School and we had to go there, instead. Besides, you know how life goes for girls here in Purity. I married my husband when I was only fifteen, that was ten year ago. And then once I started having babies…"

Ten years of marriage and only three children and her current pregnancy to show for it. I decided to ask her about it. "Why no more children? Or is it none of my business?"

Her tone was bitter when she answered. "For a while my husband grew, how can I say this politely, uninterested in me. At first I thought it was my fault, but when I asked some of my sister wives, they told me the same thing happened with them. Solomon would come to our beds for the first few years of marriage and then stop."

I understood. "He needed new blood, right?"

"An interesting way of putting it, but yes, that's about right. It's pretty true for most of the men in the compound, apparently. They get bored with their old wives and start looking for new ones. But new wives are hard to find nowadays, so they usually come back to our beds every once in a while."

That stumped me. "What do you mean, harder to find? Purity's full of young girls."

She gave me an odd look. "Sister Lena, do the math. Every other baby born in Purity is a boy."

"So?"

She laughed. "For a smart woman, you can be pretty dense, you know that? Look, in the Outside, the numbers work out okay. One man, one wife. But that's not how it works in Purity. The older men, the more powerful men, they all have between ten and fifteen wives. That doesn't leave much new blood, as you so delicately put it, for the younger men."

I frowned. "In other words…"

"In other words, Sister Lena, there aren't enough women to go around."

Well, duh. I shook my head in exasperation at my stupidity. "I guess it's obvious once you really think about it."

"That's why the men are so quick to recruit women from Outside. Even women who seem, well, *unsuitable*." She winked and I laughed with her. "The problem has always been, though, convincing a woman that moving to Purity was a good idea."

"How many Outsiders wind up staying?"

She shrugged. "It all depends on how quickly they have children. You've seen how tough it would be to leave here with kids."

"Prophet Solomon didn't have to recruit. He had access to the cream of the crop."

"Oh, yes. But I understand that Rebecca didn't want to marry him. She'd been raised Outside. There were other young girls, though, who thought it was an honor to marry the living word of God. They're my sister wives now."

"Didn't you ever feel jealous?"

She shook her head. "Maybe if I'd ever loved Solomon, but we girls in Purity aren't raised to fall in love. We're raised to obey."

"How does it work? Do you come in to breakfast one morning and see a new face in the kitchen?"

She laughed again. "Oh, no! The wives get plenty of warning. When Prophet Solomon decided to marry Rebecca, he sat us all down together and told us what he was planning. He read from all the places in Scripture where it talks about the old prophets' many wives. Not that he needed to. All us women have heard those Scriptures so often that we know them by heart."

Then her face took on a shamed expression. "Lately, though, just before Solomon was killed, he told us he'd decided to take two wives at once. Rebecca and one other girl. He reminded us he was growing old and wanted to make certain he had enough children to insure him the highest level of Heaven. And, uh, he began reading other things to us."

I sat up straight. "Like what? His 'Gospel'? Or pornography?" I meant it as a half-joke, but from her expression, I wondered if I might have been right.

She shook her head, but the embarrassment didn't go away. "No, no. He read from the Book of Genesis, about Adam and Eve and their children. He read the same passages every night for a month, right up until the night he died."

The Book of Genesis. "That's the bit about the Garden of Eden, isn't it? So what was he leading up to? Did he want you to throw away your granny dresses and run around naked?"

My attempt at humor fell flat again, because she got up and walked to the window. She stood there for a few moments, and when she finally turned back to me, I saw tears in her eyes.

"You've seen Cora, right? She used to help us in the kitchen. She looks a lot like Cynthia."

"The little platinum blond girl? Gorgeous little thing, but a bit, ah…"

"A bit slow. Yeah, her. She's Ermaline's daughter. Cynthia's full sister."

I hadn't known that. Of course, the Byzantine family structures in Purity constantly amazed me.

"Anyway, Solomon read the Garden of Eden story over and over to us, and then started quizzing us on it." She stared at me as if expecting me to go, "Aha!"

But I didn't go "Aha!" Despite the efforts of one of my more decent foster fathers, a Baptist minister, my knowledge of Scripture remained weak. I shrugged in bafflement.

Jean sighed. "One of the questions Solomon asked us was, 'Who did Adam and Eve's children marry?'"

"Beats me. Maybe God made more people."

She shook her head. "My husband's answer was that Adam and Eve's children married each other."

"Wait a minute, you mean…"

"Sister married brother. Not only that, but Solomon said Adam mated with his own daughters."

At this stage in the game, nothing surprised me very much, but to see incest trumpeted as a religious tenet appalled me. Somehow managing to keep the disgust out of my voice, I said, "Correct me if I'm wrong, Jean, but are you telling me that Solomon planned to marry Cora, his own daughter? His *retarded* daughter?" I was even too shocked to be P.C. about it.

"I'm afraid so. He told us that if it was good enough for the Old Testament, it was good enough for him. Ermaline wasn't happy and tried to talk him out of it, but she finally had to back down. What else could she do?"

I knew what else she could do. She could have killed the disgusting old pervert.

But I didn't say that. "What about the other people in the compound? What would they think of such an incestuous marriage?"

Jean sighed. "It's been done before. Martha Royal was herself the granddaughter of such a marriage. And if you want to know the truth, my own father was Prophet Solomon's brother. My husband was my uncle."

When I left the house a few minutes later, my mouth tasted sour and not from the unsweetened orange juice. Not for the first time did I rejoice that someone killed the perverted old prophet. I just needed to prove the killer wasn't my client.

All I wanted to do when I got back to Saul's was take a bath and wash the sins of Purity away from me, but such comfort wasn't to be. Davis Royal had dropped by and told Saul to send me over to the school. He wanted me to sit in on a couple of seventh grade classes, see where the curriculum stood, and suggest improvement.

"Davis came here himself?" I asked Saul, who couldn't seem to stop rolling his eyes at the prospect of me as a school-teacher.

"Yep, his own royal self. I must say, Lena, he really seems to be hot about this upcoming marriage of yours."

"And me not even related to him. Just goes to show you, some acorns do fall far from the tree."

Saul looked baffled. "What the hell are you talking about?"

Ruby entered the room lugging a laundry basket, so I waved his question away. "I'll talk to you later. Right now I'd better go over to the school. Don't want to disappoint my fiancé, do I?"

I didn't want to lose my temper further, so I avoided the class being taught by the evil old harridan who I'd heard conducting the frightening lesson on "seed." I wandered the halls until I found the seventh graders, but this class, taught from battered, forty-year-old textbooks, appeared little better. These teens would never learn about Vietnam, Panama, the fall of Communism, or the rise of terrorism. In fact, the only new books in the room were amateurishly bound copies of Solomon Royal's own religious ramblings. The teacher, a prim, elderly old woman with a skirt that literally dragged the floor, appeared dispirited. She'd apparently abandoned world history and opted for religious history instead.

As I dutifully took my notes, the teacher called on Meade. She asked him if he remembered the name of Hagar's son.

Meade remembered. "Ishmael," he said, standing up.

Could have fooled me. I'd always thought Ishmael was the narrator in *Moby Dick.*

Surprisingly, Cora sat near Meade, although it was obvious she understood nothing being said. Maybe the teachers just allowed her to wander the school at will, like Mary's little lamb. Once again I admired her beauty. On her, the compound's pale looks seemed transformed. Her skin was tinged with pink, her eyes deepened to a cerulean blue. Her glossy blond hair cascaded down to her waist in a white river. Her beauty wasn't lost on her classmates, either. The boys gazed at her with rapt faces while the girls sulked. Watching this display, Meade scowled.

What a little prig.

Rebecca, sitting next to Meade, winked. Like me, she had been less than impressed by the history lesson.

After class, I returned to Saul's to find him preparing to leave for his attorney's office.

"Court case comes up tomorrow." His face was stiff, but I could tell from the tone in his voice that he was depressed. "The whole thing's probably going to be a slam dunk, but I might as well go down fighting. Do you need anything from Zion City?"

I wanted to talk to Jimmy, and I couldn't do it here. "I need a ton of stuff, husband," I brayed, loud enough for Ruby to hear, wherever she lurked. "Can I ride along with you?"

He took his own turn at yelling. "Sister Ruby? You need anything from Zion? Laundry detergent? Bleach?"

A door opened, closed. I heard footsteps in the hall. Finally Ruby appeared, looking disheveled. She'd probably been listening in the hall in the first place, then scuttled back to her room to make it sound like she'd just emerged.

"No, nothing," she said.

Saul hooked his arm around mine. "Come along, wife."

Ruby grimaced with poorly concealed jealousy as we exited the house.

Neither Saul nor I said much on the trip to Virginia's, and the expression on his face when he dropped me off at West Wind Ranch was glum. As I stood watching him drive off, I felt the same way.

I climbed the steps into the ranch house to find Virginia and Ray holding court with a room full of Germans dressed in leather chaps and expensive cowboy boots. Yahoo, mein herr. Virginia jerked her head toward the stairs, and taking the hint, I hurried up to Number Eight.

Making the easiest call first, I punched in Tony Lomahguahu's number. No luck. The Paiute's daughter told me he was out hunting in the canyon, so I left a message for him to meet me at the graveyard at noon the next day. She assured me she'd tell him so I hung up and made the next call. Jimmy picked up on the first ring.

"It's me," I said. "Guess who just showed up at the compound?"

"Rebecca." Jimmy's concern was obvious. "My cousin tried to talk her out of calling her father but in the end, there was nothing he could do. The kid was convinced she was doing the right thing. I didn't tell Esther, though. She's got enough to worry about."

So Jimmy had visited her again. I wondered how long it would be before he proposed marriage to yet another damsel in distress.

"And Lena, we have an even worse problem," he continued. "Captain Kryzinski called this morning and told me the court's cleared Esther's extradition back to Utah. Sheriff Benson's deputy is on his way down here as we speak. You have to wrap this case."

He added that he had tried the online investigative services again, but couldn't find additional information on anyone at the compound. "I've done everything I can, and now it's up to you."

"Gee, thanks." I gave a bitter laugh, then told him about my latest misadventures with Earl Graff. "So you can see that I'm not at the top of the Polygamy Pop Charts right now. Except for Davis and a few women, hardly anyone is talking to me, let alone telling me their deepest secrets."

Jimmy moaned. "Maybe you should come back. We might be able to figure out some other way to help Esther." His voice carried no conviction.

"No can do. I'm here for the duration." I was just about to hang up, when he stopped me.

"Lena, there's something…There's something…"

More bad news, I was sure. "What?"

"Remember you told me to keep an eye on that South Mountain Citizens for Clean Air case?"

"Yeah, I remember. So how's my favorite firebug? Still in business?" In my concern over Rebecca, I'd almost forgotten about that case, but now Miles Alder's face rose up before me like the Ghost of Christmas Past.

"No, he's not still in business."

I didn't like Jimmy's tone. "What do you mean? Did he get picked up again?"

"Lena."

Then I knew. "Miles is dead, isn't he?"

A pause, then, "Yeah."

"Oh." The room blurred momentarily. How strange. I'd thought I hated the spoiled creep. But for all the grief he caused the world, he'd been little more than a kid.

While I collected myself, Jimmy filled me in. "From what the Phoenix P.D. could tell me, Miles tried to start another fire in the storage yard. He got a pretty good one going, but then something happened. By the time the firefighters got there, the kid had third degree burns over eighty percent of his body. He lasted two days."

With great effort, I held my voice steady. "How's his father doing?"

"That's the really weird part, Lena. Dwayne Alder acts like it's all the police department's fault, that if they'd done their job, none of this would have happened."

I wasn't surprised. Like most parents, Dwayne Alder couldn't admit the role he'd played in creating such a troubled child. And Miles himself, with the usual teen's belief that he would live forever, had been incapable of foreseeing the consequences of his own actions. As Jimmy gave me details I didn't want to hear, I thought back over my own troubled teenage years. The shoplifting, the promiscuity, the anger. It was a miracle I'd survived.

"Poor Dwayne," I said, breaking into Jimmy's description of Miles's melted face.

"Poor Dwayne? That man could see a chicken and say 'cat.'"

"Denial. After all, it's probably rough realizing your kid might still be alive if you hadn't stuck your head in the sand."

"I guess."

We chatted a little more about other doomed kids we'd known, and finally hung up, each as depressed as the other. I needed to make another phone call, but I didn't like my luck so far. So I sat there just staring at the phone for a few minutes, part of me nagging to make the next call, the other part holding back. The nagger won. I punched in one more number.

"Happy Trails Dude Ranch," Slim Papadopolus answered.

I forced cheer into my voice. "Hi, you sexy thing. It's Lena. Dusty back from his little sojourn in Vegas yet?"

The long pause should have told me everything I needed to know, but like someone with a hangnail, I couldn't stop picking at it. "Spit it out, Slim."

"Lena, you know Dusty."

"Yes, I do. And that's why I'm asking you straight out. What's going on?"

"I promised I wouldn't tell."

"Sure you did. Give it up?"

A sigh. "If you make a promise under duress, is it still a promise?"

"Of course not. Where is he?"

Another sigh. "Hell. I hate to be put in the middle of these things, but this just isn't right. You've been awful decent to me in the past. Too decent for me to let this go on."

By "the past," Slim was referring to the time I'd proved his son had been innocent of the hit-and-run that killed a toddler. He'd been foolish enough to loan his car to a drug-addicted friend, but his foolishness didn't add up to manslaughter. "I can take it, Slim. Tell me."

Another pause. "Well, I told you he was in Vegas."

"Yeah, but I noticed you didn't say he was alone, either. Who's he with?"

"Some hottie from New York he met here on the ranch."

"A redhead, right?"

"Lena, you know Dusty's got a thing about redheads. Anyway, they flew to Vegas a couple weeks ago and nobody's seen him since. He hasn't even called. If I don't hear from him within the next week, I'll have to give his job to someone else."

That wouldn't bother Dusty. With his good looks and easy charm, he snap up another dude ranch job in a heart-beat. "Slim, do you think they got married?"

"That's what the rumors say. Nothing Dusty does sur-prises me anymore."

Or me. I thanked Slim for his honesty and hung up the phone with as much dignity as I could muster.

But hey, what difference did it make, right? I'd never loved the man. Never.

So why was I crying?

The sun was setting as Saul and I arrived back at Purity, and as soon as I lit from the truck, I ran into the house, grabbed the notes I'd taken at the school, and headed for Davis's house.

It was Prayer Time. Davis, surrounded by his wives and a sea of his blond-haired children, sat in the chair in the living room, a big black book in his hand. Relieved, I identified the book as a standard-issue Bible, not Solomon's screed, and took this as further proof of Davis's reforms.

"Sister Lena!" His handsome face beamed in delight as I joined Sissy on the sofa. She appeared less happy than he. Maybe she really loved him.

"I'm finishing up here," he said, leaning over to pat one child's head.

"I just dropped by to share my notes on the school with you," I said.

He stood up, tucked the Bible under his arm, and told me to follow him to his den, leaving Sissy looking more miserable than before.

As soon as Davis and I settled onto his big leather sofa, I started in. "You need new textbooks. Those things the teachers are using are not only outdated, they're falling apart. Not that it matters at this point, anyway. There's so much religion being taught over there that there's hardly any time left over for the supposed subject. It's not history they're teaching, Brother Davis, it's Religion 101. Speaking as a future teacher of Purity's children, I'd like to pull all the religious teachings out of the schoolroom and confine it to Prayer Time."

He crinkled his blue eyes and leaned toward me. "Actually, they're teaching something more like Prophet Solomon 404. But I understand what you're saying, and I agree with you."

"You do?" My entire body began to tingle. I tried to convince myself it had nothing to do with the warm hand he'd placed on my knee.

Davis leaned even closer. "Oh, yes, Sister Lena. An uneducated compound is an unready compound, don't you agree?" The hand began sliding up my thigh.

"I agree." My voice sounded choked. Soon the hand would enter forbidden territory.

His voice purred. "Still, Sister Lena, Purity *is* a devout community so I can't entertain the idea of erasing all religious instruction from the curriculum. But I've been reading up on the Catholic system, and I've begun to think we here at Purity might emulate some of their techniques. Have an entire class devoted solely to religious principles, but keep it out of the other classrooms."

"It sounds fine." I could barely talk, I was so intent on what his hand was doing. I wished Dusty knew how much this gorgeous man wanted me.

As Davis's lips approached my ear, his voice grew huskier. Never had I felt so all a-quiver over educational reforms.

"Sister Lena, I'm going to need your help if my plan is going to work. I want you to go back to the school tomorrow, take some more notes, then report back to me. I'd do it myself, but, well, I'm in the middle of this big mess with the Circle of Elders. What happened to Sister Cynthia can't be allowed to happen again. Marrying children is not only illegal, it's grotesque. I have to prove to the Circle that even they are subservient to the Prophet of Purity." In contrast to his soft, busy hand, his voice took on a harder edge. "And *I'm* the Prophet of Purity now, not my father."

His hand left my lower thigh, and a moment later, I felt fingers unbuttoning the front of my high-necked dress. For a brief second my treacherous mind gave me a vision of Dusty's face, but after a brief hesitation, I willed the vision away.

"Yes, Prophet Davis," I whispered. I didn't have to fake the passion in my voice.

Chapter 19

Saul left for court the next morning the same time I left for school. My disgust at the weak curriculum only slightly eclipsed my self-disgust. How could I have responded to Prophet Davis's caresses, even for a moment? Certainly the man was handsome, and certainly, he knew his way around a woman's body, and certainly, it had been a long time since Dusty—that unfaithful devil—had touched me in the way Davis had. But damn!

What would have happened if I hadn't suddenly remembered the gun strapped to my other thigh and pulled out of his arms, making a fake-shy excuse? Worse yet, what would have happened if I hadn't been wearing my gun at all? Would I, like the old Sinatra song put it, have gone all the way?

I trotted across the compound amid a flock of giggling, long-skirted girls, cursing myself silently. Perhaps the stress of living at the compound had blurred the boundaries of my past and my present, sent me back to my lonely teenage years when I'd gone too far with too many high school boys just for the temporary ecstasy of feeling needed. Later, in an ASU psychology class, I'd learned sexually abused girls often became promiscuous, so I'd forgiven myself. But that was then and this was now. I was no longer a vulnerable teenager seeking acceptance in the sweaty back seats of muscle cars. I was a grown woman with better sense.

Supposedly.

I hurried to the first class. During the previous day, I'd recognized two teachers as Solomon's widows. Hester, a thin-faced woman only slightly younger than Ermaline, taught math, and Desiree, a plump teenager little older than her students, taught English. I spent the morning taking notes in case Davis checked up on me, then sought out the two teachers during recess.

We sat beneath the school yard's only tree, a struggling cottonwood whose puny branches looked like they might fall on our heads any moment. The older children stood around talking, while the younger ones played on the swings and slides. Rebecca, bless her, never once looked my way.

I broke the ice by asking about Rosalinda's baby. "Just beautiful!" And Hanna's baby? "Doing poorly." Then, after making a few diplomatic comments about the school and expressing Davis's interest in it, I began to draw the women out. They were Solomon's widows, after all, and we'd cooked biscuits side by side.

"Given the materials you have to work with, I think you women have done a fine job," I said, holding up the ragged textbook I'd put aside to take to Davis. "I'm just surprised that Prophet Solomon, with all his resources, didn't allot more money to the school. I mean, he seemed so concerned about every little thing here in Purity."

Hester gave me a sour look. "I wouldn't say *every* little thing."

Some jealousy there, perhaps? I wondered how long it had been since Solomon had visited Hester's bed. Not in years, I bet.

"Well, you know what I mean. He really cared about the compound, so I'm sure he kept an eye to the future of its young people."

Hester shrugged, making the shoulder seam of her ill-made calico dress slip further down her arm. I wanted to tug it up, but refrained. "The only time we ever saw him was during meals and at Prayer Time. He didn't really have a lot to say to us about anything. Except God and children, of course."

Desiree, younger and still willing to make allowances for neglectful behavior, nodded sympathetically.

"But didn't Prophet Solomon design the school's syllabus?" I asked. "What could be taught and what couldn't?"

"Sure he did," Hester said. "Problem was, he designed it around the things he found interesting, not the skills our young people might need as they established their own families. For instance, I wanted to take some of the children into town and teach them how to shop frugally, but he wouldn't allow it. He didn't want them out of the compound, not even for a minute."

"But Sister Hester, *God* told him the trip would be a waste of time!" Desiree protested.

That sour look again. "Everything our husband said and did originated with God."

I wondered where Hester's cynicism came from, and then I remembered. She'd probably attended public school, maybe even gone all the way through high school. Desiree had probably dropped out when she'd married, maybe even at fourteen. Cynical or not, though, Hester was right. The best way to strong-arm people into doing anything you wanted was by convincing them you spoke for God.

Catching my expression, Hester added, "Once our husband made up his mind, he never changed it. A couple of years ago when we were allowed to watch certain TV programs, he decided that purple dinosaur, Barney, had been sent by Satan to tempt children into believing that their own feelings and ideas were important. It upset him so much he drove into town for a stuffed Barney toy, and had each child in Purity tell it, 'Satan, I renounce you.' It was all pretty silly, if you ask me, but he didn't think so. After every child renounced Satan, he made Margaret, who was only three, burn it on the trash heap. The poor little thing just sobbed and sobbed because she'd believed Barney was her birthday present. I tried to tell him he was breaking her heart, but he didn't care."

Even Desiree looked uncomfortable at this, but true to her nature, she tried to explain it away. "Sometimes the Path of Faith is hard."

Hester vented a bitter laugh. "One of our husband's favorite sayings. He used it to make us do things we didn't want to do and threatened us with hellfire if we defied him."

In a flat voice, Desiree quoted someone, probably the Prophet. "'A wife should be a willing servant to her husband, for he is her only pathway to God. Without her husband's guidance, she will never find Heaven.'"

Hester didn't buy it. "Maybe that's true, maybe not. He used that same argument with the Circle of Elders, too, when they wanted to take a different course than the one he'd ordered. In the end, I'm not sure they were convinced he spoke for God's interests, either."

I had one more question. "I know the Circle is having trouble with Brother Davis, and I've got a pretty good idea how that's going to turn out, so what happened when the Circle ran afoul of Prophet Solomon?"

"They had to do what he ordered, of course," Hester said. "After all, the Prophet is God's mouthpiece. And you don't go against God—until his mouthpiece gets assassinated, that is."

Desiree gasped.

I almost did, too. "Sister Hester, are you telling me you think one of the Circle shot Solomon? And might now be after Davis?"

She didn't back down. "Do you really think that shot at Davis the other day came from some fool hunter? Our men handle guns better than that. I think Purity's new prophet had better watch his step and stay away from that canyon. I also think he'd be smart to chop down that mesquite grove around his house so nobody can use the cover to sneak up on him."

Desiree looked appalled. "That's a wicked thing to say!"

Hester grunted. "Tell me that in a few months, dear, but you mark my words. Unless Davis drops his reforms, he'll never live past Christmas." Then, as if believing she'd gone too far, she made a big show of checking her watch. "We should go back in now. Recess is over."

As we herded the children back into the classrooms, I reflected on what I'd just learned about Solomon. Take away the religious cant, and the portrait that emerged was that of a totally self-serving man. While I'd heard no tales of outright physical cruelty on Prophet Solomon's part, he'd manipulated his wives and children, and the entire compound.

But someone had seen through him.

Just after recess it began raining steadily. While the parched kitchen gardens probably rejoiced, the rain increased the dangers of flash flooding. Saving myself about a half hour by taking Paiute Canyon's dogleg to the graveyard was no longer wise, so I decided to leave earlier than planned. As soon I as noted Desiree didn't know the difference between an adjective and an adverb, I excused myself from her English class and splashed across the muddy compound to Saul's. I borrowed a raincoat and scarf from a suspicious Ruby and, telling her I loved walking in the rain, began the slow, wet slog across the desert.

Although the nasty weather guaranteed there would be no hunters around to pry into my movements, the price for such privacy came high. The overland road to the graveyard added two miles to my journey, and before I'd even cleared the compound, mud caked my Reeboks, weighing me down. For a while, the road paralleled the canyon, so I listened to the music of water as it burbled along what was now little more than a tiny stream. How long before it turned into a torrent?

After a half hour, the road hooked east along the dogleg and began a slow, gentle climb over a ridge dotted with desert rue. Here the road became rocky. Once the road topped the ridge, I paused to look back to see Purity in all its squalid splendor. From here the houses and trailers resembled a wagon train tightly circled to ward off foes. But this appearance deceived. Purity had no foes. The established Mormon Church, after expelling the polygamists, had washed its hands of the entire problem. Beehive County's district attorney wouldn't prosecute men like Prophet Solomon or Earl Graff, and even the county sheriff returned Purity's runaways. There was nothing I could do except save one little girl: Rebecca.

I turned my back on Purity and crossed the ridge to find the Paiute already waiting for me.

Tony Lomahguahu, hunkered under a huge black umbrella, looked thoroughly miserable. "I sure hope this is important, Miss Jones. I left a warm fire back at the house."

"It's important." The weather was too foul for pleasantries, so I started right in. "Mr. Lomahguahu, I know something's very wrong in Purity, but I simply don't know enough about these people and their history to figure it out. Will you help me?"

Lomahguahu stared at me for a moment, silent. The wind, stronger here, lifted wisps of his thick gray hair. I waited.

Finally, he said, "Have you lived in the noise of the city for so long that you have forgotten how to listen?"

I bit my lip to keep back the churlish answer that sprang to my lips: listen to what? Rain slapping against mud?

But I didn't want to alienate him. "I'm not sure I ever knew how to listen. That's why I've come to you. Something doesn't add up here, and it's probably connected to the Prophet's death." I pointed toward the graves of Martha Royal's children. "You said 'Listen to the children.' Well, one of the women has lost too many, I think, for it to be a coincidence. Is that what you were hinting at?"

The Paiute glanced at the sky, where a thin blue line appeared on the western horizon. It broadened as we watched. The rain would end soon, but the canyon would remain dangerous for days. Good. That would keep Davis away from it, and maybe he'd live long enough to put those reforms into action.

"Mr. Lomahguahu? Did you hear my question?"

His face hinted at impatience when he finally answered. "You believe this woman may have something to do with her children's deaths, but how would the Paiute know anything about that? We lead our lives, the people of Purity lead theirs. Little passes between us. But I can say this. If you cannot listen, then you must *look*. All the information you need is there. But like so many white people, you are blind. In your *busyness*, you have forgotten how to use your eyes."

With that, he got up and without another word, walked back toward the Paiute reservation.

I would have chased after him but I knew better. He'd discharged his debt to Jimmy's people, and now he was through with me. He'd not wanted to become involved with the polygamy mess in the first place, and after everything I'd seen during the past couple of weeks, I couldn't blame him.

The rain stopped. In no hurry to repeat my long hike over the ridge and back down the soggy road, I spent the next hour wandering through the cemetery. The oldest graves, high on the ridge and silhouetted against the sky, were those of the area's pioneers, polygamists even then. Below them, marching toward the present, I found graves with the same names recurring. Royal. Corbett. Leonard. Waldman. Graff. Heaton. As I studied the markers, I began to see a pattern. In the 1800s and at the beginning of the nineteenth century, young women didn't live long. Many were buried with infants, signaling they'd died in childbirth. These sad deaths diminished in the 1930s, probably because of better prenatal care. Young women's deaths dropped sharply again in the 1970s, which, if I remembered correctly, heralded the advent of Purity's clinic, proof that it did some good.

Then in the 1980s, though, the incidence of infant and child deaths began to rise again. Dramatically. For the past five years, the number of dead children had escalated alarmingly, illustrating that Martha was far from the only woman who'd lost several babies.

Or murdered them.

I remembered Andrea Yates, the overwhelmed Texas mother who'd drowned her five children in the family bathtub. Were these rows and rows of dead children the desperate acts of women like her, whose bodies and minds had been pushed beyond their resources? Were the women all covering up for each other? And had Prophet Solomon, like myself, finally figured out what the women were doing?

And had one of them killed him to keep him silent?

Then I remembered Hanna, the battered-looking woman who'd barely been able to limp her way across Ermaline's kitchen. She'd recently given birth to a baby everyone described as frail. Were the women merely setting the scene for another infanticide?

I set out for Purity as quickly as my mud-encrusted feet would allow.

When I arrived back at the compound the streets were almost deserted. Cautious, I went around to the clinic's back door, which was almost hidden from sight behind a collection of outbuildings. Good. If I was right, my discovery would put me in grave danger, not from the compound's men, but from its women.

I opened the door only to be faced with a steep staircase. Ignoring that for now, I walked down a long hallway lined with narrow, unpainted doors, even though the rough wood provided a sticky playground for dozens of tiny fingerprints. In keeping with the compound's cheapjack construction, none of the doors had locks. So much for privacy. No carpet, no tile, covered the clinic's bare floorboards, either, and the odor of Lysol in the air did little to mask the sour smell of urine.

I was surprised to hear the voices of so many babies and children. They didn't sound especially sick, but what did I know? Then I remembered the great size of the clinic. The building didn't function simply as a maternity ward, but as a hospital for all manner of ills. Perhaps these children suffered from something communicable, such as chicken pox or measles. The dead prophet hadn't believed in modern medicine, just the power of prayer, so the compound's children had probably not been inoculated against the diseases that ravaged their ancestors. Perhaps these were children who were being kept isolated until they were no longer infectious.

Still, the fact that the Prophet and his followers would allow their children to risk the more serious side effects of measles—deafness, blindness, and the mental retardation that already existed in Purity—made me grind my teeth. Why couldn't I hear God grinding His? However, uninoculated children weren't my problem at the moment. My immediate task was to find Hanna and her baby. What if the baby appeared to be in danger?

I had no choice. Even though my job here was to find out who murdered Prophet Solomon and not to rescue babies, I couldn't let the little creature meet the same fate as had the others in the cemetery. If I had to figure out another way to help Rebecca, then so be it.

As I crept along the hallway, my wet shoes making squishing noises on the bare boards, I wondered which of the many doors hid Hanna. Forcing myself to focus, I stopped and listened for an infant's cries above the happy babble of older children. Nothing. Either I was too late, or the baby merely slept. I prayed it was only the latter.

Then I heard it, coming from toward the front of the building. *There.* A thin wail. Weak, but proof Hanna's baby was still alive.

Vowing to keep it that way, I followed its cries.

I had almost made it to the door behind which I'd guessed Hanna lay when I heard another baby in the room next to it. Then another baby from the room on the opposite side. Oh, hell. The place was crawling with infants. It made sense that, with all the pregnant women I'd seen walking around the compound, several had given birth more or less at the same time. The chances of my homing in on the right room had begun to lessen, but if I walked in on someone, I'd just tell them I was dying to see Hanna's sweet little baby.

My lie prepared, I opened the first door. The room contained little furniture except for a large chest and the row of high-sided bassinets lined up against one of the unpainted walls. The bassinets, some with pink ribbons attached to them, others with blue, appeared empty, and I had almost closed the door to continue on to the next room when I heard a small sound coming from one of the blue-draped bassinets. A baby, doing baby-type things. Alone. I remembered the different eating "shifts" at Ermaline's. Some of the mothers hadn't finished eating, which meant that their babies wouldn't be brought to them until later. A stroke of luck for me. Still, I would have thought the babies would stay with their mothers all the time, but perhaps Solomon, the clinic's designer, felt some separation gave the mothers more rest.

Come to think of it, though, such a compassionate idea didn't sound like the Solomon described by his wives. Still, perhaps this baby was Hanna's. Perhaps she lay in a room down the hall, dreaming of ways to end its tiny life.

I tiptoed over to the bassinet and peered in.

It found it hard to believe something so tiny could live, but the little white-haired creature appeared brimming with health and energy, thrusting his fists out from his blue blanket as if boxing the air. Entranced, I cooed softly at him, but he ignored my presence and kept jabbing at empty space.

As I leaned over to make sure he was all right, I frowned. Something didn't look right.

Then I saw.

The baby hadn't been making a fist, as I'd first believed: he'd been born without fingers.

I bit my lip to suppress a moan and stepped away from the bassinet. This was probably Hanna's baby, then, the baby described as "sickly" a frequently employed euphemism for birth defects.

Sad, but not tragic. I'd simply find Hanna and tell her that she didn't have to kill him, that the government offered a bevy of no-cost programs to the families of such children. Prostheses would even help him lead a normal life. He could grow. He could be happy. Hanna would understand. Like all mothers, she'd want to help her child in any way possible.

Like all mothers? I remembered my own mother raising a gun, aiming it me, screaming "I'll kill her! I'll kill her!"

No. Not like all mothers.

Hanna could be a good mother, of that I was certain. She had what it took, the patience, the compassion. I'd seen her with other children in the compound, bending over them, cooing at them as foolishly as I had, holding them tenderly, speaking to them with love.

Please, God, let her not be a child killer.

I reached out and touched the baby's cheek. He turned, latched onto my fingers with his mouth and began to suck.

"I'll save you, little one," I whispered. "I promise."

I froze. Why did those words sound so familiar? After a few moments, they swam up from my deeply buried memories, the memories of an uncomprehending, four-year-old child.

I heard my mother's voice.

I'll save you, little one, I promise, she'd cried.

No! Impossible! My mother was a killer!

Brushing away the memory, if indeed the words were memory, I withdrew my fingers from the baby's mouth.

He wailed crossly as I left the room. I'd find Hanna, talk to her, tell her about the help the baby could receive, tell her to reconsider. And then I'd watch her eyes. If I saw a shadow there, any warning sign, I'd come back for the baby and sneak him to Saul's. Then we'd drive him to Zion City and…

And what? Turn the baby over to Sheriff Benson?

Better to worry about the details later. For now, I needed to find Hanna.

I looked down the long hallway, at all the doors. Heard women's low, murmuring voices, the tiny cries of infants. The clinic bustled with brand-new motherhood.

Deciding to start directly across the hall, I opened the door upon a bed-lined room, only to see a solitary blond girl of around fifteen—not Hanna—nursing a pink-blanketed infant. The girl looked at me in surprise.

I forced my voice to sound casual. "Hi. I'm looking for Hanna."

"Hanna. What'd I hear...?" As she looked down at her baby, the blanket slipped and I saw white hair. Another albino? Or just another blond? The baby had all her fingers, so I exhaled in relief.

After kissing the top of the infant's head, the girl frowned at me. "Somebody said somethin' about her at lunch but I wasn't payin' much attention. She had some kinda problem with her baby, I think." The frown faded, replaced by a smile. Hanna's woes forgotten already. "Ain't my baby pretty?"

"Adorable."

She frowned again, as if it hurt her to think. "Oh, yeah! Somebody said Hanna went upstairs, that's where she is! I'm Sister Kathy. And this little sweetie is Sister Jennifer. I was goin' to name her Susan, after my mother, but Brother Jim, that's her father, he said no, that he wants all his kids named with a J. Ain't that just the smartest thing?" She beamed, thrilled to be married to a genius.

"Brilliant." I edged toward the door. "Upstairs, you say?"

"You can't go up there without special permission."

I stopped. "Does Hanna have permission?"

"Oh, yeah. She's up there all the time." She began cooing at her baby, already forgetting I was there.

After closing the door behind me, I took a deep breath. The behavior of the young mother troubled me, but I didn't have time to examine it. The women's voices at the end of the hall rose in laughter, and I heard the rattle of dishes being stacked, the clink of cheap flatware. Soon they'd leave the lunchroom, making my escape with the baby difficult, if not impossible.

I needed to hurry.

The stairs were steep, but I noted with surprise that unlike the hallway and rooms below, they were thickly carpeted in a deep, industrial gray tweed. To keep down the sound? The same dense carpeting stretched down the hall of the clinic's second floor. I noted fewer doors here, probably denoting larger rooms, but in contrast to the doors downstairs, most of these appeared to have locks. Then I remembered. The Circle of Elders met up here, right next to the armory.

I squared my shoulders and opened the first door on the building's west side, only to find a long, bare room running almost the entire length of the building. It didn't contain one stick of furniture, not a diaper, nor scrap of paper. The walls and ceiling, however, had been covered with expensive soundproofing tiles. A chemical smell signaled that the room had been recently refurbished.

The next room, also soundproofed, proved smaller, but it contained several bunks, cribs, and chests. A bank of mattresses of varying sizes lay stacked against the far wall. The entire setup baffled me until I remembered the large number of pregnant women I'd seen since coming to Purity. The compound expected one heck of a population explosion, and soon.

It made sense. How many men lived in Purity? One hundred? Two hundred? If each man had three pregnant wives—a conservative figure—then within the next couple of months, at least three hundred to four hundred babies would be born at the clinic. Still, why did the room contain cribs, not bassinets? Surely the babies went home with their mothers within days. Although the cribs and chests looked like Salvation Army rejects, they still represented considerable expenditure.

Shaking my head in perplexity, I crossed the hall. Upon opening the first door, I knew I'd found the Circle of Elders' lair. A long, broad table with ten mismatched chairs took up the center of the room, but I hardly gave it notice. What fascinated me were the locked gun cabinets filled with shotguns and rifles, as well as a sprinkling of single-action revolvers and several small automatics. But along with those run-of-the-mill weapons so many Arizonans tote openly, stood a lethal arsenal of Berettas, Ingrams, Fabriques, Galis, Heckler and Kochs, even a few Kalashnikovs, Steyrs, and M14 Clones.

Nobody used those babies on rabbits.

Not wanting to be caught here under any circumstances, I left the room and closed the door firmly behind me. Just what the hell were the polygamists planning, an armed insurrection? Or were they just the usual Western gun nuts? Then I remembered Jacob Waldman and his call for blood atonement. I remembered the murders committed by a famous polygamist clan now serving time in prison. And I remembered Waco.

But then a door opened from one of the soundproofed rooms down the hall, allowing the babbling voices of children to drift my way. I scurried back into the armory, leaving the door slightly ajar so that I could peek out.

Two granny-dressed women exited the room, one elderly, the other a teenager. The teen sobbed hysterically, and if it hadn't been for the supporting arms around her waist, she would probably have fallen. As the older woman helped the teen down the stairs, snatches of their conversation floated back to me.

"…God's will."

"…can't stand it…"

"Pray with the Circle, they'll…"

"…too weak."

In her focus on the distraught teenager, the older woman didn't pull the door completely shut, and my hopes began to rise. Could Hanna be in there? If so, she had plenty of company. I hadn't heard such a racket since serving breakfast at Ermaline's. No wonder the clinic's top floor had been soundproofed. I hurried down the hall to the room, hoping to find Hanna before either of the women returned.

When I pulled the door back, I froze on the threshold, stunned at the sight before me. The room, every bit as large as the one across the hall, swarmed with children of all ages, from toddlers to teens. Something terrible was wrong with every one of them.

Many of the children had been born without eyes. They lay in their beds, their faces lifted, uncomprehending, to the white-tiled ceiling. Others, tethered by leather straps to iron rings set in the reinforced wall, jerked spastically. A few, born with heads too small for their bodies, drooped on the edge of their bunks, their faces as vacant as their microcephalic brains.

Hanna sat in one of the room's many rocking chairs, holding a microcephalic boy tenderly in her arms. Like any good mother, she sang to her child.

Hushabye, don't you cry,
Go to sleep you little baby,
When you wake you will see
All the pretty little horses.

This child was no baby, though. He had to be at least ten. No wonder Hanna cried all the time.

I backed out of the room before I, like the teenager, began sobbing, and as I fled down the stairs, I wondered which child had been hers.

Oh, stupid, stupid, stupid! Why hadn't I figured all this out before? With the incest rampant in the compound, the generations of uncle marrying niece, grandfather marrying granddaughter, sister marrying brother, the chances of congenital defects had to be at least double the rate of the rest of the population.

The people of Purity were genetic train wrecks.

Chapter 20

As I left the clinic by the same door I had entered, I reassessed my suspicions. No wholesale murder of children was taking place in Purity, just the kind of inbreeding that doomed them to early deaths—if they were fortunate enough to live past infancy.

I thought back to the blind girl I'd seen at Ermaline's house. Judy hadn't been abandoned in this warehouse for the deformed. Why not?

The answer was obvious. Judy was a girl, and a girl, no matter how serious her congenital defects, could still be bred. All she had to do was lie there while her sixty-year-old husband sowed his seed. Besides, with Purity's adherence to polygamy, the compound needed more girls than boys. This was probably the main reason the compound had put up with my poorly disguised independence and bad temper. Although I was—according to Purity standards—well on my way to cronehood, I could still pop out a few babies before my ovaries gave up, thus contributing fresh genes to the compound's badly damaged gene pool.

But the little boys, ah, they were a different story.

It hadn't passed my notice that most of the children in that room had been boys, and I thought I knew why. To take a wife, to breed, to add money to Purity's coffers, to ascend to Highest Heaven, a man had to be mobile. Because of their complete inability to take up a polygamist man's duties, those little boys I'd seen with the most serious congenital birth defects—microcephaly, spina bifida, profound retardation and cerebral palsy—were warehoused from birth. While their fathers collected extra government benefits.

What a life. I leaned against an outbuilding and tried not to throw up.

Hanna's son. What would happen to him? Would he, like so many of Purity's damaged little boys, live out his life in one room?

I decided to confront Davis. With all his flaws, he wasn't as bad as the rest of the men in Purity. He had a heart. He'd rescued Cynthia, carried her in his own arms back to her fool of a mother. I knew I could make him see reason, possibly even put a halt to the institutionalized incest that doomed so many children to brief, miserable lives.

Not wanting to waste another second, I hitched up my skirts and hurried through the rain to his house. I didn't even bother knocking, just rushed in. "Brother Davis?" I yelled. "I need to see you!"

Sissy came out of the kitchen. She took one look at me and gasped. Then I remembered my raised skirts. My, my. How easily polygamists became shocked over normal things like a woman's legs. To spare her blushes, I lowered them. "Sissy, where's Brother Davis?"

She shook her head. "I'm afraid he's in his den counseling someone. He can't see you now."

I shoved past her. "I don't care if he's counseling the Pope. I'm going in."

"No! Counseling is a very private time, a spiritual time." She clutched at my dress and attempted to drag me back.

I batted her hand away and kept moving. "Get your hands off me, Sissy, before I slap you silly."

"Sister Lena, I wish you wouldn't..."

But I was already at the den, already opening the door. What I saw there shocked me even more, if possible, than the scene at the clinic.

Brother Davis Royal, the Reform Prophet of Purity, was counseling someone all right, if you call running your hand up a seven-year-old girl's thigh *counseling*. I recognized those moves from my own experience with him the day before. He'd go for her blouse next.

I didn't bother keeping the outrage from my voice. "What the fuck do you think you're *doing?*"

The little girl gave a frightened squeak, jumped up, and headed out the open door, blond hair and long skirts flying. Sissy, whose face had become as white as Prophet Davis's perfect teeth, grabbed her and hustled her away.

Davis turned to face me, his face flushed. With passion? For a child? Or with anger because I'd interrupted his good time? "Sister Lena! Such language!"

"Don't criticize my language, you miserable child molester!" For a moment my hand itched for my revolver, but he wasn't worth going to jail over. Especially not in Utah.

His mouth attempted a half-smile. It failed. "I can explain."

"There's nothing to explain. I thought you had some kind of decency, but you're no better than the rest of the Circle."

He shook his head as if under attack by bees. "No, no, you've got me all wrong. I'm no rapist, and I'm certainly no child molester. Being new to our ways, you've simply misinterpreted what you've seen."

Did the fool think he could make me question the evidence of my own eyes? Then I remembered: Davis was his father's son, and therefore no stranger to manipulation. He probably thought if it worked for Daddy, why not for him?

His voice grew oily as he reached for my hands. "Sister Lena, you saw how badly the situation with Earl Graff and Cynthia turned out. She never had the chance to get used to his touch, so on her wedding night, when he attempted certain things, she panicked. Don't you agree with me that such an event could seriously scar a woman's soul? Of course it could! That's why a man who really cares for a woman's happiness begins preparing her while she's still a young and impressionable girl. Take Sissy, for example. If I'd waited until she was thirteen, it might have been too late! She could have turned her very healthy sexual nature toward another man. But by preparing her the same way I had just started preparing that other little girl, Sissy fixated on me. Don't you see the compassion in my method, Sister Lena?"

"Sister Lena thinks you're a freak." With that, I jerked my hands away and gave him the same karate chop I'd delivered to Earl Graff.

Leaving Davis writhing on the floor, and a horrified Sissy leaning against the wall, I rushed back across Prophet's Park to Saul's house. The mud-spattered truck parked in front of it told me he'd returned from court.

"I'm calling the cops!" I yelled, as I jerked open the front door. "And then I'm getting the hell out of here!"

Saul sat on the sofa, his face immobile. Next to him, Ruby had been crying.

"Yeah, you sure are getting the hell out of here, Lena," he said, quietly. "We all are. I lost in court this morning, and I've been given forty-eight hours to remove my clothes and furniture from this house."

With an effort, I put my rage on hold. "They only gave you forty-eight hours?"

"Yeah. After that, the Circle of Elders impounds every-thing else. You gonna help me pack?"

I shook my head and told him about what I'd seen at Prophet Davis's house. Then, while Saul beat his fist against his palm in rage, I called Sheriff Benson and told him every-thing, too.

"You want to press formal charges?" Benson asked when I finished. The anger in his voice weighed more toward me and what he dismissed as my "foolish undercover crusade" than at Prophet Davis's actions.

"My god, man, I interrupted an incident of child moles-tation in progress! Of course I want to file charges."

"Then I'll come right out."

Somewhat gratified, I put down the phone.

My feeling of gratification vanished two hours later, however, when Sheriff Benson came back to Saul's after interviewing everyone involved.

"The girl denied your entire story, Ms. Jones," Benson said, his face rigid with dislike. He wouldn't even sit in the chair I pulled out for him. "The girl's mother denied it and so did Prophet Davis. You're the only person who says it happened. In fact, Prophet Davis is thinking about filing a complaint against *you.*"

I jumped out of my own chair. "Complaint? Complaint for what?"

"Assault. False accusations. Oh, if you're found guilty you probably won't go to jail, but you'll be liable for a hefty financial judgment. It's happened before." Was I wrong, or did I hear satisfaction in his voice?

"That's insane!"

He shrugged. "If I remember correctly, you used to be a police officer, so you should know that when you start throwing around charges like you're doing now, you'd better have witnesses. That's how the law protects innocent parties from the accusations of people who have an agenda, such as your self."

Saul stepped forward, his face hard. "Sheriff, are you hinting that Lena is lying?"

Benson flashed a big smile. Considering the circumstances, it appeared wildly inappropriate. "Now, I didn't say that, did I? But I'll tell you this, Mr. Berkhauser. Prophet Davis said Ms. Jones has been out to get him ever since she proposed to him and he declined."

"Declined, my ass! I'll have you know he couldn't wait to get his hands on me!"

Benson's smile didn't budge. "Frankly, I think Prophet Davis's story makes more sense than yours. My years in law enforcement have taught me that a rejected woman frequently takes her revenge by making accusations against the man who rejected her. There are other things I've noticed about you, Ms. Jones, that call your credibility into question. When I first met you down in Scottsdale, you seemed much too willing to take the part of an obviously hysterical woman who had her own ax to grind. The next time I see you, here you are, living in the very community she ran away from, chasing after Prophet Davis, telling me stories about rape, child molestation, and who knows what all. Now, I have one final question. You seem to be a deeply troubled woman, Ms. Jones. Have you ever considered therapy?"

Only Sheriff Benson's uniform kept me from slapping that maddening smile off his face.

After Benson left, Ruby, who had been sitting quietly in the corner with her hands folded primly on her lap, finally spoke. "Don't look so shocked, Sister Lena. What he just said about you being crazy, that's what all these men in Purity say when their wives get upset, except for Brother Saul, of course. I'm bettin' Sheriff Benson says it to his own wives at least once a day."

Saul and I both stood in the middle of the room, staring at her.

"*Wives*, did you say, Sister Ruby?" Saul asked.

"Wives. He's got three, at least he did last time I called over there. Two of them are my own daughters."

"*What?*" Saul and I both shouted in chorus.

She leaned forward in her chair. "Neither's all that happy with him, but it's not a woman's job to be happy, is it? After all, he doesn't do…" She paused and blushed. "He doesn't do ugly things to them. Oh, they could have done a whole lot worse."

"Benson's a polygamist," I said.

"Of course he is, Sister Lena. Howard Benson's mother was Prophet Solomon's niece. He was raised right here in Purity."

Saul groaned. "My God, if we'd known that..."

I shushed him with a gesture. I wanted her to continue.

Ruby didn't disappoint me. Now that she'd finally taken the plunge and started giving her opinions, she didn't want to stop. "I knew him when he was a little boy. I didn't like him much then, either."

"But you let your daughters marry him." I tried to keep my voice level.

"Let? *Let?*" Her voice rose to a decidedly unmeek level. Sister Ruby was pissed and she didn't care who knew it. "There was no *let*, Sister Lena. My husband fixed it up with Brother Howard's father years ago. I didn't have no say and neither did my girls."

Saul put a hand to his forehead and groaned. "You knew all this but let Lena call him anyway?"

She stuck her chin out. "I heard what Sister Lena was saying about the little girl and Prophet Davis, and it made me mad! Touching a seven-year-old girl down *there* ain't right, even if you are the prophet. Sin is sin. Now, I know Brother Howard doesn't like Sister Lena much, but I thought he'd still do something about the little girl. Him saying Lena needed therapy, well, that was just pure nastiness. None of the men around here wouldn't ever let their females get that kind of help. They'd be too scared of what might come out."

Whoever said still waters run deep had undoubtedly met Sister Ruby.

I sat down heavily. "I'll be damned. Not only do you believe me, you actually care."

She looked at me with no more affection than before. "I think you're a terrible, pushy woman, Sister Lena, and you don't know your place. But you don't lie about anything important."

That night I lay in bed, staring at the ceiling and wondering what to do next. My cover was well and truly blown and I still didn't know who'd killed Prophet Solomon. Sheriff Benson, whose ties to Purity proved stronger than his ties to the law, had told Davis who I was and what I was doing in Purity. Not that it made any difference anymore. Before Benson had left, he'd said his deputy had called from Scottsdale, promising to return Esther in handcuffs the next day. As a parting shot, Benson told me her murder trial would probably begin before the first snowfall.

Rebecca was beyond help.

Just before dawn, I finally fell asleep.

A harsh light filled the bus, tinting my mother's face almost as yellow as her hair. The gun she pointed at my head looked to my four-year-old eyes the size of a cannon.

"I'll kill her!" she cried. *"I'll kill her now!"*

"No, Mommy!" I screamed, just as her foot nudged me in the stomach. Then I heard the rattle of the bus's door opening. But why? We hadn't slowed down.

"See! I'm killing her! Right now!"

Someone grabbed my mother, moved the gun. There was a struggle.

Then the gun went off. With a scream, my mother kicked me in the stomach, sending me flying toward the open door.

Just before I lost consciousness on the street outside, I heard my mother scream again.

"I failed, God forgive me, I failed!"

I awoke screaming the same words.

Chapter 21

"God forgive me, I failed."

As soon as the words tore from my throat I recognized them as lies. No. I hadn't failed. Not yet. I still had one more day left in Purity, a day to find out who murdered Prophet Solomon. A day to return Rebecca to her mother.

Yes, my mother had failed. Maybe she had even seen my eyes still open as I tumbled from the bus and into the loving arms of the Mexican woman who saved me.

But I *wouldn't* fail.

This wasn't my past. This was the here and now, and I had enough time to find a murderer. Yes, remaining here now would be more dangerous than ever, but so what? I'd faced down danger before and won, starting at the ripe old age of four.

The problem was, almost everyone in Purity had a solid motive for murdering the Prophet. His wives didn't love him, his children feared him, and he'd intimidated the Circle of Elders for years, living in splendor while they grubbed around in slums. I crawled out of bed and headed for the shower, thinking hard. While I fiddled with the taps, I tried each person's motive on for size. *Cui bono?* Who benefited from Prophet Solomon's death? Who had motive, means and opportunity?

I showered in cold water, hoping the shock would help me think. As I scrubbed away my goose bumps, I revisited my belief that the new prophet of Purity remained the most likely murderer. With his father out of the way, Davis inherited the Purity Fellowship Foundation's tax deductible millions. But if Solomon hadn't died in the canyon that night, would the power shift have eventually changed? Earl Graff, leader of the Circle of Elders, desired the more tractable Meade to be named prophet. Possibly an aging Solomon, pressured by more threats of blackmail, might have finally caved in, designating Meade his spiritual heir whether the boy liked it or not.

Earl Graff could murder without a qualm, of that I was certain. But how had he benefited from Prophet Solomon's death? He was the chief proponent of the Meade-for-Prophet-Party, and the old man's death had ended his dreams. Then again, someone had taken a shot at Davis recently, too. It wouldn't have surprised me if Earl's finger had pulled the trigger.

Purity swarmed with murder suspects. In one of his Alzheimer's fugues, Jacob Waldman could have killed Solomon, but why? Then again, people suffering from dementia didn't need rational motives, did they?

Abel Corbett, Rebecca's father, couldn't be left out of the equation, either. Yes, we'd all been told the old prophet had promised him a couple of young girls in exchange for Rebecca, but what if Solomon had reneged on the deal at the last minute? Could the about-face have made Abel angry enough to kill? As I thought about Abel's less-than-stellar track record at fatherhood, an even more intriguing suspect entered the picture.

Noah Heaton, the dwarfish thug who'd been frustrated by Solomon's refusal to give him any wives, looked good for it. Now his wedding day was about to arrive, along with his new wives' welfare checks. Brother Noah had certainly cashed in after Solomon's death.

Noises down the hall interrupted my thinking. Saul was up and headed for the kitchen, Ruby trailing behind him. Thinking about my pseudo-husband and sister wife drew my mind onto a track I'd been avoiding. Saul's own motive for killing Solomon remained second only to Davis's. Solomon had bilked Saul out of his life savings, leaving him stranded in Purity with an unloving wife.

For that matter, how about Ruby herself? She'd told me that Gaynell, her first husband, had died after Solomon's faith healing failed. Although Saul had described Gaynell as somewhat less than kind, Ruby wouldn't have been the first woman to have loved a brute. Even the Marquis de Sade's wife had remained loyal to the bitter end.

Even Cynthia couldn't be ruled out as a suspect. Her father had ignored her desire to attend college, and instead promised her to Earl Graff. If the old bastard had still been alive, I might have been tempted to kill him for that myself.

I finalized my list of female suspects with the person I least wanted to be the killer. Virginia Lawler, the owner of West Wind Ranch, the woman who devoted her life to helping girls escape from the polygamy compounds. Virginia's present life might be an ongoing act of contrition, but I wondered if she found her efforts eased her nightmares. Remembering my own nights, I shuddered. Dreams could make you crazy. They could infiltrate your waking life until you could no longer tell fantasy from reality, right from wrong.

Disturbed, I turned off the taps, stepped out of the shower, and dried off. Maybe I didn't like it, but Virginia had means, motive, and probably opportunity. And then driven back to West Wind Guest Ranch in time for cocktails. Like most ranching types in Arizona and Utah she was probably comfortable with hand guns and rifles, but in the end, what did that prove? The same could be said for every single man, and possibly some women, in Purity.

The real question here was, would Virginia have been heartless enough to allow another woman, a mother, to pay for her crime?

I refused to believe it.

I returned to my room, dressed quickly, and went into the kitchen, where Saul sat eating his Special K as Ruby watched him, her face unreadable. Neither spoke, but at least she'd set out the breakfast fixins'. Her orderly life was about to change, but Ruby just kept plugging along. It was almost admirable.

Then again, *would* Ruby's life change? Granted, Saul was still her legal husband, but did she plan to leave the compound with him? Or would she remain in Purity, hoping that the Circle of Elders would find her a new husband so that she could continue to live near her children and grandchildren?

Thinking about it hurt my head, so I dumped a pile of Special K into my bowl and drowned it with milk.

"Rain's stopped," Saul finally said into the silence.

"Good. I'm going for a walk, but when I get back I'll help pack." Getting out of the house would help me think and I had precious little to pack, anyway. Some underwear and maybe one long-skirted dress. As a souvenir.

I bolted down the cereal and after a quick goodbye, headed out the door. It was still early enough that I crossed paths with Meade on his daily journey across Prophet's Park to Ermaline's house for morning prayers.

He smiled, looking more like his mother than ever. "Would you like to join us in prayer, Sister Lena?"

Apparently Meade hadn't heard about the scene with Davis the day before. There was no reason he should have. Even though the two shared the same father, I'd never seen them together. I also doubted Sissy had told him I'd caught her husband fooling around with a seven-year-old girl. In my experience, child molesters' wives usually covered for them.

I shook my head. "Thanks for the offer, Meade, but I'm persona non grata over at Ermaline's these days."

"Sona non gratis?"

Of course. Latin was hardly a required subject at Purity School. "An unwelcome person," I translated.

"Oh, that's no problem, then. Sister Ermaline has to do whatever I say, so if you want to pray with us, you just come on. I know that you and your husband have to leave Purity tomorrow, and I'm figuring you need the solace of prayer more than ever."

What a sweet boy. But something he'd just said intrigued me. "Brother Meade, what do you mean, Sister Ermaline has to do whatever you tell her to do?"

His smile didn't change. "Because I'm a man, and Sister Ermaline is just a woman."

Not such a sweet boy. "Yeah, well, that's all very nice, kid, but I think exercise will do me a lot more good than your sexist prayers."

With that, I hitched up my skirt in front of his horrified eyes, and began jogging down the muddy track that led toward the graveyard. I looked back once to see Meade still standing in the dirt circle, staring after me in disbelief.

Once out of the compound, however, I felt a pang of guilt over my behavior. Why blame the kid for his goofy beliefs? He'd been brainwashed, too, and in a way was as much a victim as anyone else. Then I remembered Cynthia's battered body. No, not quite as much as everyone.

As I splashed along the road near Paiute Canyon, I heard the roar of the water. Two days of rain had funneled through the Vermillion Cliffs, creating one of the area's notorious flash floods, so I made certain not to go too near the edge while I ran. After an hour, I decided to take a short break. I slowed to a walk, and moseyed over to the rim, gazing into the canyon as untold tons of muddy water foamed toward the Colorado River. Small trees, ripped loose from their precarious hold on the canyon's walls, bounced along the torrent like daredevil surfers. I even saw a dead antelope borne along in the wake of a mesquite, its head bobbing loosely in the current. I hoped its death had been quick.

Other small corpses floated past, animals too small or frail to escape from the flood. Rabbits. Quail. Unidentifiable bits of feathers and fur.

I don't know how long I stood there watching water and death flow by, hoping those tiny deaths might lead me to understanding. But I when I finally turned away, I found myself no closer to solving Prophet Solomon's murder than before.

Chapter 22

When I entered the compound, I noticed most of the older children had already made it to the school, leaving only a few stragglers to wend their way through the rusting pickup trucks in Prophet's Park. Cynthia herded Cora and several younger children along, so intent upon watching them that she actually ran into me. The impact dislodged a small paperback from her apron pocket.

I retrieved it, but not before reading the title. *The Mayor of Casterbridge,* by Thomas Hardy, the story of a man who sold his wife and child and lived to regret it.

"Interesting choice," I said. "But whatever you do, don't let anyone here see you reading this."

She looked around nervously, then hurriedly stuffed the novel back into her apron pocket. "Saul once brought me something that listed the two thousand most important books ever written, so I've been working my way through them. I think I've got about nineteen hundred left." She paused, and her voice sounded heavy. "I guess I'll have to make the Hardy last until Mother lets me go to my aunt's house in Salt Lake."

Until? I didn't like the sound of that. "Come with us tomorrow," I urged. "I'll drive you to your aunt's. Why wait?"

She looked down at the children clustered around her feet, her sisters and brothers. When she finally met my eyes, she whispered, "Oh, Lena. How can I leave them?"

I understood. For years escape to Salt Lake City and the University of Utah had been her dream, and dreams were safe. Now, on the brink of freedom, those dreams looked scary.

Inspired, I bent down and picked up one of the children, a little girl of about four who so closely resembled Cynthia that she could have been her full, biological sister. As I kissed the child's blond head, I asked "Think she'll wind up marrying Earl Graff?"

Cynthia gasped.

Even Cora screwed up her face. "He's nasty." Then she began playing patty-cake with a younger girl.

"She sure got that right," Cynthia said, recovering. "But Lena, if I leave, who'll help the kids around here?"

I shifted the little girl, who had grown heavy in my arms. She giggled, and leaned against me, which made me look more closely at her. Adorable, but with the same vacant eyes as Cora. I closed my eyes for a moment, waiting for the wave of rage to pass. When it did, I opened them again.

"She's retarded," I said.

Cynthia nodded. "But she'll be fine. She'll still be able to make a life. You know how things are around here."

I sure did. But I wondered about her. "Have you ever been upstairs at the clinic?"

She looked baffled. "No. Why would I? That's where the Circle of Elders meets."

Just what I'd suspected. The soundproofing was evidence that the male rulers of Purity wanted to keep the compound's genetic problems secret, perhaps fearing that if the girls and young women knew the extent of the defects caused by inbreeding, they might start refusing to marry their relatives. As it stood, though, the females' continued ignorance gave the males exactly what they needed—unlimited power.

Well, I could do something about that. I told her the clinic's ugly secret.

"And it'll only get worse," I finished up. "Cora and this little girl here, who will they marry, Cynthia? Their cousins?

Their *brothers?* And what kind of defects will *their* children have? Now that you know what you know, are you going to stick around and watch the show, just like everybody else?"

Cynthia, who had grown ashen while I recounted what I'd seen on the second floor, looked as sick as I felt. "That's why the Circle of Elders won't let most of us go up there! Just some of the older women."

"And women like Hanna, women with such low self-esteem that they probably believe their children's problems are *their* fault."

With that, I set the little girl down and left Cynthia to think about the future of the children she loved.

I continued across Prophet's Park to Saul's house, where I found him knee-deep in boxes he'd picked up at the grocery store in Zion City. Thumping sounds from the bedroom told me that Ruby had started packing in there.

"What a mess," Saul grumbled, as he carefully stacked his old vinyl 78s into one of the boxes.

I grunted as I headed for the shower once more. "It's a mess, all right."

In the shower, I turned up the hot water as high as I could stand it. As I scrubbed, mud from my morning run created a dark whirlpool around the drain, vaguely resembling the dirty water in Paiute Canyon. I pushed that memory away, preferring not to dwell on the animals lost to the flood. Closing my eyes, I let the hot water needle my body. I'd seen so much sorrow centered around children lately. Esther. Virginia. Hanna. Even Miles and Dwayne Alder. Could there be anything more horrible than to lose a child, even when the child was a half-crazy criminal?

I tilted my face toward the spray, hoping to wash my memories away. Minutes later, the memories remained, but at least my sore muscles stopped aching. As the tenderness and tension fell away so did my mind's resistance. By the time I'd stepped out of the shower, I knew who'd killed Prophet Solomon.

And why.

Oh, it had all been so obvious. So obvious that I wondered how many people in Purity already knew the truth. But truth and law didn't mean much to them, did it? For decades they'd covered up rapes, wife-beatings, and infanticide, so there was no reason to believe they would suddenly feel compelled to run to the authorities over a matter they'd consider private.

No, Purity liked to solve its own problems in its own way. Even when the solution was simply to do nothing.

Sheriff Benson shared their moral lethargy, too. Like the rest of the Arizona Strip's polygamists, he cared more about keeping his illegal lifestyle intact than he did serving the law. Tony Lomahguahu had called it right; some people preferred walking in darkness instead of seeing the light.

I dried quickly. After putting on a clean granny dress, I hurried down the hallway, pausing once to make certain Ruby was still busy packing in the bedroom.

"Where's your tape recorder?" I asked Saul.

He looked up from a box filled with papers and gestured toward the desk. "Top drawer. What do you need it for?"

"To tape a murderer's confession."

He blocked my hand from the drawer. "Hey, wait a minute. What do you mean, *tape a murderer's confession?* If you've figured out who killed Solomon Royal, you'd better get on the phone to Sheriff Benson, not play some kind of cops and robbers game with that thing. You could get killed."

I shoved his hand aside and opened the drawer. "Call Sheriff Benson again? Don't make me laugh. Besides, I know what I'm doing."

"That's what the fly said to the spider just before he became the spider's dinner."

I drew the tape recorder out. "Saul, this is the only way. Otherwise, Esther goes on trial for murder."

After a moment, Saul took the recorder from me, scrabbled through another drawer, and fished out new

batteries. When he'd finished reloading it, he handed it back.
"I'm going with you."

I shook my head. "It'll only work if I go by myself."
Turning away, I unbuttoned my high-necked dress, and
tucked the recorder securely inside my bra. Facing him once
more, I told him how he could help.

"I want you to go ask Davis and everyone in the Circle
of Elders for help in loading your truck tomorrow. Tell them
it'll get us out of their hair quicker. During the conversation,
mention that I think I know who killed Prophet Solomon,
but act like you don't believe me. Complain that I've even
decided to go over Sheriff Benson's head, right up to the
county attorney, maybe even the state attorney general. That
should shake them up."

Saul wasn't happy about my plan, but he followed my
instructions and left immediately for Earl Graff's.

He returned within minutes. "I did what you wanted,
told Davis, Earl Graff, Vern Leonard, just about everybody
I could think of. It may come as no surprise to you, though,
that we'll be loading the truck ourselves."

"What'd they say when you told them I knew who the
murderer was?"

"They didn't even ask who."

Because they already knew. "I'll wait for a few minutes,
give them time to spread the word, then I'll get started."

Saul sank onto the sofa, his face drawn with worry. "Is
there anything I can say to stop you? If anything happens to
you, I'll never forgive myself."

I patted him on the arm. "With Prophet Solomon dead, the
murderer isn't all that dangerous anymore," I assured him. I'll
be all right, you'll see. And just in case..." I slapped my
voluminous skirt, which hid my ever-present .38. "I'm a very
good shot. Believe me, Saul, compared to some of the other
things I've gone through in my life, this will be a piece of cake."

As soon as school let out and children and teachers had
started streaming toward their homes, I went out on the

porch and began to sing a few bars of "Mustang Sally." Then I stepped off the porch, lifted up my skirts, and danced the Funky Chicken to my song. Once I had been noticed by as many people as possible, including a few shocked women standing in front of their houses, I set off toward the graveyard.

I called to Graff, who'd just emerged from his house. "Since this is my last day in beautiful Purity, I think I'll go for a walk, maybe pick a few wildflowers and take them up to the graveyard."

Once out of sight of the compound, I began listening for footsteps behind me. At first I thought my plan might not have worked, because the only noises I heard were the roaring of water in the canyon, and above, the harsh cries of hawks on the hunt. But once I crossed the ridge and started down the final stretch of road to the graveyard, I heard the thud of a rock, dislodged from its place, skittering down the slope.

My plan had worked after all.

By the time the murderer finally caught up with me, I was sitting on a rock, staring at the graves of Martha Royal's children. I had already slipped my gun out of the holster and put it next to me, covering it with my long skirt. And I'd reached inside my bra and switched on Saul's tape recorder.

Smiling, I turned and looked into the face of a killer.

"Hi, Meade. Would you like to know how I figured out you murdered your father?"

Fourteen-year-old Meade Solomon looked nervous, but to it came as no surprise to see him unarmed. After all, I was just a woman.

Meade's flushed face almost matched his red flannel shirt. "Brother Earl's right. You're crazy." But his deep voice failed to carry the conviction he desired.

"Nah, I'm not crazy, Meade, but you may be. After all, you killed your father because he was going to marry Cora the same girl you wanted to marry."

"Don't be stupid. Cora's my sister."

I shrugged. "She was Solomon's daughter, too, but that didn't stop him. The men of Purity have been marrying their sisters and daughters for a long time, haven't they, Meade?"

Meade's voice broke then and he sounded like the boy he still was. He nodded. "Yeah, but so what? The Bible tells us it's all right. That ain't why Father Prophet and I...I said hard things to him, things a son shouldn't have to say to his father. But I was right! I called him selfish, I told him he didn't care nothing about Purity, he only cared about himself." He eyes, which had been stoked with the fires of self-righteousness, became sad. "Nothing I said made any difference, though. When I was through, he told me he'd decided Davis should be the next prophet, not me, and then he ordered me to leave Purity. He said I could go anywhere I wanted in the Outside, even to one of the other compounds, but I couldn't come back here as long as he lived."

The morning sun was at his back and I couldn't see his face, but I heard the tears in his voice. Like Cynthia and so many other of Purity's children, he feared life on the Outside. I almost felt sorry for him.

"You couldn't leave, could you, Meade? You knew you weren't equipped to make it in the outside world."

He sniffled. "Purity's my home! Living here is the only way I can ever ascend to Highest Heaven. You understand that, don't you? By telling me to me leave, my daddy was sending me to the lowest pit of Hell. I couldn't let that happen. I *had* to kill him!"

"So you followed him that afternoon when he went hunting. And you shot him."

He nodded miserably. "Yeah, I acted like I was trying to make it all up with him, like I was taking back everything I'd said. And then I grabbed the shotgun and I did what I had to do. I did it for the good of Purity!"

I was certain he believed it, too. But I found one item in his recital troubling. Meade hadn't killed his father in the heat of the moment, like I'd originally thought; he'd planned the whole thing. The crime hadn't been a spur-of-the-moment act, after all. It had been Murder One.

Still, I wanted to give him the benefit of the doubt. "By killing your father before he banished you, you figured you'd still be able to get into Highest Heaven, right? And murder or not, everything would be all right if you turned away from your one sin and walked a righteous path for the rest of your life."

Meade shook his head. "No, no. When I shot Father Prophet, it wasn't murder. It was blood atonement."

"Blood atonement? What do you mean?"

He drew himself up and his voice became deeper, more Biblical. "Brother Earl says I'm the true prophet of Purity, not Davis. So when I do anything, I'm doing it for the good of everybody. My father was a false prophet, and he didn't have any right to keep my bride from me, not after God gave me a revelation that Cora should be my first wife."

Another convenient revelation that Purity's men—and boys—of Purity used to excuse their crimes. "Oh, I get it. The Devil didn't make you murder your father, God did."

Meade kicked at a rock. It bounced off an infant's grave. The movement had turned him into the sun, which now illuminated his face. He didn't look so angelic anymore.

"You're an unbeliever, Sister Lena, and a wicked woman. But I guess you can't be blamed. Women are weak vessels, always open to the wiles of Satan. But Satan can be cast out! Let's pray together. I'll lead you from the road to perdition and put you straight on the road to salvation."

"Thanks anyway, Meade, but I happen to like the road to perdition. The scenery's better."

His scowl make him look like a typical teen. "That's sacrilegious!"

"And blood atonement isn't?"

He looked shocked. "Blood atonement is one of the tools God gives men to right wrongs, Sister Lena."

I motioned to the tiny graves. "What wrongs had those babies committed when your mother killed them?"

His eyes flickered. "I don't know what you're talking about."

"Yes you do. Your mother couldn't stand raising any more babies, could she? So how'd she do it? Suffocate them? Or did she drown them like kittens nobody wants?"

For a moment I didn't think he was going to answer, but after heaving a deep sigh, he said, "I don't know how. All I know is that after Father caught her at it one night, he barred her from Highest Heaven. He could do that, you know. He was still God's chosen prophet, at least he was until he turned against me."

I could imagine the scene. Martha, leaning over the tiny body, Solomon discovering her. The curses, the tears. But no matter how deep his rage, Purity's prophet would never have turned the demented woman over to the authorities, not when he believed he had the power to separate her from the rest of her children throughout Eternity.

"Your father told the Circle of Elders what she'd done, didn't he? That's why after he died, they sent her to live in that trailer with Brother Vernon. She was being punished."

Meade nodded miserably. "Sister Esther figured it out, too, and before she left Purity, she threatened to tell the sheriff if it ever happened again. But it didn't happen again. My father banished Mother from his bed."

Another piece of the puzzle slid into place. "You hated Esther for that, didn't you? So you didn't mind when she was accused of your father's murder."

"Sister Esther had no right to tell anybody on the Outside anything about Purity!" he cried. "'Specially not after my father took care of Mother's problem!"

But Esther didn't take it to the Outside. Purity's habit of secrecy proved too ingrained, and she never told anyone, not even me. Would it have made any difference if she had?

"Meade, those babies were your own brothers and sisters. Don't you want some sort of justice for them?"

He began kicking rocks again, throwing hate-filled glances at me. As if shifting position, I stretched my hand to the side and patted my spread-out skirts, feeling for the comforting contours of my .38.

Meade didn't notice. "You think I'd tell the sheriff on my own mother? What for? Women are prone to sin, but their sins can be forgiven as long as they remain obedient plural wives. I'm going to fix it so Mother can ascend to Highest Heaven, right along with me and my brides and all my children."

And what a nice family reunion that would be.

Since Meade was obviously in a talking mood, I asked him about something else that had been bothering me. "Tell me about your uncle Jacob," I said, curious about Esther's father. "Did he kill one of his daughters when she refused to marry some guy he picked for her?"

Meade stopped his pacing. This subject didn't make him half as nervous. "Yeah. She'd been reading some stuff over at that public school in Zion City we used to go to, some stuff about genes or something. She said marrying her uncle wouldn't be right."

Receiving confirmation of my suspicions would probably prove irrelevant in the end. So much time had passed that the chances of bringing Jacob Waldman up on murder charges weren't good, especially considering his condition. Same with Martha Royal. Yet I'd been proven wrong before. Perhaps with the right prosecuting attorney...

First things first.

"Meade, you know we need to do something about all this, don't you?"

I didn't like the sly look that crept across his face. "Don't be silly. I told you all this stuff because no one around here will take your word for anything, especially after all those crazy charges you made against Davis yesterday."

"You heard about that, did you?"

"The Circle of Elders tells me everything."

Of course they did. After all, Earl Graff and his henchmen believed that Meade was God's chosen prophet, not Davis.

Time to play my hand. "Meade, I know that my word doesn't count for much around here, me being a woman and all. That's why I taped this entire conversation." When I opened the front of my dress and pulled down my bra, it was a tossup as to which horrified Meade the most, finding out our conversation had been taped, or seeing so much bare womanly flesh.

Meade shrank from me as if I'd turned into Satan himself. Then he recovered and held out his hand. "Hand that tape over, Sister Lena. I command you."

Poor little Meade. He still didn't get it. I wasn't one of Purity's subservient women. I never had been.

"The tape stays with me, kid, but here's what I'll do. I'll go with you to the county attorney. When you talk to him, leave your own feelings for Cora out of it, just tell him you were so overcome by revulsion that your father wanted to marry his own daughter that you just kind of lost your mind for a minute."

"Give me that tape!"

Meade stepped closer to me and drew back his fist. I forced myself to remain seated on the rock, betting that as disturbed as he was—and he was plenty disturbed—he was no Earl Graff. Meade didn't respect women, but he wasn't incapable of feelings for them. A nice moral conundrum, that.

"You're not going to hit me, Meade. I'm just a poor, weak woman, remember?"

I'd pegged my man. Or boy. Meade backed away and lowered his fist. "You can't use that tape in court, anyway. I saw it on a cop show once before Daddy locked the television up."

I smiled up at him. "Oh, sure, Arizona takes a dim view of this sort of thing, but Utah has allowed this sort of confession to be entered into evidence on various occasions. You screwed up when you killed Prophet Solomon on the Utah side of the state line."

Actually, I knew no such thing about the admissibility of taped evidence in Utah, but I was betting that Meade didn't, either. The whole idea of my little trick was to get Meade to come with me to the county attorney's office and *then* make a taped confession which would stand up in court.

I hammered my point home. "Bear in mind, Meade, for this to work you have to bypass Benson, because as you said, he's one of your own. But if you go to the county attorney with me and tell the truth, I'm betting you'll get off with just a short stint in Juvenile Hall or even some nice mental health facility. You'll be back out in no time."

It made sense to me. What were a few months compared to the length of the average life? If the worse happened and Meade wound up in Juvie until he turned eighteen, well, he could live with that.

But I'd forgotten that even a week looks like forever to a teenager.

When I saw the expression on his face, I knew I'd miscalculated. "You want me to live on the Outside? Never! I'd rather die!" With that, he turned on his heel and took off for the flooded canyon as fast as he could run.

I sat in shock for a brief second, then dropped the tape recorder and hitched up my skirts. But as I raced after Meade, the skirts fell down again to my ankles, tripping me. By the time I recovered and caught up with him, Meade had already reached the canyon's rim, where he stood looking down at the torrent.

Frightened for the first time, but not for myself, I grabbed him around the waist. "Don't, Meade."

The boy was no taller than me and painfully thin, but having lived most of his life on Purity's hardscrabble land, he proved stronger than he looked. He twisted in my arms and hit me on the forearm with his elbow. Although I didn't release my grip, the movement ripped the thin fabric of his shirt, and I found myself holding nothing but a ragged piece of red flannel.

As I snatched at him again, he began running along the edge of the canyon, looking down as if rethinking his original intent. This slowed him enough for me to come close to grabbing distance again after only a few yards. I dared a quick glance down. This part of the canyon was less steep than other areas, and its sides sloped gently toward the current, creating an almost navigable bank. Almost, but not quite. The thing was still a death trap.

Meade threw me an odd look, almost one of cunning. Then, just as I reached for him, he scrambled down the rocky side of the canyon toward the deadly water.

"Don't, Meade!" I screamed, as I slid down the slope after him. But the water roared so loudly that I could hardly hear myself. All I could do was keep stumbling after him, hoping that he wouldn't trip, wouldn't fall—or jump—into the maelstrom before I could grab him again.

The slope, covered with rocks slicked down after two days of rain, proved treacherous. At one point, I had to grab onto the low branches of a scrub oak in order to keep my footing. Meade wasn't as cautious. I saw his mouth open in a shout as he tripped, then fell, only inches from the water. Screaming for him to hold still, I let go of the scrub oak and edged toward him, intending to help him toward the flatter portion of the bank.

It almost worked. I grabbed him by his thick leather belt. When he smiled up at me I thought I'd succeeded.

Then he kicked me in the face.

Shocked, I let go of him and began sliding down the bank on my belly. Just before I fell into the water, though, I twisted onto my side and grabbed at a drooping mesquite. Both hands connected with a low-lying branch, but even as I wrapped my fingers around it, my legs continued into the water, where the current sucked at my skirts and threatened to sweep me away.

"Help me!" I screamed toward Meade, who looked down at me from a safer height.

His smile told me that he wouldn't, and I realized how badly I'd misjudged him. Meade was no impulsive teenager. He was a prophet, and prophets planned everything—including murder. He'd never intended to commit suicide at all. No, he'd faked his despair in order to lure me to my death.

Solomon's last hunting party had probably been Meade's idea, not his own.

Something, a log, probably, banged into my legs, snagged against my skirts. When it finally skated away on the surface of the current, it took my skirts with it.

Leering, Meade crawled down the bank toward me, shoving his muddy face close to me so that I could hear his every spiteful word. "Nice legs, Sister Lena. Not that I care. You're a soiled vessel and not worthy of me." Then he got to his knees, reached up, and began to uncurl my fingers from the tree limb.

But Meade didn't know how strong all those hours in the Scottsdale gyms had made me. After taking a deep breath, I hauled my bare legs out of the water and kicked the little monster in the balls. With a surprised grunt, he began to roll toward the water. Just before the torrent swept him to his death, I released my left hand from the tree limb, leaned over, and grabbed his belt.

"Hold still, Meade!" I yelled, but the fool kid kept struggling, not truly realizing that escape from my grasp meant certain death. If I let go, he would either drown or get his brains bashed out against the canyon walls. By the time the water spit him out, there wouldn't be enough left for his own mother to identify. Gritting my teeth, I managed to drag him closer to shore.

Yet still he fought against me, and attempted to paddle out into the current. "Let me go!" he screamed, his voice a high tenor against the current's deep-throated rumble. "God will save me! I'm his Chosen One."

And I was the Queen of Romania.

The harder Meade struggled, the tighter I held on. But as his denims became waterlogged, the drag on my arms increased. The fingers of my right hand, still wrapped in a death grip around the mesquite branch, began to cramp. My left arm, the only thing that anchored Meade to life, developed a tremor.

How long could I hold on? How long could I dangle here, suspended over the water, clinging to this crazy, struggling boy? I wasn't Wonder Woman, just a burned-out ex-cop with a bullet in her hip, a woman neither as young or courageous as she used to be. What difference did it make, anyway? If I let Meade go, I wouldn't have to come back to Utah, give my testimony at some long, protracted trial. Just think of how much money Meade's death would save the taxpayers! Meade was no good to the world, anyway. He'd already committed one murder and attempted another. What was to keep him from coming back to Purity, after his release from his vacation in Juvie, and starting a blood atonement massacre against all his foes?

Then, the darkest of all temptations slithered into my heart. Given Meade's genetic makeup, how many deformed children would he sire upon his sisters and cousins before he was through?

How many more Coras would he create?

The tone of the current grew louder, deeper, and I turned my head upstream to see what had created the difference. A felled cottonwood tree, its trunk at least two feet in diameter, as yet unbroken by its journey. Headed straight for Meade.

I tugged at him, but my strength was gone, and even though he'd swallowed enough water to slow his struggles, I could barely maintain my grip on his belt. There was a good chance he'd already lost consciousness. Maybe he wouldn't even feel the tree as it slammed through his brain.

Then I could let go.

But no. I couldn't.

It made no sense, but I refused to let him go while he still breathed. I wouldn't consign the living Meade to the flood's rough justice. If the cottonwood wanted to take him, it would have to take us both.

"It's a good day to die, Meade," I said through gritted teeth. "A good day for us both."

I prepared to die.

But then I heard her.

Save the child! Nothing else matters! Save the child!

My mother's voice, drifting back to me across the years.

Shocked, I jerked back, and as I jerked, Meade moved with me. Encouraged, I summoned my strength for one last try.

With a mighty heave, I slung him back onto the bank just as the cottonwood roared past.

Chapter 23

As soon as Meade coughed up all the dirty water he had ingested, I got him onto his feet and half-pushed, half-dragged him out of the canyon, back to the graveyard where I'd left my gun.

After I'd stuffed the tape recorder back into what was left of my bra, I gave the wobbly boy a shove. Then, at gunpoint, I marched him across the desert to the Paiute village and Tony Lomahguahu's house.

I didn't even care that thanks to the raging water I was almost naked.

After all, I did have nice legs.

Chapter 24

"Are you sure you want to keep that ratty old chair?" Virginia asked Saul, as she and Leo helped him load the La-Z-Boy into the big U-Haul we had rented.

The Circle of Elders watched us, furious, from Prophet's Park. A few feet away from them, in lonely splendor, Davis stood alone. They were all still furious over Meade and his mother being arrested, because as it had turned out, even Sheriff Benson hadn't approved of murder.

"I'm not leaving a damn thing in this place that I don't have to," Saul said. "I'm even taking the toilet paper for the new house."

As I'd begun to suspect, before Saul moved to Purity he'd managed to squirrel away a tidy sum in Phoenix, away from Prophet Solomon's prying eyes. The money had been deposited in his son's name, accruing interest for years, and now there was enough for the down payment on a fixer-upper in Zion City. Like other Purity exiles and escapees, he planned to immerse himself in the growing anti-polygamy movement. And he wouldn't be doing it alone. Jean Royal and her children were leaving with him. As soon as Saul's divorce from Ruby was finalized, the two would marry.

On the way back from the county attorney's office the day before, Saul had told me, "Remember those two widows that I told you asked me to marry them? One of them was

Jean. That's one fine woman, Lena, and she wants more children. You know how I feel about that."

After I'd finished hugging him and almost running us
off the road, I gave him a sly grin. "So who was the other
widow, stud? You going to marry her, too?"

His grin faded. "I wouldn't marry Ermaline on a bet."

Ruby would remain in Purity. As she had explained to us
when we tried to get her to leave, her children and grandchildren lived there. Besides, she said, when she saw our
faces fall, in Purity her future was assured. The Circle of
Elders had already found her a new husband: Vern Leonard,
who after Martha's arrest for murder wanted a new wife.
And while Ruby wasn't thrilled about the prospect of living
in one of Vern's beat-up old trailers, she'd decided the sacrifice
was worth it to remain close to her family.

I understood.

But Cynthia, at least, had recovered from her last-minute
apprehension. She'd ride with us as far as West Wind Guest
Ranch, where her aunt would pick her up the next day.
Ermaline, still apologetic over the role she'd played in
Cynthia's violent rape, had even helped the girl pack.

As Cynthia heaved a box of clothing into the van, yet
another book fell from her apron. This time, though, she
picked it up leisurely.

Saul grinned as he read the title. "*Your First Year in College.*
Now, that's what I call thinking ahead. You better write me
and Jean when you get settled, you hear?"

Cynthia gave him a quick kiss on the cheek, stuffed the
book in her apron pocket again, and loaded another box.

I snuck a look at Davis Royal. The sun was behind him
so it was hard to read his face, but I still thought I saw some
regret there. There was none on my side, though. Some day,
I figured, I'd read about his death in the newspapers, probably in some "hunting accident." There was a chance, I
thought, that Davis might bone up on his own shooting
skills and get Earl Graff first. Either way was fine with me.

If they wound up killing each other in the same bloody shootout, great.

For that was the only way Purity, and all the other poly-gamy compounds on the Arizona Strip, would ever be shut down. The previous day's events at the county attorney's office had made that all too plain.

As soon as Tony Lomahguahu's wife had bundled us into warm blankets, Meade, so certain that he'd acted for God, began to talk freely about the murder. He was still talking when the ambulance whisked us both away to the hospital. He kept talking there, too, even when Robert Heckaman, the portly county attorney, stood over his bed. Heckaman was flanked by two deputies, one of them holding the video camera which, I was assured, would produce evidence admis-sible in court.

Things had moved quickly then. With me still wrapped in a blanket, Heckaman escorted me back to his office and phoned a Beehive County judge. As I listened on his speaker phone, the judge promised to sign papers ordering Esther's release from the Zion City jail, where she'd arrived only that morning. The entire process would take no more than a few hours.

But Heckaman's cooperation stopped there. No matter how hard I begged, he said he couldn't do anything about the situa-tion in Purity. In fact, his words oddly echoed Sheriff Benson's.

"You have to look at it from the legal point of view, Ms. Jones," he said, tapping a pudgy finger on his glass-topped desk. "Who is the complainant here? You? If so, the only two people you can personally lodge a complaint against are Earl Graff, for assaulting you, and Meade Solomon, for trying to kill you. Sheriff Benson has already assured you that your complaint against Davis Royal isn't going to fly."

I refused to give up. "But surely I can file a citizen's complaint. Polygamy is illegal. So is rape, wife beating and child molestation, not to mention welfare fraud."

He shook his head, making his double chins wobble. "As long as the women of Purity don't consider themselves injured parties and lodge their own complaints, the law can do nothing."

"You can't be serious."

Heckaman sat back in his chair, his belly spilling over his belt. "I wish I could help you, but this kind of thing has been going on for more than a hundred years out here. That business with Tom Green and his wives, that was just an aberration, a publicity-seeking fool who got what he deserved."

I pointed out that the women of Purity hadn't come forward because the Church of the Prophet Fundamental had convinced them they'd go to Hell if they didn't follow the church's orders, but Heckaman just shrugged.

"Religious freedom, Miss Jones. The United States Constitution guarantees it."

Since compassion didn't seem to be working with the county attorney, I tried another tack. I reminded him of the genetically damaged children, and the enormous cost to taxpayers they represented.

Heckaman seemed slightly more interested in this aspect of the problem, but it still didn't fill him with the fire of reform. After mumbling something about having a social worker stop by to check on the children confined to the Purity Clinic, he hustled me out of his office, but not before I saw the photograph hanging on the wall, positioned next to a stuffed large-mouthed bass. It was a studio portrait of three serious-faced girls no more than thirteen or fourteen, each wearing puffy-sleeved granny dresses. A beaming Heckaman stood behind them, encircling all three with his arms.

"Your daughters?" I didn't even try to keep the sarcasm out of my voice.

His own voice had been unperturbed. "Have a nice trip back to Arizona, Ms. Jones."

It had been all I could do not to spit in his face.

No, Prophet Davis and the Circle of Elders would never have to worry about that particular county attorney. The polygamists were perfectly safe.

Heckaman kept one promise, however.

I smiled at Esther as she helped Rebecca load the rest of her things into the U-Haul. The shadows under her eyes had vanished, and her cheeks, so sunken the last time I saw her, bloomed again.

"Did you say good-bye to your daddy, sweetheart?" she asked Rebecca.

Her daughter nodded. "I told him he could come visit me in Scottsdale, but I wouldn't visit him here, not ever. I told him I didn't like his friends."

Esther smiled at me over Rebecca's glossy head. "How can I ever thank you? And Jimmy. Without you two..." Her words trailed off, and for a moment, the old shadows returned.

I reached around Rebecca, grabbed Esther's hand, and squeezed. "I was just doing my job. Gun for hire, and all that."

Her eyes filled with grateful tears, not for the first time that day. "Just a gun for hire. Yeah, right." She gave my arm a squeeze.

I cleared my throat. "Um, Esther, speaking of Jimmy, how is he?"

I knew perfectly well how Jimmy was doing, having talked to him three times yesterday and twice today. He'd discovered who had been stealing microchips from a Scottsdale plant, had cleared several applicants for jobs in the high tech industry, and gone to Miles Alder's funeral, where he'd helped comfort Miles' grieving father. In short, during my absence from Desert Investigations he'd kept the money rolling in.

What I needed to know, though, was how Jimmy's love life was doing.

"How's Jimmy? Uh, how would I know? I haven't seen him since they extradited me to Utah. I, uh, I've talked to him on the phone some, though."

But Esther's blush answered my unasked question.

We finished loading the big U-Haul just before sunset. Virginia's husband would drive the U-Haul and Saul would ride along with him, leaving the rest of us to ride in the ranch's van. We were just about to climb in when we heard someone yell.

"Wait! Wait for me!" It was Sissy Royal, dragging two suitcases. "I want to leave, too!"

Davis, obviously as surprised as the rest of us, stepped away from the shade of a rusting car and started toward her. "Sissy! What do you think you're doing?"

She wouldn't look at him, just kept her eyes on us, just kept dragging those suitcases across Prophet's Park. When the Circle of Elders parted to let her through, I couldn't help but notice a smirk on Earl Graff's face.

"Sissy! You come back here!" Davis began to run toward her.

I saw the fear on her face. Sissy knew Davis better than I did, knew what he was capable of.

I reached Sissy before Davis did, and grabbed the suitcases slowing her down. "Head for the van, Sissy."

She looked at me, gave one last quick glance at Davis, then hitched up her skirts and ran toward the van.

Davis stopped about ten feet from me. The look on his face made him almost appear ugly. "Bitch," he said.

I smiled. "Thank you for the compliment, Brother Davis." Still smiling, I picked up Sissy's suitcases and took them to the van.

"Okay, Virginia, let's blow this joint," I said, as I helped Sissy inside.

"Consider it blown." She stomped down on the accelerator, making the van kick up a cloud of dust as we barreled toward the gate.

As we streaked past the school yard, I could see Cora—the inadvertent cause of so much unhappiness—swinging blissfully on the swing set. Her long white dress swirled around her like a swan's wing, and the setting sun touched her yellow hair with fire.

But her eyes, like those of so many children I'd seen in the Purity Clinic, remained vacant.

Author's Note

Polygamy in Arizona and Utah is very much a reality, and authorities estimate the numbers of polygamists at between 30,000 and 50,000. Most of their compounds, such as those in Hildale and Colorado City, straddle the Arizona/Utah border, thus muddying each state's jurisdiction issues. Some polygamists, though, live openly in larger cities such as Phoenix and Salt Lake City (Associated Press, May 22, 2001).

POLYGAMY'S HISTORY: Utah (and much of Arizona) was founded by Mormon pioneers who practiced polygamy. Although this practice was officially disavowed by the Mormon Church in 1890, and was outlawed in 1896 as a condition of the territory joining the United States, it remained very much alive in outlying desert communities. However, in 1953, the Arizona National Guard raided a large polygamy compound at Short Creek, Arizona, (now named Colorado City) on the instructions of Arizona Gov. Howard Pyle (Utah authorities had declined to take part in the raid). The adult polygamist males were briefly jailed, but because the women—who had been trained to obey the men's every command—refused to testify against them, prosecution failed. The women also protested that without the males, they would have no means of support. Photographs of these impoverished women, surrounded by large numbers of children, ran in newspapers across the United States. Readers, mostly unaware of the serious abuses of polygamy toward women and children, saw Pyle as the hard-hearted destroyer of families. His political career was effectively ruined. The polygamist males were eventually released from custody and returned to their polygamist lifestyles. Since 1953, there have been no more raids into the polygamy compounds. No politician wants to lose his job, as did Pyle, who then sank into obscurity.

CRIMES ASSOCIATED WITH POLYGAMY: What few prosecutions have taken place in the past fifty years have not been for polygamy, but (with one famous exception) for the crimes which continue to surround polygamy: sexual assault, battering, welfare fraud, and racketeering (C.G. Wallace, Associated Press, July 16, 2001). Violence toward girls and women is common, but escaping it is uncommon.

Many polygamist women are forbidden to use birth control; their husbands keep a chart of their fertile days in order to impregnate them more easily. The ideal among many polygamy sects is for every woman to have one baby per year until her childbearing years are over, thus insuring her husband's place in "Highest Heaven." And more welfare income.

When a girl does escape one of the polygamy compounds, county law officers usually return her to the compound. In April of 2001, a 15-year-old girl ran away from her polygamous family, telling authorities that her parents were about to force her into a marriage with the much-married Warren Jeffs, the No. 2 leader of the Fundamentalist Church of Jesus Christ of Latter Day Saints (son of the then No. 1 leader, Rulon Jeffs). Despite her pleas, the sheriff's department returned her to the compound, releasing a statement to the media that since the girl was a minor, her parents had the right to decide how she would live (Associated Press, April 10, 2001).

In 1998, John Daniel Kingston, of Salt Lake City, Utah, was arrested for beating his 16-year-old daughter for resisting his order to become the 15th wife of Daniel Ortell Kingston, her uncle (Associated Press, June 3, 1998). The girl, who had been beaten more than twenty times, suffered a broken nose and deep bruises on her face and buttocks. After being confined to a desert "re-education camp" for recalcitrant women and children, she eventually submitted to the sham marriage. She finally escaped by staggering several miles through the desert to a gas station, where she was helped by concerned customers. Her father and uncle are now serving prison terms for incest and felony child abuse, but not for polygamy.

BIRTH DEFECTS ASSOCIATED WITH POLYGAMY: Because of their tight-knit and secluded compounds, the pool of possible mates among the various polygamy clans remains small. This frequently leads to incestuous plural marriages. Sometimes, though, that incest is purposeful. The Kingston clan (cited above) was founded by Charles Elden Kingston, who—after experimenting with breeding dairy cattle—set up a similar breeding program for his own numerous children. To this day, members of the Kingstons are allowed to breed only with blood relatives. In an article written by Greg Burton, printed in the *Salt Lake Tribune*, April 25, 1999, Connie Rugg, one of John Ortell Kingston's estimated 65 children, said, "All my life my family told me I had to marry a Kingston. I could choose, but it had to be a brother, uncle, or cousin."

Many Kingston children are born with serious birth defects directly traceable to the sect's breeding program. According to that same article by Greg Burton, one Kingston girl was born with two vaginas and two uteruses but no vaginal or bowel opening. Congenital blindness and dwarfism are common among the Kingstons, as are microcephaly, spina bifida, Downs syndrome, kidney disease, and abnormal leg and arm joints. These children and their mothers (who are designated *unwed* mothers by both Arizona and Utah social service agencies) receive considerable medical care and welfare, all paid for by the U.S. taxpayer.

Under Utah law, it is a felony for close relatives to have sex, but this law—as is the law against polygamy—is rarely prosecuted, and then only when considerable physical force has been used upon an unwilling girl. Daniel Ortell Kingston's prosecution for incest is one of the few on record.

WEALTH AND POLYGAMY: Although the women in most polygamy sects are not allowed to inherit or own property, and thus live in dire personal poverty, the leaders of these sects are often quite wealthy. Reporter Lou Kilzer, in an article in the *Denver Rocky Mountain News*, August 14, 2000, connected the Kingston sect's holdings to organized crime. The Kingston business empire includes casino gaming equipment such as slot machines and video poker (bought from Mafia-controlled companies in New Jersey), coal mines, accounting firms, finance companies, pawnshops, bail bond firms, poker parlors, and huge cattle ranches (one 160,000-acre ranch in Nevada formerly belonged to actor James Stewart). Estimates of the Kingston sect's wealth range from $150 million to—by one of their business competitors—$11 billion. According to Kilzer's article, the 1,000-member sect is currently headed by Paul Kingston, a Salt Lake City attorney with 32 wives and more than 200 children.

THE TAXPAYER FOOTS THE BILL FOR POLYGAMY: A *Los Angeles Times* article written by Julie Cart, dated Sept. 9, 2001, assessed polygamy's cost to the U.S. taxpayer. She cited U.S. Census Bureau estimates which found that every school-age child in Colorado City, Utah, was living below the poverty level. This level of poverty is unlikely to change, since many polygamists—who are unwilling to have their children influenced by "outsiders"—have pulled their children from public school. Cart's article also cited wide-ranging tax fraud, since polygamists rarely declare the full extent of their income.

This income-hiding behavior was highlighted in the 2001-2002 bigamy and child-rape trial of Tom Green. Court documents revealed that Green's five wives had been supporting him by selling magazine subscriptions, and yet the family was collecting large welfare payments. The child rape charges emerged from findings that Green impregnated one wife when she was only thirteen—with the permission of her mother, who was *also* married to Green. To date, the child's mother has not been prosecuted for aiding in child rape. Green is now in prison; his wives and 29 children are living on government assistance.

In Cart's article on incest and polygamy, Cart stated that the combination of birth defects, poverty, and the lack of education have overtaxed the already strained public service agencies of both Arizona and Utah. In fact, Cart found that Medicaid pays for more than one-third of the babies born in Utah, and plural wives account for a disproportionate share of those births. According to an article by Tom Zoellner in the *Salt Lake Tribune*, June 28, 1998, fully 33 percent of the residents in the Hildale and Colorado City area are using U.S. Dept. of Agriculture food stamps to feed their families (the average in Arizona is 6.7 percent, and in Utah 4.7 percent). The town of Hildale was also awarded $405,006 in federal housing grants to refurbish 19 homes on polygamy sect-owned land. Colorado City and Hildale rank among the top 10 in the Intermountain West in reliance on Medicaid and government-issued food.

WHY POLYGAMY ISN'T PROSECUTED: Proving a polygamy case continues to be difficult, since most polygamists' wives refuse to testify against men they consider their husbands. Proving child rape is difficult, because as seen in the Green case, the parents agree to the illegal "marriages" of their children. Until recently Utah law permitted girls to be married at age 14. The children themselves have been taught from birth to obey blindly the dictates of their parents and sect leaders. More crucially, the girls are moved back and forth between compounds, or back and forth over the Utah/Arizona border when necessary, thus making establishing the location of statutory (or actual) rape, almost impossible.

In addition, many of these child marriages are consummated in Mexico, where many of Arizona's and Utah's polygamy sects have set up satellite compounds beyond the reach of U.S. jurisdiction.

Complicating the polygamy issue is solid suspicion that the polygamy compounds have stockpiled large caches of guns and explosives in the caves near the compounds. Few politicians want another Waco.

However, in some cases, Utah and Arizona county prosecutors simply decline to prosecute. In a front page article in the *Salt Lake Tribune*, published May 20, 2001, Mohave County (Arizona) Attorney William J. Ekstrom Jr., said, "We don't view polygamy as a prosecutable crime. There is no driving desire to prosecute people for these types of things. We see it as consensual relations between adults."

PROSPECTS FOR CHANGE: Most women and girls in today's polygamy compounds are, like their predecessors, the victims of learned helplessness. Many are undereducated and have no job skills, no bank accounts, no property, and no income other than their welfare checks. In the unlikely event they ever leave the compounds, they are poorly equipped to find jobs and support their children. The few women who have managed to leave the compounds usually leave their children behind, an agonizing choice.

WHAT YOU CAN DO: The polygamists depend on public and governmental apathy to keep operating. The only people empowered to change this sad state of affairs are the governors and elected officials of Arizona and Utah. Write them. You can also write your own U.S. Senator or U.S. Representatives, demanding that the federal government stop using our tax dollars to finance polygamy. You can also help support Tapestry Against Polygamy, an organization founded by women who have fled the polygamy compounds. The group can be reached at (800) 259-5200 or www.polygamy.org, the site where they post current polygamy abuses and proposed legislation.

WHY THIS MATTERS: In a *Los Angeles Times* article by Julie Cart, published Aug. 25, 2002, Arizona State Representative Linda Binder, an anti-polygamy activist, complained that her efforts to pass legislation curbing polygamy in Arizona have met with resistance from other elected officials. Binder said, "We have a situation here that is unconscionable. We have the Taliban in our back yard."

Betty Webb
Scottsdale, Arizona
August 31, 2002

To receive a free catalog of other Poisoned Pen Press titles, please contact us in one of the following ways:

Phone: 1-800-421-3976
Facsimile: 1-480-949-1707
Email: info@poisonedpenpress.com
Website: www.poisonedpenpress.com

Poisoned Pen Press
6962 E. First Ave. Ste 103
Scottsdale, AZ 85251